Embers in Our Souls

STEFANIE CASTRO

For Meghan and Ashley: Thank you for feeding my soul when mine felt empty. This one's for you.

Content Warning

This book contains sensitive topics relating to adoption, death of family members, and mental health. The main male character will discuss his experience with Post Traumatic Stress Disorder due to time served in the military.

If you need more information on some of these topics, please feel free to visit organizations similar to those listed below:

The Wounded Warrior Project and Compassionate Friends

Spotify Playlist

Please use the QR Code below to find the Spotify Playlist or click the link here. Listen and enjoy!

Tyler

Numb. That's the only word to describe how I'm feeling right now. Even sitting in my favorite part of Nevada, I can't feel the calm I usually find in the natural beauty of this spot. The Memorial Bridge at the Hoover Dam is the place I find to be the most peaceful in the state. Whenever my mind feels over-whelmed, I'm automatically racing to get here. The minute I got my motorcycle license, it was the first place I came.

Today is no different. I finished up at work, excited I had the afternoon off; only to get home and discover it is no longer mine. Everything I hate about my parents simply washed over me as I took in my surroundings.

I've always loathed that dingy trailer, but today it took on a whole new meaning. Of course, Sharlene and Ricky were nowhere in sight. They were always cowards, fleeing to the nearest bar to drink away the money they made either at the casino or on alcohol. As if that money was going to burn a hole in their pocket if they saved it for an emergency—or their son. Being a responsible adult is probably one of the hardest concepts for them.

I look down at the crumpled note in my hand, the reminder of the parents I was given at birth. I tamp down the lump in my throat, feeling the unease as I reread the words my "mother" wrote. I know it was her because of the penmanship, but I have no doubt my "father" shares the same cruel sentiments she decided to impart me with:

Tyler, you've been dragging us down for years. You don't deserve the last name we gave you.

I came home to find this note taped to the door of our trailer, along with a large bag of my belongings sitting outside. They didn't even have the decency to let me pack my own things. I was kicked out of the only place I've called home, when I simply had to survive eight more days there.

Honestly, good riddance to that hellhole and to them. This was the reminder I needed to leave this state and not look back. Once I cross state lines, I'll never fucking return. It's been my intention for years to leave, I've just been biding my time, saving wherever I can, working at an auto body shop since I've been of age. Now with my diploma in my hands and my plan in place, I've got nothing keeping me here.

I'm the result of a teen pregnancy—why they kept me I'll never understand. Living in Las Vegas, where everyone comes to see the shining lights and chase the dream of winning big, I've been wishing to run away. Tomorrow, I'm granting my own wish when I start my road-trip toward Fort Benning, Georgia. It's earlier than expected, but I'm learning nothing in life goes quite as we plan. It will be a long road ahead, but I'm determined to make it.

I look over toward where my bike is parked, hoping she has it in her to make it across all those states to get me where I need to go. I worked hard to get her, saving up the way I did. The guys at the shop helped me find the best deal. She was my biggest purchase ever. I'll have to give her up at some point, unless someone takes her in when I go overseas while in the Army.

I see a few visitors passing me, stragglers from the last tour taking photos. The heat from the day sticking around, even though the sun isn't even as strong as it was when I first got here. Nevada heat hasn't hit the highest point, but I know in a few short weeks, it will be triple digits.

I bring my ball cap down further, covering my face, hoping to avoid eye contact with the public. I've never been known for my winning personality, so this just helps keep people from starting a conversation. I don't feel like having anyone approach me, my mood worse than usual.

I grab my phone to check the time. Shit, I've been here for nearly three hours. I've been lost in thought for far too long. The moment I'm stuffing my phone in my back pocket, an older woman walks up to me.

"I'm so sorry to bother you. Do you mind getting a quick photo of us please?" She gives me a wide smile to soften the blow.

I fucking called it. Apparently, my scowl wasn't enough to give the "fuck off" vibe.

I tamp down the eye roll and groan when I look her way. My irritation is palpable, but from the smile on her face, she must not be very good at sensing social cues. I'm about to grab her phone when a voice calls from behind me.

"Oh, I can take the picture for you. You don't want to see how bad his pictures come out. It will be out of focus."

It's the only voice that soothes my troubled nerves. Indiana Ranton saunters over, her smile radiating our surroundings. She's the last person I expected to see today, yet the one Nevada resident who shares my great love for this spot, despite being a tourist trap.

As the only girl that has left me speechless on more than one occasion since the day puberty took over my hormones, it's hard to believe I won't see her on a daily basis. I've known her since kindergarten, but I didn't really appreciate her beauty until middle school, when looking at a girl did something to me. I came back from summer break in seventh grade, and she made my heart rate accelerate in a way I never could understand. After that, I was a changed person. Not that I ever told her that.

Let's just say, if people were to look at her, they'd see the sun, while looking at me, they'd see the darkest night. When she walks into a room, she radiates happiness, while I scowl. I'm the leather jacket and motorcycle riding guy at school. I made teachers cringe when they saw me on their student roster. That's not an exaggeration—teachers told me that on more than one occasion. Indiana was our valedictorian. We couldn't be more opposite if we tried.

We never ran in the same circles. She was the girl that always did her homework. I was the kid whose dog ate it— although I never had a dog. In other words, Indiana and I were never meant to be friends. Then one day in sophomore year I came up to my spot here at Hoover Dam's bridge and found good ole Indy sitting here looking up at the sky, listening to music.

We formed a kinship that day; one I never expected. I'd say she never predicted it either. Almost like the dark with the light colliding and what it produced was the most beautiful of sunsets. Our souls felt like they were searching for each other and when we became friends, the world righted itself, at least for me, and I was happier.

I laughed, which was something I didn't do often. I looked forward to waking up each day, and even going to school didn't feel like a chore. She made me feel seen, and I loved what we had formed. These secret meetups were something I looked forward to throughout the week.

At first we started finding ourselves meeting here, then we'd plan out our days to see one another. Those became my favorite days actually; my *Indy Days*, as I called them. She was my favorite person, my treasured pastime. Until her mom discovered her whereabouts—primarily who she was with—and banned her from coming back. Diana Ranton is controlling and difficult, something I always found to be the opposite of her daughter.

That's the problem when the angelic girl who has never done anything wrong hangs with the bad boy; you can't combine the two because there's always a risk of contaminating the good girl. I'm the risk—and I knew it too.

I dreamed of tattoos and motorcycles. I wanted to drink and party, right along with skipping class. I was the villain in this storyline, per Mrs. Ranton, and she'd never allow her princess to be poisoned by the likes of someone as horrible as me. Her parents knew my reputation at school, along with the tumultuous trail my parents had left throughout the years since I was younger. I didn't fight it when Indy pulled away and stopped showing up to our meeting spot every week. My Indy Days were gone, and so was my sunshine.

By senior year of high school, we'd cut contact completely. She'd give me slight smiles in the hallway, but that was about it. She'd gone back to her old life, as if I'd never existed. She had her boyfriend at school, and I had to focus on getting the hell out of dodge. The only time I saw her give me attention was when I had a girl on my back as I rode off on my motorcycle. I'd spur her on with a sly smile and wink. Indy's eye roll always gave me the satisfaction I was looking for.

Now, keeping the bill of my hat low, my eyes stay trained on her while she snaps the picture of the family in front of us. The way the sun is hitting her long, rich, auburn-colored hair, I see the hints of caramel, gold, and brown undertones mixed perfectly throughout her strands.

She hands the phone back and says goodbye. I simply jut my chin in the group's direction, not paying any attention to the tourists or the direction they go. Indy has large sunglasses on, so I can't see into her eyes right now.

"What brings you out here?" I ask her.

When Indy and I first ran into one another on this bridge years ago, it was when something was bothering her. After we lost touch, I continued my visits to the bridge, sometimes in hopes she'd still come, others because I've needed to clear my head.

"I needed to get away," she sighs, looking down at the ground and kicking a few stones.

"Yeah? Want to talk about it?" I put my hands in my pockets and start walking. It was something we used to do until we could find a comfortable spot to sit.

"You want to hear my problems even after all this time? I mean, we haven't really been friends for a while." She shrugs.

"Just because we haven't spoken doesn't mean I don't consider you a friend, Indy. You can talk to me. What's up?"

Finding a place to sit, she takes a moment, looking around, almost contemplating if she wants to share. At first, I think she's going to reconsider and keep walking. Then she takes a deep breath and finally relents and takes a seat.

When she pulls her sunglasses off, I realize her eyes are puffy, as if she's been crying.

"Shit, Indy. You've been crying. What happened?" I reach out and touch her cheek.

Her chin quivers and she gives a slight shake of her head. "I feel like my world has just been rocked. I don't know what to do about it, Ty."

She looks away again. It's only then I realize a tear is falling down her cheek.

"Did Derek hurt you?" I feel my molars grind.

Derek was her boyfriend up until a few weeks before graduation. They broke up right before prom. I heard through the gossip mill he started dating one of her close friends and it was a whole thing between the senior class. He was always a dick. But, then again, everyone at the school—Indy aside— was a jerk in my opinion.

"No, it has nothing to do with that. He's an asshole, but I knew that already. I wasn't planning on marrying him or anything, even if my parents loved him." She laughs, but there's no substance behind it.

"Then what is it?"

"Ugh, this is so hard." She looks up to the sky and wipes the stray tears that are now falling uncontrollably. "I don't want to cry, but once I start, I can't stop."

"It's okay to cry. It's just me," I tell her. There was a time we used to tell each other everything. She would even pass me notes between classes. I loved those little moments together.

"Well, I've been sick. It's been going on for the last few months. At first, I thought it was nothing. And sorry for the overshare, but it's been this weird digestive thing. I won't go into too much detail. But I was sort of ignoring it. You know, thinking it was stress because of exams, and then the whole thing with Derek. Then there was college applications, and getting ready to move into the dorms. The whole nine yards; it was all piling on." She gestures with her hands in a circular motion.

"Well, this morning, I was nearly toppling over in pain. My stomach was really bad, so my parents got worried and they took me to the emergency room. To give a little back-story. You know my brother, Bryce?"

I nod. I've seen him in passing, but he's four years older than us, so I don't know him well. He's in college studying something way too complicated for me to try to understand well.

"Well, he did this complex assignment a while back regarding genetics; he only did it on my parents and himself. Turns out he and my parents are type O blood. Then today, while at the hospital, they did bloodwork on me and once they got those back, I saw I'm type AB." She swings her gaze at me. "Tyler, if both my parents are type O—there's no way I can be their child. Not biologically at least. So, I confronted them about it. And it's true; I'm adopted."

Right then, two tears escape down her cheek. The look of devastation nearly cripples me. "Oh, Indy. I'm sorry." I pull her to my chest.

She sobs into me and I rub circles over her back. I kiss the top of her head.

"They've lied to me all these years. This whole time, they could've told me and they haven't. They've asked for honesty and respect from me. They've asked for so much from me and they couldn't even give me honesty in return. Why, Tyler? Why couldn't they just do that much for me?"

Her questions and heartache are valid. I have no answers for her. So, all I do is hold her and continue rubbing reassuring circles as she cries. And she sobs into my chest even harder. I hold her until I feel her breaths even out. I wish I could've held her in my arms forever, the warmth of her body in my arms feels like home to me, something I didn't realize I was missing after all these years.

She pushes at some strands of hair that have clung to her forehead. "And it's not that I'm upset that they adopted me because they've given me a great life. It's that they've given me such restrictions to my life. They're so strict. Look how they treated you!" She throws her hands in the air in protest. "I've lived a confined life in many ways. I've even been punished when I went outside the lines, but they couldn't even be straightforward about my own past. How is that fair?"

"Did they give an explanation as to why they made that choice?" I ask her.

"They said they got scared I would leave them or not love them." She rolls her eyes. "That feels so unfair though. They never gave me a chance to form that opinion. I hate that they did that to me. You know?"

I nod because that's unfair that they pushed her life into a corner without her knowledge or consent. Especially as she got older.

"I have friends that are adopted, and their parents made their adoption story so positive. It doesn't have to be a negative thing. I just don't get it."

"Your feelings are valid. I'm so sorry." Her green eyes have a halo of gold, then in the center it's brown. It's the most unique eye color I've ever seen. Now that I know she's adopted, it makes sense why she looks so different from Bryce. Her brother has the darkest hair and eyes compared to her, although their fair complexion is similar.

"Were you able to get any answers about your health? I mean, it seems you need to figure out what's going on there?" I ask her.

She shakes her head. "No. I left in such a hurry. I got a ride-share to my house and grabbed my car. Then I came straight here. Bryce called me and asked me to fill him in on what happened. I guess our mom called him in hysterics." She rolls her eyes and continues, "And he wants to know if I'm running away or something."

"Is that what you're going to do? Run away?"

"I mean, I feel like I've lived a life by their standards, and I sort of don't want to anymore. Remember I told you I didn't want to be a surgeon like they wanted? I mean, that's their life. They're cardiac surgeons and I was doing that to stay in the family business, but I don't even want to do that."

"Yeah, you mentioned that, but then said you had grown to like the idea of it. I think someone at school said you got into some big school in California," I tell her.

"Yeah, I got into Central Coast University. It's a big deal. A huge deal. But that's their old school, where they met. It's their life, not mine. I was doing it to make *them* happy. But it's not what I want. And I'm sick of living the life they want for me," she tells me.

"What do you want then?"

"I want my own life, as hard as that might be. I think that's what I need to do— find my own happiness," she says.

"Then do whatever's needed to achieve that. You won't be able to live a fulfilling life until you run after the life you want."

"But how do I do that? How do I go after that with a health issue now? I mean, I need insurance. I'll need a job and I still want to go to school, but I won't go on their dime. I'm going to do it on my own. I'll put myself through the future I see for myself, even though it's going to suck." She drops her head into her hands.

I look out over the view, the calm in front of us providing the serenity we've both come here to find. This day has had so many winding turns, each one with its own obstacles.

"What if I gave you a solution to the insurance part?" I look over at her.

"What do you mean?" She looks over at me in confusion.

"I can at least help with one. But it will require a bit of rebellion on your part." I give her a sly smile.

"What kind of rebellion?" She laughs.

"The kind that's more my style than yours." I nudge her with my shoulder.

"Oh gosh. I'm scared to ask more."

"Do you trust me?" I ask her.

"You've never lied to me before," she says, her smile growing.

I stand up, putting my hand out for her to grab.

———

Hours later, we lay together in a hotel room; laughing, making promises, and holding each other. Wrapped together in the hotel sheets, I memorize every little piece of her. I'm cataloguing each touch, each motion, each second, because I have no idea if I'll ever get to feel this close to Indiana again.

Then I grasp her left hand in mine, and the feel of our wedding bands touching is a reminder of our little secret. I'll carry it with me as we start our lives; moving in separate directions after this. But I'll hold a piece of tonight with me every step of the way.

CHAPTER 1

Indiana

PRESENT DAY

"MAMA, I want to see Harley on Saturday," Noah says as we drive to school.

I sneak a peek at him, his dark brown eyes laser focused on the cars as they pass us.

"Sure, baby. I'll call her mom later. Maybe we can go to a movie. Ooooh, we can get popcorn and I'll make sure to get extra M&Ms and pour them in my bucket." I see him scrunch his nose without looking my way.

"I don't like sharing popcorn with you," he confesses.

"You don't like my popcorn?" I mock gasp.

"M&Ms and popcorn don't mix," he protests.

Little does he know, I've had this argument all my life with his dad. Part of me loves that his disgust was passed on to him because it's a constant reminder he lives on in such fundamental ways in this beautiful child.

"Wow. Next you're going to tell me pineapple doesn't belong on pizza!" I say as I turn into the drop-off line at the school.

"Yuck, Mom! So gross." He sticks his tongue out like he's going to be sick.

I pull up to the row of cars and stop, where I swing to look back to Noah. He's unbuckling and grabbing his things.

"Noah, baby, have a great day at school. I love you so much, even if you don't love M&Ms in your popcorn and pineapple on your pizza." I wink at him.

"Love you, Mama." He's already hopping out of the car and joining some friends he sees outside. I wave to his teacher as she ushers him into the kindergarten yard.

I feel my heart squeeze, knowing my heart will live outside my chest for the next few hours while I'm at work. Adopting my brother's son was the best decision I ever made. Noah is a carbon copy of my brother and in moments like these, I'm reminded of how much I miss Bryce with my whole heart.

It doesn't matter how much time passes; the ache remains as painful as it was the first night I found out my brother was taken from us all those years ago.

I can still hear the wails from my mother on the other end of the phone when my father called to tell me a drunk driver hit Bryce's car while he was driving home. Noah was home with a sitter, thank goodness, but Bryce was killed on impact.

The numbness I felt in that moment will stay with me forever. Despite the issues I've had with my parents, I pushed them aside in that period of my life to come together for the sake of this child that needed a family. Noah was only eight months old at the time, however, he had to adjust to so many changes that went on within the family structure that had acclimated between us.

Looking back, he adapted so well while all of us were crumbling. I was living in Chicago at the time of my brother's passing. I was just starting to adapt to life as an adult, thinking independence was going to be this fresh start in the real world, with a career I was truly falling in love with. I was acclimating to a life without someone I was painfully aching for who left me behind.

Gaining custody of Noah wasn't something I expected, but I welcomed it because I never wanted him to feel unloved. Unlike the secrecy my parents chose with my own adoption, I'm constantly telling Noah about his father; openly discussing what a hero I saw Bryce as throughout my life. But, Noah's biological mother leaving him behind shortly after he was born is something I shield him from as much as I can.

Although we started off living in Chicago, we're now solidified with a life in Boston. We moved here a little over two years ago, after my grandfather branched off a section of his publishing house, opening Medstone Publishing. I'm the editor-in-chief and I've never felt more alive in a role as I do with this one.

I always thought once I started working with my grandfather, I would one day see myself publishing my own work. At one point, I envisioned myself as an author, writing a New York Times Bestseller. But after I interned one summer behind the scenes with an editor, I realized this is where my heart was destined to be. I've come alive in this role, and this move only brought out more of my creativity.

Before Noah, though, I was lost. My relationship with my parents has gone up and down throughout the years for various reasons, currently on the downshift due to how they handled my gaining custody of their grandson. At this point, I've prioritized Noah having a relationship with them, putting my own needs aside.

Since Bryce passed away, our only connection has been focused on Noah and him alone. They continue living in Las Vegas, but they primarily come out to Boston to visit. When possible, I try to fly out to see them, but it's becoming harder to accommodate that trip.

As the years have passed, I only seem to be more disappointed in the people I'm supposed to care about. The move to Boston was bittersweet. My grandfather confessed he was sick, and when his health took a turn, he put the wheels in motion to get the expansion for Medstone Publishing open here in Boston. Losing someone as supportive and inspirational as my grandfather was hard on me, but I feel his strength carry on in me with each step forward that I take. Once I moved to Boston, I realized how much I was struggling to find peace in Chicago.

Although my brother never lived in Chicago, it was hard to shake off the heaviness of his loss and becoming a single parent. Every inch of the city was painted with memories of a struggle instead of remembering those times as ones I cherished.

Sure, we had growing pains trying to figure things out on our own, but Noah and I did it together. Something about the experience of coming to a new city was freeing. Much like when I moved to California more than a decade ago for a year of college, it gave us the opportunity to start a clean slate. My heart needed it more than I realized and I think Noah did too.

———

"You think Roger might be *the one*?" Kalli deadpans.

"Yeah," I tell my best friend, although I don't think I'm as convincing as I hope from the look on her face. Kalli is too observant and knows I'm not in love with Roger. She can tell I haven't been in love with any of the guys I've dated since I met her.

"We're talking about *your* Roger, right? The same guy I met on our double-date?" Kalli eyes me as she takes a sip from her coffee mug.

She's sitting in my office as we have our ritual morning meet up. We have to schedule this in every day because our schedules are absolutely packed. Kalli is our chief legal officer at Medstone and the minute we met back in Chicago, we clicked. We've been inseparable ever since.

She transferred here from our Chicago office eighteen months ago, and having my best friend with me to tackle this city has been one of the reasons I've loved this transition as much as I have. She's sharp as a tack and I love how great she is at her job. The issue is, when it comes to knowing when I'm pretending, she can read me like a book.

"Why is that so hard to believe? Roger could be it for me," I say, avoiding her pointed stare.

She nearly spits out her coffee. "Because it's Roger, Indy." She rolls her eyes. "The guy is as exciting as a fucking encyclopedia. Plus, you haven't committed to anyone since Noah came into the picture and now you're into *this* guy? Explain yourself."

"First, that's rude. Second, maybe he's different. Maybe he's made me reevaluate things." I give her a pointed glare.

"Come on, Indy. You're the least romantic person I know. Also, I've met the guy. There's no way that guy can even find your clit, let alone your G-spot, babe. He can't be your forever guy," she chastises.

"Tell me what you really think," I tell her as I take a bite of my breakfast burrito.

"Listen, he's cute. I'll give him that much. I thought he'd be fun. But at dinner, he spent ten minutes talking our ears off about an Excel spreadsheet. I mean, it's fucking *Excel*, Indy. Does he scream 'MICROSOFT!' when he climaxes? How did you come to this conclusion?" She lifts a perfectly manicured eyebrow at me.

I try not to make a face at her comment because she's not wrong. Roger did spend most of the time talking our ears off about Excel. He's a data analyst at a large firm in Boston and he's got a hard-on for the damn software on his computer. I thought Julian would at least find it interesting, but even I caught his eyes glazing over.

"I just think he's stable for Noah and I," I confess.

"I see. And you think that's how you should gauge this?" She sits back in her chair and crosses her legs.

"Well, don't you think that's the responsible thing to do?" I laugh nervously. The way she's looking at me is unsettling.

"Don't you think you should find someone that rocks your world *and* brings stability? I think that would at least be more fun. That's what Julian does for me." The way she's looking at me, I know she's going into overshare mode.

An image of Tyler pops into my head, but I'm quick to erase it from my mind. Damn Tyler Hunter and the way he ruined me for other men.

The minute she opens her mouth again, I groan, knowing this story will be awkward.

"The other night, I put the baby to bed and Julian couldn't wait until we got into our bed…" The gleam in her eyes is downright sinful and she's having way too much fun making me uncomfortable with this story. "… so when I was in the kitchen washing some dishes, he lifted me on the counter, spread my legs, ripped my panties off, got down on his knees, and feasted on me like I was his last meal."

I swear I nearly choke. "Jesus, Kalli."

"I know, right? I nearly saw the light, girl." She smiles at me, fanning herself with her free hand.

"Why do you tell me shit like this? Maybe, now that I think about it, can we scale back on the storytelling?" I admit.

"Oh stop. You watched me give birth to Vivienne. It's too late now." She waves her hand in the air.

"What was the point of your story, exactly?" I ask my bestie.

"That there's no way 'Routine Roger'"—she emphasizes with air quotes—"is going to be your forever guy. You need someone that will rock your world, Indy." She shakes her head as she takes another sip of coffee.

She holds her gaze on me and I narrow mine because she just wanted to share her story. She's so damn dirty, which I know quite a bit of because she's always telling how we should publish more authors that have steamier books with dirtier scenes in them.

Roger and I met about seven months ago in a coffee shop down the street from my place. He lives in the building not far from my townhome. When we first met, he seemed really charismatic, but I don't know if he simply had an extra boost of caffeine that day or what. He's nothing but kind, although, he is a bit dry.

"Why are you even with this guy?" She looks at me like I have three heads.

"We have a lot in common!" I throw my hands in the air.

"Oh, really?" she throws back.

"Yes."

"Great. Lay it out for me then." She's not going to budge until I give her something.

"We both love Boston," I immediately explain.

She stares back, looking bored. After a few beats, she scoffs. "Are you fucking serious? That's it? Your list is one thing. You both love Boston? You know what? Julian and I both brush our teeth. Then we knew we had to get married because we had the same brand of toothpaste. When we fight, we always come back to that basic principle and all is right in the world."

I swear, I really hate that she's a lawyer. "Fine, we love the Boston Gaels, which is unique because I'm not from here, and we also love lobster rolls," I explain.

"You're killing me right now." She brings her thumb and index finger to pinch the space between her eyes. "So, you like the same baseball team here in Boston—wow, what a concept—and you like the same food. Shocker! You've been dating for a little over half a year and you don't even have him hang out with Noah. Why is that?" She looks at me and narrows her eyes.

"It's safer this way, Kalli," I say.

"You always say that, yet you never expand. You've dated guys, yet you never really let them in. Now, all of a sudden, on this one who is as complex as a potato, you're thinking he's the one? I don't get it." She's still eyeing me, thinking I'll break under pressure.

Dating someone like Roger feels safe because I can compartmentalize how I feel about him. The connection feels harmless, which is easier for me. I can't feel deeply for anyone like I've done in the past, but I also need stability.

"*Earth to Indy,*" Kalli singsongs.

"Hmm?" I say.

"You can't pick someone because of security. You have to take a leap, butterflies and all," Kalli says, her expression full of remorse.

I've never told Kalli anything about my past with Tyler. She has no clue how much of my heart I've given to the boy back in Vegas. I leave that part of my life behind me. She thinks I'm closed-off because I've just been through too much with my adoption and losing my brother. Plus, she knows how terrible my parents have been, especially my mother. It's easier that way and I've never let her believe otherwise.

"I know, but I also have to make sure Noah and I have a stable future ahead. He needs that. And I want him to have a male figure in his life. He's been through enough," I tell her, taking a sip of my coffee.

"It's not only about what Noah has been through, Indy. You've been through it too. And I'm not just talking about losing your brother. Everything you went through with your parents, finding out about your adoption, that's traumatic. Not to mention your health. That alone is a lot. Stop shoving everything under the rug." She grabs my hand and squeezes.

Kalli has never let me forget it's okay for me to have feelings about the trauma I've suffered. She encourages me to talk through my emotions, emphasizing how important it is that even if something happened years ago, it impacts us for years. Unfortunately, she has no idea how much of my past is still seeping itself into my present and it has nothing to do with my adoption, my health, or my brother's passing. It has everything to do with a boy I gave my heart to eleven years ago.

CHAPTER 2

Tyler

"IS that a maybe on the smutty books?" Malloy looks at me while I finish my last few minutes on the treadmill.

It's an unusually muggy day in Boston for spring. We had originally planned on meeting up at my house. I had a whole day of filming laid out for my social media page, but scrapped those plans and we're now at the gym.

"Dude, you know I don't care to read that stuff." I stop the machine and towel off.

"You're missing out. Baylee and I try the kinkiest shit. Especially when it's Kennedy's book choice for the month." He smirks and I respond with a look of disapproval.

"Don't knock it 'til you try it, man." He shrugs as we walk to the weights.

"Why are you trying to get me to join your book club? I thought this was sort of your thing with the girls."

Malloy is one of my closest friends. On top of that, we work together at the firehouse. I'm the newest to join the crew —the probie, short for probationary, as they say in the firehouse—but he's taken me in. We formed a solid friendship early on.

This book club he's trying to get me to join was started

with his close friend Abby and their mutual friend Kennedy. Both of whom are engaged to identical twin brothers, River and Clay, who happen to be firefighters at our station as well.

River, Kennedy's fiancé, is probably the most energetic and ridiculous character I've ever met. Clay is more reserved than his twin, but when they're both together, the two can get into some pretty heated arguments. Who am I kidding? They exhaust me when I have to be around them. Recently, their disagreements center around Clay's infant daughter, Gabriella, who we call Ella. River lives for three passions in this world—Ella, Kennedy, and Lola; the last of which is his dog. I'm still not sure in what order.

"I think it would be fun for you to hang out with us," Malloy continues, grabbing a set of weights.

I stare at his reflection in the mirror, not buying it.

After a few seconds, he gives up whatever internal struggle he's having and confesses, "Fine. They're ganging up on me, okay? Since Baylee joined book club, the three of them are fucking coming after me. I'm outnumbered and I can't take it." He starts his reps, but I don't miss the look of desperation he gives me in the mirror.

Baylee is Malloy's wife; they just got hitched a few months back and the guy is smitten. His complaints don't fool me. He is one hundred percent infatuated with his wife, despite the hard road they had getting to this point.

"What do you mean they're teaming up against you?" I ask him, grabbing weights of my own.

"It's exactly how it sounds. The three of them have started some sisterhood of their own; and now, I'm some outsider. When we discuss the book, and the guy in the story does something dumb, I get these looks from them like I'm part of it. They call me out and start acting like I represent all of the male population. They'll be all like, 'Malloy, why are you guys like this?' Or they'll simply state, 'Why can't all of you be more like Frankie from the book? He buys flowers every week.' It's exhausting, Hunter. I can't take it."

"So, you want to torture me in the process? No thanks," I tell him.

"Well, the books are great. I wasn't lying about that." He's whining now.

"Malloy, you're borderline pathetic," I say as I look around, hoping people can't hear him. It's embarrassing.

"I'm seriously at my wit's end with it. This week, we talked about a book Baylee chose and after the discussion, all of them were so heated over it, Baylee gave me the silent treatment. She wouldn't even have sex with me."

"Okay, I don't think I need to know about your antics in the bedroom. Honestly, I don't care," I tell him, wiping the sweat off my forehead.

"Oh, so I have to hear about River's shit, but you can't hear about mine?" he continues.

"I promise you, hearing anything about River's personal life with Kennedy behind closed doors is never a desire of mine either," I say, grabbing some water. "But, speaking of River, why don't you ask him to join?"

"Absolutely not. Could you imagine him in book club? Then imagine him with Kennedy. I just got a visual and my head already hurts," he says as we begin walking to the bench to start another round of exercises.

"Yeah, you make a fair point. Would Clay work?" I ask him.

"No, he's not interested. I started hinting at it, but he's not into these kinds of books. He tried reading one for fun with Abby a few months back, but he started calling it soft porn and she got fucking pissed at him. It didn't end well." He makes an uneasy face.

"I have no solution for you then. Sorry friend." I smack him on the shoulder.

"Yes, you're just being difficult. You could join and help me even things out a little bit," he tells me.

"My evenings are booked." I shrug.

"Every evening?" he asks me, unconvinced.

"Yes, every single evening," I lie.

"You're such a fuckface." He laughs as he spots me. "And for your information, the books are good. That part wasn't an exaggeration. It's just the harassment is getting to be a bit much. I'm a sensitive soul, Hunter."

"Mmhmm," I grunt.

Once I'm done, I sit up and wipe my face. "I know, Malloy. I was just telling the guys, I caught you wiping a tear from your face when we were watching an ad with those puppies trying to get adopted."

"Hey, they were cute. And I thought we were taking that to the grave."

I put my hands up in surrender. "Chill, I'm kidding. I was getting choked up too. Seriously though, I'll consider book club. But I'll admit, Kennedy sort of scares me still. She's a bit intimidating."

Kennedy is the CEO of the Boston Gaels and she turns heads the minute she walks into any room. If anyone is going to handle River's antics, it's Kennedy Sparen. Her strong personality can handle anyone in a boardroom, but most importantly, she can put her fiancé in his place any time of the day.

"Kenny's harmless. I promise, she's a total softie." He waves me off as we switch places.

"Really? So, you never felt like she was a bit terrifying?" I look down at him with a questioning expression.

"Well, yeah, of course I did. She's a badass, but she grows on you. And I definitely don't call her Kenny to her face… anymore. But she's loyal and handles River better than anyone I've ever seen; better than Clay, which is pretty impressive. Also, don't tell her I called her a softie. I don't think she'll consider that a compliment."

He begins his set while I chuckle. "Malloy, you're proving my point right now." I honestly don't know how I ended up with this interesting mix of friends, but in such a short amount of time, they've pulled me into their blended family, and I've never felt so seen.

———

"How are things going in Boston?" Jerry asks while sipping a mojito on the beach on our FaceTime call.

I was stationed with Jerry and Scarlet's son George, who was soon dubbed Georgie, while in the Army. Georgie was four years my junior, and I took him under my wing when he was put in my unit.

Although I ranked higher than him, we formed a friendship the moment we met. Georgie had a quick wit about him and we bonded over our love of motorcycles. He told me about his closeness with his parents and I envied that, as I had grown up in a household that was the complete opposite. I could tell he truly loved spending time with Jerry and Scarlet, his calls with them sparked emotion from him that provoked a deep respect for them. It was something I envied amongst the three of them.

When I confided in Georgie about my upbringing, he invited me to his hometown to spend a long weekend with his family. I thought I'd feel like the oddball out, but the moment I crossed that threshold, his parents welcomed me as one of their own. I never felt more loved than I did amongst them. Jerry and Scarlet embraced me with the kind of love a parent should from the beginning and I've allowed it to blanket me ever since.

Georgie's kindhearted nature was what I think my dark personality needed and craved. I don't think I ever longed for a sibling before, but around him, he felt like someone I could confide in. He was a brother I never thought I needed, yet I was gifted with nonetheless. Whenever we took time off-base for a weekend or could travel back to the States, we'd travel together to visit his parents. Sometimes we'd meet up with them somewhere to see them if they were traveling around Europe. I felt a connection to their family, and they never made me feel like I wasn't part of the bond they had formed. Georgie was my brother for all intents and purposes.

While stationed overseas, we were on patrol one day when our squad came under fire. The chaos was loud and uncontrollable in that moment. Georgie was shot and killed in front of me. I had moved from where I was standing for just a second, leaving him in my spot. He took the bullet that was intended for me, and that's something I will have to live with for the rest of my life. I never thought we would leave the compound as a unit and return missing one of our own. The aftermath of that day impacts me in ways that I spent a long time denying. That single bullet catapulted my life in a whole new trajectory.

Nothing ever felt the same after that. My world crumbled from that moment on. It took years for me to see the world with the same light, but I suffered for a long time; the survivor's guilt nearly crippling me.

Looking at Jerry, it's like life is giving me the gift of seeing what his son would have looked like years down the road. They are carbon copies, although, a light dimmed in Jerry the moment Georgie died. But with the sun shining on his skin and Scarlet by his side, I can see the travel has lifted their spirits a little.

"It's finally warming up. I've been able to get the bike out again," I say. "It's nothing like that view you've got though." Jerry knows I had to sell my motorcycle before going overseas years ago, and I crave the way I feel free, letting go when I take off for a few hours on a bike ride.

The motorcycle sitting in the garage was Jerry's until recently. I take it out throughout the warmer months, but it's too dangerous to ride when Boston's cold weather greets us come fall. He gifted me the bike when I moved out here, something he once dreamed of doing for Georgie. I can still remember the tears pooling in his eyes the day he handed over his prized possession, proclaiming how thankful he was that his son found a friend like me.

He turns his head toward the ocean behind him and smiles brightly, lifting his glass. "Well, I would have to agree with that, son."

Something tugs at my heart when he calls me *son*, knowing that these two people have felt more like parents in the few short years I've known them than the actual people who share my DNA. My smile is genuine as I look at him through my screen.

Jerry has been working remotely for a while anyways, so he can work anywhere they can find internet. He started out as a general contractor, but he now oversees his own business. Since becoming the boss, he manages everything from his computer. This gives him the freedom to work from paradise, as he's doing at the moment.

Scarlet sold her business shortly after Georgie's death; her heart wasn't in it anymore. Prior to his passing, she ran a successful home design company. She was highly sought after, with a long list of clients when she decided to walk away. Technically, Scarlet and Jerry don't need to work anymore, with enough savings and investments to keep themselves afloat. But Jerry says he enjoys staying busy with his company, even if it's just remotely. He mostly handles the contract agreements and phone calls with clients so that his team is free for the hands-on portion of the job.

The only problem was, the heartache they felt being in this house was overwhelming. When I confessed I was hoping to settle down after traveling throughout the States for a stretch of time, they asked if I would consider caring for their home. I had been looking for a place to live and I jumped at the chance help them out.

I've been living in their house since they decided to travel the world, leaving me behind to care for their home in Boston. When I got back from the Army, I had seen and experienced far more than anyone ever should. I never thought I'd recover from the devastation I'd witnessed. Therapy and months of work on myself got me through it. I'm thankful for the hours I invested in myself, and I can finally say I'm through those dark times in my life.

I've been steadily building my social media account as an influencer throughout the years since returning to civilian life. People have been following along as I work out in different locations throughout the States. Posting and connecting with the online community has proven to have a positive impact on me.

At first, I never imagined anyone would watch my content. I did it for me, hoping it would help me decompress from the stress I endured on a daily basis. And I'll admit, I've enjoyed building my following once I saw it take off. Seeing different parts of the United States was exciting at first, but the constant movement from one place to another became tiring.

Looking back from the man I am now to the young kid I once was, it's strange to see how much I've evolved. Seeing so much of the world helped me grow and I'm grateful I haven't become more bitter and recluse. I could have let the ugliness of what happened in the Army push me further into depression, but I was able to find help, which I'm grateful for. Many don't have the same story to tell. I've surrounded myself with the right people. Although, I know I've pushed one special person away; which I will admit, that might be one of my biggest regrets in life.

My social media content became a type of journaling for

me, where I got to document my life and connect with others. I never expected it to take off. I posted some videos I had from my time in the service, some of which were workouts I had saved on my phone; but most of my content is newer, focusing on how my workout routine benefits me physically and mentally.

As time passed, I started to realize I needed to settle somewhere and finally find a career that differed from military life and the social media life I had cultivated. I wanted to find a group of friends and build solid, meaningful relationships again. I had pushed many of the people I cared about away because of Georgie's passing, feeling incredibly lost when he died.

Even though I now work at the firehouse, having the social media presence helped bring steady income when I first retired from the Army. Even though the guys at the station have been making fun of the fact the female following is only growing by the day, I think keeping it up as a side-gig is something I'd like to continue.

Apparently, there's a SpaceBook group out there now named *Hunt's Prowlers*. I don't look at it, nor do I manage it, but the guys constantly read the comments when we have slow nights at the firehouse. It gets a laugh out of me how these people will become fascinated by the fact I'm working out without a shirt on.

The last time I had seen Jerry and Scarlet prior to moving to Boston was for Georgie's funeral service, five years ago. Their heartbreak was my own. And then, I shattered what little remained of my own world shortly after that day.

By the time Georgie's parents connected with me again, I was in a better place in my life and that's how I found myself in Boston. Being here gave me the opportunity to start fresh. They gifted me a chance to find myself again in a community rich in culture and life, something I was craving more than I realized.

"Where did you go, Hunter?" Scarlet asks, eyebrows knitted in concern.

"Sorry, got lost in thought," I tell her, a smile tugging on my lips.

"Oh? Is it about a girl?" Scarlet waggles her brows.

"Scar, don't make the boy uncomfortable," Jerry says, shaking his head.

"What? The boy is young and so handsome. I bet he has a line out the door. What's the big deal?" She puts her hands on her hips.

"Don't give him the third degree. This isn't one of your romance novels." He takes a drink of his beer and sits back in his chair. "Speaking of which, have I told you, Scarlet reads porn now?" Jerry makes a face. "Ow, what was that for?" He rubs at his upper arm after Scarlet smacks him.

"I do not read *porn*, old man!" Scarlet seethes at him. "I read romance novels that happens to have sex in them."

Jerry brings his face closer to the camera. "It's porn. I read some lines when she was in the water earlier. It's dirty." He chuckles and it's hard to keep a straight face.

"Really, Jerry? So, you like reading my smutty books? Wanna buddy-read them with me?" She looks over, intrigued.

"Buddy-read? What's that?" He looks confused.

These two are as bad as Clay and River. I rub my hand down my face then snap my fingers. "Hey, remember me?"

"Sorry, Hunter." Scarlet looks back at the camera. "Jerry gets jealous I give my book more attention than him." She rolls her eyes, but gives him a small smile. "But seriously, is there anyone special in your life?"

"No special someone. Still getting used to everything at the station. I'm liking it a lot though. A few more months before I'm no longer a probie."

I joined back at the end of summer, so I have a few more months until I reach my one-year mark. I thought it would be a bigger adjustment for me to fit in, but the guys welcomed me right away. Personally, I hang out with River, Clay, and Malloy, but even those who I'm not close to outside of the firehouse have been easy to bond with.

"I'm glad you found your fit in the city. Boston is a great place. Have you made it to a Gaels game yet?" Jerry asks.

"Not yet, but I'm hoping to go soon. I actually happen to know someone that works at the organization. She's engaged to one of the firefighters at my station." I grab ingredients to make a protein shake.

"Well, we're going to let you go. I need to take a dip in the water. I can feel my skin burning under the sun," Jerry says as he fans himself with his magazine.

"Before you go, Scarlet, what book were you reading?" I ask.

"Oh, look who's into dirty books after all," she says with a satisfied look on her face.

I roll my eyes. "It's not for me. It's for my friend. He's actually in a smutty book club."

"Sure. I bet you'll be in that club soon enough." She winks at me.

She reads off the name and I write it down on a piece of paper. We say our goodbyes and the moment the screen goes blank, the silence is deafening.

I've gotten used to the silence throughout the years. It's something I chose for myself and the longer I'm alone, the more used to it I've become. It doesn't mean my mind doesn't wander to years ago, when I saw it leaning in a different direction.

There was a time I let myself fantasize a bit; imagining I would come home to something different because I'd let my heart soften. I'm not the hardened person I once was from years ago. My Indy did that.

All the letters she sent me slowly started to chip away at that cold exterior of mine. She helped me find a piece of myself I didn't know I was capable of offering the world. I started to dream of a lighter life. I started to believe I could have a brighter future; something my parents never let me accept I was worthy of.

The moment my thoughts drift to Indiana, I can't help but wonder what her life is like today. I know the last connection I had with her, she was in Chicago. She had a whole life ahead of her and I have no doubt she's flourishing.

I know now I handled my grief over Georgie wrong with Indy, but pushing her away was all I knew at the time. I was hurting, the pain all-consuming. She's a ray of light and I would have dimmed it.

Fuck, I would have torched it and her entire life had she allowed me to stay near her back then. Thinking back to that time in my life, I wish I could go and do it all differently. But that's the hard part of our past mistakes—when the fog clears, we see our miscalculations differently.

If there's one lesson I learned when I started to fall in love with Indiana Ranton, it's that I could never let her experience the kind of loss I had. Even if I never confessed my true feelings for her before I shattered her world, my pain was worth saving her from the same fate.

CHAPTER 3

Hunt's Prowlers

SPACEBOOK GROUP

HUNT'S
PROWLERS
SPACEBOOK GROUP

Jenni0898
Could he be any hotter?
#absfordays
#tattoosarehot

oceangal48
I wish he would hunt for
me instead 😊 #imsingle

bostonluv28
I live near the park he posted
that video at! Ugh!
#workingwomanproblems
#hottestguyever

HUNT'S
PROWLERS
SPACEBOOK GROUP

Huntsangels69
@huntsamillion why couldn't you have picked to live in Cali? Boston is so far from me! #westcoastisthebestcoast

Sierra447
Does he need a personal assistant to wipe that sweat off his chest? I volunteer as tribute. #ilovehim #hunterlover

CHAPTER 4

Indiana

"I **LIKE** the direction this cover is going, but there's something missing," I tell my marketing team. "Since this is the third book of the series, and we know it's supposed to be seductive if the last book was any indication, then it should allude to such," I explain as I look at the illustration in front of me. Even though I'm the editor-in-chief I have a bit of an eye for design. Plus, having intimate knowledge of the stories can give me a unique perspective on how the aesthetic can attract the right reader. So, I like to give input on the cover design when I can.

The team is quickly jotting down notes as I look over the design. "This is our most popular series since we opened in Boston and I want to make sure we get this cover right. Maybe add a little more color over here"—I point to a spot to the right—"to make it pop, you know?"

"I'll send these notes over to the cover designer and I should have a new mockup to you by end-of-day," one of them says.

"Sounds good. And make sure—" I'm interrupted by a knock on the door when my assistant, Angela, walks in.

"Ms. Ranton, I apologize for interrupting, but Noah's school just called and there's an emergency." Her nervousness is unmistakable in her tone.

I can't help the way my pulse spikes at her words.

"Did they say what the emergency is?" I can't help the way my voice hitches. I'm usually calm, but when it comes to Noah, there's always an extra layer of caution reserved for him.

"He was stung by a bee and he's having an allergic reaction. That's all they said. They asked that you head over there right away," she says and I'm already moving toward the conference room door with my purse in hand.

We discovered Noah is severely allergic to bees on a trip to visit my parents last summer. Since then, I've become well versed in allergic reactions, carrying an Epi-Pen everywhere I go.

Moving quickly, Angela is updating me that she will cancel my afternoon and reach out if anything urgent comes up. I hate to admit, I'm barely listening to anything she's saying. I'm furiously pounding on the elevator button, hoping it will quicken its arrival, knowing it's making no difference whatsoever.

Once the metal doors open, we jump in. I inform Angela I might need her help grabbing items from my office to drop off at my house if I end up working from home tomorrow, but I'll keep her updated on Noah's status when I know more. I shoot a text off to Kalli regarding what happened, in case she hears it through office chatter.

The moment we get to the garage level, Angela keeps up with my fast pace until I reach my car and she bids me good-bye. The school isn't far from the building, luckily keeping my drive short. I pull up to a parking spot and hurry into the school. When I see the firetruck, my anxiety kicks up a notch, my steps taking on a quickened pace along the concrete.

I've had my cell in my hand, worried they would leave without me from the school. I'm kicking myself for having my phone on silent when I was in my meeting earlier; that's why Angela got the call from the school instead of me.

I walk through the front office, and someone is waiting for me as soon as I open the door.

"Ms. Ranton, let me walk with you to the nurse's office. The EMTs arrived and are caring for Noah. He's in good hands. He received Benadryl and the Epi-Pen you provided us, but he is still having a reaction to the bee sting," she's explaining as we move.

I keep my gaze forward, my jaw clenched. He must be so scared and all I want to do is wrap my arms around him. I see commotion in front of us as we near the nurse's office. From what I can see, Noah is already on a gurney, and I speed up.

"I'm here. Noah, Mommy's here. Baby, I'm so sorry!" I call out as I approach. The minute I reach him, I take hold of his hand; but when I see his face, I hold in my gasp. He's completely swollen, his eyes nearly fully shut.

I'm stunned by his appearance. I knew he was having an anaphylactic reaction to a bee sting, but I assumed it was on an extremity. This reaction is more severe than the last time he was stung.

"Noah, sweetie, I'm here. I'm so sorry," I say, moving my hand through his hair. "Does it hurt?" I ask.

He nods his head, his eyes welled with tears. I assume the swelling is uncomfortable. I see his chin wobbling, but then he whispers, "I get to ride in an ambulance." I can tell he's doing everything possible to sound brave, but his voice is shaking.

"Yes, you do. I'll be right there with you, okay?" I tell him, unsure if he can see me with all the swelling around his eyes. "I'll make sure I'm right there with you." I squeeze his hand reassuringly.

I look around, hoping someone will tell me what the hell happened that he looks the way he does. The gurney is being packed up with supplies and I'm hopeful we'll start getting him loaded into the ambulance.

It isn't until I sweep my gaze over to my right that I see blue-gray eyes staring back at me. I've only ever seen that exact shade once in my life.

"Ty?" I feel like the wind has been knocked out of me. This day is already draining me emotionally and now the last person I expected to see is standing in front of me.

"Indy…"

I feel my body go numb. I don't know why I had convinced myself I would never hear his voice again. It's silly, really, because eventually we'd have to meet up. We have a history and a mess to clean up. Yet, if the goosebumps forming on my arm are any indication, he's throwing me off balance by simply saying my name.

My brain and my body aren't on the same damn page. I'm supposed to hate him, remember?

I look him up and down, trying to compose myself. It's obvious from his attire he's one of the firefighters helping Noah. How the hell is this happening right now? He's in my world, in a way I never expected. For years, I compartmentalized him; being so far away, never expecting him to stand so close to me again. Now he's here, close enough I could touch him, although he feels so much further than ever before.

I don't want little ears hearing this conversation, so I quickly whisper to Noah, "Mommy is going to find out what's going on, but I'll be close by." He nods while another paramedic is caring for him.

I walk over and stare at Ty, looking him up and down, still wondering if I'm conjuring him from my imagination. This can't be possible that after so much time, Tyler Hunter is standing before me at my son's school.

"Do you two know each other?" I'm startled from my thoughts by another gentleman from Tyler's unit.

"Um, yeah, we, uh—" But I'm cut off when Ty decides to speak for us both.

"Yeah. She's my wife," Tyler says to his colleague. Luckily, he isn't loud and I don't think Noah heard him.

Tyler's confession seems to stun his coworker, confirming that he must keep it as close to his chest as I do.

"Always full of surprises, huh, Hunter?" the firefighter says, more with a look of amusement than disappointment. I wish I could share the sentiment, meanwhile, I feel like I might see my breakfast resurface.

"River, let's not make a big deal of this right now," Ty says under his breath. I can see Tyler's face is stoic, likely grinding his teeth like he did in high school. I guess some things never change.

"Hey, your secret is safe with me," his coworker, *River*, says as he walks away.

I stand there for a brief moment longer, staring back at a man I thought I once knew, feeling completely exposed, but I finally snap out of it and remember where my focus belongs.

"Indy, I—" Tyler begins.

"I can't do this right now." There's more bite to my words than I usually use as I straighten my spine. My thoughts float back to the past and the harshness Tyler had the last time he chose to interact with me. Too bad he never let me communicate back. Ties were severed after that.

I can see my coldness surprises him. The last time we saw each other, the Indy he remembers was light and free. It was one of the last times I felt like a person that truly lived in a world where my shoulders weren't weighed down by grief. The world was bright and full of possibilities.

My eyes stare back at the man I once loved. There's a rigidity that begins to snake down my spine, filling me with icy strength as a way of protecting myself around Tyler Hunter. Noah is my only concern, and he needs me to be whole for him. I cannot stretch myself thin for a man who tossed me aside like the next day's trash.

I turn around and walk toward the person who matters most in my life and grab his hand. It feels like everything starts moving at lightning speed in that moment. The gurney is pushed toward the ambulance and we hop inside. I keep giving Noah reassuring words to calm him down, hoping my own words will settle the uptick in my heart rate after seeing Tyler.

Once we're settled, I expect the doors to close for us to head out, but Noah's small voice whispers, "Where's Hunter?"

"Oh, um, I think he's going in the firetruck, sweetie."

Before my words have time to register, Tyler calls out, "I'm right here, buddy."

He's making his way into the patient compartment, which is confined as it is. I can't help the way my body goes still at the sound of his voice. I keep my back to him as he addresses Noah and the woman taking vitals by his side.

"Polly, sorry to make it even more cramped back here. I got it approved with the captain to tag along," Tyler says.

"No problem, probie." She winks at him and my traitorous heart feels that pang of jealousy, wondering if there's something between them beyond a working relationship. It doesn't matter, though, does it? I have to try and remember whatever is going on in Tyler's life is his business. He made that clear to me years ago. I was nothing to him then, and I'm nothing to him now.

"Hey, champ," Tyler greets Noah as he sits nearby. "I'm going to ride along with you just like I promised. How's that IV?"

"It's okay." Noah lifts his arm and wiggles it around. The hives are still all over his face and neck, but haven't gotten worse in the few minutes I've been around him. My poor boy is still puffy and unrecognizable around his eyes, but I'm hoping they can give him more medicine at the hospital.

"Why is he still so swollen, even with all the medication you've given?" I ask Polly while inspecting Noah.

"He got both doses of his Epi-Pen and Benadryl at the school. Once we get to the hospital, they'll evaluate him and see if he needs more medication, like steroids or if more anti-histamines are needed. The fact that we were able to keep more swelling and hives at bay is the most important," Tyler interjects before Polly can explain.

I can feel his eyes on me, but then I notice him in my periphery turning his attention toward Noah. "You feeling any difficulty swallowing or speaking?"

Noah shakes his head.

"That's good," Ty says, then swings his attention back to me with a reassuring smile.

I let out a breath, my gaze remaining on Noah. My hand runs through his hair. I lean down and kiss his hand. "You're so brave. I love you so much." I smile at him.

"I love you, Mommy," he whispers back.

Noah only recently started calling me Mom, claiming he's now a big boy. I've noticed he only calls me "Mommy" when he's scared or sick. I miss his chubby little hands squeezing my cheeks, but I will admit I would do anything to hear him call me Mom right now and have him feeling one hundred percent. At least he wouldn't be in the back of an ambulance.

When I pull away, I look over and catch Tyler looking at us, a pensive look on his face. I wish I could read his mind right about now. He doesn't know this side of my life. The last time we connected I was still the old Indy, untethered to a child, and only broken because of parents who lied to me.

Now there are so many pieces of me he doesn't know about, facets of my life he never got to experience. Letters I itched to write, but never did, with updates about things throughout the years because I missed him. My world went up in flames and Tyler was nowhere in sight, because he was selfish and nothing how I imagined. He isn't privy to what's going on anymore because he chose to walk away from me. Now he's an onlooker into my life—an outsider—a choice he opted for years ago because he broke my heart instead of cherishing it.

We pull up to the ambulance loading zone at the emergency room and we're seamlessly escorted through. The moment the back door to the ambulance opens, Noah's gurney is pulled out and everyone is speaking to the hospital staff. I'm trying to keep up, but I feel overwhelmed by the medical jargon being spewed from one person to the other.

Tyler and Polly are answering a ton of questions, while I stand back with Noah, holding his hand and constantly asking if he's feeling alright. The nursing staff is checking on him and assessing his hives, ensuring he isn't having trouble breathing.

We get ushered to a room and soon we're going through more questions while the paramedics are handing off their report. I watch from afar as I know I'm close to seeing the last of Tyler. A part of me is relieved because I feel like I can't breathe around him—but there's another part of me that knows I want to hold onto this. Now that I've seen him, I want to know more.

What has he been up to all these years? What brought him to Boston? Why did he leave the military? Why did he ruin me all those years ago? Why did he ruin *us*?

As if my thoughts attract his gaze, Tyler locks his focus on me.

"Ouch, Mommy. You're holding my hand too tight," Noah says.

"Oh, sorry, sweetie," I tell him. Get a damn grip, Indy.

I look up again and now Tyler is walking toward us. He makes his way into the room.

"Listen champ, I've gotta run. But you were so brave out there. Promise me, no more fights with bees. Got it?" Noah gives Tyler a small smile in return, even though I can tell the hives are impeding him from giving him a full one.

"Promise," Noah says.

Tyler brings his focus to me next. "It was good seeing you again, Indy," he says.

"You too, Tyler. Thanks for everything you did for Noah."

He stands there an extra beat, and a part of me wishes he'd tell me how much he's missed me since we last saw one another. That romantic side of me, the one that I know is buried deep inside and didn't fade away years ago, is begging Tyler to swoop in and kiss me. But then that bitterness resurfaces, and I remember the feeling I got that day when I felt worthless holding that last letter. It felt like a brick in my hand.

I steel my spine again and stand taller, composing myself in front of this man that shattered my heart into a million pieces. Finally, he nods and turns around. I watch his retreating form as he leaves, and it takes everything in me not to chase after him.

———

"Aunt Kalli, you can't do that!" Noah declares.

"I beg your pardon? I sure can," Kalli says yet again.

I swear playing UNO with Kalli is worse than any child in the history of ever.

"I need an intermission," I put my cards facedown and stand up to stretch.

"Okay, kiddo. Your mom and I need a breather. She can't hack it with top UNO champs like us," Kalli declares and I hear Noah chuckle behind me.

"Don't gang up against me, you two," I say, even with my back to them.

"Can I watch my iPad for a bit? I'm a little tired," Noah asks.

"Sure, baby." I grab his things from the table, putting his headphones on, with his iPad in place. The swelling has nearly completely subsided this morning, with a few raised bumps I can still see on his face. They had him spend the night as a precaution because it still hadn't resolved much last night.

Once Noah is comfortable and watching a cartoon of his choosing, I get settled in the chair next to him.

"Thanks for grabbing my car at the school yesterday. And for swinging by my place and getting me a change of clothes. I appreciate you feeding the cat," I tell Kalli.

We have a white, long-hair, Persian cat named Darth. We got him a few months back and I almost named him Snowflake because he honestly looked like a ball of snow, but it came down to a vote. Kalli was our tie-breaker and she sided with Noah when choosing—traitor.

"Of course," she tells me, checking her phone. Once she finishes typing, she tosses it aside and gives me a long look. I know something is coming. She looks over at Noah, who is engrossed in his show and brings her gaze back to me.

"Alright, I've given you enough time to recover from yesterday's trauma. Now spill."

"I'm sorry?" I give her a quizzical look.

"You're acting funny and I have a sneaking suspicion it doesn't have to do with what happened yesterday," she says as she motions toward Noah on the bed. I look over to the little boy that holds my whole world and hope to delay this conversation a bit longer with my best friend.

I feel foolish all these years later that I haven't told Kalli about Tyler. I thought I'd never have to, if I'm being honest. I fooled myself in believing there'd never be a reason to. The divorce papers were drawn up after we parted ways—when he torched what I thought was a possible future—and I chickened out.

I used every excuse in the book not to pull the trigger and send it out. Shortly after Tyler imploded what I thought was something special between us, my brother passed away and the direction of my life shifted. My brother made it clear who he wanted Noah's guardianship to be with and I needed my focus on that little boy.

Noah became my center and everything else became less important. Whenever I thought of Tyler and the divorce papers sitting in my drawer, I felt the unease creep in. The pain of it made me spiral even more, so I'd shove it deeper in the recesses of my thoughts, until I eventually let it go completely.

I'm scared she's going to be mad at me for keeping this secret about the sham marriage that I let take hold of my heart. In the end, I was the fool that lost focus of what it was supposed to be—a contract to serve my best interest. I let feelings take over and he obviously felt differently.

I'll never put myself in a position to be made a fool of again. And I haven't since. I keep men at a distance now. I keep everything at a comfortable surface-level so I don't risk getting hurt; that's as far as I can handle things right now. Even with Roger, I'm aware giving him my whole heart is just too risky. So, if things keep moving forward as they have, I'm fine to live a stable, comfortable life and hear about spreadsheets until the day I die.

"Seriously, Indy, what's going on? You've been all fidgety since I got here," she eyes me from her seat.

Kalli knows me better than anyone and she's not going to drop this. Seeing Tyler yesterday rattled me and I haven't been able to shake the encounter off.

"I have no idea what you're talking about." I avoid her gaze. I look down at the lint that's attached itself to my leggings.

"Now I know for sure you're hiding something. Just tell me what it is. I know it's more than Noah's trip to the hospital. What happened that you're acting all strange?" she pushes.

"I—"

"Knock, knock," a red-headed woman with a spattering of freckles across her face enters the room. She flashes her hospital badge and gives us a welcoming smile. "I'm Erin and I work for the hospital registration department. I need to clarify a few things with you regarding your paperwork. Are you Mrs. Ranton?" She looks to me as she walks further into the room.

"Yes, that would be me." I wave my hello.

"Wonderful. I was looking over your paperwork. I see you checked off your marital status as married" —She brings her computer into the room. I keep my eyes focused on the woman, but I can feel Kalli's eyes on me from my periphery. I heard Kalli's surprised intake of breath at this information. Luckily, Noah is so enthralled in his show that he can't hear our conversation through to his headphones. Erin continues as if she didn't just blow up my life—"but it wasn't clear if you are the primary on your insurance or if your husband is."

My heart is thundering beneath my ribcage, and the room is suddenly feeling incredibly stuffy.

I hate that in the haste of nerves yesterday, I filled the hospital forms out in a desperate attempt to get everything out of the way, and forgot I checked off the married box on the insurance portion. I'm no longer a dependent on Tyler's insurance, but I can't lie on my paperwork.

Somehow, I find my voice despite my mouth going dry. "I, uh, I'm sorry about the confusion. I'm the primary on the insurance," I confirm.

"Wonderful," Erin says in a cheerful voice. "The nurses said your husband sat outside your room this morning, but he left before I got here. I'm sorry to bother you."

I can't help the look of confusion that must pass over my face. Was Tyler outside Noah's hospital room this morning? Why would he return and risk running into me again?

I pull myself out of my trance and wave goodbye to Erin. Little does she know the shitstorm she has just left me to deal with. I'm sure my best friend will now verbally berate me thanks to this woman's revelation.

I continue to look at the now closed door, hoping a nurse will walk in with discharge papers and distract us further. Unfortunately, the silence is the only thing that takes over the room.

I finally look over at my best friend and expect to see her seething, but instead I find a look of hurt across her face.

But now I see, keeping this secret from my best friend, of all people, has broken her heart. If the tables were turned, I wouldn't be furious, I'd find myself stricken in the same way she is looking at me right now.

I look down at my hands, shame washing over me.

I finally speak and I can hear the defeat in my voice.

"I'm sorry." There are no other words I can think of right now.

"Why would you keep this from me?" she asks right above a whisper. I can't mistake the pain in her tone.

I shake my head. "I've only ever told my brother. And my parents found out when I was in the process of gaining custody of Noah." I look over at her again. "I swear, I didn't keep it from you to be hurtful. It's something I never wanted to talk about, and I never thought we'd stay married this long."

Silence washes over the room once again. The heaviness between us is new to me because our friendship has always been the one easy part of my life that I have appreciated through all my struggles. She has held me up when life has felt like it was trying to drown me countless times.

"Well, then, I guess you're not carrying this secret without sharing it with me any longer," she says.

And that's when I tell Kalli all about the night I married Tyler, in what started as a fake marriage. Then I continue the story about a marriage that morphed into what felt like a real love story for me. That is until he disintegrated my heart years later right before I planned to confess that I wanted forever with him.

CHAPTER 5

Indiana

11 YEARS AGO

CHAPTER 6

Tyler

11 YEARS AGO

July 7, 2014

Dear Indy,

Or should I really be addressing this letter to my wife? I won't lie—it's still surreal to me that we're married. Does it still catch you by surprise sometimes?

Thanks for sending me the postcard with the update. I love that you're in California. I've always wanted to visit. I can't wait to hear more about what it's like now that you're living there.

I had to fill some paperwork out when I arrived on base and I found myself having to pause because it still leaves me dumbfounded. I think it will take time to wrap my head around what we did. I promise, that's not my way of saying I regret any of it. I'm glad I could help and I hope you're able to get the care you need for your health issues.

When we went our separate ways after your mom found out about us hanging out, I thought that was it between us. To have our friendship back feels surreal. Looking at us, no one would guess we fit; two mismatched puzzle pieces. Yet, here we are, our edges blending as one, coming together perfectly, and I wouldn't have it any other way.

I think that's what I always liked about being friends before. At school, no one suspected we were close. I never cared that we kept our meetups to ourselves. I liked having something between us that no one could partake in. All my other friends weren't the best influence, but you were always different. Unlike my parents and the administrators at the school, you never passed me off. You saw me. You _see_ me.

How is everything going on the west coast? Are you feeling any better? Did you get any answers? I hope you've gotten some treatment and found a doctor that can help you out.

What's the plan with school? Last we spoke that night I was in Nevada, you were going to start life on your own, financially. I know it's overwhelming to think about and I just want you to know how proud I am of you for taking this initiative and standing up for yourself. It's hard, but as you get used to everything there, I'm sure it will get better.

Boot camp is challenging, but it's been worth it. I've been making friends with some of the guys here and I've felt like it's been a true brotherhood. Georgia is incredibly humid compared to Vegas.

I knew that coming into this it would be hot, but when we're running in the middle of the day with all our gear, it's a whole new level of sweat. I won't go into detail, but damn, Indy; I never knew heat like this. It's so muggy here compared to back home. It feels like we're living close to the sun.

I love the idea of writing letters with you. I hope things are starting to adjust well for you.

Your pen pal husband,
Ty

CHAPTER 7

Tyler

I'M EXHAUSTED. I haven't felt an ounce of calm since the day I walked away from Indiana at the hospital.

Running into her felt like I walked back in time. All the emotions swimming through my mind from the moment our eyes connected haven't stopped. I've been restless every night and it's been hard to focus, let alone sleep.

My head is swarming with thoughts of her son, the fact that she's a mother, and the mere notion she has moved on in life. I mentally prepared myself for the possibility that Indy was living a full life with someone else, but seeing it is something completely different. While I've felt like I'm lost, stagnant in this world, still looking for my place without her and Georgie. I might be putting on a brave face in front of millions on my social media platform, and in front of the guys at the station, but deep down it's all a front.

I've worked hard in therapy ever since I got back to civilian life, to ensure I work through the trauma I was living in after watching Georgie be killed in front of me. Add in the destruction I witnessed nearly daily, I had gone through too much while I was in the military.

I'm aware that I see the difference in my truth now that

I'm trying to live a new life here in Boston. I'm balancing a new normal, that's something my therapist always reminds me of. What's portrayed on my social media and what's reality are two separate things. Although I make a decent living with content creation, building my life here in Boston started to feel empty to me and I needed human connection. The guys at the station help me feel like I can lean on people again, much like the camaraderie I had in the Army.

After I pushed Indy away years ago, I was able to self-reflect and learn from it. My grief after losing Georgie truly took me to new depths. I coped in the wrong way, and I dealt with it poorly. She has no idea what I was dealing with, nor did I take the time back then to use my words to explain. I shut down and used lies to hide my truth. Now, all those feelings have come flooding back since running into her.

Seeing Indiana succeeding in life is all the confirmation I needed to know that walking away from her was the right thing to do. I can't bring her down by telling her the truth behind what I did and ruin her life, but it doesn't take away from my heartache.

What's even more fucked about this entire situation is the fact that she's got a child while she's still married to me. After leaving the hospital, I had a moment of panic thinking Noah could be mine and Indy had kept him from me out of spite. But before I spiraled, I remembered overhearing the school nurse whisper that his father passed away while updating us when we asked about his parents' arrival.

It didn't keep me from waiting outside that hospital room in hopes of seeing Indy for a moment the following morning after my shift. I finally pulled myself away and went home, realizing I was acting like a crazed stalker and thought it best to head to back to my place. The last person she wants to see is me after the pain I put her through.

The guys and their significant others have forced me out of the house today and we're meeting at a park. They said I can't avoid them any longer since I haven't explained the whole surprise marriage bomb to them.

I'm the first to arrive at the park, so I'm sitting on the grass, watching a few families playing with their kids. It's a sunny day, not a cloud in the sky. I leave my ball cap on, shielding me from the sun, watching people run around in the warmth of the spring day.

"Hunter, hey," Clay says as he makes his way over with the stroller.

"Hi. Want some help?" I ask him as he carries a few extra items in his hands to set up stuff for Ella to sit.

"I think I've got it. Thanks though." Clay locks the stroller and starts setting up a play area for her, with a play mat that has a shaded cover for her. Ella babbles in her stroller and I stand up to greet her.

"Hi, Ella. Do you remember me?" I ask her as I tickle her feet. She gestures with her hands, then stuffs one of her fists in her mouth, smiling. Her big, blue eyes, matching her mother's, look up at me, while her dimples pop out to greet me.

"Hi, Hunter. How are you?" Abby meets up with us.

"Hey, Abby. Good. Ella's getting big." I look over my shoulder.

"She is. Time's moving too fast. I hear you've been keeping a few secrets." She winks at me.

"Geez, they're such gossips." I roll my eyes.

"You have no idea." She chuckles.

She makes her way over to the stroller and talks to Ella, unbuckling her, then pulling her out. Ella immediately latches on to her hair, pulling at her mother's long locks.

"No, no, sweet girl. What did Mama say about pulling hair?" Abby says.

"Mama," Ella says while trying to put said hair in her mouth.

Clay looks over and simply smiles. I didn't meet either of them before Abby gave birth, but I've heard stories about how rocky things were for them. It seems their relationship has been through an ordeal to get to this point. Whatever hardships they've endured, I'm glad they've made it to this point, because when I see him look at Abby, all that's reflected is love and adoration in his eyes. And this beautiful baby they've created is perfection.

"Alright, Ella, your play area awaits," he says, pride evident in his tone.

Abby puts their daughter down and she's immediately entertained with the toys they brought. We'll see how long it lasts. She's already crawling and wants to be on the go.

"Hi, everyone," we hear a voice greet us. I look over to see Kennedy with Lola. I look beyond her, but don't see River.

"Where's River?" Clay asks, a little concerned.

"He said he had to grab something, so he'll be meeting us here." Kennedy shrugs while she hugs everyone. The minute she gets to me, she whispers, "I hear you're a big secret-keeper in the group."

"Am I seriously going to be harassed all day about this?" I ask.

"Yes!" all three of them say at the same time.

I roll my eyes and give them an exasperated look. I'm about to say more when I'm gladly interrupted by Malloy and Baylee.

"The party has arrived," Malloy says, pulling me in a big bear hug. "You're a fucker for keeping me in the dark, man," he says in my ear.

"Dude, I've never told a soul, if it makes you feel any better." I look at him.

"It's fine man. I sort of had a feeling you were keeping something hidden in there. But I'll say, you are a damn mystery, Hunter. What else are you hiding?" he asks with a smile.

"I swear, that's it!" I tell him.

He pulls me into a hug. "Well, you've gotta fill us in. Tell us all about this girl."

"Let's wait for River. He'll be here soon," Kennedy says.

"Where is he?" Baylee asks as she greets everyone.

"I knew it was too quiet. Plus, Ella is being left in peace; that should've been my first clue. She's usually snatched up by now," Malloy says.

"He said he had to run an errand," Kennedy tells Malloy, shrugging.

He raises an eyebrow at her. I might not have been around very long, but even I know that's suspicious as hell when it comes to River. He must be up to something. Hopefully whatever it is takes the heat off my not-so-little secret.

We get a few snacks out and get situated. I brought a football and frisbee so we can play later. Malloy and I get a few chairs set up while Kennedy and Baylee sit with Ella on the ground. Abby uses this time to take a break and eat some food. Once things are set up, I'm standing and talking to the group, when I see River approaching. It isn't until he's getting closer that I notice his outfit. I do a double-take.

"What the hell is happening? Am I seeing double?" I ask him.

"Well, yeah. We're twins," River says as if I'm clueless.

"No shit, man. But you're wearing the same outfit, dipshit," I say the inappropriate words under my breath for Ella not to hear.

As soon as I say the words, everyone turns their attention to River, who has made it closer to our group. The moment Kennedy notices her fiancé's attire, she buries her face in her hands, mortified. Abby seems used to River's antics at this point, while Malloy's giddy, probably wishing he had a bucket of popcorn. Baylee mimics an attendee at a tennis match, her eyes volleying back and forth, likely unsure how this will play out.

"That's not the outfit you left the house in, sweetie," Kennedy calls River out.

"Yeah, I know," River answers, his focus on his twin. He's completely fucking around with Clay and he knows it. The question is why.

Clay has his lips in a straight line, not finding this game amusing at all. I'm simply watching what River's play is here.

"River, baby, what the heck are you doing?" Kennedy asks.

"I just really like this outfit, so I felt like changing." He crosses his arms across his chest.

"Is that why you called and harassed me about my outfit earlier?" Clay asks.

River continues the stare down with his brother until Clay breaks it and looks over at Abby.

"You're fucking losing it, Riv," Clay says.

"I just look up to you. Remember, you are older." He smiles, but there's nothing sweet about it.

"By two minutes," Clay says through clenched teeth. "You're a real dicksickle, you know that? Isn't this a bit stalkerish, even for you?"

River ignores his brother's comments and gets a sly look on his face, walking over to his niece. With the way both are dressed today, it's hard to tell them apart and it isn't until this very moment that I start to put the puzzle pieces together.

"Ella, baby," River says. He smiles at her. Ella looks up at him. You can see her do a double-take between Clay and River, trying to assess the situation.

"Dada," she says in River's direction and that's the win he was going for. The look of satisfaction he has across his face is immediate. He snatches her from the ground and plants kisses across her cheek, telling her, "No, sweet girl, I'm your Uncle River. That's Dada." He points at his brother.

Then he runs her through the park, making her laugh and

smile. When they come back, he puts her back down on her play mat, looking over at Clay again.

"You satisfied now?" Clay asks. "She still didn't call you that first. She's been saying that for a while now," he says.

"Oh, I know. You really think I'd take that from you?" He smiles. "But I was on a mission to do it today at least."

"Why? What did I do?" Clay throws his hands in the air.

"I spoke to Mom. And guess what she had to tell me?" He walks closer to his brother while all of us watch this interaction. He bends over and scratches behind Lola's ear. "You told her that you think Lola loves her more than me—my Lola will always love me more." He looks down at his golden retriever and blows her a kiss. Jesus.

The rest of us all groan. River is ridiculous. He's seriously obsessed with his dog. But I will agree, Lola loves his mom. I've seen her interact with River's mom and Lola is quite honestly over-the-moon when River's mom is in the room. She will sit with her and put her head on her lap. I hate to admit, but Clay might have a point.

"So you did all that over my comment to Mom about Lola?" Clay says.

"Obviously," River says.

"Seriously, Riv, you're exhausting." He throws his hands in the air. "Kennedy deserves an award for dealing with you."

"Thank you," Kennedy says, a look of satisfaction across her face.

River points toward Kennedy. "Watch it, babe. And Clay, most of the stuff you have, I have as well. You're wearing a Boston F.D. shirt with shorts. It's not hard to replicate this outfit."

As much as I'm not one to usually care for this back and forth between the brothers, maybe the distraction will be enough to distract the group from asking me about my little marriage omission. I sit back and allow them to carry on as if I'm not even here. I continue to take in our surroundings, not even getting up to grab food, even though I'm hungry. If I don't move maybe they'll forget I'm here.

Right when I think I'm out of the woods, Malloy says my name. Damn him and his memory.

"Hunter, what the hell was that about the other day? Care to fill us in?"

"Not particularly, no," I answer.

"That's not good enough," River says on a laugh, already forgetting his little stunt with his brother and niece.

"Well, there isn't much to say. Indiana and I are married," I say, matter-of-factly.

"Really, that's it? You're not going to elaborate?" Kennedy says.

"I mean, what do you want me to say? We got married when we were eighteen right after we graduated high school. We didn't tell anyone. It was sort of a secret. We did it because she was in a bind due to health reasons. She needed my health benefits and I had it to offer through the Army. Some stuff went down with her parents right about that time, so I was someone she could lean on for support. I wanted to make sure she was cared for before I was gone for boot camp. That's it."

When I look up, I see Kennedy and Abby swooning at my explanation, but before I'm able to ask why, I'm interrupted.

"Well, did you catch feelings? Have you seen her since? Why didn't you get divorced?" Those questions are from Baylee.

"Umm..." I pull my hat off and scratch at the back of my head.

"You totally have feelings for her, don't you?" Abby asks.

"It's complicated," I say.

"Dude, that means there's so much more to say then," Malloy adds.

"Okay, so it's complicated and I don't really know what to add. It's a bit hard to explain and process. It got a bit messy.

Lines were blurred in the end. Yes, I guess feelings were involved at one point. But I have no idea if they were two-sided, we never talked about it. After high school, we used to send letters while I was in the military, which is how we kept in touch," I explain.

"That's so romantic," Abby says, putting her hand over her heart. "Doesn't that remind you of that book we read a few months back?" She snaps her fingers as if she's trying to remember the title while looking at Kennedy and Malloy. "The guy had lost his memory though. It was second-chance and she has things he left behind for her. Oh, it was heart-breaking and beautiful."

Shit, is she going to start tearing up?

Then I see all three women look at me, while Malloy's mouth quirks. Fuck, I can anticipate the question before I hear it come out of Kennedy's mouth.

"Hunter, you should join book club. You would love it. Maybe this is just what you need to connect with us and get your mind off all this." I see Abby and Baylee nodding in unison, while Malloy is nearly toppling over in laughter. Motherfucker. He saw this coming from a mile away.

As if he could sense I need saving, River comes to my rescue, "When was the last time you saw her before last week?"

"About six years ago," I answer, ignoring the book club topic.

"And things didn't end well?" Kennedy asks, apparently already distracted.

"No, I sort of put an abrupt halt on everything. I was convinced she would have sent me divorce papers right after that. But she didn't. And I didn't push for them either. I honestly don't know why. I just fell into this deep sorrow after suddenly losing my friend Georgie. He and I were serving together in the Army and he was like a brother to me. I didn't really care about a lot of things after he died. I realize now it was wrong to push Indy away, but it's all I knew at the time. It was my way of coping."

"Why don't you try to get ahold of her now? Maybe you can try to mend things," Baylee explains.

"Well, the guys and I saw her last week and she has a son now. I think it's pretty clear she's moved on. So I think that's all the sign I need. Now the only thing left is to sign divorce papers."

Just thinking of divorcing Indy feels like rocks settling in my stomach and it's heartbreaking for me. I feel a love for her that is everlasting and I have no idea if I can close that door forever.

CHAPTER 8

Hunt's Prowlers

HUNT'S PROWLERS
SPACEBOOK GROUP
Jessica23
I think I saw @huntsamillion at Boston Common this weekend. He was throwing a football, and I wished I could be that pigskin.
#huntinthewild
Bostongurl1997
@huntsamillion has been quiet lately. What's the deal? I need me some workout videos!!
#iwatchfortheweights #jk #needmesomehunt
Jamie778
I miss @huntsamillion
#huntwhereyouat

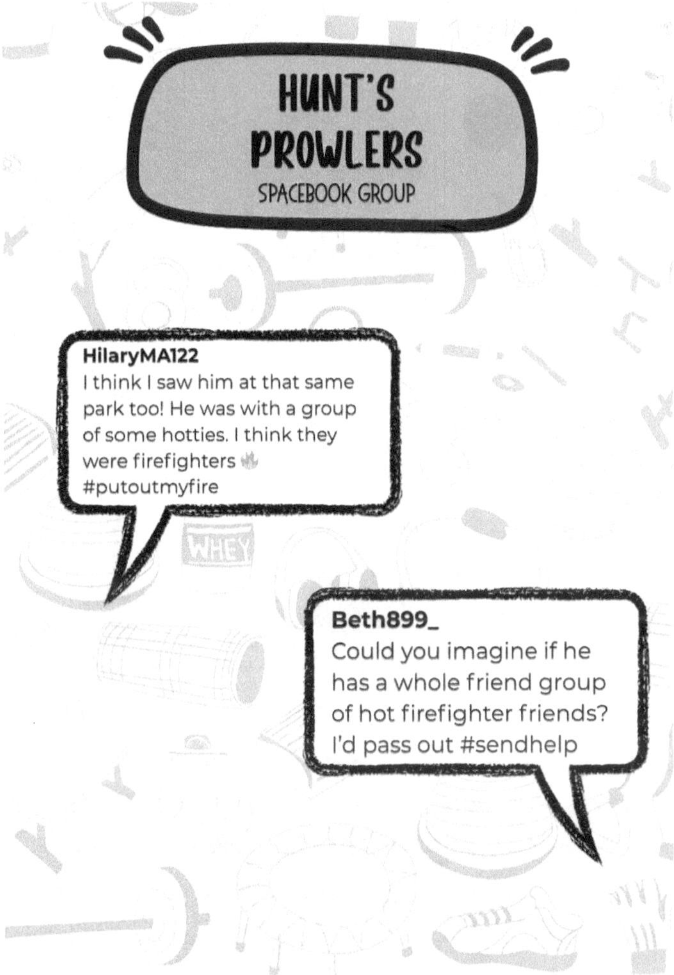

HUNT'S PROWLERS
SPACEBOOK GROUP

HilaryMA122
I think I saw him at that same park too! He was with a group of some hotties. I think they were firefighters #putoutmyfire

Beth899_
Could you imagine if he has a whole friend group of hot firefighter friends? I'd pass out #sendhelp

CHAPTER 9

Indiana

11 YEARS AGO

August 3, 2014

Dear husband/ pen pal Tyler,

I agree, I'm still getting used to the fact that we're married. But at the same time, I'm comforted by it. It's hard to explain. I don't know what it is about you, but when everyone saw you as a storm, you were my calm breeze. Something about your presence soothes me. Whenever I felt my heart racing I'd rush to our spot over at the Dam, and the moment my eyes found you, I felt at ease.

What you're doing for me, I will never be able to repay. You're giving me the ability to feel independence. I've never been able to live on my own, to feel free from the responsibilities my parents put on me. I don't know if I've said thank you before, so I'm saying it now. Thank you, Ty. I mean it. You've done something for me that I don't know if many would have. Not even Derek would have done this, and he was my boyfriend.

My brother is letting me crash at his place this year, while I figure things out. He's actually moving to Oregon in a year, so I've got a timeline to get my life in order.

Little confession though—my brother found the last letter you sent and he saw how you signed it. We've been caught and I had to explain everything to him. I'm sort of surprised he isn't more upset. He had a few choice words, but I'm obviously an adult and he understood the position I'm in with my parents and my health.

He did tell me I could have gone to him for help if I needed it, but I explained I wanted to find a way to figure some things out on my own the best way I can right now. I trust he'll keep this to himself, seeing that things are not great between my parents and I at the moment. I just thought I'd let you know I did have to lay things out to him after I left that letter out on the counter. I guess I won't be working in law enforcement or anything like that. Maybe stand-up comedy would suit me best? Thoughts?

I found a job close to the community college,

waiting tables. I work nights, while I start summer classes, getting a jumpstart on some courses before fall semester. I'm liking what I'm doing, especially now that I'm not focusing on biology as my major.

Luckily, despite the secret revelation, my relationship with Bryce isn't a problem. My parents, however, are a different issue altogether. We've had a few fights, ending in me hanging up the phone. They don't understand why I'm so upset, whereas, I'm holding firm on the fact they lied for my entire life.

My health is still teetering a bit, especially as I don't have a complete understanding of what's going on. They're still running tests to see what I could have. They think it might be Crohn's Disease. Once I have more answers, they'll start to see what medications I might be a candidate for. It's been hard to find foods that don't upset my stomach, especially when I'm running around all day.

The doctors were thinking that a family history might help narrow things down. So, I tried finding my biological parents, but, unfortunately, my records are sealed. Maybe I can hire a private investigator to look for them when I can afford it. Aside from that, everything else is a mystery to me. It's going to take a lot more time and resources to get those unsealed so at this point, I will have to wait. It's frustrating, but right now, I have to focus on getting myself healthier. Thanks to you, I have the ability to do that.

I did a little research and found out I can send you care packages once you're done with boot camp, so get ready to accept those soon. I've got some ideas on what to send.

I think those are all the updates going on. How is everything else?

I was excited to receive your first letter and I know I'll be anticipating the next. Hope you're being careful out there.

XO-

Your tummy-troubled wife,
Indy

CHAPTER 10

Indiana

"ISN'T IT FUNNY THOUGH?" Roger drones on about his little work tidbit.

In all honesty, I can't believe we're still talking about it. The restaurant is filled to capacity and all I wish is that my Arnold Palmer were spiked right about now.

Roger and I are at lunch and I was initially excited to be out of the house after a week of shit sleep. Work has been nothing but endless meetings and late nights after I had to catch up following Noah's brief hospitalization. I'm so grateful he'll be alright, but now I'm working nonstop, and I swear my eyes are seeing double when I look at my computer screen.

Unfortunately, with this lackluster story from Roger, I'm currently fighting sleep at this table, listening to my boyfriend drone on about fucking spreadsheets, Excel, and organizing data for his latest meeting. I've zoned out as he goes on and on. Am I a bad girlfriend? Probably. Do I care right now? No. He hasn't asked me once if Noah is okay, so my patience is waning.

He's quick to pull me out. "Ana, seriously, can you imagine?"

I honestly hate that nickname he uses for me. I mean, my name is unique and he shortens it into Ana, not that there's something wrong with the name. But to go from Indiana to Ana just doesn't sit right. Everything Roger does is bland—even the way he cuts my name down. I suppress my eye roll.

"I'm sorry, I missed that," I say, holding back a yawn.

"I said, could you imagine if they really did name it 'Mr. Spreadsheet' or 'Master Plan' like they had thought about doing? I think it would be a completely different world out there." He looks at me with an expression that's hard to read.

Is he talking about Excel now? Is he serious?

To think I contemplated bringing Noah today to finally introduce him. He'd be bored out of his mind. He's spending the day with Kalli and her family; they're going to the zoo. Vivienne is obsessed with animals and loves imitating their sounds. Noah loves showing her around and it makes me wonder if I'll ever get to add to our little family. Noah would make the best big brother.

"I mean, do you remember that little paperclip on Word documents? Maybe that's where it stemmed from. The sky's the limit, really," Roger continues.

Stab me in the eye with this butter knife. Honestly, what the fuck? I'm dying a slow death over here.

I simply nod and give him a tight smile as I take a bite of my sandwich. Since running into Tyler, I can't stop thinking about him. *My husband.* Holy shit. I'm fucking married, although we're separated for all intents and purposes, and I'm sitting here with my boyfriend. Who has no clue about this double life I'm leading. What kind of sick human being does this?

I'm terrible. I'm a horrible, miserable person. I'm leading Roger on. I'm married and I can't keep doing this with another person until I make this right. All this time, I've let this marriage go on hanging over my head. I get it was done out of convenience, but it's still a marriage nonetheless. If someone did that to me, I'd be furious.

I feel like there's lead sitting in my stomach. I can't take another bite of food. What kind of heartless person does this to another person? I've led Roger on like some sort of insensitive prick. I'm over here mentally berating him for being boring over Excel and his job, all while I'm the one that deserves to be judged. Hell, I deserve Roger throwing me to the curb.

"Ana, you look like you've seen a ghost?" Roger says, pausing mid-sentence.

I put my sandwich down, unable to take another bite. I look at him and blurt out, "I'm married!"

———

"Hey, how was lunch?" Kalli says as I walk through her house.

"I would say it wasn't great," I admit, dropping my purse on her kitchen island.

"Eek, why?" she says, pulling out a sparkling water for me.

I can hear Noah and Julian in the backyard with Vivienne.

"Oh, you know. Just the normal lunch, with a side of confession garnished with a girlfriend telling her boyfriend she's married."

"What? No! Why, Indy?" Kalli's eyes go wide.

"Because, Kalli"—I throw my hands up by my sides—"it dawned on me as I sat there, letting him go on and on about Excel almost being called 'Mr. Spreadsheet' that I was mentally judging him on the boring conversation topic, when in reality, I'm the asshole because I'm dating him while I'm married. Who does that?!"

"Hold on—Excel was supposed to be called 'Mr. Spreadsheet'? That's a fucking weird name." She scrunches her nose.

I snap my fingers. "Focus, Kalli!"

"Sorry, babe. I'm focusing. So, then what happened?"

"He kept going on and on about his spreadsheet debacle. Then I interrupted him, and I just blurted that I was married —because I really was feeling like a jerk in that moment," I finally tell her.

"Well you are married, but you sort of aren't. You haven't seen each other in years. How did he react to it? Was he pissed?" Kalli asks.

"You'd think, right? He just sat there, with a blank expression," I throw my hands in the air. "I gave him a moment to ask follow-up questions. He honestly said 'okay' at one point and I thought he'd be mad, but he wasn't. I told him I understood if he wanted me to leave, but he said I didn't have to. We finished our meal and said goodnight. He said he'll call me later as if everything was normal."

"What? He didn't break up with you?!" Kalli looks as annoyed as I feel.

"No. I'm so confused. Nothing shakes the man. I think I'm more irritated by his non-reaction than he is that I didn't tell him I'm married."

I expected at least a raised eyebrow or something from Roger. Looking back, I think I would have had a stronger reaction from him if I told him Excel was dumb or that his job is boring than the dismissal I got at lunch today. Honestly, what the hell? He acted like I told him I bought a new pair of running shoes. He couldn't give a flying fuck.

"So, you agree he should care, right?" I ask Kalli.

"I mean, you've been dating for a decent amount of time. I would expect some sort of reaction beyond an 'okay' from him," she agrees.

"This whole thing is really weird. I left the lunch feeling way off. Actually, I amend that statement. I have felt off since Tyler looked into my eyes at Noah's school." I take a drink of my water and look out the window to see my little man handing Vivienne the ball.

The way he plays with her is so sweet. I can't help the automatic smile that spreads across my face.

"You should have seen the way he mimicked her at the zoo today. I had both of them making animal sounds. Well three if you count Julian by the end of the visit." She chuckles.

"I wish I had been there. Next time I'll have to join you. She's gotten so big." Time is definitely flying by. I still remember when Noah was Vivienne's age and I was still trying to manage so much.

Noah's deep-brown eyes spot me through the window and I wave.

"I should warn you, Noah's been asking to go—"

"Hi, Mom!" Noah comes barging in. "I want to go see the fire truck that saved me."

"That's what I was going to tell you," Kalli whispers as she walks past me.

I look from Kalli to Noah. I move closer to him, sweeping his hair off his sweaty forehead, and try to distract him. "How was the zoo?"

"It was a lot of fun. The lion was so big!" He gestures with his arms to show me and I laugh.

"Wow! Did you make all the sounds with Vivienne?"

"Yes! And she tried to stand like a flamingo, but kept falling over." He giggles.

"She's so silly." I laugh along with him. I look over at Kalli. "Thanks so much for taking him with you. I owe you one."

"Of course. It was our pleasure. Thanks for helping me with Viv today, Noah."

Noah looks proudly at Kalli then over at me and scrunches his nose. He starts shaking his head. "I want to see the fire truck, Mom. On our way home."

"Maybe another day, sweetie," I start telling him.

"But we drove by and they're there! I saw them when we drove by today. Pleeeease, Mom," he insists.

"Yeah, about that," Kalli begins, "we were driving back from the zoo and apparently the station that helped him is the one by us. He caught sight of them washing the truck. I guess he recognized them. The kid has eagle eyes," she whispers low enough for me to hear that last part. "I wouldn't know, but he claims some of them were the same." She shrugs her shoulders.

I sigh and try to convince him otherwise. "Noah, they might be out on a call right now. It would probably be best to stop by another day, okay?"

"Mom, you're always working and I have school," he declares.

Man, this kid knows how to get me every single time. Using the work card gets me—and he knows it.

I look over at Kalli and she knows I'm going to cave. "Why don't I go with you both? I'll make sure Julian's good with Viv." She winks in my direction.

While Kalli is in the backyard, I'm working to ensure Noah grabs the items he brought over. I'm helping him with his shoes when Kalli makes her way to the foyer.

"Okay, all set here. Let me grab my purse," she says.

Julian and Vivienne make their way to the foyer as we are about to leave.

"Noah, thanks for being such a big help today," he says as he gives Noah a high-five.

"Sure. No problem," Noah smiles. He turns to Viv, "Roarrr!"

Vivienne lights up at the sound and repeats it to him. Soon they're both trying to outshine each other in volume until we're out the door and I think my eardrums are on the verge of bursting.

"Who knew that girl could get so loud?" I say, rubbing my ear.

"Oh, consider yourself lucky Julian wasn't involved. I had a headache a few hours ago." She laughs.

Kalli is nice enough to drive, and we pile into her SUV. While Noah seems ecstatic in the backseat, sitting in the booster seat she borrowed from me earlier today, I've got butterflies multiplying by the second as I sit in the passenger seat.

There's no guarantee Tyler will be on shift, but there's still a chance we'll bump into him. My guard's up and I really have no idea how I'll feel seeing him today. I saw him for a short amount of time the other day and I haven't been the same since then. My entire week has felt off-kilter since and this time I'll be on his turf.

By the time Kalli pulls into the driveway, I'm close to wanting to hurl my lunch. The things I'll do for my son are remarkable because I'm close to begging for my best friend to turn this car around, but I hold myself together for him.

I get out the passenger side and help Noah out of his booster. The moment he's out of the car, he grabs the drawings he made for the crew. Apparently, he used some of the extra time he had while Viv was napping to draw firetrucks and pictures of himself with those members that helped save his life that day at school.

"Don't run too far ahead, please," I tell Noah. His excitement is palpable.

"Try to take a deep breath. It'll be okay." Kalli walks up beside me.

"It just feels like a lot. I haven't seen him in so long and now I'll be seeing him twice in the span of a week, possibly," I tell her.

"Maybe luck will be on your side today. He might not be here." She brings her arm around my shoulders and pulls me into a half hug.

"Have you noticed my luck? I doubt it." I give her a side

eye and laugh. There's no humor behind it, but she laughs with me.

"Come on. I won't let you go through this alone." We catch up to Noah and walk through to the equipment bay. We find two firemen standing near the garage doors, which are open.

"Well, good afternoon, young man," a tall, red-haired fireman says. He kneels down to greet Noah, giving him a fist bump.

"Hi, I'm Noah," my son says with a big smile.

"It's nice to meet you, Noah. I'm Tucker. But the guys like to call me Malloy. What can I help you with?" Malloy asks, moving his hand through his beard.

"You came to my school. I was stung by a bee right here," Noah explains, pointing to the spot where the bee stung him.

"Oh, yes, I remember. You were pretty allergic, if I remember correctly," Malloy looks up at me for confirmation.

"Yes, he is." I nod my head. "I'm Indiana, his mother. Thank you so much for everything you did for him that day. Noah and I wanted to come by and say thank you."

Malloy looks at me a moment, then down at Noah, quickly bringing his attention back to me, his smile widening. "Of course. Indiana, you said?" He brings his hand out for me to shake.

"Yes, Indiana Ranton. And this is my friend Kalli. Kallista Francis."

"Nice to meet you both." Malloy is smiling wide, a little too happy with this encounter. He seems almost giddy at the fact we're here. I don't understand it, but soon his attention is back on Noah.

"Noah, you want to come check out the fire engine? We just got it all cleaned up." He juts his chin in the direction of the truck behind him.

"Mom, can I?" Noah looks over his shoulder at me.

"Sure, but please be careful," I tell him. "Listen to Mr. Malloy."

"Yes, Mom," Noah says as he's already looking in amazement at the truck.

"Well, hello. Good to see you again," I recognize the firefighter greeting me. Shit, what was his name? It started with the letter R.

"Hi. Rover, is it?"

"Close. It's River. Hi, nice to meet you." He shakes Kalli's hand.

"Hi, I'm her friend Kalli. I'm so sorry, do you have a restroom nearby?"

"Yes, down there and to the left." He points her in the right direction.

She scurries off and I'm left behind and hoping there are no surprises while she's gone.

"Sorry about your name. That day was a lot for me," I say apologetically.

"It's fine. Luckily you didn't say it around my brother or I wouldn't live it down." He winks. "He seems to be doing better." He juts his chin toward Noah.

"Much better. Took a while for the swelling to go down, but he made a full recovery, thank goodness. He wanted to come by and see everyone that saved him that day." I smile up at River. "Thank you, by the way."

"It's no problem. Just doing our job." River looks at Noah again, then back at the double-doors.

A few of the other guys start making their way out to the bay to greet us. They're showing Noah all the features of the truck and his face is glowing. River leaves me behind to watch them show off the truck to my son and meets up with the rest of the guys. They even let Noah put a helmet on and I snap some pictures.

All of a sudden, I feel a presence next to me. At first I

think it's Kalli returning, but the way my body reacts to the presence, *his* presence, I know exactly who is near me.

I turn around to see Tyler standing and staring at me.

"Hey, Indy," he greets me.

"Tyler. How are you?"

"Oh, just peachy. That's quite a kid you got there."

Peachy? Well, he's certainly not the Ty from high school.

There was a time when our roles were reversed. I was the light and airy one, and he was the dark and stormy presence. Now, it feels as if we've switched. My guard is up and he has let go of the darkness that once surrounded him.

I can feel my spine straighten and my veins fill with ice as I stare back at him. My heart quickens as I look at the man I thought I could give my whole heart to—the man I *did* give my whole heart to. Only for him to destroy it. Now I fight not to give into temptation.

"It's good to see you again," Tyler breaks the trance my mind has fallen into.

"Don't do that," I tell him.

"Do what?" He looks at me quizzically.

"Be nice. Don't be nice to me." I can hear the disdain dripping off me.

"You want me to be an asshole?" he asks as if it's hard for him.

"Yes, you seemed to be good at it when you wrote me that final letter. Just project that each time you see me. It's better that way, Ty," I tell him then turn around, looking back at Noah, reminding myself why I'm here.

Tyler needs to walk away. Instead, he inches closer to me. "I would love to grab a coffee, Indy."

"That's not you being an asshole," I tell him, keeping my eyes forward, watching Noah interact with the firefighters.

"The person I was in that letter wasn't who I wanted to be," he says.

"Yet, it was the version of you I remember most," I bite back.

That's the version that stuck and the person that broke my heart. I fell in love with him before that. I know that's what I felt for him and in one single correspondence, he torched my feelings for him.

He takes a deep inhale. "Indy, come on. What do you want from me?"

"I wanted everything. Today, I want nothing. I just want Noah to be happy, and I want to leave. We came here to thank your crew for what you did for Noah." I look over at him. "That's all. I honestly hoped you wouldn't be here."

My words are harsh and from the way he's looking at me, I can see I've hurt him. This isn't who I used to be. But I've built a barrier, especially when it comes to Tyler Hunter. He broke me, so I picked up my pieces and glued them back together the best way I knew how. The way they pieced back together, with the cracks and all, is just how I am now.

"Listen, we should just—"

"Hey, what did I miss?" Kalli comes strolling up, not a care in the world.

"Hey," I say, lacking her enthusiasm.

"Hi, I'm Tyler—"

"Oh. My. Fucking. God!" Kalli says. Luckily, she isn't loud enough to draw attention from the group at the truck. "You're @huntsamillion, aren't you?" She covers her mouth, but I can tell she'd scream if she could.

What am I missing?

I look from my best friend to Tyler. He has a smirk on his face and Kalli looks like she might wet her pants. Is she hopping in place like my kindergartner?

"You look like a fool. What are you doing, Kalli?" I say through gritted teeth.

"This is why you should have social media, Indy!" She

smacks my arm. Then she looks at Tyler. "Can you believe she doesn't have any accounts? I mean, who doesn't have an online presence these days?" She rolls her eyes and huffs.

Tyler looks at me, then brings his attention back to my best friend. "I appreciate meeting my fans. Thanks for following."

"Are you kidding? I love your content. That last one where you did that run, then immediately followed with a workout. Oh my gosh, then there's that time where you did a half-marathon and raised money for a little girl battling leukemia? I cried." Kalli looks at Tyler completely enamored.

Seriously, what is happening right now? I'm standing in front of the two of them, mouth agape.

"Look at her; she's lost." Kalli points at me.

"I have a social media page. It's garnered some attention." Tyler shrugs.

"*Some attention*? No. It's more than that. He has a shit-ton of followers. Don't let him fool you," Kalli says. "I'm a Prowler, you know."

"What the hell is a Prowler?" I can't help the look of disgust on my face.

"It's a SpaceBook group. You wouldn't get it." She waves me off and smiles at Tyler.

Am I in another dimension?

"I really appreciate that. It's definitely gained a lot of traction." Tyler gives her a small smile.

Who is this guy? He's acting all shy, and nothing like the bad boy from high school.

Am I living in the upside-down? And is he winning over my best friend when she was all pissed off after I told her what Ty did to me in that letter?

"We should really get going, right Kalli?" I give her a look.

"Huh?" She looks over at me. "Oh, yes, we should," she nods. "It was so great meeting you *Hunter*." She winks. She fucking winks at *my* husband.

No, Indy. DO NOT REFER TO HIM AS YOUR HUSBAND. That's how we start going down a dangerous path.

"Noah, sweetie, we should go." I wave for him to come down.

Noah starts to make his way over. I hear him thanking everyone for showing him the truck. Luckily, he's not making a fuss about leaving, which is a win in my book.

The guys thank him for the drawings and the pride on Noah's face is priceless. Although we ran into Tyler, seeing the happiness on my son's face has made this trip worth it in the grand scheme of things.

Noah recognizes the person beside me as he approaches and starts running, "Hunter!"

"Hey, buddy! Good to see you're doing so much better," Tyler greets him.

"Yes. My mom said I was super brave."

"I agree. The bravest actually," Tyler tells him.

"I made you a special picture," Noah tells him. I watch as Noah pulls a picture from his pocket. I wasn't aware he had another. It's then I see he has a folded one in his back pocket.

Tyler kneels to look at it.

"I made this one for you. My aunt Kalli helped write your name," Noah says.

"You did a good job. Let me guess—this is me." He looks over to Noah for confirmation and receives a nod. "And this is you and your mom?" Another nod of approval. "And is this a cat?"

"Yes, that's my cat. His name is—"

"Oh, can I guess?" Tyler jumps in.

"Yes!" Noah laughs.

"Snowflake?" Tyler guesses and quickly looks up at me. I suppress a gasp.

"No!" Noah laughs harder. "His name is Darth."

"Darth? That's an interesting name. Like Darth Vader?" Tyler laughs.

"Yeah! You like Star Wars too?" Noah asks, his smile wide.

"I do, actually. Why did you name the cat Darth? You like the dark side?" Tyler glances at me real quick, but his gaze returns to Noah without missing a beat.

"Star Wars is my favorite movie, and Darth is a funny name," Noah says as if it's the most normal explanation.

"Noah is obsessed with anything Darth Vader. He fell in love with this kitten, even though he possesses no Darth qual-ities. He's very sweet and doesn't belong on the dark side. Isn't that right, Noah?" I add.

"Well, Uncle Julian says he's on the dark side." Noah laughs and Kalli snickers.

"You're right. He's not a fan of Uncle Julian." I smile.

Tyler smiles at our interaction and I remember I'm in his company and my smile fades. Ty turns to Noah, "I love this picture. Thank you. I'll keep it with me all the time."

"You will?" Noah asks.

"Of course. It's the first one someone has ever made me," he tells my son.

"Really?"

"Yep. Thank you," Tyler says, extending his hand out for a fist bump that Noah returns.

Kalli and Noah begin the walk to the car and I fall in step behind them. I nod and wave goodbye to the crew, thanking them for showing Noah around.

I think Tyler is going to stay back, but I realize he's walking out with us. He's walking at my pace, however, I don't initiate conversation.

"Indy, honestly, I'd really like to grab a coffee with you. Please."

"Why?" I finally ask.

"I think we have a lot to discuss," he answers.

"Really?" I abruptly stop walking and look at him.

"Well, yes," he says.

"Okay, fine. We can meet up." I pull out my phone and hand it over for him to input his number. Once he's done so, I pocket it and look up at him. "But I only have one thing I want to discuss." I tell him, arms crossed.

"Okay, great. What do *you* want to discuss?" he asks.

"Our divorce."

CHAPTER 11
Hunt's Prowlers

HUNT'S
PROWLERS
SPACEBOOK GROUP

momma_2_viv
I met @huntsamillion and he's so sweet! #hubbahubba

Heather4_30
You're so lucky @momma_2_viv. We live many states away, but I saw him run that marathon and raise all that money for that girl with leukemia. He seems like a kindhearted soul. #cutiewithaheart

HUNT'S
PROWLERS
SPACEBOOK GROUP

Savannah_K2004
I loved his running video a few weeks ago.
It motivated me to start running again. I
started watching his stuff for the eye candy,
believe it or not, but now I'm back to
working out. #eyecandytoworkouts
#thanks #healthier

Lindsey780
He seems like a cool guy. Love
watching his videos. Wish I lived in
Boston to see him around in person.
His last running video looked
amazing. #hottiesthatrun

CHAPTER 12

Indiana

10 YEARS AGO

July 12, 2015

Dearest Secret Softie,

You're receiving this from an official Chicagoan. I just moved from California a few days ago and I'm living in a tiny apartment on my own. I won't pretend it's fun just yet because it's pretty lonely. I've never had a place all to myself.

Maybe I need a pet or something. Too bad the rental agreement said no animals allowed or I'd get a cat. I hear they're easy to have around, especially if I'm gone all day. Although, that seems unfair.

I saw the cutest one the other day. It was white and had the prettiest green and yellow eyes. I imagined her name was Snowflake.

Maybe one day. Manifesting it into existence.

How about you? Do you want a pet one day? My parents never let us have an animal. Bryce is allergic to a lot of things, dogs and cats being in the mix of those. Add to the fact my mom isn't really an animal lover.

Other than that, my first year in California was stressful, but definitely eye-opening. My brother is a messy roommate and I learned a lot about having him living with me. He's moving to Oregon in the next three weeks. I moved to Chicago sooner than I planned because my internship started a few days ago and I needed to get settled.

So far, Chicago suits me. The weather is more humid than the west coast, that's for sure. It's going to take some time to get used to. My co-workers have been nice so far. The publishing world is different from what I imagined. As soon as I started work this morning, I hit the ground running. I thought being in an office setting would feel stuffy, but it's been welcoming and fun so far.

Where are you now? Can you tell me? Is it top secret? Can you divulge such information to your wife?

The care package this time around includes some Sour Patch Kids, which I know you love, along with Laffy Taffies. I removed the banana ones because you always said those tasted artificial to you.

I know I usually include a thriller as a book, but I've decided to spice things up this month. You're getting a dirty book too. I've highlighted some of the spots I think are extra juicy for you—wink wink. Enjoy!

I think I've updated you on everything on my end. I'll let you know how school is once I've started. I'm taking a break on classes this summer before starting in the fall. I needed to take this time to settle in and just work before the semester starts.

I hope you're well. Do you ever get time to come visit the States? If so, know you can stay with me. I've got this whole apartment to myself. Oh my gosh... did I just proposition you? I completely meant that like a friend, I swear!

I'm going to stop writing before I make more of a fool of myself. Stay safe!

XO-

Your wife who is trying to look after your needs, but not like that,

Indy.

CHAPTER 13
Indiana

MY HEART IS STILL RACING as we drive away from the firehouse. While we head over to her place, Kalli keeps looking over, making sure I'm not going to break down and cry. I hold it in until Noah gets out of the car. The minute I reach back and unbuckle him, he leaps out of the car and runs inside to see Julian and Vivienne.

I stay back and finally break down. I didn't think I was going to be this emotional over finally asking for a divorce from Tyler, but apparently, I was holding back. But the second the first tear falls, a dam breaks and Kalli holds me as I let go.

It feels like I'm letting go of my past. Not just a piece of Tyler, but a piece of myself is being erased with this entire relationship. It's not like we were anything other than something completely fake. He married me to make my life easier and I accepted.

Now I'm stronger and my tears are a way of shedding that layer of my past. It feels like I'm saying a final goodbye to the girl I was—the one who had a brother, who had a boy that showed this version of himself that held the possibility of love and who was naive and never thought life could hold so much pain.

There are so many layers to why I've held onto this marriage and now it's all coming to the forefront of my thoughts. It's causing me to have a slew of feelings and the emotional toll it's taking on me feels crippling at times. I know I'll have to confess everything to Tyler at some point, yet I don't know how to put it all into words when the day comes.

Once I leave Kalli's place, I'm calmer. On the drive home, Noah and I stop to grab supplies to make homemade pizzas —his favorite meal. I grab my signature toppings—ham and pineapple. I watch Noah cringe as I put everything on my personalized pizza, savoring his snarky remarks because my brother did the same thing. Noah is exactly like his dad, enjoying black olives and pepperoni.

We finish putting the pizzas in the oven and we're currently picking a movie for the night. "Can we watch one of my dad's favorite movies tonight?" Noah asks as he scrolls through our streaming service.

"Of course. Can I see the remote?" I motion for the controller.

I find the movie I'm thinking of and press play. The opening credits begin and I see Noah's face light up when the realization dawns on him. He's seen this movie dozens of times, but I've never admitted to him that Bryce loved this movie.

"My dad loved *this* one? Just like me?" His eyes are big with amazement.

"Yep, just like you," I smile as I push back the lump in my throat. This day has been full of emotion, but at least right now it's a good feeling knowing I'll feel my brother's presence surround us as we eat pizza and hear familiar sounds of his favorite characters on the screen.

"No one likes *The Phantom Menace*! We liked the same *Star Wars* movie." My brother's mini looks absolutely delighted at the revelation.

He falls back on the couch and pulls Darth close to him. Our cat cuddles him, which is unusual for a feline. I can't help the smile that creeps up on my face, taking in the sweet sight.

The night continues on, our bellies filled, and Noah continually teasing me about my topping choices as he looks over at the pineapple on my plate. I tickle him each time he makes a comment, and he attempts to do the same to me, but I block him with a pillow.

I see his eyes getting heavy as we get close to the end of the movie. Noah tries to fight bedtime, but I promise him he can finish the movie tomorrow. Luckily, he understands he needs sleep after the long day he's had and I'm able to get him ready for bed quickly.

After I close his bedroom door, I move down the hall and downstairs toward the kitchen. That's when the realization hits me of the mess we made with dinner. These are the moments I'm hit with how exhausting being a single parent is. But no matter how tiring it is, Noah is worth it.

I move through the kitchen, washing the dishes and wiping down the countertops until everything is back in its place. Once everything is finished, I grab a glass of wine. My mind wanders back to Tyler and all the emotions that have crept in since we saw one another this afternoon.

His stormy-blue eyes keep coming back to me and all I think about is the fact that he's now the one with this airiness surrounding him, while I'm the one carrying this storm cloud over my head. He's to blame for my anger; and now these walls are built to protect myself all due to his heartless ways. I can't let him hurt me again.

That's why this divorce has to happen, but at the same time, it means digging up things I've pushed aside for so long. I throw the dish rag I've been holding on to the kitchen counter with added irritation and start walking out of the room, slamming the light switch off, as if it's deserving of my anger. Luckily, I don't spill the wine because my movements are lacking any grace.

We can't keep letting this lingering frustration follow us. It's not healthy for me. I can't move on if I don't put this thing with Tyler to bed. We need to move on from here.

Then why does it hurt so bad? Why did I cry like my heart would never recover when I was in Kalli's car?

Walking to my room, I deposit my wine glass on my bedside table, and move straight into my closet. I know exactly where my feet are leading me. I see the box that's followed me through every move. I pull down the simple square box down, pushing the dust off the lid.

I return to my bed and dump the contents on the mattress. I haven't opened it in years. I still remember the last time I closed all my journals inside, promising myself I wouldn't look back. As if I would unlock all the pain if I simply tipped the lid open slightly.

But I feel compelled to revisit my words, just for old time's sake. Apparently, I'm a glutton for punishment.

Riffling through the papers, I see other things, like the gold band from years ago, the tattered green bracelet I wore, along with the letters he sent me. There's even a highlighted book I never sent him.

It's like looking through a time capsule, if I'm being honest. I sift through everything, looking for the journal I labeled with the oldest date. It's remarkable I kept these for so long, a part of me never feeling like I could part with the feelings that I wrote down on these worn pages.

I finally find what I'm looking for, the year scribbled on the front. I pull it out and open the composition book, the cover creaking from underuse. I glide my hand down the front page, feeling the indentations of paper where the pen creased along the notebook.

I feel the lump forming in my throat, emotion pouring in as I think back at how raw and real everything between Tyler and I has always been. Even now, I know he's the only person I've ever really given my heart to. Since that day five years ago, I've put walls up.

I know I'm the one that's become closed off and distant with anyone since him. Every relationship I've had never felt right because I've found an excuse to find a flaw.

I touch my cheek to feel the moisture from a lone tear that has escaped. Wiping it, I compose myself and finally look down to read the words I once wrote about a life that feels so distant and forgotten. The girl that wrote them doesn't even remind me of the person I see today in the reflection in the mirror.

August 8, 2015

Dear Journal,

I've never been a girl that wrote in a diary or a journal, so this feels a little weird for me. But I'm reading a contemporary romance and the character keeps writing in a journal, so I thought I'd try it out.

I've always had a lot of girlfriends growing up, but life got a little chaotic for me after high school graduation and I sort of started walking my own path. I distanced myself from them and we lost touch. I miss having people to talk to, and living alone is really isolating.

I'm feeling more and more disconnected from my past life in Nevada since I found out my parents adopted me. I don't know why, but I feel like I'm living in limbo since that night. My entire life I've felt so comfortable in my skin, only to find out it was all a lie—at least that's how it feels for me currently.

I do still feel a close connection to Bryce. My brother makes me laugh and gets how controlling my parents are, especially with me. But now we are living so far apart, with me being in Chicago and him in Oregon, we will barely see one another. It's just hard figuring out life on my own.

The only other person I feel who knows me is Tyler, funny enough. We are worlds apart, but at the same time, he understands a side of me I don't have to explain. He talks to me, not through me like everyone else in my life seems to—in letters, which feels more intimate. We're married, which is a secret only my brother knows. But it's not even for love; we're married because I needed insurance so I could care for myself.

He's just that kind of a person—not that anyone would guess that from looking at him. He's brooding and sort of intimidating if you look at him. He scowls a lot. He rode a motor-cycle in high school and it was sort of hot, if you ask me. Every girl swooned over him. I won't lie, even I couldn't ignore how electrifying it was to see him walk by. He's got a presence about him. But it scared my parents, me being around him. We are polar opposites—me being valedictorian and him being the ultimate bad boy.

I haven't seen him in over a year. He's in the Army, so he's not around to visit. But the letters are something I cherish when I do receive them.

He's the one who pushed me to be independent and step away from my parents financially. If it weren't for his confidence in me, I don't know if I would have had the courage. I moved to a new state and cut myself off from them, instead of going to California and attending the college they chose for me. They wanted me to follow in their footsteps, going to the same university as them for medical school. I would have lived out their dreams, versus having dreams of my own.

My parents love me, there's no doubt. But many of their aspirations have felt like ones they've wanted me to live for them. I started to reflect on the fact they never really asked me what I wanted out of life. Once I moved out and financially cut ties, I realized I had very different dreams than my parents put on me.

Studying medicine wasn't something I ever wanted for myself. Now that I've gotten a taste for the publishing world, I might want to be an author one day. Seeing my name sprawled across the cover of a book sounds exciting to me. I could see myself as a best-selling suspense author or something along those lines. It thrills me to think about and that's what a career should be.

If it weren't for Tyler Hunter, I would be living someone else's dream. I'd possibly be resentful and likely hurting. As much as many around me in high school thought he had this rough exterior, he's only shown me a softer side. My parents misjudged him, pushing him out of my life.

But since he's been back in mine, all he's shown me is this tenderness that fills me with anticipation when I see his writing sprawled across an envelope.

I'm starting to realize that with each letter he writes, maybe this marriage isn't fake after all. I think I'm starting to catch feelings and it's becoming a little more real with each stamp I put on those dang envelopes.

I close the journal abruptly, my heart pounding with the memory of writing those words. I remember my heart opening up to him so easily that summer and I never questioned how carefree it was for me back then. I welcomed my feelings for Tyler, without question.

I shove the journal away, my heart feeling the confusion of the day tugging at it in multiple directions, but my mind is completely set on the fact this divorce *is* necessary. I need to move on or I won't be able to give Noah the future he deserves; even if in some way, it goes against what my brother wanted. Then again, my brother didn't have a full picture of what was to come. I'm no longer going to have this hanging over me. Tyler Hunter is not going to be the person holding my heart any longer, not even a morsel of it.

CHAPTER 14

Tyler

IT'S hard to wrap my head around the fact that Indy wants a divorce, even though I knew it was coming. But when I asked to see her, I thought she'd be open to a conversation.

Realistically, we should have been divorced years ago. She obviously hasn't needed to stay married for some time now. She has been independent and thriving financially for a number of years, but we've ignored it until now.

I know it's the right thing. She deserves to be free of me; I understand that. But she's been a constant in my life, even if I ruined it a handful of years ago. She's always been in the back of my mind, but seeing her recently has brought her to the forefront of my thoughts. She's all I think about when my day gets quiet.

I'm doing everything I can in this moment to focus, but I'm having a hard time. The sun is strong as it beats down on me in front of the firehouse. I committed to this, excited to launch my first recording in front of the station for my followers to see me in action.

They'll be eager to see me in firefighting gear and I know it will probably make the Prowlers wild. I don't fully follow their antics, but Malloy constantly gives me updates on what they're chattering about. I've decided to come in on my day off and film.

Not sure I'll regret this next decision, but I'm roping in Malloy's help too. Too bad I'm lacking enthusiasm as I'm sleeping like actual shit lately. It sucks that something I loved doing for the people that have shown me so much love online is giving me no joy at the moment.

"Dude, what's up with you today?" Malloy asks, wiping the sweat off his brow.

"I'm just not feeling it. I can't muster the energy to do this, but I'll snap out of it." I look around, irritation the only feeling passing through me as I take in my surroundings. I haven't told him what Indy said as she left the station the other day.

"I thought you said Cap and the Lieutenant were good with this. Have they been giving you crap or something?" He looks around, as if he's going to get in trouble.

"No, it's not about that. Indiana told me she wants a divorce." I sigh while grabbing another set of weights, giving him my back.

When I turn around, Malloy's gaping at me, shock evident on his face.

"Listen, I don't want to make a big deal about it," I say nonchalantly.

"Hunter, I know you keep things close to the chest, but you don't have to brush this off. I don't know your whole history with her, but honestly, you don't have to pretend with me."

"I'm not pretending. I'll get over it. I'm just processing is all," I lie.

"Hunter," Malloy continues.

"Seriously, Malloy, it's not a big deal at all." I urge.

"Then put the weights down and look at me and say that." He comes closer to me and crosses his arms.

I put the weights down and mimic his stance. Malloy is a

big guy, hovering over me at six foot six. I'm not a short guy at six two myself, but he's burly and built like an ox. His trimmed beard is overpowering. If I didn't know him to be the kindest human, I'd be intimidated, but he's a marsh-mallow inside.

"It just threw me off when she told me. I know it's time. I mean, the marriage is a sham, right? So, why should I care?" I shrug my shoulders, trying to play this off as indifference.

"Because I think you love her deep down, you're just not owning up to it," he says. "I don't know if you're just ignoring your feelings or you are going to let her go because you think she's better off without you. Either way, it's a mistake to walk away without fighting for her."

"Does it matter at this point? She wants a divorce. She already expressed her wishes," I confess.

"Hunter, don't be a fool." He scoffs.

"Malloy, she wants out. I'm not going to try and force this. I tried that for years with my parents. I don't need to force someone to try and love me," I finally admit.

The minute I say it, I see him soften. "Dude, your parents sound like assholes. I'm sorry that's the upbringing you got. I had a fucknut for a father, so I get half of what you're saying. But you deserved better, believe me. So for that, I truly am sorry you missed out on having someone good to look up to. But she's not your parents, Hunt. Just try to talk to her when you see her again. That's all I ask, alright?"

I nod, taking in what he's saying. He's right. I should try to explain my side of things. Hopefully she'll at least be open to hearing what I have to say, even if it gets me nowhere, I can sleep better knowing she understands why I torched every-thing between us years ago.

I turn back to grab my weights again while Malloy sets up the camera. He's started to grasp a little bit of what I do, becoming a good wingman on social media with me.

As we're about to begin, I hear someone step out from the garage.

"Don't worry, the true star has arrived!" River's voice booms. To top it off, he's got Ella strapped to his chest, her baby legs bouncing as she smiles with her baby teeth showing off at us.

"Oh, Lord. What are you doing here? How the hell did you find out about this?" Malloy groans. "And why do you have Ella?"

It doesn't stop Malloy from grabbing Ella's toes and greeting her with a high-pitched voice and pretending to eat her toes as a loud scream of joy comes out of her.

"Are you kidding me? And pass up the opportunity to become the next Station 10 star? Heck to the no!" River flexes his biceps as he struts along the sidewalk. He's been better about his language now that Ella is starting to become more verbal.

It's hard not to snicker with his antics. "What are you expecting to do?" I ask him.

"You tell me, boss." He moves his hand through his hair, as if he's a model. I can't contain the eye roll. Then he kisses his niece's head and tells her, "We'll break the internet, won't we my princess? Uncle and Ella are going to be number one on Hunter's page."

"Seriously, what in the world are you going to do with her strapped to your chest?" I ask, looking at him like he's crazy.

"Why don't you do the workout you were conjuring up in your head and leave the creativity to me, hot stuff?" He smirks. I should have known River had an idea up his sleeve the entire time.

Getting the rest of my stuff set up, Malloy instructs me where to stand and we begin. I hate to admit it, but I've never laughed so much filming before. Damn River and his charm.

———

I'm sitting at the restaurant looking at my latest post in front of the station. It is the most popular one I've ever done and my smile is instant. Seeing little Ella with the fake dumbbells River had her holding is adorable. River pretending to coach her as he carries her while lifting his own weights is—and I hate to admit this—genius. The whole thing was well-received.

Apparently Abby was fine having Ella join the post and River got her permission prior. Ella's little legs were moving and kicking the entire time. She squealed—not certain if it was due to Malloy making funny faces or from River's bouncing around while he ran around behind me.

At one point, Ella took a break and River did the workout with me, shirt off and his ball cap backwards. That smirk he wears and the dimple that pops out will be popular with viewers. He knows it too.

I know people loved his wild ways. I had so many comments about "Rowdy River" on my post, they're asking when he'll make a reappearance.

Of course, Kennedy is texting me how insufferable he's become with his rise to fame and I can't help her with that. The last text read:

KENNEDY

> Fuck this shit. If you think River was bad before—he's a nightmare now. If his head gets any bigger, they might see him from space. I'm shooting daggers at him any chance I get.

Then to top it off, I'm getting separate delusional texts from River saying:

RIVER

I think Kennedy finds my fame online sexy. She keeps giving me this smoldering look. I keep looking over and it's like she's undressing me with her eyes. I think she's going to pounce on me. I see why you're popular with the ladies. I'll keep telling her how cool this post is to get her hot and bothered.

I can't help the laugh that escapes. These two are an odd fit. It's the strangest dynamic. I'm still scrolling through my phone when I see a shadow loom over the table. I look up to find Indy staring down at me.

"Hi. Hey. Good to see you," I tell her, standing up suddenly.

"You too. Am I late? I thought we said twelve-thirty." She looks at her phone.

"No, we did. I got here a little earlier." I nod and smile.

She gives me a tight smile and I pull out the chair opposite me.

"I ordered you a sparkling water. I wasn't sure you still liked those, but I took a gamble," I tell her. "I'll drink it if—"

"No, I still do, thank you." I see her smile widen just a bit more, but then she seems to catch herself and corrects it back to a thin line. She's still apprehensive with me. I wish she'd give me a little more of the old Indy, but she's holding back. I don't fault her. It still stings though.

"Have you been here before?" I ask her. I haven't been to this place. It's a cute little bistro. I've probably passed it a dozen times, yet never come in.

She takes a seat. "Yes, Kalli and I come here often when we have time during lunch while at work." She's looking down at the menu.

"How long have you been friends? You two seem really close," I say.

"A good number of years. We actually met when she started working at the Chicago office. She transferred shortly after I did to the Boston location."

"I'm glad you have a supportive person to lean on, especially with Noah," I tell her, truly meaning it.

"Thank you," she says, a genuine smile spreading across her face.

"And Noah's dad. I overheard the school nurse mention he passed. I'm really sorry Indy. That must be hard for you—parenting on your own. How long were you together?" I've been curious about this the whole time.

The smile I finally coerced from Indy mere moments ago, drops immediately and I see sadness in its place. She looks away, her eyebrows pinched in worry.

"Indy, I'm sorry for bringing that up. Shit. You don't have to talk about him." Obviously this is a tough subject and I'm screwing this lunch up right from the start.

"Um, no, it's okay to ask about Noah's father," she says. "His dad—is Bryce. Noah's dad is my brother. I got custody of Noah after my brother passed away when Noah was just eight months old. I officially adopted him a few years back." She clears her throat and looks away, most likely hiding her emotion.

I'm taken aback by her words, not sure what to do with this information. Her brother died? When? How? Why didn't she tell me?

"When did this happen? Why didn't you—" I stop myself from finishing that question because it dawns on me right then that she's led a whole life without me that I have yet to see. In all honesty, I may never see. Because she's cutting me out of it permanently now. But I cut myself out if it the minute I lied to her five years ago.

"I'm sorry about Bryce. I didn't know."

"How could you? You left. Abruptly." She says it so matter-of-factly. But she isn't wrong. I walked away from her.

I took everything we started to build together and tarnished it. In true Tyler fashion, I blew it up. And I let her grieve alone. She had no one to lean on because her circle was so little already and I made it even smaller.

I feel like there's a rock in my stomach and I haven't even eaten lunch yet. I take a quick sip of my water, looking down at my menu. The server stops by and we quickly put in our orders.

Once the server leaves, I look at Indy, the silence between us is deafening.

"Listen, Ty, to be completely frank with you, I'm in a relationship. I've been seeing him for a few months and I think for me to continue moving forward in my life, I need to cut ties with my past. I need to begin fresh and this thing between us just can't continue. It's not healthy, you know?" She finally looks up from her rant, and I'm not sure if she had this speech memorized in her head, but she looks relieved she got it all out in the open.

"I understand," I tell her. "But don't you think we should talk about what happened all those years ago?" I ask her.

"I think you made yourself pretty clear on how you stood then," she says. "I already spoke to a divorce attorney and got papers drawn up. It's pretty cut and dry to get this done."

"You move fast," I say, the sarcasm dripping from my tone.

"Fast? You call a fake marriage of eleven years fast?" she throws back.

"I just think this deserves a little more time for us to talk. Especially since we haven't seen one another. I think I should explain myself further. It's just that—"

Right then there's commotion to my right. A pregnant woman pushes her chair back and screams, more in excitement than fear.

"Oh my gosh. Is that pee or did my water break!" I can't

help but look over and watch the situation unfold. Indy is drawn to the woman as well.

"I guess those *were* contractions I was feeling, babe!" She says that loud enough that most of the restaurant hears her. I stand up, grabbing my phone, ready to make a phone call.

I start to make my way over, knowing they might need some help.

"Hi, my name is Tyler. I'm a firefighter, off duty right now. Sorry to overhear, but can I lend a hand to get you to your car?" I offer.

"We walked here," her partner says, his eyes the size of saucers.

"Is this your first baby?" I ask, hoping his answer is yes. If so, they'll have a little more time until the baby makes their arrival.

"No, it's our fourth. But I have never had my water break. And I usually have to be induced. I've never gone into labor naturally. This is a first. We were trying to walk this baby out in hopes I could change things up," the woman says. She must be feeling a contraction coming, her hand splayed on her belly.

"You feeling a contraction?" I ask, already knowing her response.

"Yeah, it's not too bad," she says, even though she might be one of those that has been having them all day and progressing without knowing it.

"Sweetie, why are you making that face?" her partner asks.

"Oh, I just have to use the restroom." Then she whispers to him and I overhear her say, "I didn't go this morning."

Right then I suppress a groan because I already know this could get messy. I dial emergency services and ask for help at our location. Then I explain the situation to the restaurant staff. I shift to see Indiana's face look up at me in confusion.

I walk over to explain. "I think we'll have to continue this another time. I have a feeling this lady might have this baby pretty quickly, so I'm going to stay with her until emergency personnel arrive. I don't feel comfortable leaving her like this."

"I thought you said you're still in a probationary period though," she says.

"I am, but I've delivered babies before. Plus, I can't simply leave her. Look at them." I jut my chin in their direction to the panicked looks on their faces. Another contraction is already hitting her and it's only a matter of time, she's feeling even more pressure with that baby's head crowning.

"Sorry, I just don't think today's the day. Raincheck?" I tell her.

"Sure," she nods, her eyes focused on the couple behind me.

"Great, thank you," I say. "I'll text you my schedule and we can pick another date and time."

She nods and I turn around, my attention on the laboring woman.

I was not expecting my day off to go this way. The only positive is—I prolonged this impending divorce another day.

CHAPTER 15

Tyler

June 28, 2016

Dear Indy "damn-that-book-was-steamy" Ranton,

It's so stinkin' hot here right now. I can't seem to cool down. I can't say much about things at the moment, but you can guess from watching the news where we're stationed.

I've seen stuff I can't unsee and it's just been so unfortunately hard. Luckily, the guys I'm around have been like brothers to me and I'm grateful. We've started to work on some workout routines to pass the time. One of the guys here used to be a personal trainer and he's showing us some things. It's nice to pass the time doing something besides running in a circle and squats (though we still do those too).

Writing to you is my only other saving grace, honestly. Hearing from you is like watching a sunrise after the darkest storm, Indiana.

Sometimes I wonder what my life would look like if we hadn't made this pact and gotten married. Two years ago you needed me, but now, it seems, I'm in need of you just as much. I am leaning on this marriage in many ways emotionally. I long for these letters from you.

Knowing you are out there helps me carry on because it's lonely here. The nights are isolating, but the stars do shine bright without the big city buildings drowning out the night sky. Those are the moments I think of you most—wondering if you're thinking of me.

Do you think of me? Because I definitely let my mind ponder the "what ifs" of this life had I not left to pursue the Army. I sometimes let myself imagine if I was born into a life that your parents approved of, if I would be someone you could see yourself with.

I know I'm really letting my feelings out in this letter, but one of the guys confided in me regarding someone he cares about, and it got me thinking about you. The way you send me those care packages—I feel seen with you. You're the only person in my life that I feel knows me and I'm barely around you.

Those last two books you sent me were great! Were they authors you worked with? I really liked the notes you left in the margin, it felt like I was reading along with you. Some of those scenes were pretty hot, I'm not going to lie. I did picture you while reading them, our last night together still replays in my mind.

I know we aren't romantically involved, but I haven't had anyone close to me aside from you. And it got me thinking: What if you were? Then my mind just started going down that road. So now you're getting the middle of the night ramblings in this letter.

Maybe I'm saying too much, but at this point, I think it's safe to say we are each other's person to confide in when we need a shoulder to lean on, right? After two years being married and writing letters to one another, I honestly don't think anyone knows me this well. Damn, my own parents aren't even acquaintances in my life.

I hope you're doing good in Chicago. I'm optimistic the school year will go smoothly. I know last semester was a tough one for you with trying new medications. And I hope you've adjusted to the new meds well.

Still picturing you naked daily,

Ty

CHAPTER 16
Fire Hunters

PREVIOUSLY KNOWN AS HUNT'S PROWLERS

FIRE
HUNTERS
PREVIOUSLY KNOWN AS HUNT'S PROWLERS

bostonluv28
He's a firefighter? Oh my word
As an admin, I've officially changed the
name of this group. No more Prowlers,
we're FIRE HUNTERS NOW!
#firehunters #putoutmyfire
#yesplease

Samantha_Keys228
Who is that tall glass of water?
Rowdy River, you are one beautiful
man! Add in the backwards cap
and those muscles? #pickme
#slipperywhenwet #rowdyriver

BadgeLover211
I cannot believe they are
firefighters. They've gained a
new follower in me!
#firefighterlover #newmember

FIRE
HUNTERS
PREVIOUSLY KNOWN AS HUNT'S PROWLERS

Baseball_G_Boss
Hunter's cool, but not too sure this River character is all he's cracked up to be #alltalk #dimplesarelame #nothiskid

GoldenDogLuver987
He seemed like a standup guy, if you ask me. I think whomever snagged him up is a lucky person. #lucky #lotterywinner #idmarryhim #rowdyriverlover

Gingers4Life
I'm with @Baseball_G_Boss on this one. This newcomer looks like he could be a lot of work. I vote for @huntsamillion to stay with a solo gig for his page. #ditchthedimples #huntsolo

CHAPTER 17
Indiana

"HE SAID he has a really romantic night planned for us," I explain to Kalli.

"Oh, I bet he does," she says, sarcasm dripping from her tone.

"You can leave that attitude at the door," I tell her as I put Noah's toys in the bin, tidying up the house.

"How does Roger feel about your husband coming over today?" Kalli asks, tossing a handful of almonds in her mouth.

"Soon-to-be-ex-husband, remember? And Roger is completely fine about it, actually," I tell her, ignoring the fact my boyfriend seems completely indifferent to the fact Tyler is coming over today.

I even offered for Roger to be here in case he was jealous my husband would be here alone with me. Roger has nothing to be nervous or concerned about, but I thought a little jealousy would be shown. Roger remains unfazed by my revelation.

Tyler is headed over to continue the conversation about our divorce. It's been two weeks since our disastrous lunch where that woman went into labor. I contemplated another public lunch, but decided against that because I thought some other issue might arise in such a setting. This time, I'm thinking my house will be easier because there won't be any interruptions.

"My relationship with Roger is always growing and evolving. We're in a really great place right now, especially since I came clean about Tyler. It's infinitely better," I continue explaining, my smile plastered in place as I move through my living room, assessing what else needs to be put away.

"Yeah, infinitely growing like my iCloud storage. So romantic." Her eye roll can be felt from a mile away.

"I know you don't like Roger. I get it." I look over at her and cross my arms.

"Listen, it's not that I think he's a bad guy. He's actually benign overall. He's just boring. He lacks personality and you deserve someone with more character than him. When I look at you, I envision a person with some oomph. And Roger ain't that," she says.

"Well, he's what I found for me. And I think he'll be good for Noah," I say on a sigh.

Kalli gets up and walks over to me. "Indy, you've been through it. I love you, you know that. I will walk whatever path you need me to, always by your side. I'm giving you shit because that's my job, but no matter what, I'll support whatever road you choose. I love you so much, and I would walk through fire for Noah. You know that. I might fall asleep on said road though with Roger, but I'll stand by your side. Please know that." She winks and grabs the bits of trash I've found on my quest to toss in the kitchen.

"Thanks, Kalli. I love you!" I yell as she walks away.

I hesitate and then bring something up before she leaves. "Um, did you see some of the stuff Ty's followers have said about him?"

That makes Kalli rush back from my kitchen. "Indy, are you stalking your husband on social media?"

Without looking at her, I shrug my shoulders. "I just got curious what videos he posts and I was able to find them. Then I fell upon the SpaceBook group that someone created. They're, uh, vocal, for lack of a better word." I school my expression when I turn to face my best friend.

The smile she has plastered across her face is absolutely scandalous. "Oh you dirty little wife. You are so into him." She points her manicured finger at me. "What did you think of the chat?"

"Oh, I don't know, 'momma_2_viv,'" I look over at her and she laughs. She doesn't even seem embarrassed.

"What, you think I won't interact with them? I followed him before I knew your connection to him."

"You are too much."

She smiles. "Look, I think he's good for you. And I stand by my claim there's more to his story regarding that shitty letter he wrote you. I feel it in my bones," she pleads.

"You're ridiculous," I roll my eyes.

"Alright, ignore me, the wisest person you know."

She scoffs when I yell, "Hardly!"

She continues, "I'm going to get out of here before 'Fire Hunter' gets here. That man must know his way around a woman's body." She fans her face.

"Kalli! I don't think your husband would appreciate what you're saying," I tell her, even though she's not wrong.

"Stop being a prude, Indy! Julian wouldn't mind my words. That's all they are—words!" Kalli says, grabbing her purse and putting it over her shoulder.

"I hope you enjoyed your few minutes of meeting him when you did, because I will not have him running into us anymore. Tyler Hunter will no longer be a fixture in my life after today," I tell her.

"Too bad. I think, despite what you think, he's a better fit for you than Roger." She pulls her phone out and checks her messages, then looks back at me. "What?"

"Are you going to keep saying this to me?" I say, my mouth agape.

"You know honesty is my thing."

"To a fault, yes." I roll my eyes.

"Well, today is no different, Indy."

"Anything else you'd like to say before you leave?" I ask her.

"I think you should hear him out. He's asking for you to talk about what happened years ago and you're not giving him that," she says.

"Seriously? After what he did to me, you want me to offer him an olive branch?" I say.

"Well, after all this time, what does it hurt?" She shrugs.

"You're just saying that because you like his content online." I give her a look.

"That and his muscles and tattoos don't hurt," she smirks.

"You're incredible." I roll my eyes and start shoving her out my door. The laugh she gives is pure evil.

"You love me. Give me a call afterwards and let me know how it goes." She gives me a little wave as she laughs, walking to her car.

Once Kalli leaves my place, my living room is too silent and I'm reminded how much I needed her here to keep my mind occupied until Tyler arrives.

I open the drawer in the end table and find the journal I hid inside, taking a seat at the couch. There's still about thirty minutes before Tyler's scheduled to arrive, so I get comfortable, hoping to get lost in a bit of my past before he shows up. I don't know why I'm doing this to myself. This has become my new pastime since running into him. I used to write daily back then, so there are many entries to read.

July 1, 2016
Dear Journal,

I'm so confused right now. I just received a letter from Tyler and it's probably the most raw one I've gotten from him. He pretty much confessed how he felt about me—us—and I don't know what to do about it.

We write letters and we're married, but is he just feeling emotional or is he lonely? Is that where he's coming from? Is he just needing a physical release? Has he even been with anyone since that night we last saw each other? Surely he has. Ugh. I hate this.

When we first got married, although we felt a physical attraction for one another, we were going our separate ways. I had to focus on finding my independence and getting my health in order. Ty was going off to the Army, moving on to God knows where for an undetermined amount of time. Our lives were moving in separate directions.

I lived my life independently from him and I didn't think much of it. As much as we wrote letters, I never put much weight on us developing feelings. I started off my life in college dating, thinking nothing of it back then. At first, I embraced it, but then it felt strange. The more whatever this thing is with Tyler grew, the more I felt like I was doing something wrong. So I started to push dating aside in order to foster this growth with Tyler a little more.

I can act like Tyler and I aren't a thing, but it's hard not to have him in the back of my mind. How do I not though? We're technically married—legally speaking that is—and we say this started for me to get insurance and that's why we are here now, but I know it's more than that at this point. Yes, I need the health benefits, but I know my heart is invested too.

Tyler is not the kind of guy to tell someone how he feels. He keeps everything bottled up. Even when we were kids, he never really opened up to me about his feelings. Now, he just word-vomited everything. I'm stunned. And he pretty much told me how he feels without saying, "Indiana, I love you," or "I like you," but it was implied.

This is so weird. How do I respond? It feels like a huge leap in a new direction. I'm still on the fence about what to do. It doesn't mean I don't feel the same. I guess I just want to touch him. I want to kiss him and hold him. I miss him.

My phone chimes for the doorbell, pulling me away from the journal in front of me. The minute I know Tyler is here, the butterflies have once again quadrupled. These journal entries have reminded me the feelings I hid away long ago are just tucked away, waiting to be pulled up if I allow them.

As I walk to the front door, I move my hands down the front of my jeans, smoothing my clothes, the motion doing nothing to calm me down. Taking reassuring breaths, it's doing nothing to slow my racing heart, but I have to get this over with.

I reach my door and open it. The moment I see his gray-blue eyes, it feels like the wind is knocked out of me. It happens every single time I look at him, and today is no different.

"Hey, Indy," that deep voice of his greets me, his smile growing as his eyes look me up and down.

"Hello, Tyler," I say, keeping my voice as steady as possible. "Come on in." I motion, opening the door wider for him to pass.

He moves inside my house, while I close the door behind him. I follow, watching his frame move through the entry of my townhome. Tyler Hunter is no longer the person I saw years ago.

The man I saw six years ago was already stronger than the man I said "I do" to in Vegas back when we were mere eighteen-year-old kids. But now, as I take in this older version of him, nearly thirty years old now, I can see he's thicker in his upper body than he was over a handful of years ago.

I can see working as a firefighter has made him grow muscles in places along his shoulders where maybe the Army didn't before. His arms look stronger, even though he bulked up previously. He has definitely become more defined in that area. As he walks further into the house, I try not to ogle him, although I'm probably failing miserably.

Today he wears a light-blue shirt that clings to his upper body, allowing me to see the definition of this perfect man in front of me. I see tattoos on his biceps poking out from under his T-shirt sleeves on both sides; something I couldn't see when he was in uniform nor when we met up last. Although he's well defined on his upper body, his waist tapers, which I imagine forms a nice V if I were to touch him along that abdomen. I wonder if he has an eight-pack.

I think I need to turn on the air conditioning. There must be a heat wave coming today and the weather person did a poor job predicting it on the news earlier today.

"Indy, you feeling a bit hot right now? You look flushed," Tyler abruptly turns his gaze my way and catches me looking him over.

I look up, pulling myself from my thoughts. "Huh? Oh, I was cleaning up before you got here. You know, having a kid with their things all over the place. Didn't want you tripping over Legos or something," I lie. Fuck. Can he read the dirty thoughts running through my mind?

"You don't have to worry about impressing me." He smiles, almost as if he knows I'm lying through my teeth.

"Well, don't want to worry about having to call 9-1-1 again," I say, rushing off to the kitchen. "Can I get you something to drink?" I can hear my voice going up an octave.

"Water is fine. Thanks," he says. I can feel him following me and he's too close behind me. Shit, why does he have to be in my space? I can smell his body wash and it's intoxicating.

"Alright. I'll get it for you," I say.

"Indy?"

"Yeah?" I say with a squeak.

"Are you nervous?" Tyler asks.

"No! Why would I be nervous?" *I'm most definitely nervous.*

"Because you sound nervous and you're jumpy," Tyler says.

"It's just weird to have you in my home after all these years." I motion around us.

"I get that. Would you have preferred we met somewhere

else? I mean, you said we should meet here. I would have met wherever you wanted." He says it so casually.

Tyler and I remain complete opposites. Looking at him, when he looks at me with that smirk, it reminds me of that young version of him. Deep down he's still got this bad boy component about him and I'm transported right back to high school.

His hip is against my kitchen island, with his ankles and his arms crossed. There's an ease about him in this moment that feels so nonchalant, while I'm a ball of nerves. I've got walls up to surround my heart in every direction and I can sense an air of simplicity about him, like nothing affects him. I wish I could be as easygoing. I envy that so much. I continue to move through my kitchen, grabbing a cup to fill for him.

All of a sudden, he begins approaching me. I still, not sure what he's about to do. Soon, his hands are resting on the counter by my side, caging me in. He's so close, I can feel his breath on my skin. I can see the gray mixed with blue in his irises.

My breathing accelerates, while his stays even. I keep my hands by my sides, even though all I want to do is grab his shirt and pull him closer, bringing his lips to mine. I miss feeling him near me. It's been too long. And when he's this close, that's all I'm reminded of.

"What are you thinking about, Indiana?" Tyler asks me.

I love when he says my full name like that, his voice husky.

I don't answer right away, my eyes volleying between his. I just keep looking at him, both our breaths becoming more labored as we stare at each other.

I bite my lower lip and reply, "I think you're dangerous."

His eyes ping-pong between mine, his lips in a straight line. Then he brings his face close enough to mine that I think he's going to kiss me. I stop breathing in that instant and close my eyes, ready to feel him seal his lips to mine.

But then I don't feel anything, and I open my eyes to see a smirk break loose across his face. Then he says, "Mmm. That's interesting you say that because I think you and I are dangerously beautiful."

He pushes away, back to where we are a safe distance apart and I'm instantly missing the warmth of his body near mine. Why is this so fucking hard for me? I want him one second, yet I know we can't do this anymore.

I open my mouth to speak, but he interrupts me. "You said you had information to discuss before serving me with divorce papers?" he says, as if he didn't just tip my life over yet again with those words.

I take a moment to right myself, then look around my kitchen. I nod at him, but I use it as a way to remind myself why we're both here, in this moment.

"Yes, um, I do. You mentioned you wanted to talk too?" It comes out as a question.

"I thought you didn't want to hear my side of things, Indy," he reminds me.

Now I'm the one prolonging this divorce because he's thrown me and I'm really having a hard time finding solid ground. I'm feeling conflicted on so many levels.

I hear Kalli's voice in my head telling me to give him a chance to listen to his side of things. I feel myself stand a little straighter. I'm about to say something when he speaks again.

"I'm just doing what you want. I don't want to make this harder on you. I listened to what you wanted and I really want to make your life easier in this whole thing," he explains. He looks sincere as he says this.

I nod and begin walking toward the living room. Right as I turn around to explain why this divorce has taken so long for me to initiate, there's a knock at the front door. I can't help the confused look I give Tyler.

"Give me a second to see who that is." I start making my way to the door.

The moment I open it, Noah walks through it, stomping his feet. I can tell he's visibly upset.

"Noah, baby, what's wrong?" I ask him.

"Harley isn't my best friend anymore!" he exclaims as he walks through the house.

I wish I could say this is a new occurrence, but the two of them go through these highs and lows pretty frequently. Harley's mother and I have become mediators at this point.

Before I can explain Tyler's presence, Noah walks into the living room and halts when he sees Ty standing there. Noah's anger is soon forgotten.

"Hunter, did you come over to hang out with me?" Noah exclaims.

"Hey, buddy. How are you?" Tyler purposely avoids Noah's question.

"Good. Do you want to play with me?" Noah's smile is infectious.

I can see Tyler's eyes shift to me for a second before focusing back over to Noah. I give a slight nod, knowing our previous conversation will have to be put on hold yet again.

"As long as it's okay with your mom." Tyler juts his chin in my direction.

Noah swings his gaze toward me, his eyes pleading without words. I relent without a fight.

"Of course, baby. But the moment Tyler says he has to leave, we aren't going to complain, right?" I give him a stern look.

"Yes, Mom." Noah looks up to me, his big, brown eyes proud and excited.

I can see him jumping in place. I watch the interaction unfold, Noah walking over to Tyler, but I'm unable to hear what they say to one another.

Ty gets down to eye level and puts his fist out and Noah bumps it. They say a few more things to one another before Noah runs off to grab something. When he returns, Darth is prancing behind my son. With the commotion earlier, the cat was probably hesitant to come out, uneasy to greet someone new. Now he's willing to take on the challenge with Noah here to greet Tyler.

"This must be Darth," Ty says.

"Yes," Noah looks behind him. "He's shy."

Tyler puts out the back of his hand for Darth to inspect. Unlike Julian, Darth seems unfazed and moves closer to Tyler for pets. It's hard to hide my shock.

Noah beams. "He likes you! Mom, look. Darth likes Hunter!"

"Yeah, I see that." I try to show enthusiasm, but inside, I feel a mixture of emotions.

Before I'm able to let myself feel too deeply about what this can mean, my son shows Tyler the football he brought from his room and announces they're going to play. "Hunter's going to teach me how to throw a football, Mom!"

The smile on his face is infectious. I know how much he's wished to have a father-figure in his life to have these little moments with and the second he has Tyler under his roof, he asks him to throw a ball with him. Ty looks over at me and it takes everything in me not to let the smile break through that I'm fighting to contain.

He's starting to break me at the seams. I've glued myself back together after years of building these cement walls up once he tore me down. I can't let my husband see through my cracks because if I fall in love with him again—I might not pull myself out.

Indiana

9 YEARS AGO

July 28, 2016

Dear sweaty Tyler,

How are you? How's everything been for you?

I won't lie... this letter will be a venting session and I'm sorry. I have a lot to say and so much has happened. I spent Fourth of July up in Oregon to see Bryce. I was so excited to visit with him and for the cooler weather.

The humidity in Chicago is still something I'm getting used to, but Oregon was a nice break, as you can imagine. Well, let's just say, it was all a ruse to get me there because my parents were waiting for me.

Yes, you read that correctly! Bryce hadn't

planned it that way. It was originally planned to just be Bryce, myself, and his friends. A BBQ was planned at his new place—some downtime for the holiday and much-needed for me after a very tough semester.

Unfortunately, my parents decided to take it upon themselves to sabotage the holiday and try to crash it in order to bombard me. I'm so fucking pissed. Bryce apologized a dozen times already while I was there and since I left. It's not his fault. He mentioned I was visiting prior to my arrival, never expecting them to show up. But of course, they did, thinking it was a good thing to try and corner me to pull me back into their lives.

And that's exactly what they tried to do. They literally sat there, trying to shove the narrative of medical school still being the better route for a lucrative life for me. Then they tried to guilt me that they had to lie to me about the adoption, saying I wouldn't have been able to handle the truth had they told me sooner. They even said I'm too delicate to handle this kind of truth, saying my health was to blame.

It was such bullshit, Tyler; they still treat me like a child. I'm twenty years old! If they only knew I'm a married woman. Add to the fact, I'm financially independent and living across the country without their help. I'm so over them trying to control my life. It's infuriating, to be quite honest with you.

I'm furious with them right now. The minute Bryce saw them, I could see the anger consume his face, but it's hard because he's caught in the middle too. He's their child as well. He loves them and wants to see us all get along. I hate that he feels shoved between us all. This isn't his fight.

To top it off, once I got back here to Chicago, I got really sick. I was hospitalized for a few days, my Crohn's Disease coming out of remission. I was doing so well on the new meds, but the stress from the holiday probably spurred things on. I seem to be on the mend right now, but I'm cautiously optimistic. I'm just upset things got so bad with my health. It's unfortunate and I'm now dealing with more doctors appointments and new medications to adjust to.

It brings back a lot of horrible thoughts and memories for me. It's a reminder this disease will be with me forever and I hate it, Ty. I wish I could wave a magic wand and make it better. I know I don't have it as bad as others who have way worse illnesses. But it makes me feel like my parents are right—I am weak and fragile. Like their words hold truth and I can't handle the reality of my life and that's why they couldn't say anything to me. I hate that and just hearing the words they said to me repeated in my head makes me so upset.

All I wanted was a nice holiday, plus I enjoy just hanging out and seeing the fireworks. Now it feels tainted. I'm whining and I apologize. I didn't know who to tell. I didn't cower to them, but I also feel like a part of them won because the aftermath was me getting sick and it sort of proved the point that I'm a weakling.

The only good thing to come out of this trip was that I got to meet Bryce's new girlfriend. I'm not sure how I feel about her yet, but he seems happy. So I'll try my best to get along with her too.

I wasn't able to run to a store to get you snacks to send with this care package, so I'm sending two smutty books instead. I had a lot of time to highlight while I was in the hospital. Consider that an added bonus this time around. Enjoy the dirtiness.

Alright, I should go. Thanks for letting me vent.

Stay safe out there.

XO.

I don't need anyone but you,

Indy

CHAPTER 19

Tyler

IT SEEMS each time we've tried to set up a time to meet up, nothing has worked out to talk through the divorce. If I was one to believe in signs, I would say this divorce isn't meant to be.

I haven't heard from Indiana since the last time I was at her house. I played catch with Noah for about an hour until it was time for dinner. He begged his mom for me to stay, but I could tell Indy was uncomfortable with me in her space, so I came up with an excuse about needing to head out for a work thing.

I think she saw right through my lie, but she seemed okay with it. Noah is a cute kid and I wanted nothing more than to be around him a little longer. I don't know how much time he gets around her boyfriend. I also won't lie that the thought of that stings me to my core. It shouldn't because I'm the asshole that dug my own grave on that, but I'm self-aware enough to say I fucked up.

When I was playing catch with Noah, the look of excitement each time he caught the ball successfully brought a feeling of pride to my heart. I know the kid isn't mine, but fuck did it feel good to see him happy. Whatever Indy is doing with him, she's doing a damn fine job raising him. He's polite and he's fun to be around. I hope her boyfriend appreciates what a kindhearted soul Indiana is raising.

I'm meal-prepping in my kitchen, with the camera propped for content I'll post later this week. My phone rings and I look to see it's Clay.

Wiping my hands, I swipe and answer, "Hey, Clay, what's up?"

"Hey, man. Not much. Whatcha up to?" I hear sounds in the background of some giggles I assume are Ella.

"Not much. Just recording some content." I grab a few more items from the fridge to place on the counter.

"Cool. Abby's friend Marissa is in town for work and we're going out to dinner. We thought you'd be interested."

"Not sure I'm up for being set-up right now, but thanks for thinking of me," I say. I honestly don't think I'd be a great date right about now with everything going on. I haven't been on a date or hooked up with anyone since I ran into Indy.

Clay chuckles. "No, not like that. Um, Marissa's girlfriend is back in California. She couldn't make it out this time around. Marissa just wants to head out to dinner. There's that new spot in town…" I can hear some rustling like he's covering the phone, but it doesn't do much to mute the sound while he calls out to his fiancée, "Abby, what's that place we're headed to with Marissa tonight?"

"*¡Vita!*" I can hear her answer in the background.

"*¡Vita!*" he says to me.

"Yes, I heard."

"I hear it's hard to get into. I think Kennedy pulled some strings to get reservations."

"Okay, sounds good. What time should I meet you there?" I put the phone on speaker as I open a few more items on my counter.

"Seven. My mom is watching Ella and Lola. You know

how River gets with all his weird instructions for the dog and Ella will be down for the night before we head out."

We get the plans ironed out before we hang up. Something about going out, knowing it's not a date, makes me excited. I need to distract myself. Workouts, social media posts, and work at the station aren't cutting it anymore. All roads lead to Indy—I need something else. Maybe a night on the town will be just the thing to get my mind off my wife—or shall I say soon-to-be-ex-wife.

Just the thought of that makes my stomach roll. I hate the fact she will divorce me without knowing the real truth as to why I made her walk away from me five years ago. But it is what it is. She's probably better off. I'm no good for her. Whoever this boyfriend is—he's most likely a better fit.

¡Vita! is so busy that it feels like a fire code violation. From the moment we walk in, I feel claustrophobic. Kennedy looks to be in her element, but it's thanks to her we got ourselves a table to begin with. She knows Sergio, the owner of the swanky new spot.

We're currently being ushered to our table by the owner himself, who is showing us all the intricacies of the restaurant as we pass them. He has kept some of the old pieces of the building, trying to preserve old parts of Boston, while filtering in new things to make it more relevant to appeal to the newer generation.

The moment he saw me, he recognized me from my content. I promised I'd tag his restaurant in my stories tonight. The further we move through the restaurant, the more I realize how appealing this restaurant is. It has a nice feeling to it.

Abby's best friend Marissa is a whole other factor altogether. From the moment I met her, I could tell she is—a lot.

She is energetic and when she saw me, she took hold of my arm and hasn't let go. Malloy's smile grew and he hasn't stopped smirking.

I know she isn't attracted to me, but I know she's trouble with a capital T. We are walking deeper into the restaurant, and Marissa is pointing at a sconce that's high up on the wall. The glass has a beautiful rainbow effect of colors mixed in, a reflection on the wall that just adds to the ambiance of the dining experience.

I'm enthralled by the restaurant's atmosphere, I'm not looking at any of the people around me until I hear my name being called.

"Tyler?" I hear a female's voice calling.

I look to my left and that's when I see Indiana sitting at a nearby table with a group of five people in a booth. Marissa and I both stop. It's then I notice a gentleman sitting closer than the rest of those at the table. I assume it's her boyfriend.

"Hey, Indiana," I say, an easy-going smile taking over my face.

"What are you doing here?" she says, her eyes looking over at Marissa, landing on where we are joined.

"Oh, we're here for dinner with my friends," I jut my chin in the direction where Kennedy, River, Clay, Abby, Malloy, and Baylee walked off. "This is Marissa. Marissa, this is Indiana."

Marissa doesn't let go of where we are linked, but gives her the biggest smile. "It's a pleasure. Isn't this place amazing? Hunter has been promising to bring me here for the longest time. Right, baby?"

Then out of nowhere Marissa looks my way and nuzzles her face into my neck, and whispers under her breath, "Just go with it."

I keep my gaze on Indy and I can see her assessing us. "This doesn't seem like your scene, Ty."

"Are you kidding? Hunter and I go out all the time. This

guy doesn't stop showing me off. I mean, he loves dancing all over town. This is just the appetizer tonight. Right, babe?" Marissa is too fucking much. I don't know how Abby handles her as a best friend.

"Right, *shnookums*," I ooze sarcasm, but I may as well have fun with it. The hell with the serious side of this whole thing. I wanted to have fun with my night; and Marissa is all about finding amusement in this moment, so I'll join her.

"I'm Roger," the gentleman to Indy's right says.

Indiana seems to snap out of her assessment of Marissa and gains her composure. "I'm so sorry. This is my boyfriend, Roger."

"Great to meet you, Roger. I'm Marissa and this is my hot-as-fuck man, Hunter," she says as she runs her hand down my chest. She has no filter whatsoever. It's hard to contain my laugh. I swear one of the other guys at the table nearly chokes mid-sip of his beer as a result of Marissa's crass language.

I shake Roger's hand, then he proceeds to introduce us to everyone at the table.

"You know, before both of you walked by, we were in a heated discussion that both of you could help us with," Roger begins.

"Oh, sweetie, I doubt they want to get involved in that discussion," Indy says, embarrassment evident in her tone.

"No, I think they could help," Roger is adamant.

"Sure, we can help, can't we, Hunter, baby?" Marissa side-eyes me.

I shrug.

"Well, you see, at work, we have to do all these presentations. And the guys and I were discussing the exciting differences between Excel and Sheets. We are split between which is better. Indy doesn't really care between either. Do either of you feel you can weigh in on which is best?" Roger asks.

At first, Marissa and I stand there, thinking he's fucking with us, but after a few seconds, we realize he's serious.

"Oh, you're not fucking with us," Marissa responds. She laughs, encouraging the rest of the table to join in, although they aren't feeling as jovial. I'm looking between Roger and Indy, wondering what she sees in this guy because there's nothing charismatic or fun about him. This is what she has chosen in a partner?

"I guess, gun to my head, I'd choose Sheets?" she says it more as a question, whereas I remain silent. In all honesty, I couldn't give two shits. I've never thought of either platform for longer than a second in my lifetime and this guy is wasting an entire conversation while he has the most beautiful woman sitting next to him? I don't get it.

Indy has a tight smile as she watches me and I can't help, but take in the entire interaction. She knows this is bullshit and this guy isn't right for her, but she's so damn stubborn, she won't admit it. Who am I to judge though?

I'm allowing Marissa to stand by me and caress me and pretend we're dating while she has a girlfriend back home. I'm pushing Indy's buttons and I'm liking that it's getting a reaction from her. I can see it in the way she's watching Marissa's hand move along my chest.

"Listen, we've got to catch up to our friends. It was a pleasure meeting all of you. Indiana," I nod at my wife, finding some pleasure in knowing I still hold that title over her for a little longer.

She nods in my direction. I don't look at anyone else. Roger seems more perturbed Marissa chose Sheets over Excel versus my connection to Indy, but I couldn't care less at this point.

We walk away without another glance. The moment we are out of earshot, Marissa laughs, proclaiming, "I wish I had eyes in the back of my head to see the daggers she's throwing my way."

"I promise you she's not throwing daggers at either of us,"

I assure her, even though I'm keeping my sights ahead of us, looking at where they sat the rest of our group.

"Oh, sweet, sweet Hunter. You really don't know women, do you?" Marissa pats my forearm.

"I know women plenty. You just don't know that woman well. That's all."

"Let me tell you one thing. I might not date men, but I can guarantee you one thing, you know nothing about women. You're absolutely clueless about women, my dear fake date. That woman might be dating that snoozefest, but she's only got eyes for you. It's completely obvious."

I try to keep myself from faltering when she spills this information my way, but it's hard to focus on anything else. We find our group quickly. The moment I spot River and Clay, I can already tell they're arguing about something, while Malloy is probably placing a bet with Kennedy.

I move out of the way in order for Marissa to make her way into the booth, but when I do, I sneak a peek back toward Indiana's table. I catch her gaze still honed in on me, eyes laser-focused on where my hand is touching Marissa's back.

I can't help the little smirk I throw in her direction, knowing it will make her blood boil. I don't know why I'm taunting her in this way. She doesn't need more stress in her life, especially after everything I've already put her through. But for some reason, we're at this crossroads and I'm wanting to see how far I can push her to see if we might have a chance together or if we're simply beyond repair.

―――――

"I think you two should consider getting Ella a pet. She'd love having a dog. Have you seen the way her face lights up when she sees Lola?" River says as our plates are cleared.

"Yes, we've seen how animated she is, but I think we've

got our hands full with her right now, Riv," Abby says, looking over at Clay.

I watch as River pulls out his phone and starts scrolling through his countless photos of his niece and dog. He's not wrong. Ella is all smiles when it comes to River and Kennedy's dog, but I can see why Clay and Abby are hesitant to add to their family right now.

I have only heard how things weren't all butterflies and rainbows for them prior to Ella's arrival. Apparently conceiving Ella was a hardship and had contributed to Clay and Abby's divorce before bringing them back together. Luckily, thanks to a little scheming on Marissa's part—something Malloy got roped into—it all worked out in the end.

I sit back and watch the exchange between the brothers, knowing it will likely go full-circle as we settle the bill. I look around the restaurant, trying to keep my gaze from finding Indiana's table yet again. Throughout our entire meal, I was constantly wanting to look over, but tried to refrain to keep myself from coming off like a creep.

"You're looking desperate. She's still there and she's looking over here plenty. Don't worry. She's the one more curious about us," Marissa says, as if she's reading my mind.

I sigh, this thing with Indy eating at me. I rub at the back of my neck, irritated and wishing I could talk to her about everything that plagued me years ago. She seems to want to walk away from us, although the way she stared at Marissa's hand touching my skin, it wasn't like she wasn't disturbed by that connection.

We settle the bill when the server makes her way over, then I excuse myself to the restroom. I'm restless, the unease not only from tonight's encounter, but from the last couple weeks starting to mount, starting to weigh on me.

I'm about to open the door to the bathroom when I feel a hand settle on my forearm. I look back to see Indiana's gaze on me.

"How long have you been together?" Her expression is hard to read, but I can't help and assume she's jealous.

I turn toward her and cross my arms over my chest. "Indy, you should get back to your boyfriend."

"I deserve to know." Her lips are in a hard line. She's so stubborn, but this side to her is still so new to me. She's lost so much of her softness from before.

"Do you?" I'm being a complete asshole to her now. I'm annoyed I had to steal glances of her at a table with another man when all I wanted to do was pull her away and put my lips on her.

She stands straighter and I can tell she's getting angry. "Fine, don't tell me." She goes to walk away, but I grab her hand.

I pull her back up against my chest and bring my lips to the shell of her ear. "Tell me Indy, why do you want to know so badly? All you've wanted to do since reconnecting with me is find a way to break our tie. Now you want to know what Marissa and I have together? What gives? If I was a betting man, I'd say that you're jealous."

She scoffs. "You wish."

I can see her breath quicken and I can only imagine her heart is beating at a faster pace. If only I could bring my hand up against her throat to feel her heartbeat on my palm to confirm it.

I continue speaking against her ear. "It's too bad, Indy, because your boyfriend is a bit of a snooze. Can he see into your soul like I do?"

Her intake of breath is audible, but she pushes away from me right then.

"Maybe you knew me like that once upon a time. But those days are long gone, Tyler." She's shut down now, and I won't get anywhere with her tonight.

My words were meant to take her back to our last night together, but I don't regret them. She shifts herself far enough away from me so there's a few feet of distance between us. We simply stand and stare at one another.

Someone walks down the dark hallway, breaking the trance between us.

"I'm heading back to my table. I'll reach out to get something set up. This time, we should really get things finalized. We can't keep putting this off." She looks at me until I finally nod in acknowledgement.

I watch her walk off and once again, it feels like a piece of me is being carried off with her. Why haven't I learned my lesson when it comes to Indiana Ranton?

October 2, 2018

Dear cutest grad I know, Indy,

Congratulations! I'm so proud of you! I wish I could have been there to see you walk across that stage. You deserve all the accolades. Tell me all about the day.

Sorry this letter is getting to you much later after your graduation, but I was out on a training mission during your graduation and unable to write. You'll see there's something for you included with this letter as a gift.

I just returned from traveling and saw this bracelet that reminded me of you. The green beads are so similar to your eye color, I had to pick it up for you. The woman at the booth told me the colors symbolize growth, renewal, and prosperity. You're starting your new journey as a professional in the world, so it seemed fitting.

Last you wrote me, you were on the fence about having your parents attend graduation. Did you invite them after all? I know it's been hard trying to navigate things and you can always lean on me if you ever need to. Don't blame Bryce for trying to keep pushing you to make amends with them. I think he's simply wanting to build the family he had between all of you again. I can see that.

As someone that never had the dynamic all of you had, I can see where he's coming from. It must be hard. I'm not saying you're not justified to feel the way you do, but I get where your brother is coming from as well.

How's your health? I know last year was still rough, but our last few letters, you seemed to be on the mend. The last medication seemed to work really well. Is that still the case? Keep me updated. When you were hospitalized that summer, it took everything in me not to fly home and see you. It broke my heart what your parents did to you. You are the strongest person I know. Never forget that.

Have you decided to take the offer from your grandfather and work at his company full-time? I think it's a great opportunity to do something independent and from everything you've told me throughout the years, you seem to really enjoy the publishing world.

You've come a long way since that night after high school, and now, look where you are! I cannot believe you're a college grad and embarking on a whole new career. This is amazing, Indy!

Have you been able to look into getting answers to your biological parents again? I know last time you checked, you couldn't do that because of the cost and the records being sealed. Is this something you can do now that you'll have the means?

We recently got a new crew from the States arrive here. They look so damn young, all from boot camp. I forgot how fresh-faced we looked at eighteen, even though it wasn't that long ago for us.

I've taken one of the newest guys that arrived recently under my wing. His name is George, but the guys and I call him Georgie. He's so funny, I'd love for you to meet him one day. If I had I little brother I would want him to be just like this guy.

His parents are coming over here for a visit and they've invited me to join so I can meet them. I think I'm going to take them up on the offer and take that time off when they're visiting. It's been a little sad not having parents in my life since mine were shit but it would be nice to have parental figures sometimes.

I miss you, Indy. Not getting to be at your graduation a few months ago really made me realize I want to be stateside. I'm going to see when I could possibly get over there. I can't guarantee it will be soon, but maybe I can find a time to make that happen. I've used a lot of my free time to travel throughout Europe, but maybe the next time there is a break on my end, I will hop on a flight over and see you, if that's something you'd be comfortable with me doing.

Let me know if you'd be okay with me coming to visit you still. It's been too long since we've seen one another. I hope you're doing well.

Needing to see you,

Ty

CHAPTER 21
Indiana

NOPE. I don't care. Not one bit. Seeing Tyler and Marissa at the restaurant two nights ago has not consumed my every thought.

"Do you agree then?" Kalli asks, interrupting my thoughts.

"Of course I do," I answer as if I know what she said, stopping my pen from tapping against my lips as I look out my office window.

For all I know, I'm agreeing to wearing a clown outfit at Vivienne's next birthday party because I haven't paid attention to anything for the last fifteen minutes. I don't dare look over at my best friend, afraid my blank expression will give me away.

"Great, so I'll let our best-selling author know her gargoyle romance is a go, and she should scrap the mafia romance she pitched the group with the dirty sex scenes," she says, her sly smirk taking over her face when I swing a shocked look in her direction. It's then I realize she tricked me. She knew I wasn't paying attention to a word of what she was saying.

Kalli was in the meeting I missed this morning when I was

at a school performance for Noah. My assistant gave me notes that I still have to look over, but Kalli insisted on giving me the rundown on Ana Clevesky—the up-and-coming author that has hit the best-selling charts with her last two books.

Now I know why Kalli insisted on giving me the condensed version of those notes from the meeting; she knows I've had my mind in the clouds and she wanted to take advantage of it to get me to spill. I guess today I'm not doing my best at masking how distracted I am. I internally roll my eyes at myself.

I told Kalli everything that happened at dinner the other night and I've done a shit job covering up how irritated it has left me. Why am I letting this whole thing with Tyler consume me to the point that my life can't seem to move forward?

"You got me, alright? I'll be present, I promise." I throw my hands in the air.

"Hey, you don't have to explain yourself to me." Kalli puts her hands up as if surrendering. "I'd be pissed too if I saw someone with their hands all over the man I care about."

"I don't care about Tyler!" I groan.

"Why are you fighting this? You know you're full of shit," Kalli laughs. "Keep telling yourself lies. I bet if someone was making out with Roger, you wouldn't even bat an eye."

"I would too. Don't be ridiculous." I scoff.

"Sure you would, Indy. I mean, let's not forget this is the same man you're trying to divorce. Why are you getting so frustrated over this whole thing with Tyler if you're trying to detach yourself from him anyway?" She pulls her blue-light glasses down an inch to give me a proper stare down.

"I just don't understand why he didn't mention her. Also, she doesn't seem like his type, that's all. She seems a bit too strong-willed." I shrug and go back to looking out the window, annoyed that Marissa is everything I'm not.

That's the thing. The moment I met Marissa, I could tell she was confident and her self-assurance made me question if that's what I lacked for Tyler. I hate that my mind went there. Is that why Tyler chose to walk away from me years ago? Is that why someone else made him look in a different direction? Am I just not enough for him?

This is why I didn't want to be around him anymore. I don't like feeling less than because I'm sensing the cracks in my exterior. I don't like this sense of inferiority because that's not who I am deep down. I built myself back up, but the moment Tyler Hunter came back around, I started to feel the insecurities creeping in again.

Marissa is tall, strong, and vibrant. She's everything I once thought I possessed, but then Tyler crashed this world I built up in my head, and my confidence was shattered. I had to rebuild, and it's never really felt the same since then. I need Tyler out of my realm so I can go back to being Indiana without Tyler.

"Have you talked to him since the other night?" Kalli asks.

"No." I shake my head.

I've avoided reaching out, sort of annoyed and also wanting to keep my distance. I know he read into my emotions that evening and I don't want to give him more ammunition at this point. Maybe if I play it right, I can just find someone to serve the papers and get this over with. But then there's a side of this I can't avoid, which is the *why*. He needs to know the real reason why I waited so long to divorce him and it would be wrong to keep it from him. I thought we could have a conversation before moving further into the divorce, but each time I try we seem to get interrupted.

"Indy, what is your goal here?" She throws her head back, pinching the bridge of her nose.

"Honestly, I don't know anymore. I thought I did, but I think he's got the upper hand right now. The way he acted the other night, I can't shake it, that's all." When I close my eyes, all I see is her hand on his arm. Then I feel his breath near my skin, talking into my ear, and my body ignites.

I'm confused and I want things to go back to before I knew Tyler was in Boston. I'm truly fucked, my emotions taking me on a roller coaster, and I don't know what direction I want this ride to go.

"You better figure out what you want to do, Indy. Because you've got your monotone boyfriend and a hot-as-fuck husband. I vote for the hot one, as you know." She waggles her brows and shimmies her shoulders, while I roll my eyes.

"Yes, you've said as much at least once a day," I tell her. "You're forgetting Tyler and I have a past that involved breaking my heart, along with this revelation about a girlfriend. Kalli, you seem to forget a lot of crucial details. Plus, Roger can't just be tossed aside."

"You're right. Maybe tell Roger you prefer Sheets over Excel; he might break up with you and then you won't have to deal with it." She starts laughing hysterically, while I give her a flat expression. My best friend, everyone.

"Sorry, bad joke?" Kalli says, wiping the tears under her eyes. "But you sort of set me up." She realizes I'm not laughing. "Okay, this is your life. I shouldn't make a joke of it. But it's sort of ironic that you go a while not dating anyone and all-of-a-sudden you now have a boyfriend you want to get serious with *and* an estranged husband at the same time."

"Soon I'll just have a boyfriend because the husband will be in my past." I shrug and look down at my desk, trying to busy myself.

I move my mouse to awaken my computer to check new emails that have come in. Kalli finally relents and begins talking about work and we settle into a good flow of business that gets my mind off Tyler and the things that have consumed my mind for the last forty-eight hours.

An hour has flown by and before I know it, Kalli has another meeting she has to attend. Once she leaves my office, my assistant comes in to update me on more things going on within the company. I have more meetings throughout the day, meaning time goes by quickly. Luckily, Noah has a play date with a friend, so I don't have to rush after school to pick him up.

I sit down for the first time since this morning and gaze outside my window to reflect on everything without anyone chiming in on how I should feel. I look down at my oversized bag, itching to pull out the one thing that has brought me comfort recently.

I know it's wrong, but I brought it anyway. That damn journal has been calling at me to read it since I put it in my work bag while running out the house. I ran back inside my room this morning and stuffed it in, even though I know it was a mistake. The moment I started my drive with Noah chattering about his performance, I knew it was a sign of weakness.

What does it say about my feelings for Tyler if I'm longing to read how I felt about him years ago? Actually, what the hell does it really say about my relationship with Roger? Fuck— what am I going to do about my boyfriend and our relationship?

I think deep down I know what I have to do. I can't continue doing this thing with Roger. It's not fair to him, nor is it fair to me. I may have told Kalli I want to move forward to try to get more serious with Roger, but I know my heart isn't in it. Even if nothing happens with Tyler, I'm not invested with this thing between Roger and I anymore. My heart has long detached and my mind has drifted away from wanting anything to become more than surface-level between us.

I open the journal and begin reading.

October 6, 2018

Dear Journal,

I recently got a note from Tyler and it

seems he might want to come visit me. I don't know when he'll be coming by, but he's thrown it out there. What does it mean?

The last time I saw him, I was eighteen and it feels like I was a completely different person. I was unemployed, scared, very sick, and lost. Utterly lost.

Now I'm a professional, pretty much holding up on my own, and my life is starting to figure itself out. I'm a mess otherwise. I'm starting to develop feelings for my husband—well my fake husband that is. He doesn't know that, but it's the truth.

Do I tell him? Do I say, "Well Tyler, you see, throughout the years of these letters, I've gone on dates, but none of them really seem to compare to the person that I've gotten to know behind your words." Ugh. That sounds lame.

But seriously, I think I've fallen in love with him. And I have no clue how he really feels. I can make assumptions, but I need him to come out and tell me.

What if he sees me or spends time with me, the real me, and hates who I am?

This is uncharted territory for me and I feel completely confused about it all. But getting that letter a while back has left me feeling jittery —either by excitement or fear, not sure which. No *matter what, there is a high likelihood I'll see him in person and I have no idea what will happen.*

Not only that, I haven't told him that I no longer need insurance through him anymore. I have a job now. I don't need to depend on him in that way. I'm scared to tell him and then that link we have together is gone. What if I tell him and he says, "Well, then, bye!"?

Just the thought makes my stomach sink. He's been the most beautiful constant in my journey since the rest of my life went up in flames.

A call from an unknown number startles me. It's after five and phone calls at this hour aren't uncommon now that I've been promoted into this role, but they still make me jump when I'm here alone. Most people avoid picking up calls from phone numbers they don't recognize, I don't have such a luxury as a parent. I always worry it could be a parent with a number I don't have saved into my phone or an emergency from a hospital calling me regarding Noah.

Picking up in a frenzy, I bring the phone to my ear.

"Hello?" I try to sound calm, although my heart is beating at a hurried pace.

"Hi. Is this Indiana?" a male voice says on the other end.

"Yes, this is she." I don't recognize the voice speaking to me.

"Oh, yes, um, this is Malloy. Uh, Tucker Malloy. We met when you came down to the station with your son."

"Oh my gosh. Is Noah okay? Is he hurt?" I try to keep the lump in my throat from forming.

"Yes, he's fine. This isn't about Noah," he says immediately. "It's about Hunter. I mean Tyler."

Tyler? What? Is he hurt?

"What's wrong with Tyler? Did he get injured at work?" I feel the air in my lungs escape.

"No, not at work. He was injured on his motorcycle. But he's fine. Just a few scrapes. He'll be okay. But I thought you should know. I found your number on his phone. We're at Boston General." Malloy says.

"Oh, alright. I'm glad he's okay. But shouldn't you let his girlfriend know? I mean, Marissa might prefer to be called." I feel conflicted if me showing up might cause some friction.

"Marissa? Why would Marissa—ouch, Abby don't hit me." Malloy must cover the receiver because it's muffled.

"Malloy? Should I still come over?" I say into the phone, unsure if he's still on the other end. I wait a few beats until he comes back on.

Finally, he returns, "Of course, yes, I think it's best you're here."

"If you think that's best." I really hope Malloy knows what he's talking about.

I gather my things, wondering what I'm about to walk into, unsure how injured Tyler is from this accident and hopeful Marissa isn't mad I'm coming to help my husband, who isn't going to be my husband for long.

I rush into the emergency room entrance of Boston General. The waiting area is packed. I don't see anyone that I recognize as I search for a familiar face, so I head straight to the reception area.

I reach the front desk, and wait to be noticed. The woman

looks me up and down and I can tell she's already annoyed before I open my mouth.

"What is bothering you today, ma'am?" the woman asks without even looking me in the eye. She's got her face pointed at her screen, ready to put my complaint into her computer.

"Oh, I'm here to see someone that's being treated. He's already in the back," I state, hoping that will be a relief to her that I'm not a patient and an added stress to her list.

"Sorry, but you can't go back. You'll have to wait until they're discharged or sent up to a room." She doesn't even ask for a name or more information from me.

"I'm sorry, but I was told to come down here to see him," I say, slightly annoyed she won't even ask me who I'm here to see.

"Sorry, I can't help you further, but you'll need to—"

"I want to see my husband right now!" I say, impatience taking over.

I don't know where that came from. Maybe it's irritation finally spilling over with everything that's going on. It could be the boiling point after all this time. Whatever it is, this woman is getting the brunt of my bad mood and I know later I'll have guilt over it.

"Indy, he's back here," Malloy pokes his head out of the double doors that lead to the back rooms of the emergency department. I can see the smirk on his lips and I already know without asking that he heard my little outburst. *Fuck my life.*

I inwardly groan, wishing I could hide somewhere and not come out, but I've got to own up to my behavior.

"Sorry about that," I say to the woman at the front, and she just gives me an annoyed look before she watches me follow Malloy.

Malloy winks over at the woman. "Sara, thanks so much for all your help."

"Sure thing, Malloy. You better tell Hunter I want a batch of those snickerdoodle cookies when he's better." She smiles at him and I'm trying not to let my jaw hit the floor. This woman is putty in Malloy's hands compared to the ice queen she seemed to be with me prior to my outburst.

Once I move past the doors, Malloy looks over at me and chuckles. "She's a bit of a Crabby Patty until you give her sweets. She sort of loves us though." He nudges my shoulder. "So, you got a bit possessive over there, huh?"

I give him a murderous look.

"Your secret's safe with me. I promise." He smiles, but something about it looks anything but innocent.

"Why don't I believe you?" I tell him, giving him a side-eye.

We reach the room, where I find River, Clay, and Abby waiting outside. I can't help the look of confusion that crosses my face.

"Where's Marissa?" I see River and Clay look at one another with questioning expressions, while Abby looks down at the ground.

"Hunter fell off his bike, getting a few scrapes. He'll be fine. The bike was one he was fixing up. It wasn't the one he usually rides, which is good. He's inside if you want to go in." Malloy completely ignores my question about Marissa.

I look around them and nod. As I make my way into the room, I swear I hear River whisper, "You owe me fifty, Clay," but I could simply be hearing things.

The moment I move into the room, I slide the glass door closed and Tyler looks up from his phone. His eyes lock onto mine and we stand in silence, staring at one another. I notice a crack down the center of his phone, but besides that, the phone seems to be working.

I expected him to be in a hospital gown, but that's not Tyler's style. He's opted out of wearing it and is simply topless, his tattoos now on full display. I get to see his toned physique, and, indeed, he's tatted like I saw on his social media posts. But in person, it's a whole new level. *Indiana, do not drool over a newly injured man.* There is something significantly wrong with me.

I can't help the way my eyes roam along his chest, moving down his abdomen. Malloy was right, his injuries are minimal, but I can see he has some stitches along his forearm, in addition to some scrapes along his shoulders.

"Hey," Tyler whispers. "Who called you?"

"Malloy," I say. "How bad is it?"

"Nothing that won't heal."

I stay rooted in place. "You want me to call anyone else? You need Marissa?" I ask him.

He shakes his head. "Everyone I'll ever need is standing right in front of me."

At his words, my heart skips a beat. Why is he saying this to me? Why did he break my heart years ago to just come back into my life and ruin me again?

I can't risk this, especially with a kid this time.

I look down at the ground, worried the trance will suck me in and I'll never be able to pull myself out.

"Indiana," Tyler says my name in that way that makes me melt into a puddle.

"Yes," I answer, my gaze planted at my feet, looking at the linoleum of the hospital floor. The speckles of blue, gray, and green enough to keep me occupied for now.

"Please look at me," he begs.

"I think it's best I don't for now," I answer honestly.

"I think it's best we have an honest conversation for once."

"We've had many conversations for years and all that got me was heartbreak." I feel that damn lump in my throat forming.

"I think for all the words we said to one another, we never

said what we really felt. At least, I didn't." *What is he saying to me?*

"What does that mean?" I ask him.

"It means that I said a lot, but I didn't say the most important thing," he tells me.

"And what was that?" I ask, the curiosity pulling me further into him, my gaze remaining planted to the ground though.

"Indiana, are you still with Roger?" he asks me and I can't help my head shooting up to meet his gaze, my expression pained. "I won't compete with another man."

"Funny coming from a man that had another woman by his side last time I saw him," I say on a laugh, no humor behind my words.

"Marissa is back in California with her girlfriend." I can't help the slight gasp that escapes my lips at his confession, while his smirk grows.

I wonder how many people know this side of Tyler. I've seen his social media page where everyone has fallen in love with the carefree version of him. But I know the real Tyler Hunter that is all cocky. This side of him, where he throws these smiles my way, casting glances at me that feel like he's undressing me with a simple look.

"I see. Well, Roger is still very much my boyfriend," I tell him.

"Sounds like you have a decision to make then," he says, biting down on his lower lip and scratching his eight pack. It's hard not to follow his movement and he knows it.

"What decision is that?" I ask him, knowing full well I'm falling for this trap he's set up.

"Between me being your ex-husband or your husband." Then he crooks his finger for me to come closer and I abide to his request. Once I'm seated on the bed, only inches away from him, he continues, "If it's the latter, just know, I won't play this game anymore with you. You're one hundred percent my wife. No more walking around my feelings."

"Walking around your feelings?" I ask just above a whisper.

He catches his thumb over my chin and locks his eyes on mine. "That was my mistake last time. I was a coward. I'll tell you everything. And yes, no more half-truths anymore. I'd give you everything this time around. Every fucking piece of my heart would be yours, Indy."

CHAPTER 22
Fire Hunters

Bethany_2005
@Huntsamillion Feel better 🖤💊 #illkissyourbooboos #recovery

Ariana_luvs_pups
Does this mean the firefighter crew will have to do the workouts until he's better? #idontmind #rowdyriver #rideafirefighter

CharlotteCollageGal
Oh my gosh. I feel so bad. Feel better Hunter. We're pulling for you. I'll be your personal nurse! #volunteernurse

Real_NurseBoston
Looks like it wasn't bad, but riding a motorcycle isn't the safest thing to do. #safetyfirst #becareful

Sunset_Gal27
I hope he's back to posting soon. I miss seeing his cute face on my feed! Love you Hunter! #hunter4life #tylerhunter #pullingforyou

CHAPTER 23

Indiana

7 YEARS AGO

November 27, 2018

Dear secretly-loves-steamy-books Tyler,

How are you? How was your Thanksgiving? It's been a while since our last letter and I'm sorry it's taken me so long to respond. Work has been so busy now that I work full-time at my grandfather's company.

Did I tell you I'm a copy editor at the company now? I got promoted from my editorial assistant position. I'm really liking the change. It's been challenging for me and I'm enjoying the team I'm surrounded by. I've learned a lot in this new position. It has kept me busy, which has meant me coming home and crashing the moment my head hits the pillow.

I thought things would be weird once I

went from interning here in the summers to working as a paid employee because I'm the boss's granddaughter, but everyone has been welcoming since I graduated.

I told my grandfather I'm not looking for any handouts. I'm here to truly be an asset to the company and learn how to be a valuable addition. We have weekly dinners together, which I love more than anything. I've learned to keep the business and family matters separated, something that has been a key component if we want to see this relationship survive moving forward.

He's never understood why my mother kept my adoption a secret all those years, so he sees why I'd be angry with my parents. He doesn't push me to have a relationship with them, and it's something I really appreciate. After losing my grandmother years ago, I think he put everything he's had into his company. Now that I'm here in Chicago, he can have something else to focus on and I'm glad I can be here as well. I can see I get my work ethic from him. And my love of books stems from him as well.

I've gotten to read a lot of new authors, hence this one I've included in the package I'm sending you. She's an up-and-coming one that we've started working with and I thought you'd appreciate her work. This is a slow burn romance, but once the spice hits, it's hot. Don't worry, I've highlighted the good stuff. I've also included a good psychological thriller too. The candy of choice this time around are Hot Tamales and gummy bears. I hope you enjoy them.

Enough about me. I bet things are busy on your end. Anything new you can tell me about? How's Georgie? With the amount you mention him in your letters, I feel like I know him at this rate.

I'm glad you brought up visiting in your last letter, because it's been on my mind too. I have to admit, I didn't know how to address it and when you said something in the letter, I felt relieved you mentioned it. It's comforting to know we are on the same page about you visiting. I'd really love to see you whenever you find the time.

I feel like I'm rambling. Why do I feel like I have butterflies as I write this? I don't know if you remember when I offered for you to stay here if you find yourself in Chicago. That offer still stands. I mean, I understand if that's not something you're interested in doing anymore, but if you're waiting for an invitation from me, know that my door is open. I'd love to have you here. If you can still manage some time away, would you still like to see me?

If you plan to visit in the winter, just prepare yourself because it's cold. I thought I knew what cold felt like, but no matter how much I prepare for the winter months, I seem to forget and my layers ill-prepare me each time I go outside. I swear, the jackets feel paper thin. But hey, maybe we can keep each other warm while you visit.

Oh my gosh. I need to stop the direction of this letter—maybe the dirty books are getting to me.

Talking about this makes me so nervous and I have no idea why. I mean, we've been exchanging letters for years—this shouldn't be so hard for me to bring up, yet the butterflies are doubling as I continue to write.

Do you ever think about the times we used to meet up at the Dam before my parents ruined everything? I still think about that first day often. I couldn't believe it when I saw you there. The school's rebel just sitting there gazing out at the Dam like it could solve all his problems. Resident bad boy liked to sit around and contemplate life out in the calm? Wasn't what I expected, I'll tell you that.

I'll admit I'd had a little crush on you

before I met you, but after that day I was a goner. I couldn't believe you were talking to me of all people. It crushed me when I couldn't talk to you anymore. As soon as I was mad at my parents after graduation you were the only person I wanted to talk to. I didn't care what they thought of me anymore and I needed you; my closest friend. Because that's always how I saw you. You saved me that day, and many days before then.

I better wrap this up before I make a bigger fool of myself.

Stay safe out there.

XO-

Needing to see you too,

Indy

CHAPTER 24

Tyler

I'M STANDING in my garage, checking out the damage on the bike I was working on when I got in the accident the other day. Looking down at the stitches, I'm lucky the injuries I sustained weren't worse. When I look up, I'm grateful I wasn't on the motorcycle Jerry gifted me.

I got the second bike as something fun for myself, and I took it out because I needed to get my mind off Indiana. It was a stupid thing to do because I ended up swerving to avoid a squirrel on the road. Luckily, I wasn't going fast, the motorcycle sustaining minor damage. The gravel on the road led to some minor injuries and I just count myself lucky. My phone screen wasn't so lucky, although it still worked enough for Malloy to snatch it and steal Indiana's number to call her while I was being evaluated in the emergency room—*sly bastard*. Guess using my locker number as my phone passcode wasn't the most secure choice.

I only got stitches due to some larger rocks on the ground when I landed and my shoulder sustained some road rash that should heal with minimal scarring. I wasn't far from the house and my friends just happened to be driving over to my place to check on me since I've been in a foul mood with everything going on with Indiana. I guess I should be grateful they care, but it hasn't led to any answers when it comes to where I stand with her.

When she walked out after I pretty much told her I wanted to give her everything, Malloy strutted in like he was king of the world. I saw the look of satisfaction on his face and I knew right then that he called her.

"You can thank me now or later, but I usually enjoy a box of cookies and a smutty book," he told me and sat down next to the emergency room gurney I was lying in.

I rolled my eyes and laughed at his cockiness that night. It's hard to keep a serious face around him. I know he's only looking out for me. He knows how conflicted I've been with my feelings for Indy this entire time. Most of all, he understands all I've wanted is to explain myself from years ago and see if she'll give me a second chance.

Now I walk out of my garage, annoyed I won't be able to enjoy the nice weather on my good motorcycle. I head into the house when my phone rings. I note the phone number for the animal shelter appearing on my screen.

A few months ago I was lonely, so I had gotten approved to be a foster caretaker. I almost adopted a dog immediately, but with the shifts at the firehouse, I thought it might be unfair to leave a dog at home without supervision. River has his mom and Kennedy to care for Lola when he's on shift, but I have no one to do the same for me.

I hadn't heard from them since then, so I had forgotten about it. I pick up the phone, curious what they have to say after so many months of silence.

"Hello?" I answer.

"Hi. Is this Mr. Hunter?" a woman says on the opposite end of the line.

"Yes, this is he."

"Hi. This is Cora at Paws for Hearts. I see you have volunteered to be a foster caretaker. We have a little one here that needs to be cared for tonight. Are you available? He's a little pup, about a year old," she explains, rattling off the details of the dog.

The more she describes of the dog, the more my sour mood dissipates. I was expecting to sit at home thinking of Indiana and how she hasn't called me, but now I can distract myself with a little dog instead. I don't have a shift for another two days, so this will be a good way to keep my mind occupied.

Once I get the details of what I need to do, I call River to get some advice. Instead of helping me with how I should prepare, he decides to meet me at my place. Although I hang out with River plenty with the rest of our friends, I don't see him on my own very often.

Thirty minutes later, there's a knock on my door. I'm greeted with an excited River rubbing his hands together.

"Dude, are you ready for my master class on dogs 101?" River says as if he's the dog guru.

I roll my eyes. "I don't think it's that hard."

"Hunter, you're going to be begging to adopt this dog after I'm done with you." His smile is wide as he nods at me.

I laugh at his confidence and he makes his way through my house, grabbing a bag at his feet of a few toys he's brought for the little furball roommate I'm about to house for the next twenty-four hours. I'll admit, I can't wait for the distraction and fun that awaits.

———

"Holy shit, I might actually pee my fucking pants. You're telling me each time you moved your arm to get up, the dog got in position to hump you?" I look over to see Clay and Malloy crying from laughter on the couch at the firehouse as I make lunch for the guys.

Even our captain is trying to cover up his smirk behind his phone.

"This isn't fucking funny. It was the longest twenty-four hours of my life guys. I mean, if I even attempted to get off the couch, that fifteen-pound dog started humping an extremity of mine," I protest.

"Aww, poor Hunter is scared of a sweet, little dog," River pouts. "Clay, call mom. Maybe she can comfort Hunter because I think he's scarred for life."

That earns me another roar of laughter and I flip him the bird, but I can't help the smile that I try and fail to cover up. The night with that little foster dog was traumatizing, but hilarious all rolled into one. At least it got my mind off of Indy, which was the point.

"Okay, I'll admit, it wasn't all bad, but I think I'll call the fostering done for me." I say as I finish up the spaghetti and meatballs.

"That's too bad. Dogs are the fucking best," River says, wiping the stray tears from his face.

"Great, then I'll just borrow yours when I need my fix," I say. "Also, lunch is ready."

"I'm starving," Malloy says, patting his belly.

River chimes in with, "You can borrow Lola for like an hour, but that's it. She has separation anxiety from her daddy."

Clay groans and rolls his eyes.

"You have something to say, brother?" River asks his twin.

"No, I just think you exaggerate." He eyes River as he passes him to grab a plate. "You and I know she loves mom more than she loves you."

"You best take that back." River points in his brother's direction.

I lean against the counter and watch it all unfold, knowing it will progress on its own.

"No, because I think anyone that sees Lola with mom

knows the truth, including Ma," Clay says, confidence oozing from his tone.

"You're an ass. You're just jealous because I'm the fun brother," River throws back.

I feel my phone vibrate in my back pocket. The moment I pull it out, the bickering between the brothers is all but forgotten. A text from Indy is staring back at me.

INDY

Hey. You have some time to meet up and talk?

I'm looking down at my phone when Malloy sidles up next to me.

"You okay?" he asks me.

"Yeah," I answer without looking up from my phone. "Indy just texted."

"Yeah? Sound promising?" He twirls spaghetti on his fork and takes a bite.

"I guess it could go either way. I mean, she isn't asking us to talk about the divorce right off the bat at least," I say, moving my hand through my hair.

When I've gotten texts from Indy previously, she usually asked if we could meet up to talk about the divorce. I might be dissecting this simple request a bit, but she isn't mentioning the divorce this time around. That has to be good, right?

"I'd take that as a good sign, man," Malloy says between bites. "You should have seen how concerned she looked when she arrived at the hospital. That girl is not over whatever you two have together."

"Over it or not, she has a boyfriend. Plus, we have a lot of stuff we need to talk about. Our past is a bit messy and we need to discuss that before we can move forward. I don't know if she can forgive me for the lies I've told." I look at my friend, irritation evident in my tone.

"We've all made mistakes in our past. She has to under-stand that. You were going through a hard time. Regarding the boyfriend, that's a decision she has to make. But all you can do is say your piece. What I can say, Hunter, is you've been a standup guy since the moment I met you."

I nod, grabbing a plate of food myself and sitting at the table, my thoughts drifting to a time in my life when I felt more lost than found, and all I wanted to do was be a drifter. I look around the room and see a group of guys I now consider family, but it wasn't too long ago I thought I'd be on my own.

The thing is, since I started therapy, I've really tried to put my best foot forward. Malloy has gotten to see that side of me. But Indiana saw a rougher side of me when I left her behind. I gave her a piece of myself that was heartless because in that period of my life, I died alongside Georgie.

I'll admit, I was being selfish, although I thought I was being selfless. I thought being alone was best for me. Losing Georgie put me in a downward spiral in my own life. I set off on a tailspin, thinking she was better off without me. It wasn't until I saw the errors of my ways that I realized what I lost leaving her behind. But it was already too late.

Six months after Georgie passed away, my contract was up for renewal with the Army. That's when I decided not to continue serving, and I returned to the States for good. My time in the Army was behind me.

I thought coming back to civilian life would be refreshing, possibility bringing clarity, knocking some sense into me after what I did to Indiana. But all it did was cast a shadow of depression over me, further darkness taking over my thoughts. I knew I needed to seek help.

Many of the guys I was stationed with stayed in the Army, so I was on my own when I returned. I wandered on my own for some time. The only people I spoke to here were Jerry and Scarlet. I'd call and check in with them, and they'd beg for me to stay with them. But I could tell I wasn't well, so I'd continue my travels along the various states, hoping my mood would improve.

It wasn't until I sought help with a therapist that things finally improved. Rodney, my therapist in New Mexico, is the true hero of my story. Aside from Boston, I stayed there the longest, making sure I took the time to heal mentally. He made sure I cared for myself, realizing I suffered from post-traumatic stress disorder after Georgie's death. Witnessing such a horrific death, on top of so many other atrocities, took a toll on me and I hadn't come to terms with it.

If it hadn't been for Rodney's expertise, I don't know where I'd be today. He encouraged me to look at my days as positive instead of negative. I was living with survivor's guilt; something I hadn't quite come to terms with until my work with Rodney began. Georgie was standing on a part of the rig I had been at just minutes before. And for a better part of a year, I had blamed myself that I hadn't taken the bullet that took his life.

If Malloy knew the version of me that Indiana knew growing up, he might see me in a different light. He sees me as carefree and lighthearted. But Indiana sees two sides now. Where I was once brooding and mysterious, I'm now optimistic. I'm really trying to live like each day is a gift, because Georgie doesn't get to do that for himself. I know the guys at the station keep saying I keep things close to the chest—and when it comes to my past that hasn't changed, but I won't let opportunities pass me by anymore when it comes to my future.

As Rodney has reminded me—life gave me a second chance and I won't take it for granted. I need to live life to the fullest whenever possible. That's why I'm so adamant to explain myself to Indy, even if it changes nothing between us moving forward. She deserves to know where I was coming from in that last letter to her. I was wrong to do what I did, but she should know that I regret my choices.

Mentally, I was sick and I was angry at the circumstances life chose to hand me. When I wrote her, I really believed I deserved to have been gone and Georgie should have been the one living. But in many ways, I thought I was doing her a favor.

I'm not saying life hasn't dealt her a shitty hand as well, but I simply did a poor job handling everything on my end. I'll own up to it.

I just hope this text means she'll be open to a conversation and not just shut me down.

I grab my phone and open up our text thread.

> Yeah. I get off work tomorrow morning.
> Would that work?

I see the little dots pop up immediately after I press send.

INDY

Can you swing by after your shift? I'm working from home in the morning.

> I'll text you when I'm headed over.

INDY

See you then.

Sounds like I'll finally get my chance to talk to her. I know she'll most likely be upset for the lies I put her through, but she deserves to know the truth. I've carried it for far too long and from the way she's been acting, the bitterness she carries seems to weigh heavy on her shoulders.

CHAPTER 25

Tyler

6 YEARS AGO

January 8, 2019

Hey, you-make-my-day-brighter Indy!

How were your holidays? Did you do anything fun? We decorated the best we could and had some traditional food from back home. We made the best of it.

How are things going at work? From what you last mentioned, you were swamped. I hope you're adjusting to the new role. I know it's a lot more work, but I hope you're really enjoying it still.

Your goal to still become an author? Does this mean the positions you're holding would lead to that? I don't know much about the publication world so you'll have to enlighten me.

The days are long here. I look forward to

your letters and hearing about your day brings a smile to my face. Your last letter brought the biggest smile to my face, actually. Knowing you wouldn't mind a visit from me is music to my ears.

Of course I still think about our days at the Dam. How could I not? I was spending my days with the prettiest girl in school! Plus, you were such a ray of light for me in my dark life. I know you think I "saved" you, but in truth we saved each other on that Nevada landscape.

This letter won't be as long as some others, I'm sorry to say. But I wanted to get a letter sent out to let you know I'm thinking of you. Actually, I'm thinking about you more often than not these days.

I hope we can see one another soon. I have started the latest book you sent me and that book is spicy as hell. I can't stop highlighting it and the guys are giving me shit for it.

I really do love the steamy books,

Ty

PS: I swear, woman, these books you're sending me are getting dirtier each and every time. What are you trying to do to me?

CHAPTER 26

Indiana

I'M A FUCKING FOOL. I shouldn't be trusted to make decisions. Next time, I should be monitored when texting Tyler. That's it—I'll have Kalli mediate my text conversations with him when I decide to make spur-of-the-moment decisions, because this one was plain stupid. Actually, she'd probably welcome the stupid choices in this case.

I stand up and rush over to my sink, dunking my hands in the sudsy water to wash the dishes I've been avoiding all afternoon. May as well tackle the chores with the nerves I now have coursing through my veins. Noah is at the neighbor's house for the afternoon, so I can't lose myself in his laughter and antics. Maybe after I tackle these dishes, I can fold laundry.

You'd think Tyler reached out to me and not the other way around. But I'm the one that initiated the encounter that's happening tomorrow morning. And at my house, nonetheless. Nothing good will come out of him being in my environment again; Noah is already too attached to him.

I'm really finding it harder to be near him. His smell, his eyes roaming over my body, feels like pinpricks along my body. I feel like he's undressing me with his gaze, much like he did years ago when he showed up at my apartment.

Fuck, now I feel like my body temperature is increasing with the memories of that weekend with Tyler years ago flooding my mind. The plate that I was washing slips out of my grasp; my thoughts are no longer on tomorrow morning, but on versions of the two of us when life seemed so innocent.

Why am I letting him derail my life like this? Forgetting the plate I dropped back into the sink, I pick up a pan that has the stubborn grease stains and start scrubbing.

I remember after he left me behind, I had rehearsed how I would act if I ever ran into him. My mind starts to pull the fictional scenario I had conjured in my brain. I'd run into Tyler walking down the street and my life would be completely in order. I would keep my head held high and he'd regret his selfish behavior and I'd throw divorce papers in his face and never look back.

Of course it's ridiculous to believe it would happen in that way, my imagination running rampant, but working in the field I do, I read a lot of fucking romance books and that fictional world seemed to work in my favor. So yes, I loved the idea of that ridiculousness when I fantasized how things would fall into place for me when that fateful day occurred.

But now that isn't actually how things are going. I feel like he holds this imaginary power over me. No cards in my favor, and it's really frustrating. I don't want to want him, although when he's around, my hands feel like touching his cheek and caressing his chest. I want to run my tongue down every inch of his body and get lost in his touch.

I want to move my fingers through his hair, which is significantly longer than it once was. It's not that standard buzz cut it had to be for his military requirements. Those tendrils are golden and beautiful, with a volume I never expected to see as he aged.

I'm scrubbing over the same spot when my phone chimes

and I squeak in surprise, the noise jolting me. Calm down, Indy!

I look over to see a text from Kalli:

KALLI

Did you finally text your hot hubby?

I shake my soapy hands and groan. Her constant rooting for him is turning obsessive.

Can you stop calling him that?

KALLI

Honestly? No. Have you seen his posts? The fact you've been with that perfect specimen is sort of enviable.

Check your left hand.

KALLI

Ok. Why?

Is there anything on it?

KALLI

Yeah. My wedding ring.

Oh, so you are still married?

Last time I checked, you're the one who has a boyfriend and a husband, AT THE SAME TIME.

Shit, she's got me there.

Shit. Roger. I need to break up with him.

KALLI

Did you forget you have a boyfriend?

Um, no...

Instead of responding with a text, my phone begins to ring.

When I pick up, before saying hello, Kalli starts up by talking first.

"I can't believe you forgot about Roger!" She cackles.

"First of all, this isn't funny. This is a person's feelings we're talking about," I begin. "Second, I didn't forget about Roger. It's just that, I haven't really spoken to him much. He's been working long hours and we haven't had time to see one another. When he's done at the office, I'm already in bed. We aren't the type of couple to talk every second of the day."

"Indy, Roger is completely wrong for you. Even if Tyler wasn't in the picture, you should be breaking up with him. He's not your person. If you wanted to make time for each other, you would. Clearly, neither of you are really in this." I can picture her shaking her head on the other line.

I expel a breath and mentally concede to the fact that she's likely right. A few weeks ago I was all about saying Roger was *the guy*, and now I'm realizing I was making excuses to fit him in my life for all the wrong reasons. Who am I kidding? I was trying to convince myself I should be vying for the spot as his potential spouse. Settling for a forever snoozefest with the guy, if he was willing, because I thought it was best for Noah.

"Fine. Maybe you're right. But it doesn't mean what I'm doing to him is fair." I feel bad because he's not a bad guy.

"I get it. But he'll be okay. He's still got his Excel documents to keep him warm at night." She laughs on the other end.

"Stop. I obviously felt something for him to date him this long. I know it's not going to work out, but a part of me feels bad, because I know deep down he's a good person." I sigh. Roger is kindhearted and his passion for his work is simply at the forefront of his mind most of the time right now. One day,

I know he'll meet that person that consumes his heart, it's just not me.

"You're right, I'm sorry. So, what's the plan then? You going over there to talk to him? You need Auntie Kalli to come grab Noah?" She always knows what I need before I even ask for it. I'm so lucky to have her.

"Have I ever told you how much I love you?" I tell her.

"Not enough," she throws back.

"And you're humble too," I add with a laugh. "Noah is with the neighbor until after dinner. They're watching a movie together. If I need you, I'll let you know, but I'll text the mom next door and see if she can keep Noah a little longer if necessary."

"So, you're going to talk to Roger tonight? You're comfortable with that?" I know she's worried I'll be emotional going into the meeting with Tyler tomorrow.

"Yeah. It might seem I'm breaking up with Roger because of Tyler, but, like you said, I think this breakup would be happening eventually down the road. Although, I can't, in good conscience, be having these feelings around Tyler while I have a boyfriend. I know it's not right. It doesn't change some other things though, Kalli," I groan.

"You mean, all the stuff he did to you years ago?"

At the hospital, when I confessed everything to Kalli, I told her why Tyler and I parted ways. She was furious on my behalf at first, her hands balling into fists and I wasn't sure if my best friend was going to search for my husband herself.

But now, she keeps reminding me there's more to the story. Apparently, as Ty keeps saying, he has his side of things he wants to air out. So, I'm finally succumbing to the fact I should hear him out before settling things with Tyler once and for all.

"Yeah, how did you just forget how mad you were?" I ask, forgetting the dirty dishes once again and sitting at my kitchen table.

"I didn't forget. I promise you I didn't let just let it slide. But he said he wants to talk to you. I assume there's more to this story of his and I think you should listen to it. It's obviously eating at him if he's insisting. Don't you think you should?" Kalli is a true attorney. She wants all the evidence laid out before she gives her verdict. She might not be a trial lawyer, but she still likes all the facts, which makes her good at her job.

She continues, "That's why I told you not to simply hand him the divorce papers before sitting down with him. He keeps urging you to talk to him because he has something to say. What's the worst thing you'd get out of listening to the guy?"

She's right. Tyler has been asking for us to talk, for him to explain himself, and that hasn't happened. I've held on to a lot of anger, bitterness really, for so long. I'll admit that when I first saw Tyler at the school that day weeks ago, all I wanted to do was push him away. In reality, I wanted to slap him and scream for what he did to me.

The way his letter impacted me, I was never the same. His words branded me and I never walked away the same. I remember reading it that day and the numbness washed over me. As the pain impacted me from losing Tyler, a new version of myself arose, and I simply felt like I could never return to the person I once was.

Life tilted at that point for me because everything I had felt for him shifted. Little cracks in my foundation were left behind. I didn't trust my instincts when it came to what love should feel like. I felt broken in so many ways, the trust I thought I understood up to that point was shattered.

Then Bryce died shortly after, and those cracks became craters. There was no foundation to walk on anymore because my world was unrecognizable. The man I thought I loved didn't love me, and my brother was no longer here. I was left with a baby I had no clue how to navigate life with, and parents I felt disconnected to. My world was unrecognizable, so I rebuilt and everything was misplaced.

Navigating this shift at a pivotal point in my life was incredibly difficult for me. I was in pain and I wanted nothing more than to crawl into a ball and lose myself to the pain. But I had to persevere. I found a way to do so; in that quest, I built a new foundation that covered the cracks Ty's and Bryce's absences caused. This new version of myself is no longer jovial like I used to be.

In all those years, I kept putting off finding my biological parents in fear of what I might discover. Unsealing court documents can take time and effort—what if that unearths more disappointment? Can I handle that? I just don't know if I have the mental capacity to deal with it.

I haven't told anyone but I hired a private investigator to look into my biological parents. Kalli is the only person that knows he's been hired, but nothing has come from that investigation yet. Kalli knows I don't want to talk about it until there's something to discuss, so once he was hired, I let it go, leaving it in the PI's hands until something is revealed.

"Indy, you've gone silent," Kalli pulls me from my thoughts.

"Sorry," I blow out a breath. "You're right. I should hear him out. But, I'm going to be honest with you. No matter his explanation, he still did what he did. He betrayed my trust after we had that weekend together. I thought we shared a connection. And then he blew it up in the worst way. I get we hadn't really talked it out, but those few days together, there was something unspoken."

I sit there, again my thoughts going back to that day. It's hard not to feel the flutter of my heart as my mind gets engulfed by those memories. It's crazy how easily it can be transported to a time after years of suppressing them.

"I'll likely listen, but serve him with divorce papers after this anyway. I don't see how he'll explain himself out of this one," I tell her.

"I understand," she sighs. I can imagine her doodling on a piece of paper.

"I'm going to call Roger before it gets too late and Noah has to head home. You know I love you. And thanks for talking me through this."

"Of course. Good luck with the breakup. Maybe put it in a Sheets presentation." She laughs as I hang up, likely trying to lighten the mood for me.

———

Roger was coming home from work when I called him earlier, so we met up at a coffee shop nearby. It was the most cordial breakup I've ever had. I've never felt more comfortable parting ways with a boyfriend before.

When we walked back to our respective places, I expected at least a friendly hug, and as I leaned in to do just that, what happened next pretty much solidified our breakup was the right decision. I moved my body toward Roger and instead of opening his arms for me to bring my body into him, he extended his hand out for me to shake it. Like a fucking business transaction.

The worst part? I stared at it like a moron. I was stunned. No. I was speechless. Let's just say—good thing Roger is nice to look at because he needs to work on his people skills. I shook his hand and laughed. He gave me a perplexed look because my laughter morphed into hysterics as I walked away. I had literal tears as I got closer to my front door.

It's been hours and I still find myself smiling at the memory. I texted with Kalli about everything and she has sent me multiple memes throughout the evening because his behavior perplexed her as well.

Noah's home now and tucked safely in bed. He had a

good time at the neighbor's house, which always brings a smile to my face. He's always been a social child, much like my brother was at his age, but seeing him thrive despite Bryce being gone always comforts me. I worry that me being a single mom is impacting him negatively. But I must be doing something right with him because he's constantly smiling and telling me how much he loves school. Hopefully he continues to be this happy child because he's this immensely positive part of my otherwise hectic life.

I move into my room and get myself ready for bed. Of course, my vice now is grabbing a journal before falling asleep. I've gotten through them quickly because I'm a glutton for punishment, and a fast reader thanks to my job. I'm pretty much at the end of my entries. Once I'm situated against the headboard, I flip through to the page I tabbed.

I touch the paper, my writing looking so innocent and neat. It feels like a completely different person wrote this simply because this version of Indiana was so naive to the life that was going to hit her across the face in the year ahead. I want to hug this version of myself, simply to explain to her she has so much to open her eyes to.

I sit up a little higher on my bed, supporting my upper back with an added pillow, and start reading:

January 12, 2019
Dear Journal,

I'm sort of nervous. It seems any day now Tyler might come over. He hasn't told me when he'd visit, but it seems that now that I've given the okay for him to visit, he could write me and give me dates. Oh my gosh, just the thought gives me butterflies. I haven't seen him since the morning after we got married.

That whole whirlwind was a lot. We've exchanged so many words since then. I feel like we were just kids all those years ago and now here we are, adults, living our lives separately; but emotionally, it feels we are so mixed together. But in that time, I feel like I've fallen in love with this version of him. Yet, I haven't seen him at all. It's so strange. Although, I've gotten to love this side of him that I doubt anyone knows. Does that even make sense? I mean, how many people get to fall in love with someone via handwritten letters anymore? I doubt very many.

Tyler is attentive, giving, and he knows how to push me to look at myself with love and compassion. He knew what I needed when I feel like those who have known me my whole life didn't give me the same confidence. He really helped me see what I needed to succeed that night, and if it wasn't for him, I would have most likely gone back home and lived the life my parents wanted and been miserable. I wouldn't have believed in myself.

I wouldn't be here, actually. I would be in Nevada, practicing medicine. I have him to thank for being in this profession. I feel so grateful for him in many ways. It's just amazing to think that life has brought us together in the most odd way. And he's my husband, yet we've only been together once. But we might be together soon, and I'm nervous and excited. I'm rambling.

I'm just really anticipating this visit, yet I have no idea when it's happening.

I'll keep you posted on this encounter, journal.

Hopefully it happens. Eek.

CHAPTER 27

Indiana

6 YEARS AGO

February 16, 2019

Dear my forever Valentine, Tyler,

How are things going? Did you do anything exciting for Valentine's Day? Shoot... maybe I should have sent you a box of goodies or something. I've never done that. What a bad wifey I am. I'll start doing better on my end.

I worked long hours so mine wasn't super exciting. My team ordered Chinese takeout so that lessened the blow at least.

The winter came in strong this year and it hasn't lightened up. I feel like no matter how many layers I add to my attire each morning, I feel the chill to my bones. I swear, I never get used to it.

Each year I give myself a pep talk about

being prepared, and the moment the cold comes around, I'm ill-prepared for the burst of chill that hits me when I step outside my building. I'm a wimp, that's what I'm trying to say. It's crazy to think I look around and see people wearing shorts while I'm here suffering in

THE DOORBELL RINGS, *pulling me away from the letter I'm writing. I put the pad of paper and pen on the coffee table, standing up from the couch. I wonder if Ms. Sanderson locked herself out of her apartment again. She has a tendency of doing that every now and again. Last time she ran out trying to track down the delivery guy to give him a package and the door locked behind her.*

I reach the front door, looking out the peephole, and I can't help the gasp that escapes my lips. It's been years since I've seen him, but those mesmerizing gray-blue eyes can't be mistaken for anyone else's staring back at me.

What is Tyler doing here? My pulse thumps as I look back through the little hole to peer at my husband on the other side. I can't believe he's surprising me like this.

The excitement racing through my veins is hard to contain. Looking down at my tattered appearance, I'm internally kicking myself for changing out of my work attire right when I got home. Wearing a worn, oversized Metallica pajama top and heather-gray mini shorts, I look like a slob. And from what I can tell from the little bit I'm seeing reflected on the other side of this door, he looks delectable.

I move away a bit and bite my lip. I start running around my apartment, hoping I have some clean clothes lying around to look more appealing. I haven't seen him in five years. I can't let him see me looking like a couch potato.

I throw my head back and groan. I quickly cover my mouth with both hands, hoping Tyler didn't hear me through the door.

Of course, the universe doesn't reward me with such luck.

"Indy? Are you in there?"

Mother-fucking shit.

"Coming!" I yell, tossing things under my nearby furniture in hopes I can hide my mess.

There's no way to tidy up the dirty dishes in the sink and some of the other things I've got scattered. It's a Friday night and I'm home after a long, exhausting week. I find another oversized shirt, and at least it's clean. My hair is up in a messy bun, but at least I look a little more put together. My makeup is still on from earlier today. This is the real me; Tyler will just have to deal with it.

I swing the door open and Tyler stands there looking edible in dark wash jeans, a forest green sweater that tightly hugs his muscles, and combat boots. He's holding a heavy jacket in his arms with a duffle bag sitting on the ground.

I can't help but take in the specimen of a man in front of me. This is not the same person that left me behind after graduation. If I thought he was mysterious then, he's now someone I want to peel back and discover bit by bit. He's all man. He's alluring, with more muscle, and a lot more appeal. If I thought I could drool over him when we were eighteen, I'd melt at the sight of him now.

He's absolutely gorgeous. He has an intensity in his gaze, but the way his eyes are looking at me, I feel like he could set me on fire. There's nothing innocent about the way his eyes look me over, scanning my frame from head to toe. I can feel my cheeks flame.

"Tyler," I say, although I hear the gravel in my voice.

This moment has been years in the making. As if each letter has been a form of seduction and we have hit our boiling point.

I open the door further to make room for him to come inside. He picks up his duffle and slowly makes his way in. Passing me, his eyes sweep over my place, looking over every part of my open-concept place, until they land on me again.

I feel the heat in his gaze when our eyes connect. Without another word, he drops his bag and his large palms latch onto my cheeks and his lips are on mine. I forgot how soft his lips are.

A fire ignites in my belly and shoots straight to my core. Damn, I missed his touch, more than I thought possible. I tried to date while he was away, especially in the beginning when my feelings for him weren't as strong, but nothing really felt right.

Something about Tyler always fit from the beginning. Like he was carved just for me and when he touches me, it feels like he knows exactly what I need.

He moves his lips down my neck and it ignites something feral in me. A moan erupts from my lips and I move my nails down his back.

"Fuck, I missed you," he says as he licks his way down the column of my jaw. He moves my body back so I'm against the wall. "I've fantasized about my hands touching you all over." He then brings his hands down and caresses down the mounds of my breasts and squeezes them over the thin fabric of my shirt, the peaks of my nipples reacting to his touch.

My back arches and my pussy clenches, completely enamored by everything this man is doing and I'm still fully clothed.

I capture his lips again and bite his lower lip, moving my fingers through his clipped hair, wishing it was a bit longer so I could pull on it. I continue to move my hands down, enjoying the hardness of his body after years of working out in the Army. Once I get to the hem of his sweater, I start to pull on it, antsy to see more of him.

Tyler starts to chuckle, knowing I'm impatient. "Someone seems to be just as ready as me."

"Well, I didn't know you were coming, and now I want to unwrap my present." I smile into him between kisses. "Let me see you. All of you."

He pulls away and grabs his sweater up from behind his head. The moment he reveals himself to me, I'm breathless. He's more beautiful than I imagined. His skin is sun-kissed, probably after being exposed to endless time outdoors. He's toned in every area of his upper body.

His shoulders are defined, with muscles leading down to his biceps and chest. His abdomen has ripples that lead to that titillating V that I simply want to lick. It's delectable, if I'm being honest. Everything about him is absolutely giving me goosebumps, and he's only got his shirt off at this point.

I'm staring. Actually, if I'm not careful, I'll probably start drooling. I see he's got a sizable bulge in his pants that I'm having to keep myself from reaching out and stroking. Right now, all I want to do is admire because he's downright scrumptious. How on earth have we gone all this time without seeing one another?

Five years ago, when we were last together, he was already beautiful and handsome. But now, he's downright exquisite.

"Indy, you're staring," he says with a cocky grin on his face.

"Mmhmm," is all I can muster. I bite my lower lip, unable to contain the look of satisfaction. He's all man and I can't believe I get to have him all to myself. "How long do I get you for?"

"I have to head back on Monday," he says. "Why?"

"We aren't leaving this apartment," I say, then I pounce.

Tyler catches me and I hear his low laugh that soon turns into a moan from both of us when our kiss intensifies. He walks me through my apartment, unknowing which door leads to my bedroom.

I break our kiss to tell him, "First door to the right," then return to kissing him like it's my lifeline. I swear I've never found lips that have felt softer. He continues moving, then his hands move along my back and soon I hear the tearing of fabric. It doesn't register until I feel the cool air on my back that it's my shirt he's torn open.

I pull away from him. "I happen to like this shirt!"

"You were taking too long and I wanted to unwrap my gift," he says, that sly smile painting his lips.

"You cocky ass," I say.

He throws me on the bed. "If I don't see you naked in the next minute, you're going to see me more than cocky, Indy." He licks my bottom lip and I feel a shiver down my spine. His eyes are smoldering, and I wonder how dirty things will get this weekend.

Heat crawls across my body at the thought of him touching me more. I move my hands along my chest and pinch my breasts through my clothes. I bite down on my lower lip and moan.

"Fuck, Indy, I need you, baby. Do you know how many nights I've thought about you? How many times I wished I was with you? Those letters were never enough," he confesses and I feel my heart speed up.

"It's always been you, Ty," I confess and I feel the heaviness of my heart with my confession.

He pulls at the scrap left of my shirt, revealing my lace bra. He brings his arms under my shoulder blades, arching my back, licking the center of my chest. I moan and I swear I feel the wetness pool in my panties. I'm aching for him.

"Ty, I want you so bad," I tell him.

"I'm yours," he tells me. He proceeds to unhook my bra and slowly moves it off my arms, then throws it beside us, revealing my breasts. They feel heavy with need.

He brings his lips over one of my nipples, sucking hard, coercing a moan out of me that would probably wake one of my neighbors. I can't help the way my hips gyrate of their own accord. I move my nails down his back, likely leaving marks.

He does the same thing on the opposite breast and he's leaving me primed and ready for him. He moves his mouth down my abdomen and I'm panting. My gaze watches him, antsy to see what his next move is.

"Indy, you want my mouth, my fingers or my cock?" he asks me.

"All of you," I confess. After all these years, there's no way I'm depriving myself of any part of this man.

He gives me a lazy smile, as if he's satisfied with my answer, then begins his pursuit down my body. Past my bellybutton, he begins shimmying my pajama shorts off my body, my panties following suit as well.

I'm fully exposed in front of him and he stands up to look at me for a moment. I'm about to ask what's wrong when he speaks.

"Indiana, you are magnificent," he says, almost breathlessly. "How did I become so lucky to call myself your husband?"

I move my hands to cover my face, but Tyler must sense what I'm about to do, and he grabs them before I have a chance to do so. "Absolutely not. You will keep your eyes on me while I feast on this pussy of mine. Make sure your screams are loud so the whole neighborhood knows I'm making my wife feel good tonight. When I finish my meal, we're going to try some of the scenes you highlighted in those books you sent me."

Oh fuck. This man is going to ruin me.

Before I can react any further, he gets on his knees, pushes my knees open and swipes his tongue through my folds. My pelvis nearly juts off the bed. It feels so damn good. Just like he asked, I scream loudly at the contact.

"That's it, baby. You taste so good." He keeps his eyes focused on me as he swipes again, his tongue getting well acquainted with my center. The intensity of his gaze only ignites me further in my core.

He focuses on my clit, then slips a finger inside me. I can't help the sounds I'm making, my head falling back and my breathing becoming erratic. Fuck, he's good at this. I forgot how good we are together. My orgasm begins to build, like a rollercoaster going up the tracks.

"Ty, you're going to make me come," I say into the dark room.

He adds another finger, finding that special spot that makes me see stars behind my eyes. My back arches then he sucks on my clit. I move my hips at an uncontrollable pace against his face, seeking out the friction I need because this man is making me crazy.

"Yes, like that, fuck." My thighs squeeze his face in place as my orgasm rockets through me. My vision goes dark and a million little stars ricochet behind my eyes, while every part of my skin feels like it's on fire.

I'm panting as I start to come down from my release. Tyler is trailing open-mouthed kisses up my body, the wetness causing goosebumps to line my skin. I can't help the giggle that escapes, a smile of satisfaction marring my lips.

"I could watch you cum for the rest of my life," he confesses and all I feel is warmth at his words.

"Why do you have your pants on still," I complain, noticing his jeans still covering his very hard cock. I start to fiddle with the waistband of his pants, but he stands and begins to finish removing them. His socks and shoes follow along with it.

When he starts to slide his pants and boxers all the way down, his dick springs free and I salivate at the sight. Can a penis be pretty? Because his sure is.

I move to stroke his cock in my hands, thanking myself for the manicure I got a few days ago. The red polish is a stark contrast around his velvety skin. I look up to see his eyes hooded and it spurs me on to keep stroking him.

"Fuck, Indy. Feeling you touching me is everything, but I won't last. I need to be inside you. I think I'll need to have these lips around my cock later." He moves his thumbs along my lower lip to emphasize his point. *"But right now, I want to feel your pussy tightening around my dick and milking me for all I've got."*

Oh, this man and his dirty mouth. I feel wetter just hearing his words.

His hands move to circle around my throat. I keep my hands moving along his cock while he moves his mouth closer to my ear. *"How does that sound, wife? Do you want me to fuck you? You want it slow and soft, or hard and rough?"*

I fucking whimper. I swear Tyler lives up to the bad boy image fantasies are made of.

"The rougher the better," I confess.

"Good girl," he says, pulling his face a few inches away from mine so I can see a devilish gleam pull at his features.

Before I can register what's going on, he grabs me as if I weigh nothing and tosses me to the center of the bed.

"Be right back," he tells me, then stalks off, leaving me exposed.

I crease my brows, curiosity marring my features. He doesn't leave me wondering for long, his naked body returns quickly, this time with a bottle of lube, and something else that has my brows shooting up.

"Um, you came prepared." I balk.

"Well, better prepared than sorry," he says, his smile telling me he's more excited than anything. "Plus, after a few years of someone sending me highlighted dirty books, I had references." He quirks a brow and I can't help the laugh that escapes.

He places the lube on the bedside table, along with a strip of condoms. How many times are we going at it right now?

As if he can read my mind, he says, "Oh, one is not going to be enough for what I've got planned for us, Indy."

Grabbing the scarf he brought with him, he juts his chin. "You trust me?"

I nod and he grabs my hands.

He brings my arms above my head and ties my wrists to the headboard. I can't help the surge of excitement that passes through me.

"What if I want to touch you?" I ask him, my voice gravelly.

"That's the fun, baby," he says. Once he's done securing my hands, he kisses the spot where I'm bound. I expected him to be a bit rougher, but his contact is seductive and soft. It surprises me and I feel like melting right here in this spot.

He trails his lips down my arm, then moves down to my ear and jaw, goosebumps erupting on my skin. My nipples harden even more, something I thought impossible. I'm turned on something fierce. My hips begin to grind against his leg, seeking out friction. I pull against the restraints, irritated I can't touch him. I feel him chuckle against my skin and I grunt in frustration.

"So impatient," he murmurs.

"I need you," I insist.

"You have me," he says between trailed kisses along my skin.

"I want you in me. I think you said something about fucking me hard and rough." This time when I move my hips, I feel his hard cock brushing against my center and he moans. I'm soaking for him at this point and I assume he's coated with my wetness.

"Fuck, you're really making it hard for me to prolong this," he says, biting my nipple, causing me to cry out. "So fucking sensitive. I love that." He drags his tongue along my sensitive bud and I whimper.

"Tyler, please," I beg, needing to feel another release. It's been years in the making at this point and I'm at a breaking point.

He reaches over, grabbing the foil packet. Once he's rolled the condom on, I see he's ignored the lube, probably because I'm more than ready for him without it.

He sits back, his erection at attention, with a look of adoration in his gaze. With hooded eyes, he licks his lower lip.

"You're absolute perfection, Indy. Once I start fucking you, I might never stop," he admits.

"Promise?" I say, with a coy smile.

Without another word, Tyler lines himself up, and plunges in. I feel so full, so complete. We both moan in satisfaction, and I wrap my legs around his middle. He doesn't move right away. He swings his head back and cries out, just as lost in this feeling as I am.

"Fuck, Indy. I forgot how good you feel," he says and I'm still getting used to his size. He's stretching me to the point I can't even form words.

He pulls out of me all the way to the tip, then slams in again. This time, I scream out in euphoria. It doesn't take long for my orgasm to begin to build again. His cock is hitting that spot, especially the way my clit is bumping against his pubic bone. It's damn perfection.

My breasts are so sensitive, the way they're bouncing as he plunges into me is almost painful. I feel like everything is adding to this addictive feeling that's going to push me over the edge.

"Ty, I'm right there. Keep fucking me like that," I tell him.

He decides to push me a little further, grabbing one of my legs, and bringing it over his shoulder. It feels like he's pushing his dick even deeper. Holy shit, how the hell am I going to survive a whole weekend of this man?

That's it, my orgasm surges through me like a damn rocket ship.

Stars, no fireworks, go off throughout my body. I scream his name, and my vision goes blank for a second time. It's the most intense orgasm I've ever experienced.

While I'm coming down from my own high, it only intensifies for Tyler. He brings my leg down and opens me wider, pounding into me rapidly. The headboard is striking the wall at a faster rate, and I couldn't care less if the entire neighborhood can hear us. Watching this man lose himself because of me and our passion is beyond intoxicating.

His face is pulled into a euphoric trance, his brows tense. I look down to watch his dick move in and out of me; it's so fucking hot. His pace is relentless and soon I can tell he's close, only spurring me on to feel another impending orgasm of my own.

"I can feel you tightening around me, Indy. Are you close again?" he asks me between heaving pants.

I nod, unable to use words at this point.

"Come with me, baby," he says and the slapping of skin only adds to the intensity between us.

He brings his thumb to my clit and I detonate. Tyler brings his mouth to mine and my moans get swallowed by our connection. He releases into the condom, pumping into me a few more times. He falls to my side, whispering my name as his breaths are coming in heavy pants, both of us sweating and spent.

He moves his hands above me, pulling at the silk scarf, until my arms are free. My hands fall to my sides, my chest heaving to catch my breath.

I look over at him and he's staring at the ceiling.

"Shit, Indiana. You're going to wreck me this weekend." He laughs, then I'm lost as his eyes meet mine. "That was intense."

I smile at him, feeling like my whole world just flipped. I don't know if he realizes what he's done to my life, but I know I'll never be the same.

We continue staring at each other. The last five years have been about the use of words on paper, and yet, right now, it feels like no words are needed to communicate at all. Our eyes do so much of the communicating instead. Like he sees inside my soul and I inside his.

We finally get up from the bed and head into the shower. What starts off innocently to rinse off, turns dirty again when I'm on my knees and watch Tyler unravel as I take him in my mouth.

———

The next day, we head out to lunch. I hadn't prepared to have anyone in my apartment, aside from me, so I'm not stocked up on food. The moment we step foot outside, the biting cold hits us, and Tyler wraps his arms around me. It's the first time I feel protected by him. I lean into his warmth, and his hand grips my shoulder tighter.

"The diner isn't far. They serve the best patty melts," I tell him.

"You know those are my weakness." He kisses my temple and something about the gesture feels more affectionate.

"I remember." I keep my gaze forward as we walk toward the restaurant, trying to keep the flutter in my heart from taking off into a sprint.

A part of me hopes that I'm his weakness too. This isn't what a fake marriage looks like. The lines from pretend to real are starting to blur—my heart and mind aren't seeing eye to eye.

We're seated at a booth when we arrive at the restaurant. I'm pointing at a few items that sound good on the menu when someone interrupts me.

"Indy, is that you?" I look up to see an old classmate of mine.

"Oh my gosh. Hey, Chris. It's good to see you. What are you up to?"

"Not much. Got a job working at the local paper." He smiles, his eyes swinging over to Tyler.

"Chris, this is Tyler. Ty, this is Chris. We went to school together and graduated under the same major."

Ty extends his hand in greeting, then brings his arm over my shoulders. It's affectionate, something a boyfriend would do. His fingers move along my shoulders, and I can't really concentrate on what Chris is saying. I'm highly focused on the circular motion Ty's fingers are making over my sweater. It's only then I realize he hasn't stopped touching me since we left the apartment. He's been affectionate at every opportunity.

"How's everything at Medstone?" Chris pulls me out of my daydream.

"It's great. Loving every second." I smile up at him.

"That's wonderful. It's definitely better than the late night studying we had to do, huh?" Chris winks.

Tyler's fingers freeze for a mere second before continuing again, but his face looks unaffected while looking up at our visitor.

"Yeah, well, those papers were always a drag." I roll my eyes.

"Staying up late these days looks a little more fun now, doesn't it, Indy?" Tyler says, looking over at me. Yeah, he's marking his territory.

I bring my hand on his thigh and squeeze.

"Well, it was good seeing you. Tyler, nice meeting you." Chris scurries off without an answer from us.

I watch Chris walk in the direction of his table, and I'm amazed there isn't a puff of smoke behind him due to the fact he left so damn fast.

"Was that really necessary?" I ask Ty.

"Well, given the way he was undressing you with his eyes while he took a walk down memory lane—I'd say yes, Indiana, it was." He brings his lips near my ear and kisses right below my earlobe. I feel a zing with the contact.

"There was never anything between us," I tell him.

"Doesn't mean he never wanted there to be." He keeps dropping kisses on my skin.

"Tyler," I tell him, but don't pull myself away.

"Indy," he taunts.

Our server interrupts this building sexual tension and our lunch is ordered. The rest of the meal continues, no other classmates to make it awkward. Tyler fills me in on everything that he's been up to regarding his time in the Army since we last spoke—that is, everything he hasn't written about.

It seems that while most people on his deployment travel back to the States to visit family, he opts for smaller assignments that can be fulfilled. When that doesn't happen, he goes on trips to visit parts of the world he's always wanted to see or, most recently, he's tagged along with Georgie to see his family. It's been a dream of his to travel, and the Army has given him the ability to do so.

After lunch, we fight the frigid winds and sightsee. I take him to Millenium Park. Although we're bundled up, it's a clear day in Chicago. The moment we arrive, I see his eyes light up. He's never been to the city, so we walk up to the Cloud Gate statue and he pulls out his phone.

"Want me to get a picture for you?" I offer.

"Alone?" The look of horror on his face is too damn cute. "Get in with me, Indy." Without warning, he tugs on my jacket to pull me in.

Immediately, he snaps a photo and I can't help the way my smile grows. What the photo doesn't capture is the way my heart is bursting behind my ribcage.

"You two are adorable. Do you want me to get a photo for you?" a woman asks as she's walking by.

I'm about to say there's no need, but Tyler cuts me off, "That would be great. My wife and I haven't been here together before."

There goes my damn heart again. I swear, he's going to leave on Monday and take every piece of my fucking heart with him.

The weekend goes on with us fucking on every surface of my place. The man is insatiable and I realize that if I was on the fence regarding falling in love with him before, this weekend solidified it. But in-between these moments of intimacy, we talk.

We laugh, we connect, we bond. The one thing we don't do is divulge what the hell we plan to do with our marriage. As much as I *planned on being honest about my feelings, I chicken out because I don't want to break whatever we are doing. It feels too fucking good —this bubble we form over the weekend, and I need it with Tyler.*

Even though he continues being that mysterious, broody guy I knew back when we were kids, he has this other side to him as well. He smiles and laughs with me. He's romantic when we go out for a bit and grab food. He holds my hand and shows me a side of himself that I realize is everything I long for in a partner.

And sure enough, as the weekend carried on, I pushed the nagging feeling creeping up that I should talk to him about all the things I told myself I would say when he and I were face to face. Because I knew all the little butterflies that were forming inside were going to multiply and take off. I should have done something about what was going on with the thoughts I was forming because these emotions inside were strong and this was only the start.

Could we be more once he's stateside? Should we be more? "Tyler—I want to be your real wife, do you want to be my real husband? This is no longer fake for me. I love you." None of those sentiments come out though and the weekend comes to an end way too quickly.

That's the thing about being young, though. You're naive and think you have all the time in the world. Little did I know that a year later, my whole world would look a lot different—with no husband to lean on.

CHAPTER 28

Tyler

LAST NIGHT'S shift was long and hard. Had I planned this out better, I would have told her we would do this another day. But it feels like if I push this off, I might miss my shot to explain myself.

If I ask for us to wait another day, I'm scared she'll just slap me with divorce papers. Then I won't get another opportunity to tell her what was going through my head years ago when I wrote her that God-awful letter. There's still a high likelihood she'll walk away from me and never look back. But I'll feel better knowing I told her.

That's what it's about, right? Clearing the air between us is the healthy, yet harder, route. I can feel the nerves multiplying as I drive over. The air-conditioning is pumping on overdrive because I'm already sweating and it's not even nine in the morning. I've been opting for my truck since everything happened on the motorcycle.

Maybe once I get this off my chest, things will finally fall back into place. Things have felt unstable. If I could choose how I wanted the chips to land, I'd wish to have her as a permanent fixture in my life. I fucked things up years ago, but I've felt that gaping hole as my punishment. Now, all I want is make things right because she's always been a breath of fresh air for me.

I still remember that flutter I'd get seeing her letters arrive when I was overseas in the Army; it would be a jolt to the system. She always brought me the energy I needed to sustain me until I'd hear from her again. There's something to say about feeling a connection to someone when you're away and feeling like you have little association to the outside world— she was my reason for breathing more often than not.

The nights were long in the Army. Knowing Indy was a part of my life, first as a friend then as something more, was so special.

The problem is, I skirted around my emotions when it came to telling her. That's where I first failed her. Then I tripped up at every passing from that point forward. Eventually, I fucked up for good with that last letter, and I never returned to her to fix the error of my ways.

I don't deserve her forgiveness, but I'm hoping she'll find it in her to forgive me anyway. If she grants me more than that, it'll be a win. Plus, the more I've seen her recently, the more I'm reminded of why I cared for her back then.

She's sewn into the fabric of me and I've grown into who I am today because of what we had all those years ago. I've learned to be a better man thanks to her, although I see she's put up walls thanks in part to the things I've done to her.

The moment I arrive at her place, I take a breath and park. Unlike Jerry and Scarlet's place, where they are set in the suburbs, Indiana lives in a townhome in downtown Boston. From the last of our letters we exchanged, she was still not on the best of terms with her parents, so I assume she continues to rise up on her own merit.

I can't help but look at her surroundings and think how proud I am of her and all she's done for herself. Not only that, she did it while raising her brother's child. Not the easiest of circumstances, yet she found a way to make her life successful and one she can be proud of. The pride that builds inside me for her and everything she's overcome and achieved is overflowing.

Indy was so scared of the future that night we crossed paths at the Hoover Dam, yet here we are, eleven years later, with our foundations set. She's found a new dream and flourished in her own way. This life is hers and hers alone.

I step out of the truck, grab the coffees I picked up on the way, and move a hand through my hair, taking a deep breath in hopes of calming myself down. No matter what goes on after this, I have to make peace with the fact I'll do my best in explaining myself. Much like Rodney told me throughout our sessions years ago, I can't change my decisions. I have to own up to my mistakes and hope she sees how I've grown from there.

I was distraught and angry, taking it out on anything and everyone around me. I left my life in disarray. But Indy was the easiest person to hurt and I did that. The saddest part was, I never sought her out to fix it, mostly out of fear of what she'd say. I needed to work on myself first, then I used the excuse of time, feeling like she had moved on.

Seeing her all over again all these years later has been flooding my thoughts and consuming my emotions. I realize now we can't just leave everything unresolved. Plus, just the few times we've seen each other, I can feel the attraction we have like a live wire.

I've never experienced what I had with her with anyone else. I've looked—damn have I searched for it with another woman—no one grabbed at my heart the way Indy has, nor do I think anyone will.

Especially the way I've watched my friends fall to their knees and become victim to their partners—I know there's only one woman that has taken hold of my heart in such a way. Indiana Ranton is the love of my life and I not only let her walk away, I pushed her as far from my vicinity as possible, and made sure she'd never come back.

As I stand in front of her door, my heart is hammering in my chest and my mouth is dry. I'm not sure I'll be able to speak when she swings that door open.

I ring the bell and wait, hearing her hurried steps on the other side. The minute she swings it open, it feels like I'm transported to six years prior, to that night I surprised her. That weekend when everything changed. That weekend when it confirmed everything—when I knew for certain I fell in love with my wife.

Her hair is up in a messy bun, although this time, she has glasses on, and she seems she's in a bit of a rush. I take in her outfit—again she's in an oversized shirt, no band on it this time, with a tank top underneath, and shorts that reveal her toned legs.

I do little to hide my eyes from perusing the beauty in front of me. I take her in, every little inch of her a sight for my sore eyes. She's barefoot, her toes manicured a hot pink, something that hasn't changed in all the years I've known her. She's always loved that color, even when we were teens.

"Hey," she says, her tone a little clipped. It catches me off-guard.

"Hi. You okay?" I can't help the way I look at her a little confused. Did I miss something between when I texted her after leaving the station to right now? "I brought coffee."

I hold my hand up to show off the peace offering, but it does little to break her icy exterior.

"Thanks. Sorry, but I got pulled into a last-minute meeting. Come in." She motions for me to follow her in. "Let me try to wrap this up. Why don't you have a seat and I'll be right out?"

She gives me a small smile, but then she disappears off down the hall to what I assume is her office or room. I go into the kitchen and set the coffee cups down, not sure what to do with myself as I wait for Indy to return.

Soon I feel a little body move next to my legs. I look down and discover Darth zig-zagging between my calves.

"Hey, little guy," I say, bending down to offer a scratch under his chin.

He leans into my affection, his purrs getting loud the longer I scratch him. I proceed to pet him behind his ear. He leans in further, enjoying the attention. Soon, he's sprawled on his back, letting me give him a little love on his belly. This cat is more dog than cat and it's hard not to smile at the way he's letting me give him so much love today.

He's got bright-green eyes, and a flat face. Darth lets me pick him up and I'm cuddling him when Indy comes out to greet me again. She stops in her tracks.

"Hey. Look who came out to greet me," I say, my hand scratching under the cat's chin, his purrs now loud enough for both of us to hear.

"That's surprising. Darth has really imprinted on you." Indy walks over and points to the coffees to see which is hers. I jut my chin at the one I brought for her. "Thanks for grabbing me one. I needed something fancier than the Nespresso I made this morning."

"Everything okay at work?" I ask, seeing she's only slightly less stressed than she was when she answered the door.

"Already putting out fires and it's not even ten in the morning." She rolls her eyes. "We had an author go rogue in an interview and the PR department was not happy. Sort of causes an uproar, but I couldn't go in today so I had to handle it from here."

"We could've rescheduled. I don't mind," I say as I let the cat jump from my arms.

"That's appreciated, but you're not the reason why I had to be home. I have my infusion for my Crohn's medication today; I do it with home health. The joys of chronic illness," she says on a sigh. "Anyways, my nurse was supposed to be here earlier, so I was running around getting my workout done, then getting Noah to school. But then my nurse had to push the infusion to later. Add this emergency at work, it threw off my whole morning. I don't like when my schedule gets discombobulated." Indy moves through her kitchen, filling up her water.

"I remember," I say, sipping my own coffee.

She looks over her shoulder, drawing her eyebrows together. I don't know if it bothers her that I know her so well. Or maybe she doesn't like that I remember these little parts of her.

"Do you want to sit down in the living room? It might be more comfortable," she offers.

I nod and grab my coffee. I follow her, where I see Darth is now perched in a cat tower near the window.

Indy sits down on a portion of the sectional and I take a seat further away, giving her some space. I wish I could sit closer to her, but I'm treading lightly.

"I'm going to jump to the chase, Tyler. I feel like each time we get together we get interrupted. I don't want that to happen this time. And something about you—honestly us—I feel like I have a weak spot when it comes to you. I want to hear you out before we move forward with the divorce."

So, she's planning on moving forward with divorcing me. Something about that leaves me feeling unsettled. I look down at my cup of coffee. I don't know why I feel a part of my heart break knowing this thing with us will be ending, but I was naive to think it would continue. What I did to her was a betrayal, even if it was a lie on my end. She didn't know that, and she's lived believing I was something I wasn't.

"I hurt you and I'm sorry," I start. "I wasn't in a good place when I wrote you that last letter."

She sits there, her eyes trained on me, her back straight, and I can see she's trying hard not to react. Then she looks down at her cup, fiddling with the lid. She stays silent, so I continue.

"If I'm being frank, I lied in that letter," I tell her.

Her head snaps up, surprise etched on her face. "What? Why?"

"I wrote that letter shortly after losing Georgie. I spiraled. I was numb and reacted badly. I allowed my emotions to guide me and I pushed the best thing in my life away from me instead of keeping you closer." I keep my eyes trained on hers, hoping she feels the sincerity in what I'm saying.

She sits there, not wavering from her spot for a few beats, until she finally stands and walks off. I'm thrown by the reaction. I follow her frame with my gaze, wondering if she's simply done with this conversation, but soon she's back with a piece of paper in her hands.

"So, you're telling me that this letter"—she holds out what I now see is *the* letter—"these words you wrote me meant nothing? What part was the lie Tyler? There were quite a few things in that letter that I take issue with."

I open my mouth to respond, but she cuts me off.

"Let me rephrase, Tyler. Because for you, what was apparently a lie, what was written as a result of pain; something that was numbing, and an emotional reaction; you're telling me this letter is something I should ignore? Because this letter set me off on a new path in my life. It launched my heart into a new direction."

She throws the letter in my direction and it falls at my feet. I see my writing staring back at me. I look down at it; the person I was when I wrote it feels like someone else, it seems to me like that was a lifetime ago; yet I know, to her, it probably feels like yesterday. I grab the paper, which looks worn, as if she's reread it a million times. It tugs at my heart, the thought of her holding this page in her hand, doing exactly that. I pull my gaze back to meet hers.

She continues, "I haven't been the same since the day I walked to my mailbox to find that envelope waiting for me. I have never looked in the mirror and seen the carefree person that once existed before receiving that letter. You did that, Tyler. You cut that version of myself out of my life. So now you sit here and tell me to listen to your words and accept them as the truth? Give me one good reason why?"

Tyler

5 YEARS AGO

January 25, 2020

Indiana,

Things have shifted a lot around here and I'll admit, I've changed along with that. I'm no longer feeling the same about things as I was before. I think that after so many years being far apart, I'm realizing we are doing a huge disservice to one another. And recently, things have evolved.

You deserve to live a life where you have a connection to someone, and so do I. As much as what we had growing between us was special, and I'll admit, I was hopeful we could see things flourish into something more once I was back in the States, my heart has shifted.

When away for a weekend, I met someone.

We hit it off, and one thing led to another. It happened and it was out of my control. I don't know how to explain it, and it wouldn't be fair for us to continue what we have going on, even emotionally, when I have feelings growing for someone else. I have to put a stop to our letters.

We knew that this connection we started was all a farce. You have an entire life, a career you're building in Chicago. This marriage is one you needed, and I don't fit into that life you're living. I know you mentioned the insurance has been better than the one you'd receive through your current job, so please continue on it for as long as you need.

We had this incredible physical connection—I mean, the sex was intense—it was what we both needed. It really scratched the itch we had growing between us. But I think we both knew it was all this could be. I don't think we ever expected our relationship to go beyond the phys-ical aspect, but we were too afraid to admit it.

Emotionally, I can't, in good conscience, continue doing this with you and these letters anymore. It wouldn't be fair for either of us. This has to be the last exchange between us. I hope you know what an incredible support you've been for me throughout the years, giving me the ability to feel cared for as I've felt seen on my loneliest nights while deployed.

Once you're ready, send divorce papers and I'll sign them. I understand if you're mad, you have every right to be. My heart is no longer invested in that way and you should find someone to love and cherish you in the way you deserve. You deserve more than me.

Take care of yourself.

Tyler

CHAPTER 30

Indiana

I'M SHAKING. The emotions I've been feeling are overpowering as I learn the truth Tyler is confessing. I'm simply staring at him, in utter shock.

"The only true parts of that letter were that something special was blooming between us, and that things had shifted for me emotionally. My feelings toward you never wavered, but I was a mess inside," he explains.

I've gone silent. I don't think I can speak, the only thing I want to do right now is scream. I want to rip my hair out and I want to yell at Tyler for being such an idiot. Because he burned everything we had built together to the ground.

"Indy, say something," Tyler urges, eyes pleading with me.

He shut down, plain and simple. I get it. He had lost his friend in the worst way—right in front of his eyes. I understand it was traumatic, and I won't even pretend to understand how that feels. But how did he go from losing Georgie to writing me that letter? How did he think that was the solution? And why did he wait this long to talk to me about this?

"I can practically hear you thinking from here," he tries again. I can hear the frustration in his tone.

I nearly grind my molars. He's been sitting with this information since the day he wrote me that letter, yet I've had minutes to process it. He needs to be more patient. Give me a fucking moment.

"I know you're mad—" he begins a third time, but I interrupt him.

"Mad? No, I'm not fucking mad, Tyler. I'm furious. I'm disappointed. I'm so angry, I want to throw something. I'm so full of emotion, it feels like my heart is going to burst out of my chest." I stand from my spot on the couch, unable to sit still. I begin pacing the living room, moving my fingers through my hair.

"I get you were upset with Georgie's passing. I get you two had this special bond and losing him must have felt like losing a piece of yourself," I say.

"It was an unimaginable loss," he says.

"Unimaginable?" I stop in my tracks. "Funny, because I experienced a loss just like that shortly after you did. The thing is I didn't get the choice to push someone I cared for away because he had already pushed me away. I was alone. I could have really used a shoulder to cry on, but instead, you had made the decision for me and left me."

That shuts him up, so I continue, "You know, Tyler, I'm sympathetic to the fact you suffered with Georgie's death, but you aren't really doing a good job explaining why you did it in this way. Why not just be honest in the letter? I mean, why go through the lengths of an elaborate lie? You didn't think I could handle it? You thought I would be so lovestruck that I'd keep coming after you?"

I bark out a laugh, but it lacks any humor.

"I guess I just wanted to solidify the fact that you wouldn't keep writing or something," he says. "I mean, I wanted you far away from me. You have to understand. I wasn't myself, Indy. I wasn't thinking straight. I didn't want something to happen to me while we were still doing this whole letter writing thing. Then what if you were left with having to deal with my remains? I saw what that did to Georgie's family. It broke them, Indy." He stands, the destruction evident on his face.

"I mean, I was at his funeral and it nearly broke me. I almost hopped on a plane to Chicago right then, but I thought I'd chicken out if I did this face-to-face, so I opted for a letter instead. I knew it would be the easiest way to see it through. I just wanted to make sure you weren't on the receiving end of bad news like Jerry and Scarlet were. Because that funeral was fucking awful." He hangs his head and I see the defeat in his posture.

"So, you speak for me now? You can predict how I'd react? Plus, isn't that something we should have talked about first? I mean, I'm old enough to understand how to handle it. And I was mature enough then. But that letter simply took all the good things you brought into my life and burned them to the ground, Ty. Don't you see that?" I hold back a sob.

"It tarnished everything. That letter"—I point to the letter he's now holding in his hands— "didn't help me move on, it obliterated my ability to love anyone else. You were the mold for me when it came to love. Then you became the kiln for all the trust issues I developed; I didn't want to try with anyone else after you. I simply lost the recipe and gave up. Add in the fact I lost my brother shortly after you walked away from what we had built together and I was completely broken. There's no way I could endure the possibility of losing people in my life again. I didn't just build walls around my heart—I built a fucking armed fortress around it."

His eyes lock on mine and he watches me, his Adam's apple bobbing. The emotion grows thicker as we continue hashing out the lengths of this letter.

"I thought I was helping you, Indy. I swear, I thought it was for the best. I was in a bad place. Then after I got out of the Army, I got therapy and realized I was suffering from

PTSD. My behavior was a defense mechanism. I worked on myself, opening my eyes to the fact I made decisions I shouldn't have. I'm sorry. If I could change things, I would. Your feelings are valid. Being mad at me, the way you're looking at me... fuck! It's gutting me right now. But I get it. I deserve it."

He hangs his head, and I have to hold myself back from going over there and comforting him. But there's also this part of me that's furious right now. For six years I've sat here, relentlessly nitpicking over that letter, wondering what I could have done to push him away. I thought I had done something wrong to cause this huge shift between us. My love for this man in front of me was overwhelming, to the point where I felt the air in my lungs nearly collapse as I read his words on that fateful day. To now be standing here, learning that it was all a farce; I'm shaken by the turn of events.

He has no idea how I'm feeling inside. If he thinks I'm looking at him with pain in my expression, he only knows the half of it. The lengths to which his actions broke me after I got that letter and the months and years that followed were hard to overcome. The way my whole life crumbled afterwards has taken so long to recover from.

"Tyler—you have no idea the aftermath of your actions. The way I've had to find the self-confidence in a relationship again is something I will never be able to explain to you." I don't even know if it's worth admitting that I never truly recovered from the blow of that letter.

He continues to hang his head, weaving his fingers through his hair. "Indy, I was an asshole, okay?"

"No, not okay!" I yell, standing up, throwing my arms out.

Tyler flinches. I surprise myself with my raised voice, but how can he simply act like this is something I can just listen to and push aside? Not all is forgiven after the explanation he's given me.

I take a deep breath and try to settle myself before I open my mouth to speak again.

"Listen, Ty, I understand you were going through something and I appreciate how hard it was for you. I'm so sorry you lost Georgie. I know, from the letters you wrote, how much he meant to you. Hell, it breaks my heart that you suffered and you didn't trust our connection enough to simply come to me and let yourself go through that with me. I would think—" I bring my hands to my hips and look up at my ceiling. "No, I know I would have stood by you, no matter what turmoil you were going through."

I feel that lump in my throat forming and I push it down. I will not let my emotions push forward. I need to get through this without crying. I've waited too long to say my piece, just like Tyler.

"But you hurt me too. Your actions had many consequences. I'm not going to just let you sit there and tell me you were suffering and let my pain go unnoticed. You took the time to write those words and send that letter, and said to hell with my feelings. Not only that, you recovered later and never took the time to come back to explain yourself. You just carried on. No matter how I look at this, you just come off selfish in my opinion." I feel that traitorous tear slide down my cheek and I'm quick to swipe at it with the back of my hand.

"Indy, that's not at all what happened. My best friend—my brother—was shot mere feet away from me, in the spot I had just been sitting in. It should have been me. For some time, all I thought about was how that bullet was meant for me. I wasn't in my right mind, I was in no place to be making life-altering decisions.

"By the time I understood what was going on with me, I felt like you had moved on with your life. I didn't want to risk opening up all these emotions again, especially if you had made a life for yourself. I didn't deserve any more of your time." Tyler's standing and I can see he's pleading with his expression, but he makes no effort to move closer to me, probably scared I'll reject the proximity.

"So, you had no problem breaking my heart, but you were hesitant to make amends? That makes no sense, Ty. It seems you wanted a clean break, then you could fuck whomever you wanted," I bite back. The moment I say it, I see his stunned expression. I sound like a jealous wife now. Honestly, I don't even care.

I know why I say it, because it was one of the million things that passed through my thoughts throughout the years. I always wondered if he just wanted to sew his wild oats and I was holding him back.

Seeing him again and realizing he is an internet sensation had my mind running rampant. I know he gained popularity on his social media account after returning from his time in the Army, or so Kalli told me. That morsel of information has sat with me for the last few weeks, and now that I'm piecing everything together, I'm starting to wonder yet again if that's a piece of the puzzle. Maybe being with me was just too inconvenient.

"Is that what you really think?" he asks.

"Honestly, Tyler, I really don't feel like I know you. I thought I loved you after years of writing you. I thought I knew you. Letter after letter felt like a piece of your soul was being given to me. But, if you could tell a lie so easily in that last letter maybe you were just feeding me lies all along; telling me what I wanted to hear so you could have a place to come for a weekend off. I don't know what to believe anymore. Thanks to you, I barely know what's right from wrong. I question my instincts when it comes to love, especially when it comes to you. The only thing I know is my brother's dead, you chose to leave me, and my world is Noah now."

I wrap my arms around my waist, the vulnerability in this moment feels like it's mounting over my shoulders.

"Indiana, you can't really think you don't know me," Tyler pleads. "Everything, aside from that last letter, was all true. That weekend we shared together six years ago was me. My lo—"

"Don't you dare say those words to me. If you couldn't say it then, don't you even think of breathing those words now," I point at him.

Now I can't keep the tears from falling freely down my cheeks. "This was a mistake. I can't do this." I hang my head and sigh.

"This was a lot to digest. Maybe we meet up another day, and we can talk it over once you've had time to think about what I've told you. I know I've said a lot and I'm sorry, but I—"

"No, Tyler. That's not what I mean. I can't put myself through this. I thought I could try to see where this went, either with a friendship or even something more. But I can't. I know you were dealing with intense grief and mental illness, but that doesn't excuse the harsh things you said in your letter. It also doesn't explain why you never reached out to me before now." I look away, the heaviness of this whole interaction catching up to me, then finally bringing my gaze back to meet his. "I don't think we should see each other again. I think this is it between us."

"Indy, no. Please," he says, moving toward me. I can see the pain in his eyes.

"Tyler, you did this to us. You ruined this five years ago," I remind him. "I'm just making it official. I'll make sure you receive everything you need to get the paperwork going."

There's a knock at the door.

"That's my nurse." I swipe at my tears. "You need to go."

"Indy, I never meant to hurt you like this," he says.

I scoff. "Honestly, I don't believe you."

He passes Darth and scratches behind his ear. My usually prickly cat leans into his touch and purrs. I'm not sure cats are as good at judging character as people think.

I open the front door and my home health nurse, Doris, is waiting for me, her big smile dropping when she sees the state I'm in. Tyler nods at her as he passes the threshold. I don't miss the way she takes him in, watching his tall, muscular frame.

He steals another glance at me, then moves along. I open my door wider for Doris to walk in, trying, and failing, to put the morning behind me.

"Who in the world was that beautiful man?" Doris asks as I close the door behind her.

"A piece of my past," I say as my heart breaks once again. "You ready?" I move further into my place, depositing the empty coffee cups into the trash.

"Any chance that tall glass of water is coming back?" she says with a little laugh.

Doris is a woman in her fifties and she has been my home health nurse since I started getting my treatments when I moved to Boston. Given that I've spent a lot of time in and out of hospitals, I'm pretty particular about my nurses. I've had nurses who try to talk politics the second they get through the door, it makes the long infusions very awkward. It's hard to spend hours with someone you don't get along with. But from the moment I met Doris, we formed a bond.

I wipe another stray tear, pushing a smile forward. "I don't think so. Sorry to disappoint," I tell her.

"Oh, sweet girl. Let's get you started, and we can get a good documentary on. Maybe a nap after you pre-medicate is just what the nurse ordered. Sound good?" She smiles and I return it the best I can. "But first, I think you need a hug. Come here."

She opens her arms wide and I move into them. That's another thing about going through the health issues I've endured—I get really close to those that care for me. They become like a second family and Doris is no different.

The problem is, I thought Tyler Hunter was my family too and I trusted the wrong person for far too long. And after this morning, I realize I have to completely say goodbye to him. Even though I thought I said goodbye to him five years ago, my heart is now fully breaking knowing he'll be gone for good. It's in this brief moment of reflection that I realize I didn't get to say my piece. I didn't get to lay out all my reasons why the divorce didn't come sooner. As much as life got hectic, there's more to that story.

I let myself shatter for the last time in Doris's arms, crying as she rubs circles on my back. Maybe I'll finally feel free to love again, because Tyler somehow held my heart for the last eleven years, even when I thought I had let him go.

CHAPTER 31

Tyler

GETTING BACK from Indiana's house, it was hard to settle down. I was pacing inside the house and simply got frustrated. So, I grabbed the keys to my bike and took a ride. I thought I needed more, but I was desperate to feel the wind against my body.

Something about the awareness on the road, the need to be hyper-focused when riding, helps my mind relax, stripping me of the anxiety of the outside world. I can't find that when I drive the truck. I don't let my mind wander like I did last time, which was my first mistake when I got in that accident.

I'm now sitting on the bench at a park, staring out at Boston Harbor. I've replaced the bike helmet with a ball cap, my aviators shielding me not only from the blinding sun, but from being recognized.

Now that my followers know I'm in Boston permanently, they seek me out. I'm gaining more attention on my page. Since I posted my workout at the firehouse, it's gained popularity. River's antics, along with his niece in tow, have only upped the views to my content. Kennedy said he's been insufferable at home, but I know she takes it in stride, telling me her fiancé is pestering her about his fifteen minutes of fame.

Thinking about their relationship only makes me ache for what I was hoping I could build with Indy. That's the thing—I was delusional. I was dreaming of something after the stupidity of years ago. I know I ruined it, but I was hoping after she heard my explanation, maybe she would have a better understanding of where I was coming from.

I was foolish to believe she'd understand my point of view, because that lie was utter bullshit. Rekindling anything with her was a fantasy. I was an absolute moron to believe she was simply going to hear what I had to say and just come running back into my arms.

I hear movement behind me, so I look to my left to find Malloy approaching.

"So, you're the reason why my phone has been buzzing nonstop?" I say, bringing my focus back on the water in front of me.

"Guilty," he says, sitting down next to me on the bench. "I take it things didn't go so well with Indy?"

"You take it correctly. How did you know where to find me?" I never told him I'd be here.

"I stopped by your house and saw you weren't there. I saw the truck in the driveway, but you didn't answer the door. I put things together from there." He looks out to the water. "Lucky guess you'd be here."

Malloy and I work out frequently together at this park. I can see why he would look for me here out of all the other places.

"I fucked up the one good thing in my life," I admit, finally allowing defeat to seep in.

"I doubt that," he says and I feel his gaze shift to me.

"No, she made it clear this is it. I thought she'd hear me

out and maybe give this a chance. Fuck, Malloy. How could I have been such a fool?" I remove my baseball cap and guide my fingers through my hair. My frustration is mounting the more I think about how royally I messed things up.

"Maybe she just needs to calm down a bit after she digests what you told her." He sighs, scratching at his trimmed beard. He looks like he wants to say more, but holds back.

"What is it?"

"Something just doesn't make sense to me. I mean, when I went through things with Baylee, you seemed to know I fucked up and you called me out," he begins.

"Yeah, so?" It comes out with a bit more bite than I intend.

"Dude, calm down." He puts his arms up in surrender.

"Well, whose side are you on?" I can't help but ask.

"I'm on the side of love," he says with a wide smile.

I roll my eyes and groan. "You and your romance books."

"Don't knock it till you try it, my man." He winks. *Little does he know.* "Anyways, as I was saying. You said you got treatment once you left the Army, right?" I nod. "So, once you figured out what you were experiencing, I don't really understand why you didn't talk to her to clarify your reasoning."

"I told you. I wanted her to—"

"Yes, yes, you wanted her to live her life. But still, you seem to be stuck on that. But it doesn't make sense. You wanted her to move on, yet you want her to forgive you. I think, in reality, you really were and technically, still are, scared. You carry fear of what she would say. And today you faced that fear, and what you feared the most happened. Unfortunately, she didn't give you what you ultimately wanted, which was forgiveness and a second chance."

I keep staring at him.

"You did something wrong. And I know the place you were coming from was one where you were pushing her away. It was fucked up, but I won't pretend to understand how you were feeling. I mean, you were experiencing something so out of the norm for anyone here to comprehend. You lost someone right in front of your eyes; in the most horrific way. The trauma of that alone is just too much. But you were all about writing her letters. I'm surprised after you got counseling you never even attempted to write her something."

I look away suddenly, hoping he doesn't catch the change in my disposition.

"What was that?" Fuck, why is he so damn perceptive?

"Nothing." I try to play it off.

"No, don't give me that. Did you write her, Hunter?" He shifts in his seat so he's completely facing me now.

"It's not a big deal because she's done with me now. She doesn't want to hear from me anymore. She'll serve me divorce papers and we'll go our separate ways for good."

Just the thought of it makes my stomach turn. There was this belief in the back of my mind that Indy and I would always have this connection and now it's gone.

"Hunter, you really are an idiot. What did you do? What letter do you have?" Malloy pushes.

"Letters actually," I admit.

"Letters? Plural? What the hell, Hunter?!" Malloy exclaims. "And you didn't lead with that when you went to see her today?" He drags his hands down his face.

"Why would I? She didn't seem to care about what I had to say anyway." I keep my gaze trained in front of me, irritated I even brought those fucking letters up. I've read them countless times already. I wondered if I should have brought them up during today's encounter with her, but decided it wouldn't have made any difference.

"Great, let me see them then," Malloy insists.

"What? Why?" Looking over at him.

"Let me be the judge of your stupidity." Did I say Malloy is my closest friend? Because he's really fucking annoying right now.

I roll my eyes, irritated by the way this day is turning out.

"You're not going to let this go, are you?" I ask him.

"No, and Baylee says I'm really stubborn when I want to be." He follows that by standing and crossing his arms.

I let out a loud sigh and stand up. "I was really enjoying this view before you got here."

"The fuck you were. You were sulking," Malloy chimes in.

We walk back to where we're parked. I get on my bike, while Malloy gets in his truck.

The whole ride home, I continue thinking about the disaster of a morning I had with Indiana, wondering about my past and how things could have been so much different had I simply been honest with her in that letter instead of burning everything to the ground.

———

After Malloy comes over and I share the letters, he doesn't let me stay home, where I would have preferred to sit around in my quiet house. He takes me out, where the guys are at *Jenson's*, a local bar in town. Tommy, who retired from our station years ago, owns the joint. He decorated the place with items that honor local firehouses around Boston.

Luckily, the guys don't bother bringing up Indy, which I appreciate. They're able to distract me with other things, even pulling a few laughs out of me with antics of their own. River and Clay, of course, start a ruckus about Ella, mostly revolving around her next milestone. River is convinced that once Ella starts walking, she'll only choose to walk toward him versus Clay. That incites bets all around.

Clay is planning a civil ceremony with Abby, but River is trying to convince him to do something bigger. Abby wants to do something simple, as their first wedding together was a large affair.

"But think about it... Lola can be in it and so can Ella."

River is all animated talking about his brother's upcoming nuptials.

"You want me to have a bigger wedding so your dog can be in *my* wedding?" Clay gives River a *what the fuck* look as he brings his beer to his lips. "You're kidding, right?"

I used to have a hard time telling them apart a few months ago, but now it's hard to mistake them. River has this gleam in his eyes, no matter when you look at him. He's always up to something, as if he's conjuring a scheme.

I honestly don't know how their mother survived the two of them constantly plotting something rambunctious as kids. I know they were both hellions from what I've been told by their childhood friend Asher.

"Listen, Brother, I love that dog, but I'm not planning my forever with Abby based on your dog." He laughs.

River's face hardens. "After all the love I give that princess of ours." He points his finger at Clay. I don't know if he's talking about Ella or Lola, but River continues, "I love that baby like she's my own. Now you talk about my Lola like she's nothing to you. How could you?"

Malloy's eyes bug out, yet his smile grows like he's wishing he had popcorn to watch this play out. This is succeeding to be a good distraction for me from how my day started.

"River, you have your own wedding to plan. And from what Kenny has said, Lola is going to be a part of your day. You're going to have your photos littered with your sweet girl. Don't worry about it." Malloy slaps River on the back.

That seems to soften River's features a bit, but he's still eyeing Clay warily. Finally, a smile breaks through and he brings his beer up for a toast.

"You're right. My Lola will be a star in due time!" We all laugh, although I'm not too sure that is what Kennedy would like to hear about her wedding day. "Also, don't let Kennedy hear you call her by that nickname. I know she hates it." River eyes Malloy.

"Oh, she loves me." He puffs out his chest with pride.

Malloy has won over all the women in the group with his reality-show-watching and book-loving personality.

"By the way, when are you coming over to watch the next episode of that love show?" Clay asks.

"It's not a love show," Malloy mocks. "It's *Love Daters!*" He scoffs. "I can't fucking wait. It's a new dating show and it looks fucking awesome. Abby and I have been texting a countdown in our group chat. Even Marissa seems excited about it."

"You're a strange one," I chime in.

"Really? I'm the strange one, love letters?" Malloy throws my way.

"Love letters?" River latches on to that real quick and I pin Malloy with a glare.

"It's nothing. I like making up weird names for him. He has nice writing is all," Malloy recovers quickly.

River eyes us both, but doesn't press further, thank fuck.

"So, you're coming over for another show then?" Clay continues, not at all annoyed that Malloy will be frequenting his house to watch this new reality show.

"We'll alternate again. Marissa plans to call in as she usually does, but she might actually fly in for the finale if that case settles in time." Malloy looks giddy.

"Marissa is pretty great to hang out with," I say. She carries a great conversation and I enjoyed having her added into the group when she was in town. I can tell she's a lot like River when it comes to her energetic ways.

"Yeah, she's a riot. She's the polar opposite to Abby. That's probably why they get along," Clay adds.

The night carries on, and the longer we're at the bar, the more grateful I am that Malloy got me out of the house. Tommy makes his way to our table to say hi and I'm able to talk to him for a little bit. I've only spoken to him a handful of times, and he's always welcoming.

The guys and I part ways, and I get home a little after midnight. Walking into my quiet house, I'm reminded how lonely life is. I need to start getting out there and dating again. This morning opened my eyes that eventually I'll need to find a connection to someone again, and it was an abrupt reminder that it can't be Indiana. As much as I thought I would get that with Indy, I need to close that door, which brings an ache to my chest.

I get ready for bed, the weight of the day catching up to me. I'm drained, knowing what's coming in the days and weeks to come. I will be looking over my shoulder, waiting for those divorce papers.

Walking over to my bed, I look at my nightstand and feel the urge to open the drawer to read the letters I shared with Malloy.

He reminded me several times earlier how stupid it was that I never mentioned their existence to Indiana. I'm a glutton for punishment, so I pull the drawer open. I expect to see them right on top, where I left them, but they aren't there.

I start moving things aside, knowing they should be there, but still come up empty. Where the fuck did they go?

No one has been in my home. I locked up before Malloy and I left to meet with the guys.

I straighten right then and know exactly who grabbed them.

Fucking Malloy. *Sly bastard.*

I grab my phone and text him:

What did you do?

MALLOY

Something you should have done a while ago.

You had no right to take them.

MALLOY

My mom always says I'm a bad listener 😈

There's no point in arguing. He wouldn't cross that line and share it with Indy without my permission, right? *Right?*

CHAPTER 32
Fire Hunters

FIRE
HUNTERS
SPACEBOOK GROUP

sarah228
Not sure what's going on with
@huntsamillion but I like this
broody version A LOT!
#hotfirefighter #imavailable
#ivebeenbad

savvy12_90
@huntsamillion seems to be
working off some steam.
Whatever it is, these workouts
are intense. #pumpuptheiron
#yesplease #loveyouhunter

Hunter_Fan_01
I'm sort of loving this smoldering version of our @huntsamillion #hottiehunter #brooding #showusmoremuscle

GoldenDogLuver987
Shouldn't River be on the feed more? I vote for Rowdy River! #rowdyriver #morefirefighters #friendsmatter #boostratings

CHAPTER 33
Indiana

MY EYES ARE HAVING a hard time staying open and it's reminding me of those nights when Noah first came to live with me after Bryce's passing. We were just getting to know one another, his routine still foreign to me. It took some time to adjust, but we figured one another out. I just remember always being awake, restless, and checking on him.

Now I'm finding myself staring at the ceiling, frustrated with the unease I'm in. I thought with more answers I'd feel somewhat more relaxed, but here I am—annoyed at where I am in life.

These restless nights I'm getting up and walking to Noah's room and watching his sweet little face as he dreams the night away. I'm reminding myself of my "why" in those moments, trying to keep focused as we go through the motions in Boston, so we can have this life that will hopefully be worth the struggles. I do everything for that little boy, because my brother can no longer see his son grow up.

But a part of me realizes my happiness may have walked out the door days ago when Tyler and I parted ways. I'm still so angry, but now that days have passed, a part of my heart is aching in other ways as well. I'm not heartless. I'm hurting for him. No matter what, he's still someone I care deeply for.

We shared many years together, even if we weren't physically together. They were emotional years where we told our stories and life moments to one another through each letter. I feel like that part is so deep and sacred. Not only that, he's a part of me, and now I've said goodbye to him.

Although I told him it's over, it's not so cut and dry. I have yet to call my divorce attorney to serve him with papers. I'm dragging my feet yet again. Why do we torture ourselves like this?

———

It doesn't matter how much coffee I ingest, it's futile. The day is dragging.

I slam the stack of papers and spin in my chair. The Boston skyline stares back at me, something I usually love to admire. I let my head fall back, taking in a breath, hoping it calms my nerves.

When will the world feel less heavy? When will life start to feel like it falls into place? I feel like since that night at the Hoover Dam, I've been chasing that solace and I haven't found it yet. Every corner has felt like another hill to climb, yet I haven't found any comfort.

There's a knock on my office door, jolting me from my thoughts.

"Ms. Ranton, you have a visitor," Angela interrupts me.

"I have no meetings right now," I tell her.

"I'm aware, but he's quite insistent." Angela's hesitation is grating on my nerves. The lack of sleep is really starting to seep into my ability to do my job.

Fucking Tyler. I knew he'd come back and a part of my heart feels a tug knowing he's fighting for us, yet annoyance creeps in at the same time.

"What does he want?" I can't help the irritation in my tone.

"Um, he says you'll want to hear from him," she says.

"Oh yeah? And why is that?" I push up from my chair, my words clipped. Angela has nothing to do with my soon-to-be-ex-husband's lies, but I can't help her being caught in the crossfires right now.

"Well, he said he has something for you that you might want to see," she says, cowering and now I just feel bad at my poor behavior. She's keeping herself slightly hidden behind the door, as if it will shield her from any verbal assault I'll give her.

I need to rein it in because Angela is too kind to deserve my poor attitude.

"Sorry, Angela, you can let him in." I wave at her.

She whispers something to the person at my door and soon, a large figure makes his way through. I'm rearranging the papers on my desk, busying myself, trying to show indifference, although my heart is going to leap out of my throat.

When I look up, I'm shocked to see someone that's nothing like Tyler walking over to greet me. We've met a few times now, but I can't remember his name. Last I saw him, it was at the hospital.

He's got to be over six-foot five, a looming presence. Red hair and matching beard complete the look; making him look more like a lumberjack than firefighter. Shit, his shoulders rival those of a linebacker, and if he had an ax, I'd picture him in the middle of the woods.

"Hi!" I can't hide my surprise.

A smile spreads across his burly face. "I assume from the look on your face, you expected someone else?" Reaching over, he extends his hand. "Malloy—I work with Hunter."

Shaking his hand, I answer, "I remember. You called me when Tyler got hurt."

"That's right," he continues, smiling. "I hope you don't mind me stopping by. I know you're probably really busy."

He looks around my office, taking in my open space. His eyes land on my bookshelf and his eyes goes wide.

"Holy shit, is that Ana Clevesky? We just read her book last month in book club," he walks over, enamored by my collection. "I devoured the entire series in three days." He bends down and surveys the rest of my books.

Is this guy for real? This lumberjack reads romance? He's kidding, right?

I can't help the snort that escapes.

He looks over. "You think I'm kidding?" He motions. "May I sit down?"

I nod and he takes a seat on the other side of the desk. "I'm not judging your taste in books. It's just uncommon to find a man reading romance. It's—refreshing. That's all."

"I appreciate you saying that." He winks. "My wife doesn't complain about it either."

"I bet she doesn't." I laugh. "And I will say Ana is really great. If you'd ever like to meet her, just let me know. She's local to Boston."

"Really? I'd love that. I know Kennedy and Abby would too," he says. I can't help the confused look on my face. He continues, "They're in book club too. We're all fans."

"Got it. Um, I hate to change subjects, but is everything okay? Is Tyler okay?"

"Yeah." He nods. "I mean, I know how everything went the other morning and I just thought I'd stop by and talk to you.

"I see. Did he put you up to this? Because I feel like Ty said everything he had to say," I explain.

"I know. But I think he left a few things unsaid," Malloy explains.

"How so?" I feel my brows pinch in confusion. "Because from what he explained, he lied to me."

"You're right, he most certainly did lie." Malloy nods, looking down at his fingers.

"Malloy, you're really not making much sense right now." *What is he talking about?*

"Sorry, I don't know how to do this." He sighs. Then he stands and grabs something out of his back pocket. Once he retrieves it, I realize it's papers. He sits back down.

"Listen, I'm a big believer that people need to figure things out on their own. But at the same time, I think Hunter doesn't have a lot of support. His parents, from the little bit he's told me, sound like absolute assholes. Then he's been here on his own. It sounded like once he found you, he was really hopeful again. I saw a gleam in his eyes I hadn't seen before.

"When he joined the firehouse, he was pretty reserved. He *sort of* smiled, but he was this closed book. He'd give morsels of himself. But with you, it seems you have these big chapters of his life that you carry. He opens up to you in ways he never has with us. It's such a gift. And when he told me how things went down a few days ago, he's gone back to that closed-off version of himself, but now, he's not as hopeful. And I think he just needs a friend to give him that nudge in the right direction. So, I'm here to do just that. He doesn't know I'm here. He didn't ask me to speak to you and bring these"—he holds up some papers—"but I'm just trying to do what I think is right."

He throws the folded-up sheets in front of me.

"It might otherwise change the outcome of how you feel. I'll say this much. Had I not fallen for my Baylee and let love in with her, I would not get to be living the life I am today. I know that sometimes life can look dark and ugly. We have choices. You have a choice to move forward with Noah. And that life might be beautiful and bright. But maybe, if you choose to look at those letters and it makes you reevaluate giving Hunter a chance, you maybe find a path with him that's even brighter… for all three of you. I'd hate for you to miss out on something more beautiful. Because I know that he's a good person. I know he fucked up. But I also know he regrets it."

I sit down, stunned that this big guy, who seems in love with the concept of love, has sought me out today to pass on these papers, and I have yet to comprehend what's written on them.

"What are these?" I pick up the folded sheets.

"I think you need to read them and find out." He stands up. "And keep an open mind, Indy."

With that he nods and walks out of my office like he didn't just pulverize my heart in the span of minutes.

January 13, 2020

My dearest wife Indy,

How are you? I hope you're doing well. We're about to head out, but I wanted to write you a quick note. I won't be able to send it out until I'm back later today. But I've been meaning to write this to you.

I've been dragging my feet on this since I saw you last March in person. The thing is, Indiana, I don't think this is fake for me anymore. This is more than an agreement for me. Everything we've done is real. I want us to give this marriage a real shot.

I've thought a lot about this and after all the time we spent together that weekend, I just feel we need to give this marriage a go. I'm not sure where things are going with me and the Army, but even if I continue forward, maybe we talk about it together. The decision should be something we decide as a unit, because I don't see a future without you by my side.

That being said, would you like to give this marriage the effort it deserves? I'm willing to be the partner you deserve. Being around you is effortless and I love everything about you.

Your letters have become my salvation on my hardest of days, I can't imagine not having you in my life on my best days. That weekend, waking up with you in my arms was the best gift. I want this, Indy. Please tell me you feel the same way.

Georgie is calling for me. We've gotta do a patrol into town.

Your hopelessly in love husband who can't wait to come home to you,

xoxo

Ty

CHAPTER 35

Tyler

July 22, 2022

Dearest Indiana,

I know receiving a letter from me is the last thing you want at this point. I understand how upsetting my last correspondence must have been. I'm sorry for the anger and sadness I've caused in your life.

You deserve an explanation and I'm hoping my words can give you a little bit of that. It won't replace the time in which I've caused so much pain in your life, but I hope it opens the door to be able to start to mend this hurt I've brought.

I was in a bad place when I wrote you that letter—plain and simple. Do you remember Georgie? I lost him not two weeks before writing you that letter. It caused me to do some pretty destructive things in my life. I pushed away a lot of people and things I loved—most importantly you.

I walked away from the best person I could have asked for. You were a gift in my life and I simply destroyed any future we could have built together. For that I will always be ashamed of my actions.

Georgie's death left me in a tailspin; the destruction causing me to deal with the trauma in a terrible way. In the end, I wrote that letter with the intention of hurting you. It was filled with lies. I took the cowardly way out, mostly because I wanted you to hate me enough not to look back. I wanted you to walk away from me, from us, and not feel the urge to come running back.

I felt like it was best you not have someone like me surrounding you, so you wouldn't have the possibility of suffering the same kind of fate as me, possibly getting news of my loss in the line of duty. After watching the devastation Georgie's parents endured, I couldn't think of putting you through that, so I panicked. That letter seemed like the only way.

Since then, I've seen a therapist and he helped me realize the errors of my ways. I was wrong and I understand that now. Writing you feels like our safe place and I'm opting for that still. It seems that has always been our safest form of communication. Even back when we were intertwined the deepest. I should have been brave and told you how I felt that weekend we spent together in Chicago. I was so in love with you that I didn't even want to voice it out loud, for fear that it would blow away.

I have no idea what your life looks like now. I hope you're happy. I hope your heart has recovered from the devastation I likely put you through. But I feel like you deserve to know where I was when I wrote that note. I never meant to put you through any heartache, but I was suffering. I didn't know how to deal with such sorrow.

I'm sorry for doing what I did. My heart was breaking, and instead of running toward you, I pushed you away.

Forever yours,

Ty

CHAPTER 36

Indiana

I **HELD** off on reading the letters until most had gone home for the day. I reached out to one of the parents to pick Noah up and take him to tee-ball practice for me. I'll need to leave in the next few minutes if I want to get there in time to pick him up.

But I'm frozen in place after reading these two letters. After reading it once through, I thought this was some sort of joke; maybe he wrote these as an attempt to win me back. But the sheets are tattered at the edges, like they're weathered after years of being bent and handled.

If Tyler is playing with my emotions, he's doing a damn fine job at it. Aside from the lie he told in that final letter to me after Georgie's death, that was never his style.

Finally, I decide to shove the papers in my purse, grabbing my keys and other items from my desk, opting to do any other work at home later tonight. I can't focus on this right now, so I'll have to shove all things Tyler to the side for now. Noah needs my attention and I'll revisit my feelings, albeit complicated, later.

Everything is feeling jumbled in my head, and my heart is hurting in so many ways. Why didn't he tell me about these letters when he saw me the other day? Had Malloy not come to see me today, would Tyler have signed the divorce papers and never seen me again? Why is he turning away from everything without putting up a fight if he had these letters?

I feel the more that was said about our destruction, the more I realize I didn't comprehend Tyler Hunter's complicated layers. Is that what I want? More confusion in my life? I feel like years ago, when I sat with him after graduation, he held the ability to make things uncomplicated. But now, things feel twisted and hard at every turn where he's concerned.

Walking out of my office, my phone buzzes in my purse. I pull it out to see my mother's name staring back at me. I'm contemplating ignoring her, but I'm only putting off the inevitable. If I ignore her now, she'll keep bugging me until I finally talk to her. Might as well rip off the Band-Aid.

"Hello?" I say, no enthusiasm to my tone.

"Indy, good to hear your voice," my mom's tone is clipped, the judgement oozing from her voice.

I try to tamper my annoyance. The relationship once again on thin ice. We had started to mend our once rocky relationship, something that brought so much happiness to my brother before his passing. Bryce worked so hard to see us build things back to something resembling what it once was. And I would say it was moving in the right direction. That is until Bryce died.

That's when things got really ugly. Actually, it was worse than I could have foreseen. When it was discovered that Noah would be under my care, full custody having been granted to me by the judge, my parents were none too pleased. In the will, my brother had put me down as Noah's guardian. My parents felt I wasn't equipped to be a mother, not just due to my lack of knowledge in the parenting department, but because of my health issues as well.

They wanted to fault me for my chronic condition and put

that front and center. The way they belittled me, their own child at that, felt cruel and unnecessary. I have never felt less loved by the two people who were only supposed to support me. In that moment, our own cracks felt like the only things I saw between us.

It was revealed then that my brother saw me in a way I never imagined. Bryce had stated in his will—through a letter nonetheless—that I possessed a strength he always admired. He felt if there was ever a need for someone to care for his son, it should be me. When I was shown difficulty in my life, I stood up to the hardship and found the determination to persevere. He also knew that I would raise Noah in a way that would mirror the life he imagined for him.

I remember the way my shoulders shook, the emotion taking over my body with the words my brother left behind in his letter. I never knew he felt this way about me. Knowing he held me at such a high standard made me feel seen, even if he wasn't here to witness the gratitude I had for his words.

My grandfather even started to pick sides, stating he would back me up with whatever support I needed if it came to it with my parents, knowing I would put up a fight when it came to Noah. I was determined to honor Bryce's wishes. He understood that I had no means to fight them alone if necessary. Luckily, my parents were all talk, although their words were cutting. Apparently, my grandfather did intervene with a phone call to his daughter, explaining the irreparable damage this would cause.

My mother listened, however, the damage it caused between my parents and me was done. Our relationship was further torn when my parents learned of my marriage to Tyler during the guardianship process for Noah. Everything came to the surface. A part of me was relieved I no longer had to keep it buried, but I saw the disappointment across their faces when they learned the truth.

I can't change the past, and I find myself counting to ten

to calm my nerves when I interact with my mother. I remind myself, time and time again, that Noah has already lost his father, I can never deprive him of his only living grandparents. In the same token, I can't simply ignore what they did to me while I was trying to respect Bryce's wishes for his son.

The way I feel like I'm being judged by my parents each time I visit them, or the little glances thrown my way as I parent Noah feel like a microscope cast over this little boy and me. Maybe they didn't mean anything by their reaction, but for me, it felt like betrayal.

Obviously, Bryce chose me for a reason I can't explain, and Noah belongs with me. Why can't they see that? So now, when I speak to either of my parents, there's a blanket of pain in each word spoken; theirs said with bitterness, and mine with resentment.

"How's Noah?" My mother asks as I move through the building, rushing to get to my car.

"Good, he's at tee-ball practice. I might lose you, I'm about to get in the elevator." I get in as the doors close.

"Shouldn't you be there?" I don't miss her judgement and I can imagine the flat line of her mouth as she says it. I roll my eyes and let out a breath, keeping myself from saying something rude. I hold back from reminding her of all the times she missed my events because she was at work operating on patients. The comment would be futile; my mother is blind to her own misgivings.

"I had to work. One of his friend's parents took him," I tell her. This would be a great time for the elevator to cut this conversation.

No such luck. Apparently, Diana Ranton is blessed with an uninterrupted call today.

"It's late over there. Why are you still working?" This time I don't hold back the audible exhale I give.

"Was there a reason for your call? Is Dad okay?" Usually

we keep these conversations centered around Noah, but I honestly can't stand the judgement. I'm too old for this shit.

"Dad's fine. I'm calling because I'm looking at the calendar and we're headed out there in the coming weeks, so you two don't need to plan a visit out here this summer."

Every year, despite the heat in Vegas, we head out their way to see my parents. Noah loves the big buildings on the Vegas strip, and I always fit in a quick trip to California as well.

"Oh yeah? Why the change?" This isn't like them.

"Your dad surprised me with a cruise to celebrate our anniversary," she squeals. "We'll be coming your way and stay a week instead of you coming this direction. Then we'll be headed to Florida for our week-long getaway." I hate how my mom makes the decision and doesn't ask me first. What if we're busy? She doesn't even specify with any dates, so I have to pull the information out of her and it's the most frustrating thing.

"Okay. Well, I'll check the calendar and let you know." I unlock my car and throw my purse in. "Send me the details as soon as possible."

"Indiana, I'd appreciate if you made time for us," my mother huffs.

"Mom, I didn't say I wouldn't. I'm just asking that you send me the information. I just want to confirm we don't have anything planned. You didn't ask me before booking anything."

Now I'm even more irritated.

"Fine. It would be nice if our only daughter would sound even a little excited about seeing us." This is typical of her. She twists things so that I'm the bad guy. I'm not going to fall for this trap she sets each time.

"I've got to go. I'll talk to you later."

"Bye."

I hang up quickly, blood boiling from the interaction and

already on the verge of tears after the afternoon I've had. She's set me off now, pulling emotions out of me I wasn't expecting.

My drive to the field is not a quick one due to traffic, so I arrive a little later than I'd like. Luckily, Noah is none the wiser, as he's playing with his friends, running around the grassy area, throwing the ball with the biggest smile on his face.

His coach comes walking over to greet me. He's a dad on the team, close to my age, and I won't lie, he's easy on the eyes.

"Indiana, right?" his coach says. I've met him a few times, yet I've always been in a rush. When they've had games, I've been with Kalli and never really stayed around afterwards to talk to him one on one.

"Yes. You can call me Indy." I smile and shake his hand.

"I'm Zach. I'm the coach." He smiles. I can't help but notice his smile doesn't light a spark in me like Tyler's does.

Don't think of Tyler right now. We're forgetting about him, remember?

Am I though after those letters?

The push-pull of my emotions is too much.

"Yes, I remember. It's good to see Noah having so much fun." I smile in the direction of the boys running around.

"Yes, they're really a good group." He looks over and smiles wider. "Um, listen. Chase is mine right there." He points to a little blond boy chasing Noah. "And I..." He hesitates and looks nervous suddenly. "... this isn't something I do often, but I noticed you a few times and I think you're really beautiful."

Holy shit. Is he going to ask me out? I can't help the blush that creeps up my cheeks. Of all the days this could be happening, today is not the best day.

"Oh, uh," I stammer. He takes it as flirtatious, while really I'm at a loss for words.

"Yeah, so I was wondering if you'd like to go out some-time." He smiles wide, hopeful even. He's got a kindness to him, and I feel awful doing this to him. I'm a mess and this guy is simply shooting his shot.

I look down at his hand, searching for a ring. He catches my eyes, then follows with, "I'm divorced." He holds his left hand up, as if to confirm it.

I open my mouth to speak, but Noah and Chase run up, out of breath, yet smiling from ear to ear.

"Hi, Mom!" Noah's practically bouncing. "Can we grab a pizza with Chase and Coach Zach?"

I smile, when inside I'm honestly groaning. I look up, wondering if this might be better than letting Zach down. I smile, shrug and say, "Sure, why not?"

I really don't feel like saying no right now and I'm too tired to cook. We've gotta eat, right?

———

That's how I find myself sitting at a local pizza place. I'm sharing a cheesy pizza and laughing with a cute coach and two adorable kids. As hesitant as I was to be out tonight, I'm having fun. The conversation has been nonstop, and I've found myself laughing quite a bit. Coach Zach is a lot of fun. Had we met at a different point in my life, I think we would hit it off, but I know my heart isn't one hundred percent able to invest itself in this. My brain is consumed by someone that I've known for far longer, even though we have way too much to unpack.

I'm smiling at something Noah said when someone clears their throat next to our booth.

That's when I realize the universe really might have a vendetta against me; at least, it does today. Actually, it's punching me in the face. No, let me rephrase, it's going a few rounds and I'm definitely losing.

I nearly choke on my bite of pizza when I look up and find Tyler staring down at me, his face hard as stone. I can see his molars grinding as his gaze swings from me to Zach, trying to figure out what the hell is going on.

He only softens when Noah calls his name and he brings his little fist out to greet him.

"Hey, buddy," Tyler says to Noah.

"Hey, pal, what's up?" Zach's enthusiastic voice calls to Tyler, holding out his hand, completely unfazed by the tension.

The irritation returns to Tyler's expression when he looks at my son's coach. He shakes his hand, with what I assume is quite a forceful grip, from the wince Zach gives.

I look at Tyler in annoyance. His problem is with me, not with anyone else at this table.

"Looks like you're having a nice little dinner," Tyler says, his tone clipped.

"I had tee-ball today, Hunter!" Noah says, his excitement palpable.

"I bet you did great." Tyler smiles at Noah, then brings his attention back toward me.

"How do you know each other?" Zach asks, his eyes volleying between myself, Tyler, and Noah.

"Hunter is a fireman! He saved me." Noah smiles wide, then takes a bite of his pizza.

"Butt on the chair, little man," I whisper to Noah.

"Is that right?" Zach says.

"Yep. Noah here was the bravest of them all." Tyler winks in Noah's direction.

"Oh, I don't doubt it. This kid is super talented. He's one of our best in tee-ball. Right, Chase?" Zach turns to his son and they both nod.

With that comment, Tyler looks at me and I can see the irritation in his expression. He waits a few beats before looking over to acknowledge Zach.

"I believe it. Noah is the very best." Then I see those stormy-blue eyes look over at me. "Indy, you have a second that I could chat with you?" Tyler asks me.

I look at Noah, then at Zach. "Would you give me a minute?"

Zach regards Tyler, then nods. He's clearly trying to read between the lines. I can feel Zach's gaze on me the entire time I walk out of the restaurant with Tyler.

The second we're outside, Tyler inches closer to me, but he doesn't touch me. We step to the left of the front doors, so Zach and the kids can't see us from this vantage point.

"The minute you're rid of me, you're already in someone else's arms?" He turns me around, walking me backward toward the wall until my back meets the brick building.

"It's not like that, Tyler. He's just his coach," I tell him. Not that it's any of his business.

"So, his 'fuck me' eyes mean nothing?" Tyler says. While he's so close, I hate how my body lights up by his mere proximity.

"That's not how he's looking at me." I can't think straight when his body is near me.

"Bullshit, Indy. He's looking at you like he wants to devour you," he states matter-of-factly.

"How would you know?" I whisper.

"Because it's how I look at you." He slides his tongue along his bottom lip. "It's been days—why haven't you served me with papers yet?"

"I haven't had time to speak to my attorney," I tell him, my eyes looking everywhere but directly into his eyes. I can't let myself get cast in his spell.

"The fuck you haven't," he throws back. He grabs my chin. He's not being aggressive. He knows I love this side of him; this assertive side where he takes charge. He brings my eyes back to meet his. "I'll ask you again—why haven't I seen those fucking divorce papers, Indy?"

I stare at him, unable to give him an answer, my voice lost in whatever trance we're in.

"You want me to give you my theory?" He cages me in, his muscular forearms right next to my face on either side. When did veins become attractive?

I hold in my moan, wishing he'd put me out of my misery and bring his lips to mine, because I can't stand the distance anymore.

"I think you're fighting this. I think you know we belong together. But you're scared. You're scared of what will happen if you choose wrong. But you know what? Nothing about us is wrong.

"Everything about us is right. It's explosive. But you keep fighting against it. Not sure how long you're going to push upstream, but once you're ready to go all in, let me know."

Then he leans in and, I swear, his lips are going to slam into mine. I know I don't have the power to resist anymore. I tip my chin, leaning into him, but he doesn't fucking kiss me. I wait and nothing happens, until he finally moves his lips just over my skin and allows his breath to skate along my neck. My traitorous body erupts in goosebumps.

I open my eyes when he pulls away, and from the smirk on his face, he knows he won.

He stares at me for an extra beat then stalks into the restaurant. A minute later he walks out with a few boxes of pizza. He glances my way, checking me out one last time. Before climbing into his truck, he winks at me and my pussy convulses because it's a fucking traitor. *If only he knew the real reason why I can't truly let go of this marriage.*

I watch him drive off until the lights fade away. I'm hopeful that I don't look flushed after that little episode.

I saunter in, and I see the remainder of the food is boxed up.

"You okay?" Zach asks, his eyes full of concern.

"Of course. Just had to catch up on a few things. We're old friends." I wave in the direction of the door.

"Oh, really?" Zach looks perplexed. "I'd guessed there was something more," he whispers.

I smile, but don't use words to answer otherwise.

We make our way out the door and Noah says his good-byes. Luckily, Zach doesn't broach the subject of that date and I'm grateful.

The drive home is quiet, Noah focused on the lights and cars outside. It isn't until he's getting tucked into bed that he asks me something I'm ill-prepared for.

"Mom?" That sweet little voice pulls at my heart each time.

"Yes, sweet boy," I say, pushing his hair away from his eyes as he gets tucked into bed.

"I like Hunter." He looks at me, his eyes starting to get heavy after a long day.

"Oh, yeah? Why do you say that? You barely know him." I honestly thought he'd mention something about tee-ball or his coach.

"Because he makes you smile." Funny. I feel like I scowl more than anything around my secret husband.

"What do you mean? I smile all the time around other people and when I'm doing a ton of other things."

"Yeah, you smile, but he makes you smile like this…" He does this funny smile where he bats his lashes and he pretends to mimic me. I can't help the laugh that escapes.

"I do *not* do that, Noah." I tickle him.

"Yes, and you get pink cheeks like Harley does around me when I say she has a pretty dress on." Oh goodness, this boy.

"Alright. I think we need to get those eyes checked." I laugh, but I'm starting to realize this kid is way too observant.

After we say our goodnights, I walk out of his room, closing his door gently.

I make my way to my own bedroom and pull out my phone.

> I don't know what to do.

KALLI

Yes, you do. You're just scared to do it.

> What if he breaks my heart again?

KALLI

So, you're just going to let life stop you from trying?

> I have Noah to think about.

KALLI

True. But you're only thinking of Noah in this. Every single step is in relation to him. You think Tyler wouldn't think of that kid?

> I'm conflicted.

KALLI

No, you're apprehensive. You're letting your past stop you from taking a step forward. You keep finding excuses instead of just trying to make him fit in your life.

> If I text him right now, I'll want to resolve things in this moment or I'll chicken out. Noah is here and I feel like I need to go somewhere and talk to him.

Her typing stops and I start to wonder if Kalli's done texting. But then the three bubbles reappear. Soon her text pops up, solidifying her best friend status.

KALLI

Be there in 20.

She doesn't even know if Tyler can meet me, yet she's

already coming over. She knows about the letters because I sent her screenshots after I read them. I'm so lucky to have someone like her in my corner. Even if Ty isn't able to see me, I know she'll simply sit with me and have a girls' night in.

Now I sit on my bed and stare at another text thread, contemplating what I should do.

I'm full of so many different emotions when it comes to Tyler. I have every reason to be confused when it comes to him. I've tried for so long to find someone else to move on with, and it has never felt right. What if Tyler is the person I'm supposed to be with, and I keep pushing this thing between us away?

I finally start typing, and I press send before I back out of it and run away.

Can you come pick me up?

TYLER

On my way.

I guess I have to face this once and for all.

CHAPTER 37

Tyler

STANDING in front of Indiana's door, I'm acutely aware this is my final chance with her. With the way my hands are shaking in anticipation of seeing her, I'm surprised I was able to ride my motorcycle here. I called Malloy to give me a pep talk on my way over.

Not sure what he gave could be considered pep. It was more like a lecture. Then Baylee snatched the phone and told me not to "fuck things up"—her words, not mine. She stated Malloy was moping around because I was sad. Apparently, I was throwing her husband off. That made me laugh. The guy is way too sensitive.

The minute I hung up, the nerves and tension returned. I thought it was our interaction at the pizza place that had her calling me. But Malloy admitted he handed off my letters earlier today. I assume that's why I've been asked to come by.

I don't want her to think I omitted those letters as a form of lying; that's not the case. I just thought she'd either hear me out and accept me back, or not. It felt desperate to start throwing more letters in her face after she asked me to leave.

I'm about to ring the bell when Kalli swings the door open.

"Uh, hey, Kalli. I wasn't expecting you."

Kalli gives me a mischievous smile. "Oh, I know. Listen, Indy's grabbing a jacket. I came by to watch Noah while you two get out of here."

"Thanks." I move my hands through my hair.

"You got this, Tyler. You've got to be honest with her, got it?" She looks me straight in the eyes. "I'm rooting for you."

I smile shyly. "I appreciate that."

"Tyler, hey." Indy makes her way to the front door, and I can't help the way my heart squeezes at the sight of her.

"Hi, Indy." I smile at her. I see a small blush paint her cheeks.

Her hair is pulled back in a ponytail, with a few strands falling down around her cheeks. Her face is clear of makeup, unlike earlier tonight at the restaurant. Her lips are fucking kissable, but I keep my distance, waiting at the stoop. I felt possessive earlier, but now I let the nerves get the best of me.

"Okay, you two. Out you go." Kalli pushes Indy out the door.

"Kalli!" Indy whisper-yells.

"I'm not getting any younger. Go, please." She gives Indy a saccharine smile, then closes the door.

I can't help the laugh that escapes while Indy looks at her front door that is now closed behind us. Bringing her gaze toward me, she seems a bit uncomfortable over what to do next.

"Shall we?" I gesture to my motorcycle that's parked at the curb.

"Um, I can drive," she says, her voice a little wobbly.

"Nope, you asked me to pick you up. I've got a spot in mind," I tell her, handing her a helmet.

She's dressed in jeans and I brought an extra jacket to protect her arms. Luckily, she's wearing closed-toed shoes.

"I've never been on a bike before," she says, eyeing mine.

"There's a first time for everything," I tell her with a smirk.

"I guess there is." Grabbing the helmet, she tugs it over her head. I slide the jacket over her shoulders while she moves her arms through the sleeves.

I'm trying to compose myself, but seeing her in this getup is doing things to me. I take a moment to take in the sight of her.

"Why are you looking at me like that?" Her voice is muffled behind the helmet.

"You look good, that's all," I say, moving myself over my bike. She follows behind me, tentative with her movements.

"You okay back there?" I ask her.

"As I'll ever be," she says, her hands a bit unsettled as she moves them along my sides.

I grab her hands and glide them so she's holding me tightly. "We're going to be moving fast. I'll need you to hold on a bit stronger than that." I move so she can feel the firm grip I have on her hands.

I turn on the engine, and begin our ride. The moment the bike is in motion, I hear a little squeak from behind me. I feel her grip tighten around me and I revel in the feeling of her hands on my abdomen.

As we move through the streets, I savor her body close to mine. Her front on my back, the warmth of her against me is something I've ached for in more ways than one. It dawns on me that I pushed this woman away from me and I will do anything to win her back tonight. I need to make sure she knows that.

It feels like forever, yet not enough time, as we move through the busyness of the city streets until we reach our destination.

I found this lookout point that faces the city skyline last year on a ride I took, and I've been coming here ever since. The moment Indy texted me tonight and asked to be picked up, I thought it was the best place to come. The sun is near setting, but there's great lighting here, even after the sun has gone down.

We make our way to a good spot where we can see the beauty of the city and I can park my motorcycle, and I turn off the engine. As soon as there's silence, I stomp the kickstand down. Indy pulls her hands off me and I miss her contact immediately.

She begins coming off the bike, and once we're both standing, we take our helmets off. Placing them to the side of the motorcycle, I sit back down, facing the back of the bike. Then I pat the back, where she was sitting.

"What?" She looks at me quizzically.

"Sit down, Indy," I tell her.

"No," she says defiantly.

"Indiana, sit down, please." I won't back down.

"That's too close." She crosses her arms over her chest.

"Sit your butt down on this bike and let's have a conversation." I pat the bike again.

She looks at the seat like it has poison on it, then looks back up at me. She's contemplating her options then finally rolls her eyes and succumbs to whatever internal battle she was waging.

She still keeps herself as far away from me as possible, but hopefully after tonight, we can put our differences in the past. No matter the mental turmoil, Indy and I need to talk.

"Hands to yourself, Tyler." Her left eyebrow cocks up in a questioning gaze as she leans her body against the tail end of my motorcycle.

"Hey, I'm a complete gentleman." I smile, but she can read me well. My mind is racing with thoughts of her on this bike and my body doing dirty things. All I want to do is move my hands up her legs. Instead, I decide to focus on the task at hand. "Why don't you tell me why you asked me to take you out."

"I read your letters, Malloy brought them by. Why didn't you tell me you had two more that you never sent me?" She doesn't seem mad, just curious.

"I was grieving. One of those letters I wrote the day Georgie died. It was right before we headed out on that patrol. I didn't feel like that version of myself anymore. Then, when I wrote the second one, fear took over. What if I sent it and you didn't take me back because of the lie I told? I feared the rejection. I ended up not wanting to." I look down at my hands. Finally, I bring my head back up.

"I just couldn't bring myself to send it. My therapist kept urging me to, but by then, I talked myself out of it, convincing myself you've finally moved on. We still spoke through video sessions as I kept moving throughout the states. I never imagined your life had imploded. And I thought that by sending it, it would have just made things worse, so I kept to myself."

She sighs and looks away. I see her swipe at her cheek.

"Indy, talk to me," I urge her.

She shakes her head, but it's hard to stay rooted in place. She looks up at the night sky, probably in an attempt to keep from letting more tears fall.

"Tell me why you're crying." I finally reach over to touch her and move a strand of hair away from her forehead.

Her chin quivers, but she remains silent. I decide to push her further. "Indiana, we aren't going to get anywhere if you don't tell me what's going on. Are you crying because of Roger?"

She shakes her head. "Roger and I broke up."

Thank fuck.

"Are you scared of me?" Shit, did I read this wrong?

"Yes, but not like that. I'm scared you'll leave me. You have to understand that I have a kid now. My brother trusted him with me. With us, actually."

"I know, Indy. And what I did—" I halt at the realization of her words. "What do you mean *us*?"

Indy looks down at her hands and takes a deep breath. I can tell by the way she's taking her time, that she's choosing her words wisely. I wait until she finally looks up at me, tears pooled in her eyes.

"That's why I've waited so long to end things between us. When Bryce died, he knew about our marriage. Remember when I told you I confided in him about our letters and all those packages I'd send you? Well, I told him how my feelings for you had grown, too. Besides you, Bryce was my best friend. I guess he wanted to know that Noah would be cared for if something were to ever happen to him." She looks up to the stars above us, the tears escaping as she closes her eyes.

When she opens her eyes again, she looks back at me, determination cast on her face. "Did you know that a will is just a wish a parent relays when it comes to custody? The true determination comes down to the judge. Bryce stated in his will that he wanted Noah left to both of us in the event of his passing."

I can't help the way my heart is pounding in my chest. I just keep looking at Indy, hanging on her every word.

"I realize now I never told you in our letters when Noah was born. And Bryce didn't know we weren't talking before he passed. That part I hadn't told him yet. I was still processing everything that happened between us. When the judge granted me custody, I explained we were estranged and you were no longer a part of my life. My parents found out during this whole process about the marriage, so it's no longer a secret in their eyes, but I've kept it to myself otherwise. Kalli only recently found out about us being married."

I nod, processing everything she's telling me. It's all starting to make sense why she didn't dissolve our marriage sooner. She wanted to honor her brother's wishes, even though I had no idea he had a son nor that he had passed.

"I know this is a lot to process, but I've been carrying this big promise in my heart for him. And in many ways, I've just held a piece of you with me, even if you broke my heart all those years ago. I've always felt like I've walked this strange line between anger and love when it comes to you. Although, I can't let my heart get in the way of Noah's well-being. It's not only about me this time, Tyler. He knows you already.

"You and I are complicated. Everything with us is so convoluted. It feels like so many lines are blurred and every time I think my feelings for you are put away, they creep back up."

I can't help the smile that stretches across my face, even though I'm processing so much right now with her confession. I'm not angry at her. I feel like I've been given a lifeline with her revelation. It sounds like I have Bryce to thank for this second chance with Indy.

"Don't smile at me," she says, annoyance in her tone. That only makes me smile wider.

"Indy, you can't be mad that I'm happy to hear you say you have feelings for me," I bite my bottom lip.

I pull her by the belt loops and tug her to me. Once she's near me, I grab her hair-tie out, then move my fingers through her strands. I push her head back, exposing her neck to me. All I want to do is run my tongue along the column of her neck, but I restrain myself.

Her breathing picks up and a shift occurs between us.

"Tell me what you want, Indy. Put me out of my misery," I beg.

"I want you to make my heart whole again," she whispers, her eyes locking on mine. In that moment, it feels like she can look straight into my soul. It's overpowering the way she can overtake me with just one look.

"But I also don't want you to crush me the way you did years ago. No more lies. No more walking away. If you want me, you want *all* of me. That includes Noah. We are a package deal, Ty."

I bring both my hands to grasp her face in an act I hope

she feels the sincerity in what I'm about to say. "Indiana, I was a fool before. I'm sorry I let fear overtake my emotions. I should have told you then that I was in love with you. You captured not only my heart back then.

"You held my soul in your hands and it has been yours ever since. I promise, if you give me this second chance at letting me love you, I will stand by your side and never leave it again. And of course it includes Noah. I never believed otherwise. Even before you told me about Bryce's wishes, I've seen you and Noah as a package deal since we've reconnected. That little boy is an extension of you. And he's now an extension of me."

Her tears return, welled up in those beautiful green eyes, but this time, she allows a smile to finally break through. She grabs my forearms and I take that as the only permission I need to pull her down to capture her lips with mine.

I feel the warmth of her on me, and it's intoxicating. After years of not having this woman in my arms, it's like a light has come back into my life. Not only that, it's like an energy I was missing in my soul.

I continue to move my fingers through her hair as our tongues intertwine. I swallow her moan, and she moves her hands up and around my back. She moves herself onto the bike so we are facing each other. Her legs wrap around me and being on this motorcycle is just adding to the sensuality of what we're doing.

"I've missed you so much, Indy. Seeing you all these weeks, unable to hold you and touch you was torture for me." I tell her as I move my lips down the column of her neck, dropping kisses along her skin.

"You drove me nuts, Ty. I've wanted you with me, yet I wanted to push you away for what you did to me," she says, sinking her nails into the fabric of my shirt.

We're hungry for each other, but being out here in the open is something we need to rectify.

"We have to get home. The things I want to do to you," I tell her, bringing my lips back to hers.

"Then get moving, Tyler. We have years of making up to do."

I growl and nip at her earlobe before pulling away. How am I going to ride home with this stiffness between my legs. She must be a mind reader in that moment because she looks down and sees the bulge in my pants.

"Looks like someone will have to readjust before we start back." She smirks and hops off the bike.

I smack her ass, and she yelps. "Wow, already getting frisky, Mr. Hunter."

"We'll see how frisky you'll get, wife." I put the helmet on her head, then proceed to put on my own. We hop on the bike and I've got us back on the road.

She doesn't make the ride easy though. On the way back, she's a lot more comfortable moving those hands around my front, making sure it's more sensual of an experience for me. Fuck, I'm having to think about things like math equations so I won't be hot and bothered.

By the time we make it to Indiana's place, I'm nearly throwing my helmet to the curb. The minute Indy takes her helmet off, the smirk she's sporting is downright sinful.

"You play dirty, woman," I tell her.

"Sorry, my hand was falling asleep. I had to keep moving it," she says, playing innocent. Then she sashays up her steps to the front door.

"Sure, I bet it was." I grab her waist and move her close to my pelvis so she can feel the effect of her movements. The gasp I hear her take in is exactly what I expected.

Kalli is waiting for us when we open the door.

"Oh, hello, lovebirds," she says excitedly. "I assume by the smiles on your faces, you've kissed and made up, finally?"

"Yes, I'd say so," Indy says.

"Perfect. I'll expect a full report tomorrow." She winks at

her best friend and waves at me. "Noah didn't wake up and I'm off, then. Good luck and be safe. Remember to wrap it up."

"Kalli!" Indy says and her friend laughs on her way out.

The instant the door closes behind her, Indiana looks at me and I whisper in her ear, "What's first, wife? You want my fingers, my mouth or my cock?"

CHAPTER 38

Tyler

WE MOVE FEVERISHLY toward her bedroom, hyperaware there's a little boy down the hall that could catch us if we're not careful. The moment we're behind her bedroom door, she locks it behind us. She unzips the jacket she has on and throws it to the side.

She pulls my shirt halfway up, then I take over the rest of the way. The moment my chest is exposed to her, I see the hunger in her eyes. The way her eyes take me in, it feels like my skin is on fire.

She bites her lip, trailing her fingertips along the ink that lines my pecs to the tops of my biceps. "These are new."

"Do you like them?" I feel nervous, wondering if this is something she finds attractive.

"Yes." She continues rubbing her hands along my chest, skimming her hands along my skin and causing my heart rate to soar behind my ribcage.

She inspects each one, the light from the city casting enough inside the room that she's able to see well. She stops when she reaches my left rib, where I have a design that's slightly hidden. Her breath hitches when she realizes what

I've had drawn. The meaning wouldn't be symbolic to anyone other than her.

When she looks up at me, her expression has softened and I move my thumb to caress her bottom lip.

"I had to keep you close somehow," I whisper.

"When did you get that done?" Her voice is hoarse, her eyes shifting back to inspect the colorful art on my skin.

The pink hollyhock flower is mixed in with all the other tattoos, but it's still distinctive. I made sure it stood out amongst the floral artwork on my body. It's the official flower of Boulder City, in connection to the Hoover Dam. As it became our favorite meet-up spot, we grew acquainted with the location and everything the tourist location had to offer. Indiana was well-acquainted with the flower, knowing so much about the dam and the history behind it.

She moves her hand along that spot down my ribs, while I trail my fingers along her cheek, admiring her beauty. I'm not taking this second chance for granted, this time to love her openly.

I move my fingers up and into her hair, admiring how it falls above her shoulders. Her eyes close as I move my hands through her strands.

I bend down and bring my lips to her ear. "Indy, I think you have too many clothes on. Plus, it's been six years without touching you. I need to make up for lost time." I nibble on her earlobe and she shivers. I love how reactive she is.

I move my hands down her shirt, and once I get to the hem, I graze her abdomen. She moans and the air around us shifts. Her breathing accelerates and I know these little touches are driving her as insane as they're sending me close to the edge.

"How fucking wet are you?" I whisper into her ear.

"I guess you'll just have to wait and see," she teases, her smile matching her tone.

I pull her shirt up over her head to reveal a black satin bra. I move my hands over it, cupping and squeezing her breasts in my palms. That's when I feel something under the padding, causing me to furrow my brows. My curiosity gets the best of me.

Luckily the clasp is in the front, so I rush to undo it, and once her breasts are freed, my suspicions are confirmed. Both her nipples are pierced.

"Fuck, Indy. When did you get these done?" I keep kneading her exposed breasts, my thumb moving across the piercings. They're fantastic.

"A few years ago. I read about it in a book and I was curious." She pushes her chest into my touch. "Mmm, that feels..." She continues moving until her body hits the edge of the bed and she throws herself onto it.

Her tits bounce and I stand there as she lies bare, her upper body exposed to me—those horizontal, metal piercings glinting in the light shining in from window.

I prowl toward her and I see her breaths quicken. I start kissing up her abdomen, ascending and keeping my eyes on her. Every inch closer to those mounds where I want to suck each nipple into my mouth.

I pull away from her skin and whisper, "You're so fucking beautiful." Then I bring my lips back to her warm flesh and trail kisses up her body again.

I jut my tongue out to her left nipple, enticing a moan from her, while she pushes her chest against my face. I have no doubt she's sensitive as fuck. I follow up with a slight nibble, then bring my lips to the opposite breast. I give it the same attention. She's writhing, gyrating her hips, needing some release.

"Ty, please, I need more," she begs.

"I know. Patience, Indy."

"I've been patient." She reaches out and tugs on my hair. The sensation turns me on more.

I sit up slightly, giving her a smirk. I hook my fingers into her pants, pulling her panties down along with them. I toss them aside, and look at the glistening pussy in front of me. I nearly groan as I push her knees apart. I'm going to take my time with her.

"You're still my wife and this pussy is mine," I tell her. She's fucking dripping.

She brings her hands up her stomach and to her breasts, tugging on her nipple piercings. I nearly come at the gesture.

Without warning, I bring my mouth to her center and drag my tongue through her folds. She knows she has to keep her volume down, so she quickly covers her mouth and tampers her moan. But her pelvis shoots off the bed, and I use my arm to push it back down.

Bringing my tongue out again, I start lavishing her. Fuck, she tastes fucking divine.

Her eyes are hooded, and she lifts her head and looks down at me. I can see she's even more turned on watching me eat her out.

"You taste so fucking good." I bring my mouth back to her center, I suck hard on her clit and she struggles to keep her body down.

I give her a devilish smile.

Adding a finger, I watch her writhe beneath my touch. She starts moving to match my rhythm, trying to chase that orgasm.

Her breath starts to quicken and I know she's close. I close my mouth over her clit and suck, pumping my finger in and out of her at a steady rhythm and soon she's coming, her thighs constricting the sides of my face.

Once she comes off her high, I pull away, looking up at her and seeing she's panting. I start to kiss the sides of her thighs and then trail kisses up her abdomen, moving along her chest. Soon, I bring my lips to meet hers, our tongues intertwining.

My cock is begging to be freed from behind my zipper. This was about her, so I will not be overzealous right now without her initiating anything.

She pulls away. "Why are your pants still on, Ty?"

She moves her hands down to my jeans, rubbing my raging hard-on over the fabric.

"I didn't want to assume. This was about you," I admit.

"That's cute." She gives me a smile. "Now enough of that boy-next-door-that-we-both-know-you-aren't business and get naked."

I can't help the laugh that escapes. "When did you get to be this way?"

"What way?" she says, helping me unbutton my pants. It's hard to reconcile the girl that once played by the rules, with who is sitting in front of me with nipple piercings and barking orders at me.

"All… demanding," I admit.

"Well, I play by my own rules now," she says confidently.

"I guess you do. So, what do you want to do, boss?" I ask, letting my pants fall, but not before grabbing a foil packet. I toss it on the bed. My boxers are the only thing left.

She grabs my underwear and pulls them down halfway before I take over to remove the rest of my clothing.

"I want you to lie on my bed and let me ride you." This woman who's taking control is fucking sexy as hell.

I do as I'm told. I grab the foil packet and sheath myself. I lay back with my hands behind my head, ready to watch her ride me and take charge. Tonight is about her showing me what she wants.

She hovers over my length and I automatically bring my hands onto her hips and squeeze. As she slides her pussy along my length and moans quietly, my muscles constrict. I squeeze her hips, my cock reacting to the way she's teasing me.

I see the smile that spreads across her face. "Next time I'll have you on your knees, watching you take me in that mouth of yours," I tell her, my voice gravelly.

She hums as she continues to move her folds along my cock, back and forth, enjoying the feeling of me between. She then bends to bring her tongue along my neck, nibbling, then whispering into my ear, "The only thing you're allowed to shatter is my fear of you leaving us. Because I won't live through that heartache again, Tyler. You're mine now."

There's conviction in her voice. She pulls her face away, enough that our eyes meet. "Mine, forever, Indy. I'll never hurt you again. I promise."

She must sense my certainty.

She sits up and without any more words she lines herself up to me and slides her warmth down onto me. It's bliss. There's no other word for it.

The minute she's fully seated, she drops her head back, arching her spine, and sighing. I bring one hand from the column of her throat down her sternum. Then I bring that hand to one of her breasts, teasing one of the piercings.

She starts to slowly move, grinding her hips, sparking a moan out of me. Fuck, she feels so good. The way her tightness was made for me, I was an idiot to walk away years ago. I have no idea how I lived this long without her

I move my hand further south, bringing my thumb to her clit. She moans, the sound bouncing off the walls.

"Indy—not too loud, baby." I look up at her.

Her half-hooded eyes blink, but she's lost in this feeling. She keeps her hips gyrating, speeding up, chasing that high that feels too good. My cock is loving the way her pussy is clenching me as she seeks that orgasm.

She repositions, bringing her hands onto my chest, the angle hitting her G-spot differently, her clit rubbing against my pubic bone. I pull her kiss-swollen lips to mine, swallowing her moan. This angle allows me to piston into her with more fervor and she breaks her lips away from me.

"I'm coming, oh God, I'm coming. Right there." Burying her face into my neck, she drops her arms, her breathing accelerating as her climax hits her.

I feel her tighten around my cock as she explodes, her body shaking around me. She's trying to contain the sound the best she can.

Once she's come down from her orgasm, I take over.

"Get on your hands and knees, Indy." She's panting, but moves, allowing me to get a nice view of her ass.

I slide my dick through her sensitive folds a few times, enticing a groan from her. I squeeze an ass cheek, then slap it. "Fuck, you're so damn hot. The things I'll do to this body," I promise her.

She looks back at me and I see the desire in her expression.

Without another word, I line myself up and enter her to the hilt. She grabs on to the headboard with one hand. She holds back from being too loud, but moans all the same. I can't help the way my body reacts, my head falling back, my eyes closing at the way I feel completely sated when I'm inside her.

I begin moving, the rush of endorphins flooding my system. My body takes over, like a feral animal needing to seek its release.

I keep pumping in and out of her. I feel that tingling feeling trickle down my spine and I wish I could prolong it. I want this last a little longer, letting the euphoria of her warmth wrapped round my dick last forever, but I know I'm going to combust soon.

"Fuck, Indy, I'm going to come," I say between breaths.

I'm holding on to her hips, my fingers digging into her flesh and I know she'll see those marks come morning.

Our skin is slapping, the sound, along with our breaths, being the only thing projecting off the walls as we both plummet off that cliff together. I close my eyes as I orgasm, filling the condom with her name on my lips.

It takes what feels like forever to catch my breath. We both fall onto the mattress, sated and dripping with sweat. I'm looking up at the ceiling and my smile feels like the first real one in years.

She nuzzles into my side once we've both returned from the bathroom after cleaning ourselves up. I run my fingers through her hair, my heart starting to settle into a calming beat.

"I missed you. I missed us," I finally admit.

"Took you long enough." she laughs.

"Yeah, I was an idiot."

"You were. And I'm not going to pretend what you did wasn't wrong. But I'm also not going to waste time throwing it in your face. Life's too short, Ty." She brings her chin to rest on my chest, her eyes looking directly at me.

"So where do we go from here?" I ask her.

"Forward. No more looking back." She smiles and I bring her lips to mine.

My world feels like it's starting to align again and it all begins with this woman right here. Indiana Ranton is an effortless love—I know I pushed the possibility away years ago, but now I'll hold on tighter than ever. She is the calm to any storm, and the beauty in this chaos of life. I'll never take her or Noah for granted; this second chance is the gift I've been searching for since I returned.

CHAPTER 39
Fire Hunters

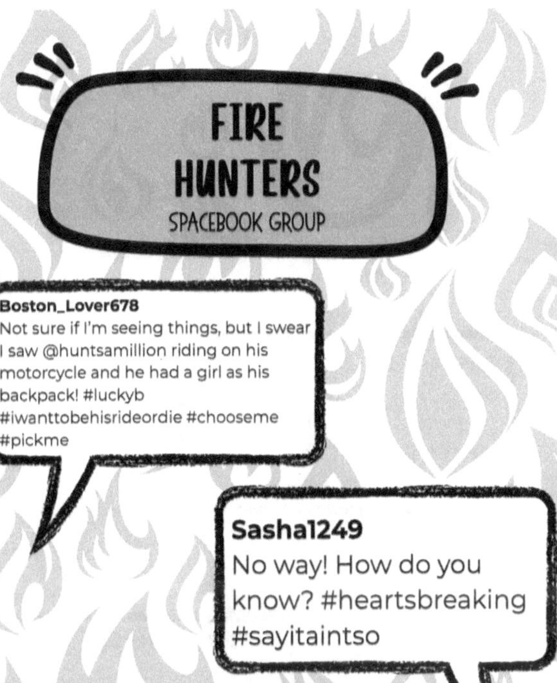
FIRE HUNTERS
SPACEBOOK GROUP

Boston_Lover678
Not sure if I'm seeing things, but I swear I saw @huntsamillion riding on his motorcycle and he had a girl as his backpack! #luckyb #iwanttobehisrideordie #chooseme #pickme

Sasha1249
No way! How do you know? #heartsbreaking #sayitaintso

Boston_Lover678
@Sasha1249 He had a sticker on his bike that was in a video once and I could swear it was the same one. I'm sure it was him. #huntersoffthemarket

Sasha1249
Wow! She better feel like she won the lottery! He seems like the sweetest. #countyourluckystars

Boston_Lover678
Are you kidding? I hope he knows how to ride more than that bike 😏 #dirtydirty

CHAPTER 40

Indiana

THIS IS SURREAL, knowing that Tyler and I are reconnecting. Not only that, but we're finally together in a way that I can see him, without hiding behind letters and years of wondering if this is real or not. I thought about letting him grovel for a longer period of time, but I've learned life is too damn short.

Yesterday morning he snuck out before Noah woke up. At one point, I panicked, worried we'd fall asleep and lose track of time, but he set an alarm and woke up before Noah would ever dream of moseying out of bed.

All I can say is having Tyler's hands exploring my body felt like returning home after years of feeling lost. The man had me seeing stars all night.

Now that my head is finally out of the clouds, reality is setting in. All things I was pushing aside yesterday are starting to filter through, mostly revolving around Noah.

As much as I let my prior relationships fizzle, this thing with Tyler feels serious from the start. Mostly due to the fact we're married and nothing about this is simple.

"Noah, sweetie, do you want the sauce on the spaghetti

tonight, or plain?" Food preferences practically change by the hour at this age.

"No sauce, please!" he shouts from the living room. Then I hear his little feet running over. Luckily, we're home at a decent time tonight because he didn't have any tee-ball practice after school.

"How many meatballs do you want?" I'm serving him a little bit of everything and I see his nose scrunch up as I put broccoli on his plate.

"You know the rules. We have to balance our plate with some veggies." I give him a pointed look.

He shrugs. "Fine. And I want two meatballs please."

Once I'm done putting his plate on the table, I make one for myself and join him.

"How was school today?" I ask him.

"It was good. We're learning about volcanos." His eyes grow wide.

"Wow. Exciting! Did you watch a video?"

"Yes. And Ms. Mendo says she's going to let us do a project in class with baking soda and vinegar." He continues talking about it, completely animated about how he'll get to see a fake volcano in class.

"That sounds fun," I tell him. I remember Bryce being enthralled by science in the same way. The older he got, the more complex his stories were regarding his classes. I have no doubt Noah will be the same way. At least right now, I can keep up with his science experiments, but I know at some point, this kid will outsmart me.

"We also learned about the temperature of a volcano and the lava!" He throws his hands up, and I laugh.

"Really? How hot does it get?" I can't help the laugh that escapes.

"Super hot. And not even the firemen can put it out. It's *really* hot, Mom," he explains, his eyes doubling in size. "I wonder if Hunter has seen a volcano erupt." He looks off in a distance.

My heart flutters at the thought of Tyler. I wonder how he'll take the news of Tyler and I together, my nerves take off at the prospect. Will he welcome the idea of me with Ty or will he be upset?

I know he likes Tyler, but dating me might bring on a new set of feelings and I'm afraid of how he'll react. He's never seen me dating anyone. Maybe I've done this all wrong all these years by shielding him and now he'll be hostile if I bring Tyler around.

I reach for my water and take a sip. Anxiety is taking over as I think about all the scenarios playing out in my head. I've really messed up and Noah could be greatly affected by my actions here if things with Tyler go sideways.

I let Noah continue on about his science class, his enthusiasm masking my anxiety attack. Luckily, he doesn't seem to notice it, along with my lack of appetite.

Once dinner is finished and cleared, we move through the bedtime routine. I let him read a book aloud. He's starting to do well with his books, needing little help from me in the last few weeks.

After I say goodnight, I walk out of his room, and pull out my phone. I quickly send a text off to Tyler:

> Hey. I hope your shift is going well. When you're done tomorrow, maybe we can find some time to talk.

I expect to get a text back at some point, but to my surprise, my phone starts ringing within a few minutes.

"What's wrong, Indy?" Tyler seems panicked.

"Nothing's wrong per se…" I start.

"Your text sounds like you're having doubts about something. So, talk to me," he urges.

"Well, I was thinking about Noah, and I'm just worried

about how he'll react to us is all." I'm walking out to the kitchen and hoping I'm talking low enough that my voice doesn't carry.

"You think Noah would be mad to know you and I are together?" Ty sounds concerned.

"I don't think so, but I've never introduced him to anyone I've dated. I honestly don't know."

"Well, there's really no way to know how this will go without telling him, Indy." It's really quiet wherever he is.

"Aren't you at the firehouse right now?" I ask him, changing subjects.

"Yeah, why?"

"It's so quiet. Are you allowed to be on a call with me?"

"Yeah, but I can't stay long. I walked toward the locker and bunk area. Your text worried me, as if you were having second thoughts," he confesses.

"I got to thinking that we aren't just going to be throwing a relationship at him, but a marriage. I started to freak out." I run my hand down my face.

"Indy, we don't have to divulge *everything* to Noah. We introduce things to him at our pace. He doesn't have to know we're married. I think we're still figuring everything out ourselves. If you're comfortable with that plan, I think that's the best course of action."

How is he so calm about this?

"Why are you being so agreeable?" I can't help but question him.

"You're forgetting I just waited years to get you back. I'll fight to keep you. Plus, don't sound so surprised." He scoffs. "I may have leaned on my buddy to get some advice."

"Malloy?" He's the only one I know well.

"No. Although he agreed with it. Clay is actually the one that suggested us taking it slow with Noah. I mean, he lost his dad at a young age. Even though his mom never dated, he had a lot to say on the matter. He had a lot of good points and I can't help but say I agree."

I feel my heart rate coming down and I'm nodding, even though he can't see me.

"So, we're good?" he questions as I sit in silence for an extra beat.

"Yeah, all good. I just freaked out," I reassure him.

I can hear him rustling on his end of the line. "Does that mean I can still see you tomorrow for lunch?"

That pulls a smile from me as I play with a loose strand of my hair. "Yes. Can you come by my office around one?"

"Of course. I'll bring some food. I know a local sandwich shop I think you'll like."

"Perfect." I feel a thrill rush through me at the thought of seeing him in less than twenty-four hours.

"Oh, and Indy?"

"Yeah?"

"You should know that dessert will be delayed until tomorrow night after Noah goes to bed."

I hear the dial tone immediately follow while my whole body ignites at the thought of what awaits.

———

It's been a week since we started sneaking around either while Noah's in school or after he's gone to bed. Today is the first time I'm going to Tyler's place while Kalli has Noah for the day.

The minute I pull up to this family home, I confirm I'm at the right address. It's a blue two-story colonial, with a wraparound porch, a swing, and a red front door. I envision the large oak trees that surround the front probably look like a Hallmark card during the holidays, with the fall leaves changing colors, along with the beautiful snow in the winter months.

Right now, the light blue paint is pristine, along with the white trim perfectly complimenting all the colors surrounding this beautiful neighborhood. I can't stop staring at the picturesque view in front of me.

I finally step out of my car, still shocked Tyler is living in this house. I remember him mentioning he's renting it from Georgie's parents. My heart tugs at the sorrow that must blanket all of them at the loss of this missing piece in all their lives.

I make my way to the front door, and he swings it open before I even have a chance to ring the bell. He's dressed in low-hanging basketball shorts and no shirt, his tattoos on full display; he's completely edible right now. The smile he welcomes me with is enough to have my heart racing.

"Aren't you a sight for sore eyes," he says, pulling me in, stealing my breath away with a kiss.

He groans as he deepens the kiss, which is far too inappropriate for something at his front door, but he doesn't seem to mind. I take in the woodsy smell he dons after a shower and melt further into him. His hair is still a little damp as I move my fingers through the ends. Once I pass the threshold, he kicks the door closed and pins me against it.

"I really missed you," he says, moving his lips down along the column of my neck.

I giggle. "I can tell."

"Being around you is never enough. Even if I had infinite hours, they'd never add up to enough with you," he tells me as he plants open-mouthed kisses along my skin.

I grab his face and bring his lips back to mine and kiss him, relishing this time we have undisturbed. I feel like when we have gotten a moment at lunch or in the evening, I know one of us has to rush off. Right now, we have a few hours together, nowhere to be, so I'll cherish it.

"If we start this right now, I may not stop, and I want to

show you around at least," he pulls away, a sly little smile on his face.

I'm out of breath, but I nod, somewhat disappointed. He grabs my hand and pulls me, giving me a tour of the house. He tells me that Jerry, Georgie's father, is a contractor and had put in the time to fix the place up.

Tyler makes sure everything is in working order while they're away. He finishes the tour in the garage, where the motorcycle Jerry gifted him rests.

"And as you know, this here is my girl," Tyler says, moving his hand along the seat delicately.

"Wow, you really pride yourself on your bike," I say on a laugh.

"There's nothing funny about Black Pearl, Indy." He's all serious now, no playfulness to his tone.

I bring my hands up in surrender. "Sorry, I meant nothing by it. But, *I'm* your girl." I raise my brow at him.

"Nah, you're my *wife*." He gives me a sharp look and I can feel the blush creeping in. "Have you ever been ridden on a bike?" Tyler's voice is gravely and he licks his bottom lip.

I knit my brows in confusion. I'm about to tell him we went on a ride the other night when I realize what he means.

"Have you ever been fucked on a bike, Indy?" He pushes one of my straps down and bites my shoulder. I let out a moan. I feel the wetness pool down in my core as I push my chest out.

He picks me up and sets me down on the seat of the bike, pushing my knees apart. I'm wearing a long dress, so he rubs the fabric of my dress, kissing me deeply, moving his hands up my torso, then grabbing and fondling my breasts. He tweaks my nipples through the fabric.

"I can see your fucking piercings through this and it's driving me crazy." He bites my lower lip and I smile, pulling on his hair slightly, enticing a guttural sound from him.

He pushes the fabric down further, freeing one of my

breasts and dropping kisses down my neck. When he reaches my breast, he captures it, circles the metal, and plays with the jewel, while watching me with hooded eyes.

I arch my back, unable to contain how much feeling his tongue on my skin turns me on.

I whimper, my brows pulling, my hips moving, seeking out friction.

He chuckles against my skin, yet continues his slow pace, moving his lips across my chest, exposing my opposite breast. I balance on the bike, trying to steady myself, while wrapping my legs around his lean waist.

I feel his hardening cock at my center and all I want is to feel him inside me.

"Someone's eager today," he teases. "Maybe I need to take you upstairs and tie you up."

"Stop finding ways to prolong this and fuck me." I'm never this impatient, but I'm wound tight now and I need release.

I start to push his shorts down with my feet, no longer playing nice. I succeed, his dick springing free.

I bring one hand behind me for support and tug on his hair, getting his attention. "I need my husband inside me right now."

The smile he gives me is downright sinful. He pulls the bottom of my dress up, expecting to find underwear underneath all that fabric. When he comes up empty, the lust in his eyes could scorch the earth beneath us.

"Looks like my wife came prepared." He pulls my hair back and kisses me deeply.

"Your wife isn't *coming* at all," I bite back.

Without another word, he lines himself up and drives into me. The moment he fills me, I yell out.

He buries his face in my neck, his breathing labored.

"Is that what your pussy needs? My cock to fill you up?"

He doesn't wait for a response and starts moving at a speed that's fast and hard.

The intensity is exactly what I need and I hold on, my nails digging into the skin on his back.

The way he's hitting that perfect spot inside me makes me see stars. No, I think I'm seeing the whole galaxy. My clit is rubbing with each thrust, my climax teetering on the edge. My head falls back, my eyes closed, and I can't help the erotic sounds that are coming out of my mouth right now.

The way he keeps chanting my name each time he pistons into me only spurs me on and I'm lost in this man. I run my nails along his back, probably leaving my mark.

I don't know how this bike is staying upright, but it's hanging on while he pumps that long, thick dick in and out of me. I don't care as long as he keeps hitting that spot inside me that has me reaching this beautiful ecstasy.

"Fuck, I can feel you gripping my cock," he whines. I can't speak because my brain is lost in this blissful state where I'm about to fall.

Feeling Tyler inside me, pumping in and out of me, while we're on his bike, feels so out of the norm, and it pushes me over the edge.

My body convulses, while Tyler brings his mouth over one of my nipples and sucks hard. I feel my orgasm go off; my body shakes, and my scream carries on bouncing off the walls around us.

Ty is holding on to my back, my head hanging off slightly as he pounds into me even harder than before, and the whole thing is unreal. He's relentless as he chases his own high. I'm still coming off my own orgasm when I feel him explode.

His movements start to slow and I take him in after he's reached his own climax. His face is sated and his eyes closed as he drops lazy kisses across my cheeks. It's only then I'm aware we didn't use a condom. He whispers my name, his motions lazy until he finally stops.

He kisses my lips softly and looks down to where we're joined. His eyes widen and reality must hit him just then.

"Shit, Indy. I didn't… I wasn't thinking."

I shake my head. "I know. Neither was I. We were in the heat of the moment. I'm on the pill and I've recently been tested."

"Me too. I'm usually careful, I swear," he assures me.

"I believe you." I move my hand onto his cheek.

He kisses me tenderly and I feel a shiver pass through me.

A calm washes over me in this moment. I think despite all the difficult moments in my life, maybe everything will finally start to fall into place.

CHAPTER 41
Fire Hunters

FIRE
HUNTERS
SPACEBOOK GROUP

Lexi_121
Just joining the group
What Adonis page have I
fallen onto?
#whyhellothere

Hunter_Fan_01
Welcome! You're in
for a treat!
#firehunterssquad

CatsRLife553
This page just gets better
and better. Did you see that
last one with the cat? I can't
get enough! #catlover

GoldenDogLuver987
Oh, I hope you get to see more of #rowdyriver. He's been the best addition to the page #riversthebest #hehasadogtoo

Baseball_G_Boss
I have to disagree with @GoldenDogLuver987 on this one, @Huntsamillion does best on his own 😵 #huntsolo

CHAPTER 42

Tyler

ONE MONTH. That's how long Indiana and I have been seeing one another, and I swear, it's been the best thirty days I could ask for. I feel like the sun is shining again on my life and I never want it to set.

Her parents are coming into town this weekend, and we have a plan to tell Noah about us after they leave. Her mother isn't a fan of Darth, so he'll be hanging with me this weekend. That gives me the opportunity to see Noah, even if it's just in the context of being his mom's friend. I can test the waters when they drop their cat off.

The doorbell rings and I run to the door. I'm a little nervous, wiping my hands on my pants. I'm usually pretty good around kids, but now that things are moving along with Indy, I feel this added pressure to make a good impression in front of this little boy.

"Hunter!" Noah shouts when I swing the door open.

"Hey, buddy."

"My mom said you're watching Darth this weekend while Grandma and Grandpa come to visit. Grandma doesn't like Darth." He scrunches his nose as he looks up at me.

"I heard. Yes, I'll watch over Darth for you. I promise to take extra good care of him. You think he'll like my house?"

"Yeah. He likes when you scratch behind his ear, but I'll show you before we leave," he says, walking in with confidence. "And he likes watching Star Wars!"

I look up and see Indy standing at the door, a soft smile grazing her lips. "Hey," she says.

"Hi, beautiful," I whisper.

As she passes the threshold, I allow my hand to skim the top of hers. I can't be around her without touching her a little.

She's holding the carrier with Darth inside, his meows soft, yet present, as they move through my home. I bring my hand out to grab the carrier for her.

"Let's put it somewhere so he can start to get acclimated." Indy says.

"Of course," I say. "Do you have water and food bowls? Because I got some just in case."

Indy looks over at me with a surprised look.

"What?" I ask.

"You got my cat supplies?"

"Well, yeah. I wasn't sure if you needed me to." I shrug.

She simply smiles at me as she opens the carrier. "I brought some, but that's really sweet. Thank you."

"Of course. I can return what I got. I just wanted to make sure he was covered. I don't want to be ill-prepared." I wink.

Noah comes running over. "Hunter has a pool, Mom!"

"Wow! How exciting." She looks at him.

"Do you think we can swim here in the summer?" If it were possible, I'd think he'd have stars in his eyes.

"I don't know, sweetie. That's something we would have to see. But, right now we have to focus on Darth." Looking at me, she smiles. Swinging the door to the carrier open, she looks inside. Darth pokes his head out, hesitant to come out, looking at his new surroundings.

Noah goes back to looking at the fenced-off pool, distracted for a moment.

I whisper to her, "If it's okay with you, I'd like for him to swim here this summer."

"Yeah?" She looks into my eyes. I nod. "Alright. That's all you."

"Hey, Noah. Your mom said you can come by this summer to swim, bud."

"Really? Yes!" He throws his arms up in the air.

I smile, it feels like a win.

Slowly, Darth starts to come out of the carrier, looking around my place. He's only staying two days, but I'm excited to have some company. Hopefully this will be a better experience than the foster puppy I had a while back.

"You sure you're good watching him?" Indy asks.

"For the millionth time, yes. I promise we will be fine," I tell her.

Noah walks over and pulls out a piece of paper from his back pocket. Once he unfolds it, I realize it's full of crayon written instructions of what Darth needs throughout the day.

This kid is fucking adorable.

———

I'm leaning against the counter and staring at the fridge. I can't stop looking at Noah's crayon-filled handwriting that I taped up shortly after he and Indy left. That's what I'm doing when my friends start walking in from the back patio door.

I'm taking a drink of my beer and Malloy pats me on the back in greeting.

"Hey, man. Thanks for having us over; glad to have a day out. Your place is the nicest to have a BBQ." He puts items down on the kitchen counter as I turn around, greeting the rest of our friends.

I give River and Clay a side hug, patting them on the back.

Ashton joined us today, he's the twins' childhood friend. He's not a firefighter with us, but he comes along when he can get away from his busy schedule. He's more reserved, but it's nice to have him balance everyone out. Plus, he has the patience of a saint if he can handle River and Clay together for as long as he has.

"Good to see you, man." I give him a hug. "How are the kids?" I ask him. He has toddler boy and girl twins.

"Non-stop. That's all I can say. They're running around and terrorizing Samara and I constantly, but I wouldn't have it any other way." He smiles from ear to ear. "I don't think I'll sleep for the rest of my life though."

"I bet." I laugh with him. "Can I get you something to drink?"

"Honestly, I think I'll have a beer, please."

"You got it. Clay, River?"

"Same, please," they both answer.

"I'll take a water, please," Malloy answers. "I'm driving these guys."

We all settle in and begin prepping for lunch. Soon, I see Darth come out of his little hiding spot, probably getting used to the noise.

"What the fuck is that?" River yells, nearly spitting his beer out.

I look over, my brows knitting. "Um, a cat. You've seen one before, right?"

"When the hell did you get a cat? And why?" He looks disgusted. "I told you to get a dog, Hunter. A DOG!" He mouths it like I'm not comprehending words anymore.

"Yes, River. I understand the difference. I didn't go out and get a cat. This is Indiana and Noah's cat. I'm watching him for them. Her parents are in town and her mom isn't a cat person. His name is Darth."

Now everyone looks confused. "Like Darth Vader?" Ashton questions.

"Yes." I roll my eyes. Seriously, why they named the cat Darth is really beyond me. I think people think the feline will be a terror due to the name. Plus, the cat is as white as snow.

"Noah is a huge Star Wars fan, and he wanted to name the cat something unique. So here we are."

"Huh, I sort of admire that," Malloy says.

"Yeah, he's super cool," I say.

"Did you two tell him you're dating yet?" Clay asks me.

"No. We're telling him after her parents leave. We thought we'd let her parents head out first, because if her parents are anything like they were when we were growing up, they'd want to see me and honestly—baby steps. They weren't my biggest fans years ago." I take a sip of my beer.

"Why? You're not giving yourself enough credit, Hunter," River says, pointing his beer in my direction.

"Listen, I know you see this version of me today, but I wasn't this stellar person"—I puff out my chest— "who seemed put together back then." I wink for added effect.

I get a few chuckles from the guys, but River gives me a stern look. "Seriously, though. Why wouldn't they accept you now? You're an adult and you've got your shit together."

"The version Indiana's parents knew of me back then was the kid from the trailer park with loser parents. I was the kid that barely made the grades, skipped class, and rode his motorcycle to school." I still feel that pang of insecurity creep up when I think about my past and Indy's parents.

"The motorcycle part hasn't changed," River chimes in with a smile on his face. "I'm still not wrapping my head around the fact that they won't accept you today. You are a good fit for her and she for you. And it's not up to them."

"I guess I just feel insecure still for things in my past. Yes, I should let it go, but I feel it when I think of them. So, when she told me they were coming this weekend, I thought it best to postpone telling them. My parents did a number on me, but Indy's parents' opinion of me had a significant effect on how I felt for years. I truly saw myself as worthless. Like I wasn't good enough for her."

"She's done quite well for herself," Malloy states. "But part of that is because of you. She wouldn't be where she is if it weren't for the way you pushed her to be independent. There's a lot to be said about that."

"She has. But people like them just like to point fingers at all the mistakes I've made, and they only remember where I came from. I'm an easy person to blame for the problems that exist between them and their daughter. That being said, we want to keep the blowback from affecting Noah. We're going to tell him once they leave. My goal is to move forward with Indy, without much drama if possible." I feel a tightness in my chest because everything I ever wanted feels like it's right at my fingertips. Like I'm finally at that point where I've always dreamed of reaching with her.

"I'm happy for you man," Malloy says, grabbing my shoulder and squeezing. "Just remember you deserve to be happy."

"Thanks," I tell him. "I'm excited to tell Noah. He's a good kid and I want to get to know him better. The little bit she's told me and that I've gotten to see, I already like him so damn much. I'll be pumped to see a different side to him as we get to spend more time together."

"Then you should definitely get the kid a dog," River says.

"Give it up, Riv." Clay rolls his eyes.

I laugh. "No way, not after that disaster with that hump-fest from the foster place."

"That was a fluke, Hunter! Look at my sweet Lola! She's an angel," River continues.

"Seriously, Riv. Enough," Clay says, as if he's talking to his own child, and not his brother.

"You sound like Mom," River retorts.

"You sound like a child and not a thirty-year-old," Clay reminds him.

This goes on, so we grab the food and start heading outside. This is exactly what these guys do. They make me feel like I'm a part of a family.

————

"I was just about to order some Chinese take-out. Would you like to join me?" I ask Indy and Noah when they come over to pick up Darth.

"Can we Mom? Please?" Noah pleads.

"That sounds nice," Indy says, her smile widening, as if she's not in on this plan.

"What do you like to eat?" I ask Noah. Indiana told me Noah loves Chinese food, so I'm ordering from a spot I love.

Noah runs over and sits next to me on the couch, looking over at my phone to look over the menu. After everyone selects their favorite items, I place the order.

"So, there's something else I was going to do before you two arrived—I was just about to cue up a movie. I don't think we'll be able to watch the entire thing, but maybe just a bit of it." I start.

"What movie?" I see Noah's eyes light up.

"I'm not too sure you'll like it. It's one of my favorite ones. It's called..." I stall a beat.

Noah's staring at me, anticipating my every move until I finally say, "*Star Wars.*"

"Really? Which one?"

"I was thinking *A New Hope.*" Not sure he'll approve of the lineup I'm going with but may as well start with the original.

"Yes! Darth loves that one," he shouts.

"Awesome," I say.

Indy laughs and shakes her head. "Okay, boys. Well, maybe we can sit and talk for a little bit first?" She gives me a look, and I nod. I'm hoping he'll be just as excited about this news as he is about the food and movie.

Noah sits with his mom while I sit opposite them on the couch. Darth is lying on what I've deemed his favorite spot since he arrived two days ago.

"How was the visit with your grandparents?" I start.

"Fun! Grammy took me for ice cream. Grandpop says he prefers basketball instead of baseball."

You have to love the honesty. I guess taking them to a Gaels baseball game won't be on the docket for them anytime soon.

"Well, the ice cream sounds like a win. And I bet your grandpop would love to see you play baseball." I smile.

Indy moves her hand through Noah's hair. "Noah, baby, we wanted to talk to you."

He looks up at her. "Am I in trouble?" His brows furrow with concern.

"No, not at all," I tell him.

"We wanted to talk to you about something good. Did you know that Tyler—Hunter—we used to know each other growing up?" she says.

Noah's eyes go wide and he shakes his head.

"Yeah, we've known each other since we were your age. Back in Las Vegas," I say.

"That's where Grandpop and Grammy live," Noah says, pride in his voice.

"Yep. That's right. And for many years, Hunter and I didn't see one another. We used to write letters to stay in touch. But then we went a long time without talking. And that day when you got stung by that bee, it was the first time we saw each other," Indy explains.

Noah stays quiet, listening intently to the story.

She continues, "And Mommy's heart felt really happy when she saw Hunter that day."

"That's what I said!" Noah interjects.

I look up at her, confused, yet I smile. "You did?" I ask him.

"Mmhmm." He nods. "I told her you make her smile."

"Yes, yes," she carries on, and I make a mental note to go back to that later. "And because Mommy feels so happy around Hunter, we have decided to see each other more."

"I like being around your mom," I say.

Noah looks at me, inspecting me and his brown eyes narrow a bit, then bounce to his mom, then back to me.

Finally, he speaks, "Okay, so can we watch the movie?"

Indy looks at me, confusion marring her features. "Noah, sweetie, do you have any questions for us?"

"No." He pets Darth, completely unfazed.

"You understand that Hunter might hold Mommy's hand or hug me?" she says.

"Yes." He doesn't look up and continues to pet his cat's head.

Her mouth hangs open, as if she's shocked at his casual nature for this entire interaction.

I shrug and move my hand through my hair, winking at her.

"Can we start the movie, Hunter? Is that okay, Mom?" Noah asks, looking up at her, shocking her to move slightly away from my hand.

"Um, yeah," she answers.

I laugh at how nervous she is and she side-eyes me, making me laugh a little harder. If looks could kill, I'd be out cold, but luckily that's not the case right now.

The movie begins and Noah sidles right next to Indy, while Darth cuddles next to me. Once the food arrives, we pause and sit at the table together.

I talk about what I did with Darth, while they catch me up on their weekend with her parents. I give Noah some stories from the firehouse that are kid-appropriate, along with some stories about traveling after the Army.

Summer is soon approaching, and Noah has a few camps he's signed up for that he's excited to start. He tells me all about how much he's loving playing tee-ball, and he wants me to come to his games. I'm well aware that coach of his is eyeing my wife, so I'll definitely be making an appearance. Plus, I really want to see him playing something he seems to love so much.

Once dinner is done, Noah runs to sit on the couch while I start cleaning up the leftovers. I tell Indy to go sit down and relax, but she insists on helping me clean up.

We're in the kitchen when I feel her wrap her hands around me from behind.

"Thank you for being so wonderful with him." She rests her cheek on my back.

"Of course. He's a good one. You're doing a great job with him. I hope you know that," I tell her.

"He's so much like Bryce. It hurts sometimes." I can hear the pain in her voice.

I turn around and let her rest her face on my chest. "Does he ask about his dad?"

She rests her chin on my sternum so she's looking up at me. "Sometimes. It's random how often he brings him up. It's painful, yet reassuring, if that makes sense. I love talking about him, but it feels like I'm taking something away from Bryce each time a milestone happens."

"I get that. He looks a lot like him," I say.

"I know. And some of his mannerisms are the same. It's weird. Noah was only eight months when Bryce passed, and yet he still acts like my brother. So strange how those things are passed on." She's looking at me but she's so far away.

"What about his mom?" I've been curious about her whereabouts.

"She gave up her rights. She couldn't handle being a mother. I won't lie, I held my breath for a while, wondering if she was going to resurface after Bryce's death. But she never did. She truly walked away." Indy takes a long breath out her nose, probably trying to steady her nerves.

I push away some of her hair that has fallen onto her face. "I know it hurts. The memories that come forward are constant reminders for you. But when they creep in, try to think of them as gifts. Little treasures from your brother. That's his way of saying hello because he's left you with a piece of him."

Her eyes start to well with tears. "Don't cry, baby." I kiss the corner of her eyes.

"I love you," she whispers. "I don't care if it's too soon after we've reconnected, but I want you to know how I'm feeling. I loved you then and I love you now."

I look at her, those mesmerizing green eyes staring back at me.

"I love you too, Indiana. My one and only love," I tell her. "The person that captured me, not just my heart, but my soul, and never let me live my life the same afterwards. I've lived trying to find myself again, but all roads led back to you, and I'll be forever grateful."

Noah's engrossed in the movie, so I lean down and capture her lips with mine, a soft kiss, to simply reassure her that what we have is unequivocal and endless.

When we pull away, I sense a pair of little eyes looking at us. When we look over, he looks away and giggles.

She smiles at me. "Sorry."

"My love isn't limited to only you, Indy."

Her smile grows and she pulls my face down to capture my lips again, and I realize how complete my life is in that very moment.

CHAPTER 43
Indiana

"IS HUNTER COMING SOON?!" Noah yells from the swings.

"Yes, Noah. He'll be here soon," I tell him. It's been five minutes since the last time he asked me.

We're meeting at the park near our place, something Tyler and I agreed on. It's been two weeks since we told Noah about us dating and so far, things have been going smoothly.

Noah has adjusted pretty well. He doesn't seem to mind the fact that Tyler has come over most nights he's off from work. I've noticed the way Noah waits for his arrival on those days, anticipating Ty's presence. I never realized how impactful having a male presence would be for Noah until Tyler showed up.

I see Noah's face split into a grin and I know my husband's arrived without looking behind me.

"Hunter!" Noah jumps off the swings and begins sprinting over. "Hi, Hunter!" The way he takes off as if it's been years and not a day since we've seen each other last.

"Hey, buddy." Tyler laughs. It's heartwarming, watching them interact. I look behind him and notice someone walking close by with a baby in his arms. It's then I recognize him to be one of his crew members from the station. There's a woman walking next to them.

Once Tyler gets closer, he bends down to plant a kiss on my lips. Pulling away, he whispers, "Hey, baby." He winks, moving his hands through my hair. "I hope you don't mind, I brought my friends along. They wanted to join us. Their daughter can't play on all the stuff at the park, but they needed to get out of the house a bit."

I smile and nod. "Of course. I remember those days."

The days are long when you're cooped up at home with a little one. With the weather warming up, getting fresh air is the best thing to do.

"Hi. I don't know if you remember me, I'm Clay. This is my fiancée Abby"—he points to the woman standing next to him—"and our daughter Gabriella. We call her Ella for short."

The little girl squeals in his arms, her bright-blue eyes are vibrant with her dark hair and dimples popping out as she looks at me. She's stunning.

"Hi, precious Ella, I'm Indy." I wave at her and she returns the gesture, although she proceeds to stuff her pointer finger in her mouth, something I remember Noah doing at that age. "Is she about a year old?"

"She will be very soon," Abby confirms. "Time is a thief." She sighs, looking over at her daughter.

Ella starts wiggling out of her father's hold and Clay starts laughing, bending over to put her down. "Alright, I'll put you down. I'll hold your hand and you can try to walk."

Clay begins to move around the park and it's comical to see this tall figure crouching down while his little girl attempts to move around, grasping on his fingers.

"I doubt his back will be thanking him later," Tyler says.

"Oh, it won't." Abby chuckles, as she pulls out a blanket. "But he'll do that for as long as it makes her happy." She smiles as she watches their retreating forms, her eyes showing nothing but love for them.

"I don't doubt it," Tyler says. "Noah, look what I brought." He holds up a baseball and bat. "Want to practice your swing?"

"You brought it!" Noah jumps up.

"I promised I would, bud." Tyler grins.

Noah starts running to the open part of the field. It's hard to contain my own happiness in this moment.

"We'll be right back." Ty adjusts his baseball cap and gives me a sexy smirk. Right then, my eyes home in on his backside, Tyler chooses that very second to swing his gaze back to me and catches me staring me.

"Hey, Indy!"

I bring my eyes to meet his.

"My eyes are up here." He laughs and I narrow my eyes in mock irritation.

I bring my focus back to Abby, who's getting some items in order on the blanket, while Clay is still walking Ella around the park.

"Do you need any help?" I ask Abby.

"No, but thanks so much." She smiles up at me. "It's so nice to formally meet you after all I've heard. I remember seeing you briefly at the hospital, but we didn't get to properly meet that day."

"Oh? So, you've heard about me?" I can't help the heat creeping up my cheeks.

"Are you kidding? These guys are worse than the tabloids." She laughs. "Plus, I'm Marissa's best friend. I saw you at the restaurant that night." She winks and now I do feel my cheeks flame. The jealousy I was sporting that night wasn't my finest moment.

"Oh." I'm mortified. "I had no idea. I was a little off that night." I try to cover up a bit, but fail.

"Indiana, you don't have to explain. Marissa is one for a little drama. She will stir it up with the best of them. She knew exactly what she was doing. And it looks like she succeeded." She gives me a pointed look, then she breaks out in a large grin. I can't help but laugh.

Changing the subject, I admit, "I've interacted the most with Malloy out of everyone in the firehouse."

She hums, nodding in acknowledgment. "I'm closest with Malloy, actually. We're in book club together."

"He mentioned something about a book club when he stopped by my office."

"Really?" She scrunches her nose. "That's random."

"It seems that way, but he noticed a collection of books on my shelf. I happen to work with one of the authors he likes. He said you and someone named Kennedy were in book club with him," I tell her.

"Yeah, we are. We take it very seriously. Baylee, his wife, is in it too. But school takes up a lot of her time, so she can't be as dedicated as we are. Who was the author he saw on your shelf?"

"Ana Clevesky." I smile.

"Are you serious? You know Ana Clevesky?" Abby gasps, dropping some of Ella's toys.

I chuckle. "Yes, I do. She's actually really down-to-Earth."

"No way," Abby says, "I can't believe that. I follow her on my socials. I can't believe you've met her. Hell, we loved her first book and I couldn't stop reading the rest."

"I'll let her know. She's a sweetheart. That will mean a lot to her." I look over to see Noah hitting the ball. My eyes stay on Tyler as he patiently throws the ball to my son.

"Hunter's a good guy. I don't know him well, but he's really become a part of our little family and I'm glad you're with him," Abby says. My smile grows and I swing my gaze back to her.

"I appreciate you saying that. It hasn't been easy, but I'm glad we are together again," I tell her. "I feel like it took years to get here."

"I know what you mean." She looks at her daughter and Clay.

"She's beautiful," I tell her.

"Thank you. She's my little miracle." I feel like there's a story behind her words, but Clay makes his way back over before I can ask for more on that.

"I think someone is going to be taking a break," he says, not sure if he's referring to himself or his daughter as he winces when he fully stands.

"Why don't you two grab a snack?" Abby chuckles.

"I think I'm going to check on Hunter to see if he needs help," Clay says. "You good here?" He bends down and brings his pointer-finger under Abby's chin to lightly kiss her lips.

She smiles and shakes her head. "I'm good. Thanks, though."

I feel like I'm interrupting something by just watching these two interact. He ruffles his daughter's hair then jogs over to meet the boys.

"How long have you been together?" I ask Abby.

"It's sort of a long story, but off and on since college. We sort of got back together when I was pregnant with this one." She taps her daughter's nose, enticing a giggle from Ella.

I smile, realizing there's no perfect road for any of us. We all have a special route to reach what is right for us.

———

Noah is at the movies with his friend Harley and her family. They invited him over shortly after we arrived home from the park. I thought he'd be too tired, but he begged me, and I couldn't resist his sweet little face. Plus, a little bit of time uninterrupted with Tyler sounded pretty good after I watched him being so sweet with Noah.

"So, how long do you think we're on our own?" Ty wraps his arms around me.

We came back to his place after we dropped Noah off at Harley's house.

"Probably a solid four hours. Harley's mom said she's taking them out for pizza afterwards. I don't know how she's got that much energy." I can't help the goosebumps that are erupting as Tyler nibbles my ear.

"I've got an idea. You want to go out on a ride on my bike?" He breathes me in and I get a flurry of butterflies as I think about getting on his bike.

I hesitate for a moment. "You nervous to get on there with me again?" He pulls away, taking in my expression.

"No." I bite my lower lip.

He bites my shoulder, and I swear my underwear is a little wetter.

He smacks my ass as he grabs my hand, pulling me toward his garage. Once inside, he grabs the extra helmet and puts it over my head.

Once he straps it around my chin, he groans.

"What?" I say, sounding a bit muffled.

"If I stare too long at you, I might bend you over my bike and fuck you again. So, we better get going."

"Really? Because of the helmet?" I can't help the perplexed look I give him through the face shield.

He grabs the chin guard and pulls me closer. "I swear, you've got me fucking hard right now and you're fully clothed."

I think my temperature just spiked a few degrees with his words. Is he sure a ride on the bike is what he wants to do? As if reading my mind, he says, "Yes, I want to do this. It will be our version of foreplay." He leans in and kisses my nose, then closes the visor.

Opening the garage, he saddles up on the bike, putting his own helmet in place. Once he's in position, he tells me to sit behind him. The moment I wrap my hands around him, I feel his warmth beneath me. That thrumming of his heart underneath my fingertips is fucking enthralling.

He yells, "You ready?!"

I nod and he starts the bike. The moment we start to move, I understand how he might find this soothing for his soul. Feeling the wind hitting me as we move along the streets calms me, and this is only my second ride on this bike.

I tighten along his middle, my thighs doing exactly as they had last time we rode, more so with each turn. I love every second I get to sit this close with him. He isn't careless as we glide along the streets, I really appreciate that about him.

The sun is starting to set and the sky has that beautiful purplish-orange color. I want to stay lost in this moment right here, my heart completely enamored by this man who has come back from where I thought I had lost him. I honestly thought I had lost *myself* years ago.

He set up his camera to capture the ride, something I assume he uses for content to post on social media. He mentioned he'll post it but not show our faces. What I'm about to do might throw his *Fire Hunters* into a tizzy.

We stop at a light, and I rub my hand up and down the front of his chest. He turns his head in acknowledgement. There's something intimate about being on this motorcycle and I'm getting more turned on by the second.

He wasn't kidding about the damn foreplay. My body feels like every cell is firing on all cylinders. If we don't head back to the house soon, I might need him to pull over so I can ravage him out here, even though prying eyes can see.

I notice him take a turn and we start crossing through familiar areas again, back to neighborhoods I recognize. Soon enough, we're turning down his street and I feel the thrill of anticipation that I'll get to strip him down once we're back in his house.

When he pulls into the garage and turns off the engine of

the bike, I pull myself off him. He must feel as keyed up as me because he's removing his jacket, then grabbing the chin strap to my helmet next.

The moment he frees my face, I grab his helmet to remove it. Once I see his beautiful features, I bring my palms to his cheeks and pull his lips down to meet mine.

He pulls me into his arms, my legs automatically winding around his hips. He moves his arms around my waist, while his calloused hands move under my shirt and jacket to touch my skin.

I moan into him, eager for more proximity. We become frantic as we move further into the house, tossing layers of our clothes. My jacket is thrown to the ground, then our shirts are next.

He pulls our lips apart to inspect the red, lace bra I chose to wear. "Fuck, you're beautiful," he says, inspecting the way the fabric stretches across my skin.

He pushes one breast free, bringing it into his mouth. I automatically push my chest into him, while pulling on his dirty-blond hair. My head falls back, my eyes closing, and my body aching for more.

He pops out my breast then blows on my sensitive skin, enticing another loud moan. "Yes, Tyler."

"You like that, wife?"

God, I love when he calls me that.

"Mmhmm," is all that comes out of me.

He pulls my hair, bringing my gaze to meet his. "You like when I call you that?"

"Yes." My tone is breathy.

He starts to nibble along my collarbone, enticing goosebumps along my skin. I start to move my hips of their own accord, seeking friction.

"I need us to be naked, Ty," I moan.

"I know, baby," he tells me. "But I also love you writhing like this against me."

I whimper.

His chuckle along my skin is downright evil, yet I crave the way he pushes me to this edge each time we are together.

We're at his bedroom door and he kicks it open. The expanse of his room is large, his bed nicely made with sage green bedding and minimal pillows. He has a few decorative pictures hung in the room, but, for the most part, this space is pretty bare.

He lays me down on the bed, still planting kisses along the center of my chest, trailing them down until he meets the button of my jeans. He undoes them then begins to shimmy the fabric down.

Once my pants are removed and I'm completely exposed to him, he starts kissing up my leg. I'm squirming, needing more of a connection from this man of mine.

"Wanna have a little fun, Indy?" I see the devilish smirk move across his lips.

I let a smile move across my face and give him a slight nod.

He moves his hands up the sides of my ribs, stopping and cupping my breasts, squeezing my nipples. "Right answer."

He kisses my lips, then pulls away too soon.

I watch as he moves to the side table and retrieves a maroon scarf.

"What are you doing?"

"Having a little fun," he says as he saunters back over to me.

I watch him, my eyes trained on the scarf in his hands.

"Turn around in the center of the bed," he instructs me.

I do as he asks. He ties the scarf to cover my eyes and my senses are already heightened. I'm sitting upright, my back facing him. I feel his lips move to my shoulder, and a shiver races down my spine. Then he disappears and I hear the sound of him removing his jeans and discarding them, followed by his belt hitting the floor.

He maneuvers me gently to lay flat on my back, my head hanging off the edge of the bed.

He brings his lips to my ear and whispers, "Good girl." The chills that race up my spine are instantaneous.

"You tell me if it's too much and you can't handle it, alright? Actually, let's come up with a safe word… how about Hoover?" I can tell he's standing over me.

I nod, but I know I'm too excited for what's next. I want this. I'm dripping for this man and we haven't even done much.

"Open your mouth for me, *wife*," he orders, his voice gruff.

My heart hammers behind my ribcage as I open for him and I feel his length slide into my mouth. It's different at this angle, so it takes a moment to adjust.

That smooth cock, the salty tip hitting my tastebuds, is only making me want him more. Although it looks like I'm completely at his mercy, he's technically at mine.

The moment I fully take him in, I hear a deep groan take over Tyler's throat. "Fuck, you take me so good," he says.

I hum my approval and that only makes Tyler moan even louder. I hear him breathing hard, probably trying to control himself.

Having my eyes covered while blowing someone is a completely new experience. He starts to move slowly, and I relish in the feeling of pleasing him. Having this control, yet not being able to see him, is exhilarating. I bring my hands to circle around his backside, my fingers digging into his ass, likely leaving marks.

"Yes, that fucking mouth of yours is perfect," he says, completely lost as he starts pumping at a more rhythmic speed in and out of me. I love how enamored he is right now.

I'm so wet and all I want is to get myself off right now. My pelvis starts to move of its own accord, although there's no friction.

I swear, Tyler is so in tune with my needs that he moves a hand down my stomach to my clit and starts to play with my sensitive bud. I moan, which only coaxes a sound of his own.

"You're so fucking wet, Indy. Sucking me gets you wet, huh?"

"Mmhmm," I agree with him.

He keeps moving his fingers through my center as I suck him off. We must look so hot right now; I wish I could see us in a reflection somewhere.

We keep moving and I can feel my orgasm building. I'm about to come, when his hand disappears and I whine. I pop off his cock.

"No," I moan.

"I need to be inside you," he says. I hear the desperation in his voice. "Get on all fours."

I move quickly, my eyes still covered.

Once he helps me into position, I feel him move behind me. He caresses up the back of my leg, then I feel the sting from the slap he delivers on the right cheek.

"This ass is so fucking perfect, Indiana. I can't believe it's mine." He squeezes it and I push it back toward him, eager to feel him inside me.

I think he's going to plunge into me, but instead, I feel his wet tongue move along my slit and I yell out in pleasure. I bury my head into my mattress, and groan.

"*Tyler*," I plead.

"What do you want?" he taunts as he flicks my clit with his tongue.

"More." He's going to be the death of me.

"More...what?" I may not be able to see him, but I can imagine he's got a smirk on his face right now.

"More of your cock and less teasing," I specify.

He chuckles, then pulls away. My heart is hammering away behind my chest. I'm about to complain again because I need some release. But in the next second Tyler lines himself up and fills me to the hilt.

We both cry out in relief. We take a few seconds, then Tyler grabs onto my hips and begins a punishing pace. There's nothing slow and sensual about this right now. We are both chasing our release after what feels like hours of foreplay.

Ty reaches around, bringing his fingers to my clit, and I detonate. My climax rips through me and my whole body convulses.

I scream his name, and with my eyes covered it feels like my senses are amplified, my orgasm bringing out all the colors of the rainbow.

As I start to come down from my high, Tyler starts thrusting in and out of me at a new pace. I know he's chasing his own release.

He's telling me how much he loves me and how good I feel. Soon his movements become erratic, and I know he's about to lose all control. I feel the moment he climaxes into me, and my name is coming off his lips.

Our breaths are labored, sweat coating our skin. We're spent as we fall to the mattress. I curl into his side, even though I know I have to get up and clean myself up. I pull the scarf off my face and breathe in his masculine scent, his woodsy smell mixed with sweat and sex.

I kept thinking Tyler would hurt me if I welcomed him back, but I'm slowly realizing he was the missing piece to making my life whole again.

CHAPTER 44
Fire Hunters

FIRE
HUNTERS
SPACEBOOK GROUP

BostonBikerChick
That last video posted was HOT 🔥
What does @huntsamillion not do? I
swear, I could feel the chemistry
between those two through my
screen #iwannabehisbackpack
#letmeridetoo

FirefighterLuver29
Oh my gosh. I've been a fan of
@huntsamillion from the start, but I
was fanning myself after that last
post! Who knew a 🏍 video could be
so damn epic! #rideordie #rideme

HunterFan526
Biker Boys or Workout guide? Whatever it is, I'm here for it! #yesplease #lovingit #hotAF #bikerboy

Savannah097
I wanna know who the lucky lady is because I want to find a @huntsamillion of my own! Maybe we'll get to meet her one day. #luckylady #bikerboy #firefighter #illtakeone

CHAPTER 45

Tyler

WALKING HAND IN HAND, we ring the doorbell. It's Malloy's surprise birthday party and Indy's coming with me tonight.

It's officially the first time we'll be going to a function where we're a couple together. We've been on intimate dates, and gone places with Noah, but we haven't hung out with all my friends. She's met them individually; however, she hasn't met all the significant others—tonight feels like the real deal in many ways.

I feel like since I joined the firehouse, I've been the odd man out, but tonight there's a sense of belonging for me having Indiana by my side. In so many ways, I've always had to shield her from others regarding our marriage, but everyone in this room knows our past. It feels freeing to be here tonight, no secrets amongst this crowd.

This evening we are coming out as a couple.

River answers the door and his smile doubles. "Well, if it isn't *the* Mr. and Mrs."

"River." I nod. I look over at Indy and she has a small smile across her face.

After a few seconds she says, "Hi, it's good to see you

again." I'm not sure she knows the difference between the twins, but at this point, she's met both of them.

"It's good to see you again. Come on in." River opens the door further to let us in.

"Is everyone else here?" I ask him.

"No. Kennedy and Abby left before we got back. They're running some last-minute errands, and we're still waiting on Sam and Ashton. Marissa's supposed to be here, so what the hell? Baylee will text when she's getting close with the birthday boy. Clay and I have been tasked with getting things ready around here." River waves his hands around the place.

There are balloons decorating the apartment, along with some signs. I notice something's missing.

"Where's Lola?" I ask River.

He hangs his head. "I had to leave her with my mom. She was devastated." He grabs his chest, I hold back a laugh. I doubt the dog was sad in any way. That pup loves being with River's mom most of the time, but I won't ruin his night.

Clay comes out of the kitchen with a package of plates he's opening.

"Hey, guys. Good to see you," he says.

"Hi," Indiana greets him. "Where's Ella?"

"She's with my mom," he and River answer at the same time.

Indy chuckles, while her eyes ping-pong between the twins.

"Dude, she's asking me. Ella's my kid." Clay rolls his eyes.

"Yeah, but we all know she favors me." River puffs out his chest.

"Sure. Keep telling yourself that." Clay gives Indiana a hug, then comes to shake my hand, but I pull him into a hug of my own.

Luckily the brothers don't take the disagreement any further because the doorbell rings.

River answers it and to my surprise it's Marissa and

another woman who I assume to be her girlfriend, Josie, from the way she's holding her near.

"Hey, Marissa." I give her a hug.

"Hunter! How's my pseudo-boyfriend doing?" She smiles, winking my way.

I laugh, then pull Indy into my side. "Marissa, I want you to officially meet my *wife*, Indiana." I feel Indy stiffen slightly, likely from the last encounter with Marissa at the restaurant.

"So, you two finally figured your shit out, huh?" Marissa has that signature Cheshire grin across her face.

"And you must be the one and only Josie." I extend my hand to her girlfriend.

"Hi." Indy says to both of them.

Marissa laughs. "You two really are stubborn little things, aren't you?"

"Leave them alone, Mar." Josie smacks her girlfriend on the arm. "They're together now. Stop causing trouble."

"What? I'm just pointing out the obvious," Marissa says.

"Let them be." Josie rolls her eyes. Then she turns her attention to Indy. "Please don't mind her. She's full of fire, but loyal to a fault. It's nice to meet you."

"Ditto. You live nearby?" Indy asks them.

"No, we both live in California. The timing worked out though. Marissa had a few days off. So I forced her to step away from the office and we came out to visit. Just happened to be during Malloy's birthday, which was a bonus. This one's a workaholic." She points to her girlfriend.

Right then, the front door swings open, revealing Kennedy and Abby, food platters in their hands.

"The party has officially arrived," Kennedy declares.

Kennedy turns heads when she walks into a room. As the CEO of the Boston Gaels, the Major League Baseball team here, she commands a boardroom and, apparently, a living room. She's wearing a form-fitting, black dress, red heels, and her smile radiates as she takes each guest in.

"I'm so glad everyone is here already. Samara and Ashton are parking right now," she announces.

We start grabbing items from their hands and set them in the kitchen. As we're pulling lids off the trays and making sure everything is set up the way the party planners envisioned, River wraps his hands around Kennedy's middle.

"Babe, just curious… if you ordered all this food, why did I see so many empty olive oil containers in the trash?"

"Well, I thought I'd do something nice for you." She pats his forearm, looking up at him.

He gives her a quizzical expression. "What do you mean? Did you make something?"

She moves out of his grasp and leans against the counter. I finish my task and grab a beer from the cooler set out for the guests. I have a feeling I want to listen to whatever Kennedy is about to say. Something about her overly sweet smile gives me pause.

"No, sweetie. You know how Abby's been teaching me how to drive a bit," Kennedy continues.

River nods and I can see he's nervous where this conversation is headed.

Kennedy doesn't drive; her parents died when she was a child in a car accident. She survived the accident and since then, she's avoided learning. She's made it her mission recently to try, so Abby has been taking her out to learn when possible.

"Well, today, when I went down to your truck, the oil was low. So, I filled it up." She shrugs her shoulders.

"Skipper, please tell me you're kidding." River's face falls and I think he might pass out.

"What? And let your precious truck run the risk of getting ruined? Not on my watch. I filled it up for you with premium oil. You're welcome!" She turns around and moves some of the napkins around.

River rubs his hand down his face and looks up at the ceiling; it sounds like he's counting down under his breath. "Kennedy, for the love of all that's holy. Please tell me you're pulling my leg."

Abby chimes in, "River, I helped her out. I made sure she used the pure olive oil. It was the imported kind."

"Abigail!" Clay says. "You didn't!"

Kennedy moves to the trash and grabs an empty container. It's a mega-sized olive oil container and she shows River. "Look, there's nothing to worry about. I only use the best for you. The car's running fine!"

"You drove it?" He pulls on his hair.

"This is fucking fantastic!" Marissa snorts. "See, Josie? I told you this was worth coming to." She grabs a carrot from the tray and takes a bite.

Ashton and his wife Samara walk in, and immediately Sam asks, "What did we miss?"

"Kennedy fucked up my car!" River throws his arms in the air.

I look over at Indy and she's watching in fascination. It's comical really. I'm leaning against the counter, as this whole thing transpires in front of us. I pull Indy into my side and kiss the side of her face.

"We were just saving you a trip to the shop, Riv," Abby says. "I think 'thank you' is what you're meaning to say." She crosses her arms.

"I'm *so* sorry," he says in mock surrender. "Thank you, soon-to-be-sister-in-law-again"—He looks at Abby. Then turns his gaze to Kennedy— "and my adoring future wife, you saved me so much time. But in reality, I think I'll need a new engine!"

He looks over at Clay and groans in frustration. Meanwhile, Kennedy and Abby look nothing but gleeful. Their grins are only getting bigger and that's when I realize this is all a joke for them.

When River looks at them, his irritation doubles. "Why the fuck are you smiling, Kennedy?"

"Because you're so easy to rile up, baby." She laughs.

"Excuse me?"

"We're fucking with you." She throws her head back and laughs maniacally. "It's a trend on social media. Of course we didn't put olive oil in your damn car."

"I fucking swear, Kennedy." He points at her. "You nearly gave me a heart attack." He pinches the spot between his eyes.

"Oh please, you're usually the one exhausting me. I may as well return the favor." Kennedy walks up to him and kisses his cheek. "I love you."

"Yeah, yeah. I love you too." He wraps his arms around her middle, then kisses her nose. "You really fucking scared the shit out of me."

"I know. I enjoyed it," she admits, a smile spreading across her face.

"A little too much, I see," he says.

Indy moves closer to me and whispers, "Is it always like this?"

I look over at her. "Wherever River is, chaos follows." I wink and pull her closer.

We finish helping with the rest of the set-up, and soon we get word that Malloy and Baylee have arrived. Everyone quiets down and the moment Malloy walks through the front door; we jump out to surprise him. The look on his face is priceless. The stunned expression on his face is one I may never forget. It's hard to catch him off-guard, but I think Kennedy and Abby really got him good with this party.

———

"You owe me twenty, Hunter." River sidles up to me.

"Damn it," I say, pulling my wallet out.

"Why?" Indy looks between us, confusion marring her expression.

"You haven't told her?" He eyes me, then looks to her, putting his arm around her shoulders. "Don't worry. I'll corrupt you soon enough. We bet on everything. And your hubby here took a bet he shouldn't have." Pointing his beer bottle in my direction. "He didn't have confidence that I'd keep my mouth shut."

"Because you almost let it slip twice on one shift alone," I confess, tossing my money in his direction.

"But I didn't actually tell him, did I?" River says, his devious smile growing.

Kennedy walks up to us, tossing money to her fiancé. "Damn, I really thought I'd win this one." She rolls her eyes dramatically. "Malloy just confirmed he was genuinely surprised."

I laugh, Indy looks amused by the interaction too.

River puffs out his chest. "See, Indiana, they don't have any faith in me."

"You suck at keeping secrets." Kennedy pins him with a stare.

"Oh really?" River starts to walk toward her, and I hear him say, "Say suck again, Skipper."

I look over at Indy and laugh. "That's pretty much the norm with River. And the betting thing is really something you should expect. He and Clay have always bet on everything. Now we're all addicts."

Malloy and Baylee approach us, and I pull him in for a side hug.

"Happy birthday, old man." I smile as I pull away from him.

"Thanks for coming tonight. I can't believe you guys did this for me." He looks around Kennedy and River's place with awe.

"Baylee, this is Indiana."

Baylee is petite compared to most, but next to Malloy, her small stature is even more evident. She's barely over five feet, with raven hair, and dark eyes. Where Malloy is burly with ginger hair, she's his polar opposite, with a black cat personality to boot. But they complement each other perfectly.

"It's so great to meet you." She smiles. "I've heard so much about you."

"Thanks for having me." Indy shakes her hand. "Malloy, happy birthday. I actually brought you something."

She told me she had something special to gift Malloy for his birthday, but didn't elaborate. I told her she didn't have to bring him anything, but she insisted.

Indy opens her oversized purse and pulls out a perfectly wrapped gift. It's the size of a book, which isn't surprising because of the industry she works in.

"That's very kind of you, but you really didn't have to," Malloy says as he retrieves the item from her hands.

"It's just a little something. I thought you'd appreciate it," she says.

"Should I open it now?" he asks.

"Sure." She looks over at me, her smile ticked up on one side.

Malloy rips the paper, and it is, in fact, a book. The moment he sees the title, he yells, "NO. FUCKING. WAY!" He looks at Indy, then yells for Abby to join us. "Abs, come here! Kenny, look at this."

"I thought I told you not to call me that!" Kennedy retorts.

"Just look at this!" he ignores her protest.

He holds the gift above his head as if it's Simba from *The Lion King* and both women gasp. I can't help but laugh because I'm completely lost.

"How the hell did you get this?" they both say in unison. They try to grab it, but Malloy keeps it high above his head so they can't take it from him.

"I have people in high places." He has a conceited smile on his face.

Both women look over at Indy and she shrugs. "Ana Clevesky had early copies available so I phoned in a favor. Told her she had a fan celebrating a birthday. It's signed too."

He quickly opens the cover to reveal it personalized with his name and her signature. "Holy shit. She knows my name," he whispers the last part reverently.

"Are you fangirling, Malloy?" I ask, containing a laugh.

"Fuck you, Hunter. You don't get it. I'm going to devour this book, Indy. Thank you," he says, closing the cover and running his hand down the ridges of the foiled design of the front.

"Actually, I do get it. Indy used to send me steamy romance novels when I was overseas. They kept me going sometimes. I've just been holding out on you with that little tidbit." He and the girls stare at me, mouths agape. "And that look right there, is exactly why I've never told you."

"You're very welcome, and you should really try a little harder to get him into your book club. He's a fangirl at heart too," Indiana says, her smile growing.

This woman is weaving herself, not only into every portion of my heart, but into my life, and I have never been happier than I am now.

———

"Saturday was a ton of fun," I say as we walk into the station that following Monday.

"Thanks again for coming, man. I can't believe I didn't catch on they were planning it." He laughs as we fall into step together. "Kinda bummed we missed the live premiere of *Love Struck*, though."

I roll my eyes at him, and know he's joking. They taped it and watched it together last night.

From what he was told, he was headed to Kennedy's house to watch the premiere of a new reality show. He didn't think much of it, because that's something they've done in the past. They always get all dressed up for the premieres to pretend they are arriving on the show with the contestants. They're ridiculous.

Malloy is one of the kindest guys I've met. He puts everyone first, and seeing him shown that kind of support and love from those around him is really all he deserves. He's still going through a rough patch with his mom's cancer, but she seems to be feeling a little better these days. It was a good time for him to take a night off.

His wife Baylee has been busy this semester, and I could tell Saturday was the break she needed from all the studying she's been enduring.

It was a relief to see Indy mixing so well with all my friends. I was glad they welcomed her with open arms, not that I had any doubts.

To say this has been a seamless transition is an understatement. I've been waiting for the other shoe to drop, so to speak, and I'm finally letting that unsettled feeling wane. A little…sort of.

I think after losing Georgie, I pushed away everything and everyone I cared about because I didn't know how to handle that type of emotion in my life. I'd never had to deal with love and loss. I was constantly anxious and feeling like my life wouldn't feel right ever again. I never let myself believe it could feel whole despite the pain I endured.

Growing up with parents that showed me little compassion ill-prepared me for a life surrounded by people that want to love me back. Being loved by Jerry and Scarlet even after Georgie was gone, showed me that unconditional love really does exist. Now that I finally have Indy and Noah in my life to love with my whole heart, I've been waiting to see how life can wreak havoc on me again. But I have to let that go. There isn't going to be something bad or negative lurking behind every closed door. And we can get through hard things together, I don't need to push people away as soon as life gets hard.

We can have our happily ever after.

"So, since you have this side-gig posting videos online, does Indy get annoyed with the comments the women make about you and your body when you post workouts without your shirt?" Malloy looks over at me.

I think about it. "She hasn't mentioned it. I know Kalli has shown her the *Fire Hunters* page, but she doesn't seem too bothered by it. She knows that social media group is out of my control and not something I put much weight on. I really love doing the workouts, but no matter what, I only have eyes for her."

"Who's becoming the softie now?" He smiles.

"I'll never be as big a softie as you, Malloy. You're a teddy bear deep down, man. Actually, not deep down, you're a teddy bear on the surface too. You're what "Booktok" would call a golden retriever."

We make our way inside where we're greeted by the previous crew.

Once we get report from them, we begin our shift— dividing our tasks and inspecting our equipment. I've been tasked with Malloy, River, Clay and a few others to check one of our three trucks. Being housed at a larger station in the city, our crew is a decent size.

For spring, it's especially humid yet again. The more we work, the hotter it's getting.

"What the hell is up with the weather today?" River complains.

"Stop whining." Clay laughs as he checks the lights on the truck.

"I can whine all I want, Clay. It's not even ten in the

morning and I need a shower." River wipes at his brow. "Hey, Hunter. When are you going to film again at the station?"

"Why? You craving some attention?" I laugh.

"I think my fans crave me." He winks.

"So humble," Malloy says under his breath as he checks the hoses. I can't help the snort that comes out. No matter how many times I work with River, he always finds a way to entertain us.

"Not sure. For now, I'm set to film away from the station. But when I plan to do another one here, I'll let you know."

"Perfect. I think Lola needs her closeup next time." His smile grows and it's hard not to smile right along with him.

"You really are obsessed with that dog," Clay says.

"Your niece is well-loved by all, Clay." He points at his brother. "You should have more respect." His glare is nothing but serious.

Clay puts his hands up in surrender. "You're right. Sorry."

I look over at Malloy, giving him a look of curiosity if this will get heated or not.

We go about our checklist, making sure the equipment is in working order.

"You know what? Now that I think about it, maybe I should be on Hunter's next live. *Captivating Clay* has a nice ring to it."

"Hey, maybe I'll have you both on my next video," I cut in.

"Really?" They both look over at me, dumbfounded.

"Yeah. I think I'll give you two a nickname together." I look over at them, "*Terrible Twos* sounds appropriate, wouldn't you say?"

Malloy snorts as I hop out of the truck and begin inspecting the tires as I hear the brothers begin bickering once again.

———

The next morning, I grab my stuff, and get ready to leave, but tired is the last thing I am. When I look down at my phone, I see a message from Indy:

INDY

Good morning! What do you say to me skipping work and coming over? 😉

I can't help the smile that forms at the thought of seeing her.

I think my morning just got a lot brighter.

I race home and I take a quick shower. I know I have a few extra minutes as she's going to drop Noah off at school.

I decide to walk outside, the warmth continuing on today. I'm sliding my shirt on, noticing Indiana's car parked on the street. She's talking to someone on the phone, her face turned down in a serious expression.

I keep moving toward her, excited to get her into my arms. You'd think I haven't seen her in weeks.

The minute she steps out of the car, I see the ashen look on her face. It's then I know something is irrevocably wrong.

I start to take my steps at a hurried pace. "Indy, baby, what's wrong? Is it Noah?"

She shakes her head, still unable to form words.

I reach her and grab her face in my hands. "Indiana, tell me what happened." She's worrying me.

"I, um..." Her voice cuts off and her eyes well up with tears. She grabs on to my forearms for support. I'm about to press her for answers when she opens her mouth again and when she speaks, I'm thrown by what she says next.

"I found my biological parents."

CHAPTER 46

Indiana

I **HATE** long nights in the office, and one of our authors is on a big deadline. Noah's home with a babysitter and I just got off FaceTime with him. He's happy as a clam, going on and on about school and what he did at recess with Harley. He's unaffected about me working late, while all I want to do is cuddle up beside him instead of being here right now.

I sit back and stare at my computer. I rub at my eyes, no amount of coffee fixing this headache that's bound to break-through.

A few more hours pass, everyone looking just as wiped as I'm feeling as we go through content in the conference room.

Once we get everything in order, we call it a night. I stand up, realizing it's already after ten. My assistant and I walk toward my office.

"Angela, I'm going to work from home tomorrow. Make sure if anyone needs to get ahold of me, you forward all calls to my cell."

"No problem, Ms. Ranton," she says, following behind me. "Is there anything else you need from me before I head out?"

"Not right now. I'll contact you tomorrow and we can go through a few more items before the Filmore meeting on Thursday." The up-and-coming author is one I've been looking forward to connecting with.

"Sounds good. Have a good night." Angela leaves my office and I finish gathering my things. I make sure I have everything I need to work from home and head out a few minutes later.

Walking to my car, I start to mentally plan out my morning. Maybe I could work from Tyler's place instead of my own. Once I drop Noah off at school, I could take my laptop to his house and do everything there instead.

I crave his presence now. For someone that was wanting to divorce Tyler Hunter not long ago, now all I want to do is blanket myself in him. I'm realizing he is everything my life was lacking. And I realize Noah agrees from the way he lights up each time Ty enters the room.

In all honesty, we both radiate happiness at the sight of my husband. We've been taking things slow when it comes to Noah, but behind closed doors, we pick right up from this starting point that we've been bound as husband and wife for more than a decade. I won't pretend it doesn't make my heart race.

The drive home is quick due to the late hour. Walking in, I note how quiet it is. My babysitter, Evette, is sitting on the couch with a cup of tea and a book.

"Hey," she says, placing a bookmark and standing.

"Hi," I whisper. "Sorry. My night was a lot longer than I anticipated."

"It's fine. Noah went right to bed. He's a good kid." She waves me off.

"That's sweet of you to say. I didn't anticipate it taking up so much of my time tonight. Thanks again," I say. "Did dinner work out?"

"Yes. It arrived and Noah loved it," she says, putting her

mug in the dishwasher. "He said Hunter makes a better burger though." She looks at me expectantly, hoping I'll give her the scoop.

"Hunter is my boyfriend," I tell her. It's hard to contain my smile.

"I picked up on that from the way Noah talked about him." I expect her to press further, but she pats my hand, then gives me a wink. "That boy seems to really like him."

I smile brightly and nod. "Yeah, he does. They get along really well."

"That's good. He had some worksheets to do for school, so we got those done. Other than that, it was an easy night. Hopefully you can relax."

She gathers her things and starts to head for the door. I follow her, thanking her for everything.

Once I say my goodbyes, I grab my phone and see a missed call from Kalli. Even though we work together, I haven't seen her since this morning when we had our routine coffee together.

I head to Noah's room and peek my head in, seeing him sleeping soundly. I let him be, not wanting to disturb him.

Looking back at my phone, I decide to call Kalli back in case it's an emergency.

"Hey," she answers. She doesn't sound upset.

"Hi. You okay?" I ask.

"Yeah. All good. I wanted to see how the night was. I know you had to stay late. Did you just get home?"

"Ugh. Yes. You know I hate when I have late nights like this." I try to avoid it because of Noah, but it's part of the job. I go through the cupboard to grab a glass to pour some wine. I need to unwind a bit. "Aren't you usually trying to go to bed about now?"

Since having her daughter, Kalli is all about sleeping on the earlier side. This is considered late for her.

"I think Vivienne is teething, she woke up an hour ago.

She's finally back down, but now I have a second wind. Julian is snoring and you know if I don't fall asleep before he starts, then I can't even think about sleeping. I thought I'd text and check in."

"I'm sorry. I remember those days when Noah was teething. It's no fun. Oh, I won't be at work tomorrow, so raincheck on our morning coffee together?" I grab a bottle of my favorite wine.

"Oh really? And where will you be? Riding some firefighter?" I can practically see her smirk through the phone.

"Maybe?" I smile.

"Such a dirty girl. I approve." She laughs.

"I knew you would. I still need to ask Tyler if he's okay with me going over there. He's on shift right now, but I'll text him in the morning. I don't want to bother him while he's focused on saving lives and all." I pour my wine and move to the couch.

Taking off my shoes, I sit down and Darth makes his way over to sit by my side. For a cat, he's quite cuddly.

"I guess things are getting serious?" she asks.

"I don't think there was ever a time it wasn't serious with Tyler and I." I look toward the stairs to ensure I don't have any little ears eavesdropping then whisper, "We're married, Kalli. It's hard to keep things anything but serious, you know? We're either all in or not."

"I get that. I love how you were all 'We're getting divorced!'" she says that with a gruff voice and I laugh. "And now you're all in love with the guy. Way to put your foot down, Indy."

"To be fair, I was lied to. And I was pissed. Not sure I was out of love with the man."

"Sure. But I can give you a hard time. What a one-eighty you did in a short amount of time, though," she chides.

"I know. I'm still trying to make sense of it myself. I think

I simply never stopped loving him. I think I convinced myself that I hated him, but the reality of it is I absolutely loved him to my core. Every single person I dated after was an attempt to replace the feelings I had for him. And I never succeeded. No one felt as impactful as Tyler did in my life."

There's silence on the other end of the line.

"Kalli, did you fall asleep?" I swear, if she's sleeping while I just divulged my feelings, I will lose it.

"No. That's just really sweet."

"Well, it's true. It doesn't mean I don't have feelings about him lying to me; and I've expressed that to him. I've made it clear that what he did was wrong and he understands that his lie caused a ripple effect on my life. But we've grown."

"I'm glad you've found your happily ever after, Indy. You deserve it."

"Thanks, Kalli," I tell her.

"I'm also glad you're not with Roger. He was so damn boring." She chuckles into the phone.

"Yes, we've established the fact Roger was as fascinating as watching paint dry." All I hear is a bark of laughter in my ear.

———

I just dropped off Noah at school. It was a rough morning today. He was dragging for some reason. Getting him out of bed was a nightmare. He has days like that and today was one of them. Even getting him to agree on an outfit for school felt like an uphill battle. And he wears a uniform. Apparently choosing from the standard green, red, or navy was a tough choice. The joys of nearly-six-year-olds.

His birthday is approaching, so I chose to distract him on the drive to school by bringing up his plans. That seemed to brighten his mood a bit. We decided to do a party at the local park, with a baseball theme. That's easy enough, although the weather is already horribly humid. Hopefully on whatever day we plan it, the shade will provide ample support.

I texted Tyler before heading out to drop Noah off, asking if I could hang out with him today. He responded saying he was all for it.

Luckily, now that I've left the school, traffic has improved, and my GPS shows I'll be at Tyler's fairly soon. I'm listening to a podcast when I get a call through my Bluetooth speaker.

I look down to see it's Theo, the private investigator I hired to find my biological parents a few months back.

"Good morning, Theo. How are you?" I say.

"Good morning, Indiana." His gruff voice greets me.

"Do you have some updates for me? I haven't heard from you in some time." Theo warned me since I first spoke to him, it's usually quiet until he has news for me. I was antsy in the beginning, but since I've been consumed by reconnecting with Tyler, I haven't really put much thought into locating my biological parents.

"Actually, I do. Do you have a moment?"

"Yeah. I'm just driving right now," I tell him.

"You sure you don't want to call me back? We can do this via video call if that's better." He sounds hesitant.

"Theo, it's fine. I've got a packed week ahead. I want to know what you've found out. Have you been able to get some information?" I can hear the hope in my own voice.

"Alright, I was able to unseal your records and discover the names of your parents and their most current address."

I feel the uptick to my heart rate as he says this.

"Okay..." I feel the shakiness in my tone.

"Are you sure you want to go over this now while you're driving?" Theo confirms.

"Of course. It's fine, Theo," I say on a nervous laugh.

"I found out you were born at Boston General," he begins.

That shocks me to hear that I was born right here in Boston. "I'm from Boston?"

"Yes."

"What small world," I say on a sigh. I'm nearing Tyler's place so I slow my pace as I continue my drive down the residential street.

"Your parents were young when they had you. They were both in high school; they were sixteen years old when you were born."

I arrive at Tyler's place and park, my hands trembling as I grip the steering wheel. My mind is still reeling at the possibility that I could be closer to my biological parents than I ever imagined.

"Theo, are you saying my parents are here? In Boston? Now?" I ask.

"It's a possibility from what I gathered. The last known address I have for them is 1585 Quixley Avenue," he says.

I look down at my map and I can feel the blood drain from my face. Theo's about to continue, but I finish the sentence for him.

"In Cambridge?" I say.

"You know it?" he asks.

"What are their names?" I ask instead.

"Sycamore. Am I missing something?" Theo sounds hesitant.

I look over at the house I'm parked next to. It can't be. The coincidence in all of this is just too much.

"Theo, what are their first names?" I ask, and I can hear the thrumming of my heart in my ears.

"Jerry and Scarlet," he finishes, but I feel like I knew that answer before he ever said it.

It feels like the world around me is spinning. "Did you happen to do any other digging? Do I have any siblings?"

"As a matter of fact you did, a brother; but I'm sorry Indiana, he passed away." He sighs. Theo knows Bryce died and now he has to tell me another sibling has passed before I've ever met him.

"Was his name George?" I ask.

"Okay, Indiana. Who's informing who now?" I can hear the confusion in his tone.

"Let's just say, I think my life has played a sick twist on me." I take a few deep breaths as I see Tyler walking over from my periphery. "Theo, thanks for your call. I'll be in touch. I need a moment to digest the information for now."

"Sure. I'll send over the information we just discussed," he says and we end our call.

Somehow, I keep my tears at bay and exit the car. I have no clue how I look, but I feel like the contents of my breakfast might reappear.

When I turn to face Tyler and see the way he's looking at me, it's clear that he can tell something isn't right. I don't know what I'm going to say. This entire time we've been more connected than ever. He's not only known my brother, but he's been interacting with my biological parents.

He takes hurried steps toward me and grabs my cheeks, looking into my eyes. It takes everything in me not to breakdown.

"Indy, baby, what's wrong? Is it Noah?"

I shake my head, but my heart feels like it's going to shatter in a whole new way. I have so many questions and all I want to do is fall to the ground.

"Indiana, tell me what happened."

"I, um…" I feel the tears in my eyes and I grab onto him for support. "I found my biological parents."

I see a smile breakthrough his face and the relief is palpable for him. I wish I felt the same way.

"Indy, that's amazing sweetheart. You must feel such comfort now, right? Did you just find out?"

He's still looking into my eyes and I wish I felt the way he does. He feels reassurance while all I feel is confusion. Where he feels like floating, I feel like a weight has been set on my shoulders.

I nod, the words not forming.

"Why do you look so sad?" He pulls me into his chest, kissing the top of my head. "Is it bad news? Did something happen to them?"

I don't answer, just breathing his scent. He just showered and I'm cherishing it right now. His warmth is centering me while I feel like I might fall. I don't know if this will change things between us. Losing Georgie was catastrophic for him years ago.

What if he leaves when I reveal this news to him now? What if he lets me go because this is all too much?

"Can we go inside please?" I need to sit down. I can't do this standing outside where everyone can see us.

Tyler looks confused, but he doesn't argue as he draws me closer to settle into his side. Once inside the house, he pulls a chair out at the kitchen table for me. I sit down, the shock still overwhelming my thoughts.

"Indiana, you're scaring me. What's going on? What am I missing?" He moves a chair in front of mine, putting his hands on my knees and squeezing them.

I look down to where he's grasping me and I just hope he's still intact after I confess what I've learned. It's surreal to think we've been connected for so many years, and this added layer that's been hidden without either of us knowing won't destroy us.

What if I hadn't started looking for my real parents? I haven't even started to deal with the fact that I know who my parents are and I can meet them. There are so many parts to this right now.

I look over at the table and the lump in my throat grows. Is this where they had family dinners? Why did Georgie get them and I didn't? I feel a tear slip and that's when I feel

Tyler's thumb swipe it away.

I swing my gaze back to meet his.

"You're breaking my heart, baby. What is it?" he says and the look of pain reflected in his eyes guts me.

"My parents," I say and a sob breaks loose, "live at this address."

CHAPTER 47

Tyler

I FEEL like the room is spinning. That is not what I expected Indy to tell me when she said she had information about her biological parents. I can't help the way my face twists in confusion.

"I'm sorry. What?" It's all I can muster in response.

"I know it's crazy. Before you and I reconnected, I hired a private investigator to look into unsealing my adoption records. Apparently, it's pretty damn hard. He called me when I was driving over here this morning and revealed my parents gave me up when they were teens."

She looks down at her hands, twisting them as if she can't settle down. "I thought maybe it was a misunderstanding or maybe this was an old address for them. But Theo—that's the name of the PI—he said their names and that's when I knew. He said their names are…"

"Jerry and Scarlet," I say.

"Yes. Jerry and Scarlet Sycamore. And that they had another child named George. It all came together."

Her tears are falling freely now, and I can't lie, I'm fighting to contain my own emotions. But she needs me to keep my composure at a time like this.

How could Jerry and Scarlet put Indiana up for adoption, only to have George a few years later and keep him? I have so many questions of my own. I can only imagine the number of questions filtering through Indy's mind at a time like this.

"Please don't leave me," Indy whispers.

I halt the endless thoughts racing through my mind when I hear Indy's words and look up at her. "What?"

"Don't use this as an excuse to leave." She looks so scared as she confesses what she fears most.

"Why would I leave?" I finally say, foregoing my chair and kneeling by her side.

"Because when things got hard last time, you did exactly that," she says softly.

"Indy, I told you before. I wasn't in the right state of mind years ago. I was traumatized by what I witnessed. I got help; I'm stronger now. I did the work to get where I am today. I want to be everything for you and Noah. Always."

More tears stream down her cheeks and she nods, which I assume means that was the answer she wanted to hear. I grab her hand and we move to sit together on the couch. I pull her onto my lap, and she buries her head into the crook of my neck. I can only assume she's experiencing a feeling of relief with this weight off her shoulders; yet she's unearthed a new set of questions regarding the why behind her adoption.

Once I feel her body settle, I pull her away slightly so our eyes can meet. Even with her eyes puffy from the tears, she's still the most beautiful woman I've ever seen. I wipe away the stray tears that continue to fall.

It's ironic how years ago, I pushed her away because I didn't want to hurt her further. I pushed her away because of Georgie's death, yet she was one of the closest people to him without knowing it. He's been close to me this whole time.

I'm staring at Indy under a new lens now. "You look like him," I tell her.

She takes in a breath. "I do?"

"I never really noticed it before. I never imagined there was a connection, but now that I know, I see it. In the shape of your nose, the color of your hair, but most of all, the color of your eyes," I say, kissing her temple.

I move my hands along her face, admiring her beauty, but also loving that she has a connection to a family that has become such a huge part of me.

"Georgie had the same greenish-brown eyes as you. I guess you both got a mix of your parents. Jerry has brown eyes, and Scarlet's are a vibrant green."

Her chin quivers.

"I've never looked like anyone around me before." A small smile appears on her face. "Do you think they'll want to talk to me?" She looks so small. She looks down again, almost like she's nervous to know my answer.

I bring my forefinger under her chin to bring her gaze back to meet mine. "They are the sweetest people I've ever met. I have a feeling they'll want to get to know their daughter."

"Then why did they give me up and not George?" She looks so defeated.

I can't say I blame her for wondering. The same question is going through my own mind, but I know there's likely a good explanation.

"We can sit here and wonder until we're blue in the face, but I think we should talk to them," I tell her.

"I'm scared. I feel like I did years ago when I found out I was adopted." She wraps her arms around herself and stares off into the room.

This house holds so many memories for a family that should be hers, yet never got to be.

"I won't pretend to know what you're feeling right now. But I will say this: don't assume you know the whole story. Let's reach out to them, alright?"

She looks back at me and nods. "I don't know what to do.

Should I call them? I mean, it feels weird. What if they never wanted me to find them?"

I blow out a breath. "What does your gut tell you to do?"

"I think seeing them for the first time in person would be the best thing. I don't want to see them on a video call. I want them to talk to me face to face if that's something they're willing to do."

"Want me to reach out to them to come back?" I ask her.

"You'd do that for me?" she looks surprised.

"Indy, I'd do anything for you. Haven't you figured that out yet?" I move my hands through her hair and lightly kiss her on the lips.

"What will you say?" She looks nervous.

"I'll have to say something about you. I can't just tell them to come home with no explanation of why."

"Okay. Yeah, that makes sense." She nods, but she still seems unsettled.

She moves her body to hug me and I wrap my arms around her. "I'm scared, Ty."

"I know, baby. But you're not alone," I reassure her.

We sit together as I make a call to Scarlet and Jerry. As expected, there is shock and a lot of tears on the other end. I look over to see Indy biting her nails, a habit she had when we were kids.

Once I'm done explaining everything to them, Jerry speaks first and I hear the emotion in his strained voice.

Only three words come out: "We're coming home."

With that, I turn to Indiana and tell her she'll be meeting her parents in a matter of days. She wraps her arms around my neck and cries quietly. I think it's in relief, but also holds some apprehension for what's to come.

CHAPTER 48

Indiana

"I'LL BE RIGHT NEXT to you the entire time," Tyler reassures me for what feels like the millionth time as he parks his truck along the curb.

I'm looking outside the window at the house where I know my biological parents are inside waiting for me. I only nod in acknowledgment. I can't help the butterflies that are multiplying inside my stomach. The anticipation is killing me.

It's been four days since that phone call from Theo. Due to the stress of the last few days, I've had a Crohn's flare up, requiring me to stay home this week to recover. Kalli has been worried about me since I received the news, calling Tyler to make sure there isn't anything else she can do. I've been restless waiting for Jerry and Scarlet to arrive. Aside from his shift two days ago, Ty has been by my side providing support in whatever way possible.

Noah has been none the wiser in all this, having the best time with Tyler at our place, cooking and playing at the park after school. They've been watching movies, making me dinner, and playing board games. School is out soon, meaning his birthday is fast approaching. Aside from sending invitations out, I've barely done a thing. Once this meeting happens, I need to get things done for Noah's celebration. I can't drop the ball for my sweet boy.

Tyler cuts the engine and we're left with silence. "Indy, baby, look at me." He grabs my hand and squeezes.

At night, he's held me and let me feel the comfort I need while I've processed the emotional roller coaster this news has hit me with. I truly believed Tyler was going to freak out and run away, but I didn't put enough weight on the fact that this was going to hit me hard.

After Tyler hung up with Jerry and Scarlet, a wave of emotions washed over me and I felt overwhelmed with how this was going to change my life. I don't know if I'm prepared for the explanation they're going to give me as to why they gave me up. Add to that, why they chose to keep George only a few years later.

"Come on. You can do this." He picks up my hand and kisses my knuckles. I look over at him and give him a weak smile.

"What if I can't?" I ask him, my voice cracking at the end.

"You've been through so much worse, Indy," he tells me. "I know you can do it. Plus, you're not going through any of this alone, remember? You've got me and Noah every step of the way."

I nod, looking down.

He drops my hand and grabs my cheeks with his palms, leaning over to drop his forehead to mine.

His eyes settle on me and all I feel is lost in his gaze. "Indy, you are the strongest woman I know. Whatever happens in there, it won't change that. No matter what you find out today, you'll leave with answers about your past. But it won't change who you are. You've grown to be a capable, beautiful, and strong person. That's what everyone sees because that's what you are. Noah sees it, and so do I. Don't let their decisions decades ago make you feel otherwise."

Just like he did eleven years ago, Tyler reminds me that I can do so much more than I give myself credit for. I smile and bring my lips to his. At first the kiss starts softly, then I deepen our connection.

"I'm glad I married you all those years ago," I tell him after I pull away.

He weaves his hands through my hair, stealing another brief kiss, before he opens his door. He makes his way around the truck and opens my passenger door, extending his hand. I take it and step out of the car, smoothing my dress.

When I take a breath, hoping to calm my nerves, I look over at Ty and give him a small nod. No matter what, today I'll get the answers I've been seeking regarding my birth parents. If I get to form a relationship with them, that will be a bonus.

Since finding out this connection with Jerry and Scarlet, Tyler has been nothing but attentive with me. He's been dividing his time between staying here at the house and being with me. Luckily, he picked me up today to accompany me here, so I don't have to confront my biological parents on my own.

We clasp our hands and start walking toward the front door. We're about to ring the doorbell when the front door swings open. A gentleman greets us, and Tyler's face breaks out in a reserved smile.

Tyler stands beside me, his hand on my lower back, letting me feel his strength, as I walk toward the only two people that can give me answers. The man at the door has his focus solely on me. A woman is behind him, her eyes watching my every step. My breath hitches as I stare at the only people I've ever met that are biologically related to me.

"Hi," I say in a whispered tone.

"Hi, Indiana," Jerry says.

"Indiana," Scarlet says, moving forward so she's in full view.

They both look tired, maybe from travel, but I'd assume from days lacking sleep. This news has caused anxiety for them too.

"Jerry, Scarlet, can we come in?" Tyler interjects.

"Of course," they're still staring at me, but move out of our way for us to pass through. "Why don't we sit at the kitchen table?"

"Sounds good," Ty grabs my hand and interlaces our fingers.

We make our way through the house and I know how awkward this has been for them. There's a layer of tension, excitement, and apprehension as we walk to the table.

"Can I get anyone something to drink or eat?" Scarlet offers.

"Why don't I grab some waters and you three sit down." Tyler looks at me and I give him a slight nod.

I move to sit down, the awkwardness settling back between us at the table. Tyler brings the drinks to us, then rests his hand on my leg, which has started to shake nervously.

"How was your trip home?" Ty begins. I notice he's trying to calm me down.

"Everything was pretty good. I thought they were going to lose our luggage, but, in the end, that wasn't the case." Scarlet fiddles with the side of her cup.

From the way the two of them look at me cautiously, they're just as nervous as I am. Even though I'm pushing thirty, I feel like a child in this moment. It's like I'm a little girl; my parents sitting across from me, waiting to say something to explain my behavior. Except, I'm waiting for them to say something to explain theirs.

Looking at the two of them, I realize what a mix of the two of them I am.

Tyler said George had a funny personality, always making jokes and trying to make the guys around him laugh. In all the pictures, his grin is wide. There was something welcoming about him in all the stills I got to see. My younger brother was in his combat uniform and fatigues in the photos Tyler showed me. As I walked through the house after finding out my relation to him, I appreciated the photos with a new perspective. But sitting across from Jerry and Scarlet now, I see them in a whole new light. Now that I'm sitting across from Jerry, I can tell George favored our father.

"George looked a lot like you," I say.

Jerry smiles, his eyes quickly moving to Tyler, then back to me. "Yes, everyone says that." He looks down at the table. "George may have looked like me, but he was one hundred percent Scarlet." He looks over at his wife.

I can't contain it any longer and I blurt out the question that's been nagging me the entire time. "Why did you give me up? Was I not good enough?"

The small smiles that both were holding drop and I can see the disappointment push through their features.

Jerry exhales and I can tell whatever pain he's holding is let go in that breath. "Absolutely not. I know how it must seem, but—"

I interrupt him, "You gave me up then had George. I need to understand why. It makes no sense to me, after just four years you'd keep him but let me go. Explain it to me."

I see Scarlet and Jerry look at one another, then turn their attention back to me. I can see the pain radiating across their faces.

Scarlet takes a deep breath, looking down at the table and smoothing her hands on the lacquered wood.

"Jerry and I are high school sweethearts, but our parents weren't too happy we were dating." She looks over at him and gives him a small smile that holds so much love. He grabs her hand, and she seems to find the courage to keep going.

"We started dating freshman year and got pregnant when

I was only fifteen with you; I gave birth when I was sixteen. Both our parents deemed we were too young to be parents. We had no means at the time to go off and get jobs. We tried to prove we could, but we knew nothing about life."

She hangs her head and I see her swipe at a stray tear on her cheek.

"Scar and I wanted so badly to take you away and start our little family, but we also wanted what was best for you. So, we listened to our families. They told us you'd be given to a family that could give you so much more than we ever could. We were promised it was going to be an open adoption. We were so naive to the process, Indiana. All in all, we were ill-informed." He sighs, running his hand through his salt and pepper hair.

"Once a few weeks had passed, and I had recovered a bit postpartum, I had asked if I could write a letter to your adoptive parents to request a picture. That's when I discovered it was, in fact, a closed adoption. I broke down. I went through a pretty dark time after that. We both did." She looks at Jerry, more tears streaming down her cheeks. "The way my parents lied to us regarding your adoption was unforgivable. I tried finding you, hiring people, but I had no luck on my own. I just waited, hoping one day you'd come looking for us."

It's then I feel the moisture on my own cheek coming down, the tears falling freely at her words. I try to swipe them away, but there's no use. New tears are replacing the old. I feel Tyler bring his hand over my knee and squeeze.

"We got pregnant with George a few years later and we were out from under the scrutiny of our parents by then. We had jobs and were living in a small apartment in the city. Not a day went by that we didn't think of you," Jerry explains.

"Did George know about me?" I ask, curious if my brother knew he had a sister out in the world.

Scarlet shakes her head, swiping at the tears that fall, and I feel the bile creeping in all over again. "No, and please let me explain." I have the urge to pull myself out of my chair and walk out of this house. I feel unwanted all over again—discarded. George was their golden child, too perfect to be tarnished even by the knowledge that I existed.

"How can you say you thought of me every day since letting me go, when you never even told George you had another child before him?"

"Because my mother made me feel ashamed every single day after I had you. I thought about fighting back and contesting the adoption after what she had done. But she verbally berated me after you were born. I wasn't even sure Jerry and I would make it. I'm surprised we did after the emotional turmoil she put me through. I was left feeling belittled and emotionally frail.

"At one point, I thought you were better off without me, without your own mother. And, in some twisted way, I didn't want Georgie to judge us if we told him. Jerry didn't think he would once he was old enough, but my mother's hateful words just kept echoing in my head." She has to pause to catch her breath, her sobs are so powerful. Jerry wraps his arms around her, whispering into her ear to comfort her.

I feel her pain in my chest as I hear sorrow through her words.

Jerry carries on the story, "Scarlet's mother was not the kindest woman. Out of everyone, she was the most vicious. Her words cut the deepest. And she made it very clear she didn't want Scarlet's pregnancy to impact the image of the family. She kept Scarlet hidden towards the end of the pregnancy, making Scar finish up school with tutors and such. Emotionally, Scarlet was a shell of herself." He kisses her temple and the love the two of them have after so many years together is commendable.

He continues, "When Scarlet told me she was pregnant again, I hate to admit—I was terrified. When we couldn't find a way to connect with your adoptive parents, it left both of us empty. But Scarlet was heartbroken in a way I never imagined. So having George was something I made sure our parents weren't able to touch, especially her mother. I was very protective of her. And when George was born, we stayed far away from our families. We stayed in the city, making sure we made do with our own money and succeeded independently from our families' wealth."

"Everything we have in this life is from our own successes. As much as my parents and Jerry's come from an affluent background, we never wanted any part of it. It felt dirty after what they did to you. Our lives were never the same after they took you from us." Scarlet looks broken after her revelation.

"You were a piece of us that we lost all those years ago, Indiana." She looks at me and I feel the pain etched all over her face. "And now we've said goodbye to your brother, someone you'll never get to meet, and someone we'll never get a chance to see again. But the fact we get to connect with one of our babies again is a gift we'll never take for granted. That is if you'll accept us in your life."

I see Tyler swipe at his face in my periphery and it's then I realize there isn't a dry eye in this room right now. We've all been affected by the events of this family. The tidal wave from years ago has brought us here and now we're weaved together in this incredible way. I'm not quite sure how it's happened, but I feel like it's somehow all meant to be.

"So where do we go from here?" I ask them.

Scarlet moves her hand through her hair that is a similar shade to mine, although hers has a few more grays due to her age.

"Indiana, why did you come looking for us?" she asks.

"I wanted to find a connection to someone that was related to me," I answer honestly. "My whole adult life I've felt like I was walking alone. I've been looking for you off and on since I found out I was adopted. I wanted to see if there were people out there that I had roots with." I look at Tyler and squeeze his hand in mine.

"If you're still looking for that connection, we'd like to be that for you," Jerry says. "We know it might take time, but we'd like nothing more. We see this as an unexpected gift."

It's hard to wrap my head around the fact that Tyler has been a connection between us for years, yet we had no idea.

All this has been so much to digest. From the minute I sat in that emergency room and found out I was adopted, I feel like my life has so many unforeseeable turns. Now I'm sitting here, finally meeting my biological parents and I have this big decision to make.

I can hold a grudge, something I did for so long with my adoptive parents and it continues to be exhausting and painful. I don't want to do that anymore in my life. I want to move forward and build something new and beautiful with these two people. I'm tired of hurting and building walls.

Since I've brought Tyler back in my life, I've gotten to feel what it's like to heal again. I didn't get to meet them sooner because I didn't have the financial means to do so on my own, but now they're here with me and I don't want to miss another second letting them in to form new memories in my future.

"I think having you be a part of my life sounds like a beautiful way forward."

I stretch my hands out and they both grasp on. Looking into faces that resemble mine feels like a connection I've longed for over a decade and I feel a flutter of hope in my chest at the possibility of finally feeling like I belong.

CHAPTER 49

Indiana

"I **TOLD** you he'd have a fun time," Tyler wraps his arms around my waist and kisses my neck.

I can't help the laugh that escapes as I lean into him. The kids are running around the park as the sugar high kicks in from the cake they just consumed. I kept the party simple, opting for a piñata, having Tyler play baseball with the kids and some other games around the bases.

The way Noah is running around laughing, it seems to be a success. "You're right. I was nervous for nothing. I just wanted everything to be perfect."

"And your parents didn't have a coronary over us being together." Tyler laughs when he looks at me. I can't help but narrow my eyes in his direction.

Earlier today, when my parents called to wish Noah a happy birthday, Tyler walked by and my mom caught sight of him in the background. That prompted the discussion of our relationship right then and there. It wasn't how I wanted the reveal to go, but I'm glad it's out in the open. I'm not a child anymore, so I don't know why I care about my parents' approval.

Since discovering the truth about my biological parents,

Jerry and Scarlet have stayed in town, prompting Tyler to stay with Noah and I quite often. More and more, his things are starting to add up at my place. I'm beginning to think we should probably have a discussion about him making this a permanent stay.

"Hey, I have a bit of a surprise for Noah," Tyler says as he kisses my cheek and heads in the direction of the parking lot.

I look behind me where he's taken off. I see Kennedy walking up and she's not alone. Standing next to her is another gentleman who's wearing a baseball cap and a Boston Gael's shirt.

What is Tyler up to?

I hear a mom squeal as she sidles up beside me. "Oh my gosh. Is that Nash Ripley?"

"Who?" I look at her, confused.

"You're kidding me, right?" I swear, she could have hearts in her eyes right now.

I swing my head back to the man in question, still clueless as to who's walking over.

One of the kids catches sight of the gentleman and starts running toward him. "Nash Ripley? Is that really you?" The kid starts jumping and pointing. "Noah, you know Nash Ripley?!"

Noah is playing with a baseball and the moment he sees this Nash person, his jaw falls open and said baseball falls to the ground while he's still as a statue. How am I completely lost right now?

Tyler makes his way over with Kennedy and, apparently, Nash Ripley, while I'm still connecting the dots. "Hi. What's going on that you've stunned my kid?" I laugh.

"Indiana, I'd like you to meet Nash Ripley, the Boston Gaels's star pitcher," Kennedy says with a bright smile. "We thought it would be a fun surprise for the kids and for my favorite six-year-old." She winks in my direction, and I'm stunned. We both know she doesn't even know Noah and I want to cry that she would do such a thing for my little guy.

Noah must reboot because he finally comes running over, smiling from ear-to-ear. "Hi, I'm Noah."

"Hi, Noah. I'm Nash. I hear you're turning six years old," Nash puts his fist out for Noah to give him a fist bump.

"Yeah, I am!" Noah's enthusiasm is palpable.

"Well, what do ya say we get out there and play ball. I hear you love the game." Nash starts walking out, looking at some of the other kids, all of them hanging on his every word. The moms are following, drooling over this person I've never heard of.

Tyler saunters up next to me; I link my arm through his. "How did you pull this off?" I whisper.

"You see, I'm sort of in love with Noah's mom, so I'll do anything to see her smile," he whispers.

"Ah, well, you're winning major points," I laugh softly.

"You think I'll get lucky later?" he whispers into my ear.

"Oh, most definitely." I waggle my brows in his direction. "Maybe even twice."

"Totally worth it then," he lightly smacks my ass as we follow slowly behind everyone.

———

"Goodnight sweet boy," I say, as I close Noah's door.

Before I leave his room, I can already tell his eyes are closing. He's exhausted after the fun-filled day he had. His party was beyond successful. He'll remember this birthday for years to come. Not sure we can top it, but we'll have fun trying.

I'm about to head downstairs to look for Tyler, when I hear the water running in the bathroom. I decide to leave any cleanup we have in the rest of the house for later and opt for joining Ty.

I walk in the main bedroom and lock the door, stripping my clothes as I walk toward the bathroom door. I open it, noting the steam throughout the small space. Tyler is humming a song I can't distinguish and it makes me smile.

My body is vibrating to be touched by him and I haven't even caught sight of his naked body yet. He hasn't sensed me in the bathroom, so I open the door and step in, startling him.

"I thought I'd join you and maybe start my thank you on my knees." I smile, biting my lip with mock innocence.

He moves his wet hair from his face. "You won't get any complaints from me." His eyes roam my naked body and I love the way he takes me in as if it's the first time he's seen me. His dick is growing in front of me and I love that I pull this reaction from him. "You look fucking edible, Indy."

"I could say the same about you." It never gets old, watching his muscles on display like this, with that defined V and the happy trail leading to his cock. I lick my lips, ready to have my mouth filled with him.

He brings his hand down and strokes himself, using his other hand to reach out and caress my breast, fiddling with my nipple and piercing. It pulls a whimper from me.

"I can't get enough of this body of yours, wife," he says, then pulls me closer and locks his lips on mine. I open for him, our touch desperate.

When he pulls away, he asks me, "When are you going to let me make it official again?"

I look at him in confusion.

"I want a ring on that finger, Indy. I want the world to know you're mine." He uses my hair to pull my head back and plants open-mouthed kisses down my neck, my hands raking through his hair.

"I'm already yours," I remind him. I push him against the tile wall, taking control of the situation. I had a little plan when I came in here, and I don't want to lose track of it now.

I start to drag my tongue down the column of his neck

and down the center of his chest. I bring my lips to one of his nipples and then to the opposite side. I bite down, an audible groan bouncing off the walls of the bathroom. It urges me on knowing I do this to him.

"You dirty girl of mine," he taunts.

"You like me dirty," I say back.

I continue my descent and lick, using my nails on the sides of his body while my tongue trails down his center until I'm on my knees.

I stroke his cock, pulling a moan from him. His head falls back against the tile, and his eyes roll back. I love watching him lose control, all while I hold this power over him. I bring my mouth over the head of his dick, and he lets out a curse.

I keep my eyes on him while I take him further. He pulls my hair off my face as the water is falling around us. I feel him at the back of my throat, and I spread my legs wider. I'm so fucking turned on right now.

I start bobbing my head, setting a rhythm, and his eyes take on a look of pure lust as he simply looks down at me. He keeps telling me how beautiful I am, but soon his words drop off, and his breathing gets heavier.

"Fuck, Indy, just like that," he says, his hips moving and I know he's getting close.

I keep sucking him off, determined to see him lose himself. "If you don't stop, I'm going to come."

I don't relent, my mouth on a mission to see him combust. I use my hand to start playing with his balls. His body tenses and I watch him simply let go. I feel that power while he's at my disposal.

Once he's slowed down, he pulls out of me, and helps me up, and brings my lips to his, kissing me hard. He proceeds to push my body against the tiles.

"You are fucking incredible," he says, grabbing my hands and placing them above my head. "Now, I'm going to make *you* see stars." And he does just that with his head between my legs.

CHAPTER 50

Tyler

HOURS LATER, we're lying in bed, sated while Indy rests on her head on my chest. I love feeling her hand wander along my chest, savoring that zap of energy that coasts along my skin as we connect.

"Ty, do you ever think about having kids?" She moves to rest her chin on my chest and looks at me.

I move her hair from her face. "Yeah, of course I do."

"So, the way your parents were never pushed you to not want them?" she asks, and my mind wanders to my horrible upbringing and how I would never impose that on my own children, including Noah.

"No. I mean, there may have been a time I was concerned I'd be like them, but I don't worry about it anymore."

She smiles brightly up at me.

"I take it that's what you wanted to hear?" I smile back.

"Well, yeah. My ovaries might be relieved to hear that." She returns her cheek back down on my chest.

I can't help the chuckle that escapes. "I've always liked the name Jonas."

"Um, veto," she says almost immediately.

"Why?" I protest.

"Indiana and Jonas? Think about it." A long silence stretches out.

"Let me spell it out for you. It's too close to our names being linked to Indiana Jones—no thanks. Again, veto."

I look at her for an extra moment then start laughing. "Okay. I hadn't thought about it, but yeah, I guess that wouldn't be good."

She keeps staring at me, not amused. "Imagine River with those names together. We'd never hear the end of it. No thanks."

"Yeah, you're right. Okay, okay." I run my hands down her naked back.

She's almost asleep when I speak again.

"Indiana?"

"Yeah?"

"Happy anniversary, baby," I tell her.

She looks over at the clock, realizing that today marks the day that we got married eleven years ago. It's sort of serendipitous Noah was born so close to our wedding anniversary. This tiny little family of ours coming together, making our hearts whole again, something neither of us could have seen coming after years being apart.

"Happy anniversary, Tyler." She pulls my body closer to her, sealing my lips to hers.

"If I've done one thing right in my life, it was being at that dam all those years ago. Maybe things haven't always aligned in many ways, but in that moment, they sure as hell did. I love you so damn much. Thank you for taking me back." I kiss her again, softly. We're savoring each other as we lay here together.

So many little moments brought us together, yet also broke us apart. I'm forever grateful those fractures of life found a way to heal themselves because I would be missing this beauty in life.

I'm working outside of Indiana's townhouse. It's got a great view, so it makes for a perfect backdrop. Noah's at the neighbor's house and Indy's still at work. She should be home soon, but I thought with sunset approaching I would record some content on a livestream today.

I'm finishing up when I catch some movement from my side. I look over and see Indy walking in. She knows the drill by now when I'm filming content and stays on the sidelines. She's never shown her face in any of my videos. The only one she's been in she had her helmet on.

"Hey, everyone. I thought today was as good as any to introduce you to someone special."

I see Indy's eyes go wide. She probably thinks I'm going to out our marriage to the world, but I'd never do that without her consent. We had the conversation off camera regarding if I ever wanted to introduce her. This is just me showing the world that I'm taken by the most beautiful girl in the world.

"You see, my heart has been captured by a certain someone. I think everyone probably knows by my last video that someone remarkable has come into my life. Well, I wanted you to officially meet her." I reach my hand out for Indiana to grab it. She shakes her head, smiling shyly.

She knew I was going to do something more official for my followers, but probably never fully thought through the reality of being shown on camera.

"Come on, baby. Say "Hi" to everyone. They want to see your beautiful face," I encourage her.

Indiana finally relents, coming into view for everyone to see. The moment she does, her smile is shy and her face is red like a tomato.

"Isn't she just gorgeous? This is the love of my life, everyone!" I kiss her cheek. "It's official. I'm off the market—well, forever." I look at her and she looks stunned.

I bring her lips to mine, my body sweaty and she doesn't seem to care.

I see hearts and comments moving along the screen, then I end the live stream.

"I can't believe you just did that." She doesn't look mad, just shocked.

"Well, it needed to be done. I didn't tell them we're married, but I don't want anyone thinking they should shoot their shot." I give her a quirked brow, then kiss her shoulder. "How was work?"

"Good. I'm tired though. I just want to change out of these clothes and curl up on the couch."

"Sounds like a nice plan. Let's grab Noah and I can make something for dinner." I smack her ass.

"I like that. Are you dessert?" She winks.

———

The next week, I've got a whole spread of breakfast out for Noah. Indiana had to head into work early, so I offered to take him to school.

I know how picky kindergartners can be and Indiana has told me he always changes his preferences up, so I wanted to be prepared this morning. Looking around, I'm realizing I may have overdone it. It's too late now, as I hear his hurried footsteps moving along the stairs.

"Hey, Hunter. Wow! That's a lot of food." Noah's eyes look over at all the food I've laid out on the counter. Yeah, I've definitely overdone it. He's only six and I made enough food to feed the crew at the firehouse.

"Good morning, bud. You hungry?" I walk over to the kitchen table and pour some orange juice. "What do you want to eat? I made a few options."

Grabbing a plate, he walks around the kitchen island, assessing all his choices. "French toast, please." He points at the piece he wants, and I place it on his plate.

Once he's seated, I load some scrambled eggs on my own plate and sit opposite him. We sit silently for a few minutes, until Noah looks up at me.

"Hunter, are you living here now?" I'm mid-bite and I'm grateful I wasn't in the middle of swallowing my food. I would have needed the Heimlich after that question.

I chew my food for a long while, then finally answer, "No. Why do you think that?"

"Well, you're here a lot. And we hang out with you all the time. I like having you around. Darth likes you, too. So, I just thought you lived with us. And you cooked me breakfast today and you're taking me to school. Sometimes you sleep-over." He keeps eating his breakfast like his question didn't throw me off course. Of course, Indy isn't here to help me maneuver this.

"How would you feel if I *did* live here?" I hope Indy doesn't hate me for having this conversation with him, although he was the one to bring it up.

"I think it would be awesome. We could watch *Star Wars* and you're a way better cook than my mom." He sets his fork down and leans in as if he's going to tell me a secret. Damn, this kid is too much.

"Don't tell my mom this, but she burns one side of my toast sometimes. I don't like telling her because I think it would hurt her feelings." Fuck, my heart may have just exploded.

"Your secret is safe with me." I wink at him.

He goes on eating his breakfast with a little smile on his face until every last bite is consumed.

"I take it you liked it?" I ask him once he's cleared his plate from the table.

"Yes." He smiles up at me. "Thanks, Hunter."

"No problem, Noah. Why don't you go grab your backpack and we'll head out. I have your lunch right here." I hold up his lunch bag in my hand.

"Alright." He runs off, but pokes his head back in the kitchen as I'm loading a few dishes in the dishwasher.

"Hunter?" he says.

"Yeah, buddy?"

"I do think it would be fun to have you living here. You make my mom happy. And you make me happy too."

Before I can even answer, he runs off to get his things and I swear, I stand completely stunned in place. Forget my heart exploding. It may have simply walked off into the other room because a little boy just took hold of it.

CHAPTER 51
Fire Hunters

Ocean_love231
That live was so damn sweet! Love them together! #wherecanifindmeahunter #huntingforawinner

HuntersMine098
All the good ones are taken. #findmeawinner #huntsamillion

VermontFallGirly
Does he have any friends? #imavailable #pickme

Megs985
The gene pool for their kids will be so cute. #theyresopretty #lovethemtogether #huntsamillion

GoldenDogLuver987
Eh. I think River is way hotter than @huntsamillion. I bet he'll have cuter babies. Anyone wanna to take that bet? #feelinglucky #rowdyriverlover

Huntsamillion
I'll take that bet 💸 #youvegotadeal #bringiton #imontoyou

Tyler

THREE MONTHS LATER

Dear Indy,

Waking up next to you has been nothing but a gift these last few months.

I've been wandering this life aimlessly since I walked away from you. Being with you and Noah has been my why. You've claimed my heart in a way I never thought possible, although if I'm being honest, I think you've carried a piece of me since we were young.

I'd be fooling myself if I said I wasn't in love with you from the moment I heard your voice. You've found a way to connect yourself to my soul and I haven't been the same since.

I know we bound ourselves through marriage over a decade ago for convenience. How about now we finally show the world how deep our love stretches? We met when we were young and formed a friendship. We fell in love through letters. Then I made the biggest mistake of my life and tore us apart; and now I don't want to let time separate us any further. Let's not waste any more of what we have left and let's start living.

I want every second moving forward to be planning the family we envision together. Let's celebrate this life we have with Noah, our friends, your parents, and everyone else that deserves to witness what we've chosen as a unit.

I love you beyond myself. I love Noah and I can't wait for the endless tomorrows with both of you.

Finish reading this letter and join me in the living room. I've got a surprise waiting for you.

I love you to eternity.

Forever Yours,

Tyler

I feel my heart pounding as I wait for Indy to read the letter. I've been waiting in the living room with Noah. She sleeps in on weekends that I'm not working and I've had this plan for a while now.

I took Noah to help me pick out a ring for her a few weeks ago, and we came up with a plan to ask Indiana to "marry" me last night. He doesn't need to know the logistics of our marriage from years ago, so I kept that to myself. All he needs to know is that I'm asking for his help today.

His smile stretches across his face because he knows what I have planned for this morning. Last night we went out on a guys' trip as Indy was working late. She was none the wiser, thinking we were simply hanging out together while I had the day off.

We finally hear her moving around in the room, so we scurry to get in position. Noah's giggling, as I try to tamper my nerves. Even though we're married on paper, I've never officially proposed to her. The velvet box feels like a weighted brick in my pocket.

"I hear her, Hunter." He beams up at me.

"I know, buddy." I ruffle his hair as I move up beside him. "Okay, you know what to do?"

"Yep." He smiles brightly, that upper left tooth missing from his grin. I know things will likely not go as planned with a youngster at the reigns of a proposal, but that's the fun in all this. I'm surprised he's kept anything a secret this long.

I look over to find Darth looking unamused in this whole thing. Noah thought we should dress Darth up for the occasion. So, he's in a little bowtie and dapper top hat, which hasn't been the easiest to keep on. He's stretched out on the couch, licking his paw, unfazed for now.

"Grab Darth," I instruct Noah.

"Oh yeah!" He nods. The cat looks perturbed being dragged into this whole scenario after he got settled in a comfortable spot on the couch. If a cat could roll his eyes, Darth likely would.

Setting the white furball down, Noah adjusts the bowtie in place. "Perfect!" Noah says.

I hear the door open upstairs and I up look to see the woman I love staring down from the railing.

I'm in a suit, while Noah is in a button-up and slacks. For nine in the morning, it's probably a lot, but it's all I could come up with. I wanted something she wouldn't expect, and it's hard to surprise Indy with our hectic schedules and having Noah in sports most weekends.

She's holding the letter I wrote her in one hand and she swipes at a stray tear. She has a haphazard smile on her face. That has to be good news—at least that's my hope.

We're standing in a row, even Darth keeping his place in line. She looks at us and lets out a soft laugh.

"This is a nice welcome." She walks down the stairs.

"Good morning, sweetheart," I tell her.

"Yes, good morning." Noah puffs out his chest, trying to look more grown up and that pulls a laugh from both Indy and me.

Noah walks up to his mom and grabs her hand, pulling her toward me. She bends down and gives him a kiss on the cheek. "Mom, come. We have surprises for you."

"Oh, okay, sweetie." She winks, continuing her walk over to me.

Once she reaches me, Noah brings her hand to rest in mine. I lean into her and whisper, "You look beautiful."

"I just woke up and now my eyes are puffy from reading your letter," she whispers.

I've never seen a more beautiful sight.

I get down on one knee, my heart once again racing.

"Tyler." She cups my cheek with one hand.

"Indiana, for years I have loved you, yet I haven't been able to find the courage to tell you. I have kept those words inside and hidden. I don't want to live a life where no one knows how much I love you anymore. I want everyone to know you are mine and I am yours. I want to wear my love for you out in the open." I bring my lips to the inside of her palm and kiss it. "Will you officially become Indiana Hunter?"

She's nodding, with tears running down her cheeks. Finally, she says, "Of course, Ty. I love you."

Standing, I wrap my arms around her waist, while she brings her arms around my neck. I hear Noah cheering. I reach for him, and I feel this little family of ours celebrating in our bubble for a moment together. It's everything I've been searching for, and I finally get to have it.

———

Jerry and Scarlet offer their house two weeks later for an impromptu lunch we've posed as an engagement party. Indiana's parents even flew in from Vegas.

Prior to the engagement, Indy did take some time to let it all out regarding past frustrations with Diana and Gary. She told them how hard it has been since Bryce's death and the pain they caused her when she became Noah's guardian.

At first, it seemed there'd be some pushback, but finally Diana and Gary listened. The conversation was productive, and I feel there might be some healing occurring in the relationship.

This brought a new conversation between Indiana and her parents—that of her finding Jerry and Scarlet. I could tell that was a tough subject for her, but I'm proud of her for tackling it. It was necessary before this gathering today so there wouldn't be any animosity between her sets of parents. It seems, from what I can see, everyone is getting along.

"Maybe it's time to say something. The butterflies are eating me alive, Ty," she whispers.

I pull her lips closer, loving the way she feels against me.

I shout into the crowd, "Hey, everyone. Thanks so much for coming today. We're so happy you've joined us."

We've gathered many friends from all around, even some that she went to school with and coworkers from Chicago as well.

Everyone cheers, holding up their drinks and whistling. I

see Noah jumping up and down, trying to see over those that are taller than him. River moves him closer to the front.

"We have a little surprise for you all; Indy and I have actually already tied the knot. We did it in a civil ceremony. We're excited to start our next steps forward, with Noah by our side." I reach out and Noah comes bounding over.

"Let's hear it for the new Mr. and Mrs. Hunter!" River calls out, his beer high up in the air. Everyone else joins him and I feel that pride swell in my chest.

I look down at Indiana as I wrap my arm around her. I see the glint of my wedding band, the same ring I had that night years ago, finally resting back on my ring finger, shining back at me.

People come up to congratulate us on the wedding, surprised we tricked them with the engagement-slash-wedding. We wanted this to be an intimate affair, really focusing on us with Noah, and bringing everyone together for a gathering afterwards. Because we have been married for years and no one knew, we thought it best to simply have a party to celebrate the continuation of this union together; of love and happiness that we are excited to see blossom as the years move forward.

The night goes on, with laughter and love. I feel surrounded with the found family I know we both felt we missed. As much as things were strained with Diana and Gary, I think with time, things will start to heal for them. I walk over to where Indy is dancing with Noah.

"Join us." She laughs. They reach out for me to hold on to their hands.

The three of us are dancing until Noah sees Kalli and Vivienne walking by.

"I want to see Viv!" And before we can say anything else, he's running off.

I pull my wife into my arms and breathe in her vanilla

scent that I love so much. "I can't wait to live on forever with you."

"I can't wait either," she tells me, her smile growing across her face. "I really am at peace right now."

"Same, baby." I kiss her cheek.

"Sorry to break things up, lovebirds, but it's tradition to do a money dance." River walks up to us, putting his arm around us.

"Um, we weren't planning on doing that," I tell him.

"Sorry, you don't get a vote." He smiles, pulling both of us into him. "You see, I have plans, and I really need this to work out in my favor."

I roll my eyes, knowing he probably has money on this. "Riv, no."

"Yes, it's happening." He pushes me to one side, Indy to another. I see lines have formed, meaning he already spread the word prior to wrangling us into this.

I see our firefighter crew has lined up to dance with my wife, while a horde of women are ready to dance with me, Scarlet being the first one. At least I see Noah is the first one lined up to dance with his mom.

I look over and notice River is waiting for Noah to finish the first dance with Indy. I scrunch my face in confusion.

"That friend of yours is up to something," Scarlet says and I bring her into my arms.

"He's always up to something," I say, twirling her.

Each dance goes seamlessly. I get a piece of advice from each person. I'll say Abby has kind words when she dances with me, while Kennedy is just as ridiculous as her fiancé. Most of her advice is dirty.

"I hope you ravage that woman tonight," she finishes saying, her smile pure evil.

"Um," I say.

"Oh, I know you've got another side to you, Hunter. I mean, you're probably not as freaky as Malloy, but don't tell me you haven't gotten a little carried away on that bike of yours."

I must blush because right then she pushes away and points at me. Of course, Marissa is next in line and she looks over at her. "Look, I told you. He's a freak in the sheets. I knew it. How is he not in book club with us?"

"It's always the quiet ones," Marissa chides.

"Isn't there a time limit on these dances?" I question.

Kennedy tosses her hair off her shoulder and gives me a sneaky smile and a wink. She might be worse than River. Either that or she's learning from him.

I look over at Indy and I notice River is monitoring her dancing. What is going on over there?

"Marissa, I know you're in on why River is so invested on Indy's money dance over there. What is he doing?"

Marissa looks away.

"Marissa, tell me." The minute I hear her explanation, I stop what I'm doing and find myself walking toward my wife and River, unsurprised he's as immature as he is.

Fifteen minutes later I'm in the kitchen with River, Malloy, Baylee and Indiana. I should add, there's a penis purse filled with cash on the table.

"What the hell, River?" I protest, arms crossed at my chest.

"I don't know why you're so pissed." The fucker is smiling.

"Indy, how are you not upset?" I look at my wife, who's counting said money.

She shrugs, a smile pulled at her lips.

"If I may speak, Noah was unaware there was a penis purse on the premises." Malloy has his hand up as if we're in a classroom.

"Seriously, Malloy, I expected better from you," I say, which pulls a snort from his wife, Baylee.

I look over at her and she covers her mouth.

"Sorry," she says, muffled behind her palm.

"Ty, sweetie, Noah is completely unaffected. He danced with me, then ran off with Kalli. He didn't see the purse, which did not come out until after I had my dance with him. River pulled this phallic thing out for me to use once there were no children present. I promise, sweetie." She puts her hand on my forearm and soothes my irritated nerves.

"I really cannot believe you pulled this out at a wedding," I tell him. "What is wrong with you?"

"When else would I do it?" He looks at me like I'm the crazy one.

"Seriously?" I question him. "Never, River. The answer is never. It's fucking hideous." I hold up the crocheted purse. Who makes something so ugly?

"Listen, someone very close to me made this for my wedding. And I was kind enough to extend this for your use tonight." He says with the most sincere expression.

Fuck. Seriously?

Right when I'm about to apologize, Malloy starts laughing and then Baylee follows suit. River's serious expression fades and his smile pokes through.

"You mother fucker. I almost fell for that sob story!" I throw the purse at his chest.

"Hey, it's true that someone made this though. But it was for Samara's wedding. And Kennedy now has to use it at our wedding. It's a long story!"

"So how is it at my reception?"

"Our reception," Indy corrects me.

"Sorry, baby," I say, squeezing her hand.

"It was in my car, so I thought I'd spice things up."

"Yes, River, because our lives were so boring. The adoptive parents flying in to hang with the birth parents at their home wasn't juicy enough. Add in the twist that I served with Indy's long-lost brother—that wasn't enough?"

"Well, maybe I didn't think it through." River throws his arms in the air.

Baylee stands next to River. "My dear River was just trying to be a good friend." She starts patting him on the shoulder, even though she's ridiculously short so she has to reach up to do so.

"You guys are absurd, you know that?" I tell them.

All of them, including Indy, respond, "Yes!"

"Indy, I didn't mean you." I drag my hand down my face.

———

As we say our goodbyes, our friends wave as I walk my wife to the motorcycle waiting in the driveway. We don't have plans for a honeymoon, saving for a big trip during one of Noah's breaks from school.

For now, we'll spend the night at a hotel. I grab the helmet and slide it over her head, still feeling my body hum at the sight of her. She's changed so she can climb behind me on the bike.

Everyone is cheering for us. Noah runs up to say goodbye. He hugs his mom, and she tells him she loves him. Then he comes up to me, and I bend down, wrapping my arms around his little body. He tells me he can't wait to see me tomorrow to toss the baseball with me at the park.

I pick him up and tell him I love him, something I started doing a few weeks back. The way my love for him has grown is something I didn't see coming, yet it feels completely natural. I truly love him like he is my own.

I asked if it was okay that I told him I loved him and he told me it was okay. I know it might take time for him to tell me he loves me back. I don't expect it to be overnight that he feels the same.

He pulls his face away from me, bringing his little palms to bracket my cheeks. It's then he whispers, "I love you, Hunter."

The tears are instant and I hear Indy gasp behind me.

I pull him close to me again, my tears releasing down my cheeks. "You are my everything, buddy. Thank you for loving me."

I feel him tighten around me. I never knew love could feel like this.

Once I let him go, I ruffle his hair and he runs off to meet up with Kalli and Julian, Vivienne clapping her hands in Julian's arms. Everyone in the crowd is cheering and waving.

Indy and I get ourselves settled on the bike and I rev the engine. I feel her wrap her arms around my middle and we start to ride off into the night.

Feeling that evening air move along us, something I once did to calm my nerves, I now do with the woman I love behind me. She soothes me now, with and without my motorcycle.

When I ride now, it's toward her, or it's only to sunsets that include her. I no longer need to find solace; she's my comfort. She's my soulmate and my missing piece. I never thought I was going to find what I was looking for after I walked away from Indiana Ranton.

Little did I know marrying Indiana all those years ago was the start of my beginning, and she will forever be my end.

THE END

Also by Stefanie Castro

THE BOSTON EMBERS SERIES

Embers in the Outfield

Embers in Our Past

Embers in the Dark

THE IF ONLY SERIES

If Only You Knew

If Only You Fell

If Only You Hurt

Acknowledgments

I got the inspiration to write Hunter and Indiana's story back when I started *Embers in Our Past*. Little did I know, my life was going to take many drastic turns when I would sit down to write this story.

When I say this book was a labor of love, I'm not exaggerating. My heart and brain couldn't meet in the middle for the longest time. The words were lost somewhere in the complexities of my life. Pulling the story out from my soul is exactly what had to be done.

I leaned heavily on two people to help me through this struggle. Meghan and Ashley were my rocks through this because I had to navigate the writer's block I was facing. The story was there, buried deep inside, but I simply couldn't find how I wanted to tell this love story properly to my readers. In the end, I think the time I gave myself to write it may have allowed it to become better and stronger. What sprouted was something more developed and beautiful between Hunter and Indiana.

Ashley, my editor extraordinaire, is one that has allowed me to blossom tremendously since we started working in a professional manner. Not only that, you have allowed me to shift my thinking as an author, and to see my books with a better eye as I write. I appreciate your keen eye and insight. Thank you for bringing a refreshing viewpoint to my work and always being honest when you read my stories. I love working with you. It is always fun, there's always a laugh, and I constantly walk away knowing my writing will be stronger.

Meghan—my Christmas wife—who is my positive light, and the one that will always go to bat for my books. You are a cheerleader for authors, and I feel honored to have you in my corner. Thank you for being you. I appreciate the kindness you bring in my life and for simply checking in on me on days I'm quiet. You believe in me, even when I don't believe in myself. Thank you.

Joanna—thank you for being a sounding board for my characters and letting me spoil the surprises on all my books before I even write them. Each one of my plots will never be new to you and I apologize, but I really do thank you for going through each scenario with me. Because without you, I would never get to figure out if things sound right. With Indy and Hunter, you were the first to let me talk out their love story. I thank you from the bottom of my heart.

No matter how many books I write, I have to thank my family. They tolerate the endless moments I'm grabbing my laptop and running off to write the next chapter. I know it feels like this is never-ending and I apologize I'm lost in the next fictional story. Thank you for never complaining and always understanding my demanding schedule. Thank you for your kindness and love as I navigate this lifestyle. I know the life of an author feels like it takes over every corner of our lives, especially as I work endless hours. I love you and appreciate the fact you give me the space to be creative.

This year, I had the amazing opportunity to attend a book conference in central New York where I connected with some incredible people in the community. One of those ended up being Cynthia, who has pioneered new ways to get my name out there in the author world. Thank you for everything you have done for my work so far and I look forward to what's ahead for us. Thank you for your perseverance and tenacity in this industry.

Christiana from Concepts by Canea, you are one of the most talented artists I've gotten to work with. I love when it's time to work with you because we have so much fun together. These illustrated covers are gorgeous and seeing Indiana and Hunter join the mix completes the series perfectly. Thank you for bringing your creativity to characters, and making this process seamless and fun. It's a joy seeing the covers and adding the spice of the NSFW artwork as well!

A special thanks to The Author Agency for all the hard work you bring in hyping me up during the release of my books. You're a great support and I appreciate your input when I have questions along the way.

I can't really say enough about my Beta readers who are kind enough to give so much feedback about the storyline and characters. I appreciate the time and effort you put into reading my rough draft. Also, thank you for the notes you send me. You have no idea how much every single moment you spend giving me your reactions to my fictional characters means to me.

And to my ARC readers—thank you so very much for taking the time, not only for reading my stories, but for signing up early for a copy of my book. I know what it's like to wait for an advanced copy, but to know you did that for one of my books is something I treasure. I appreciate you more than you even know and I take that with me. You contribute to filling my cup with joy and I am endlessly grateful for the way you hype me up and cheer on my characters!

To my readers and hype team: I am endlessly grateful for each and every one of you. Thank you for reading my work and loving my characters. I pour everything into building these worlds for you to enjoy and I hope you get lost like I do. I love bringing complexity, mixed with real life, to those I write and I hope you feel that as you read my stories. Thank you for taking the time to pick up my books. It means so much to me that you have chosen something I have put together because I know there are so many options out there.

I have to take a moment and touch on a topic that is near and dear to my heart. Indiana's chronic illness is something personal for me. I was diagnosed with Crohn's disease when I was twenty-two years old. Prior to that, I had ulcerative colitis, suffering back when I was just eighteen years old. At this point, I have lived longer with a chronic illness than not, so I felt compelled to interweave that into this storyline.

Highlighting chronic illness in this book was a way to bring awareness to readers without making it the only piece of my FMC's life. I wanted to find a way to show her live a life without keeping her from being able to thrive. Indiana found a way to move forward and soar, which was really important to me. There were many moments where my illness tried to bring me down, but I persevered, and I was determined to do the same for Indiana. If you'd like to learn more, please visit The Crohn's and Colitis Foundation or click here.

This series might be done, but I promise there are many things in the works for the future.

Here's to many more book boyfriends in the future,
Stefanie 💋

Embers in Our Souls

Stefanie Castro

Copyright © 2025 by Stefanie Castro

Visit the author's Instagram on @stefaniecastro.author and website authorstefaniecastro.com

ISBN: 781-966504-02-3 (eBook)

ISBN: 978-1-966504-03-0 (paperback)

All rights reserved.

Embers in Our Souls is a work of fiction. Names, characters, places, and incidents are all a product of the author's imagination. Any resemblance to actual events, locations, or individuals that are living or dead is coincidental.

Except as permitted under the U.S. Copyright Act of 1976, no product of this publication may be reproduced, distributed, or transmitted in any form or by any means, stored in or introduced into a retrieval system, including photocopying, recording, or other electronic or mechanical methods, without the prior written permission of the above author of this book.

No AI use or training: Without in any way limiting Stefanie Castro's exclusive rights under copyright, any use of this publication to "train" generative artificial intelligence (AI) technologies to generate text is expressly prohibited. No AI was used to write Stefanie Castro's publicized and copyrighted material. Generative AI is created with stolen copyrighted materials and threatens the livelihood of all writers, creatives, and artists.

Editing by Ashley Matthews of Smashin' Edits

Cover Designer Christiana at Concepts by Canea

Links and Social Media:

Email: stefanie.castro.writes@gmail.com

Instagram: @stefaniecastro.author — https://www.instagram.com/stefaniecastro.author/

TikTok: booklovingnurse — https://www.tiktok.com/@booklovingnurse

Goodreads: Stefanie Castro — https://www.goodreads.com/user/show/108038362-stefanie-castro

Facebook: Author Stefanie Castro – https://www.facebook.com/profile.php?id=61551400180728

❀ Formatted with Vellum

Stefanie Castro is a Registered Nurse, certified doula and yoga instructor. She specializes in the field of obstetrics and loves everything about her career. She is a first-generation Brazilian American and is fluent in English, Portuguese and Spanish. Stefanie is a wife of 19 years and mother to her son and daughter, along with her very rambunctious Cavalier King Charles Spaniel, named Rusty.

She has grown in her love of reading throughout the years and now it's hard to find her without her Kindle by her side. Her favorite foods are popcorn and sushi. She is also very excited about Christmas and begins plotting next year's decor on December 26th. Stefanie has started two book clubs and is avidly reading whenever she has a free moment in her day. She loves to cuddle on the couch with her dog, along with a great book and a cup of tea.